W9-CML-063

WITHDRAWN

BECOMING a Queen

Dan Clay

ROARING BROOK PRESS

NEW YORK

Published by Roaring Brook Press
Roaring Brook Press is a division of Holtzbrinck Publishing Holdings
Limited Partnership
120 Broadway, New York, NY 10271 • fiercereads.com

Our books may be purchased in bulk for promotional, educational,
or business use. Please contact your local bookseller or the Macmillan
Corporate and Premium Sales Department at (800) 221-7945 ext. 5442 or
by email at MacmillanSpecialMarkets@macmillan.com.

Library of Congress Cataloging-in-Publication Data is available.

First edition, 2023
Book design by Aurora Parlegreco
Printed in the United States of America

ISBN 978-1-250-84309-8
1 3 5 7 9 10 8 6 4 2

For my mom and dad

The Worst Night of My Life

The sequins scratch my upper thigh and I wonder why I agreed to do this.

I had a bad feeling from the start. Two weeks ago, in the bleachers, as the crowd flooded in for the JV basketball game, Haley Stewart held up three black body-hugging dresses with strands of fringe that wrapped around like stripes on a slutty candy cane. The dresses were so short, so tight, they wouldn't pass dress code even if girls were wearing them.

Six-foot-one Joe Thomas was skeptical. "Is this a joke? There's no way Cole's thighs are fittin' in that thing."

Damien Cole, too, was reluctant. "All three of us wear these itty-bitty dresses? I don't know, girl."

I stood still. Any motion seemed liable to give me away. I tried to mimic Joe's and Damien's hesitant expressions, tried not to give away how desperately I wanted to wear that dress, how vitally I needed to wear that dress, how my heart could not possibly continue beating if I knew that itty-bitty dress existed in this world and I was not the one wearing it.

And if you want something that badly, it's bound to be bad for you.

Now, two weeks later—waiting in the wings as a packed auditorium heckles an empty stage, busting out of my dream dress like a partially popped can of Pillsbury crescent rolls—*I need to get out of this dress*. The lining under the sequins feels like chicken pox. The arm holes are too tight, like I'm wrapped in fishing wire. One thing is clear: This is a terrible idea.

The thing is, I had no choice. At least that's what I'll tell my parents. That's what I'll tell my boyfriend. I had no choice. Seconds before the JV basketball game started, Haley, who's been a teenager since she was six years old, drew on the same authority that gets her dates with upperclassmen and extensions on math homework. "It'll be hilarious, and we're not actually asking you, we're telling you that we picked you and you're doing it," she said, as decisive as a slammed locker. "Me and Beth will finish '*rollin'* on *the riverrrr*' really slow, and then the music goes fast, and you'll run out from offstage and start the dance."

"And then we'll snatch our talent show trophy," Beth added, with a rhythmic shoulder shimmy.

I blame my brother, actually. "If you wanna do it, do it, bud. Who cares what other people might say?" he said. "Be yourself! Your full sequin-y self."

How could I have ignored so many warning signs?

First of all, our dress rehearsal was too much fun. Squeezed into skintight dresses, we twirled around like giddy schoolgirls playing princess dress-up. Joe and Damien were even more enthusiastic than I was, spinning on their tiptoes, the fringe of their dresses flying like helicopter blades, while I, the only one dainty enough to fit into Haley's heels, practiced strutting like a supermodel.

If you're over twelve years old and you're having that much fun, unassisted by drugs or alcohol, something bad is about to happen.

And second of all, the dress rehearsal was too good. Say what you want about straight dudes, but Joe and Damien had practiced that choreo to perfection. "Nah, man, you gotta *flop* your wrist to the side, like a little baby swan. Boom-boom-*kat!*" Joe instructed. "Stick your arm up and *flop* the wrist. *Bam*. On the beat. See? *Fierce*." He demonstrated about a dozen wrist flicks while I processed how bizarre it was to have Annondale's starting power forward telling me my wrists weren't floppy enough. Eventually, we nailed it. Every move.

And anyone who's been in a single spring musical knows that the only way to have a good performance is to have a *bad* dress rehearsal.

Now, in the wings, we wait for our cue. Damien adjusts his dress, smooths down his fringe, straightens out Joe's wig. "Bro, you were not born to be a blonde," he jokes.

"Listen, we can't all be as pretty as Davis," Joe says, giving me a backslap that hurls me off my heels. Damien steadies me, and the three of us wrap our arms around each other. "All right, fellas, let's make this a night they'll never forget."

The background track starts. Low, slow notes from a single guitar. Haley and Beth enter from stage right. The audience explodes before they even sing a single note. Haley, with a raspy whisper, tells the crowd how we never do anything nice and easy.

I'm so certain things are about to go horribly wrong that I'm not even nervous.

"*Let's do this!*" Joe shouts as we burst into the lights.

People tell you to be yourself, as if it's possible to have any idea who that is.

I count about a thousand different selves. There's the person I am at school and the person I am at parties. There's the kid who makes loud jokes in the lunchroom and the kid who can't say the first hello. The me who wants to have abs and the me who wants to eat Froot Loops out of the box. There's scared me in gym class and silly me at theater camp, plus hundreds and hundreds more all fighting for prominence inside one skinny battlefield known as my body.

The real me? Who knows? They're all real and they're all fake. The secret is controlling who sees what.

And now the entire city of Annondale is about to see the me who wanted to wear this dress. And that is some super gay toothpaste that can't go back in the tube.

I'd mentally prepared for every possible scenario except what actually happens: It's the greatest three minutes of my life.

Under the blinding lights, my heels feel like wings.

The dance moves dance themselves. Rapturous applause—miraculous applause!—lifts us toward the sky while I wonder if it's possible that my smile is wider than the stage. Perhaps a reward for going to church every Sunday for sixteen years: my first miracle.

The satisfaction is so consuming I don't even think to laugh at my earlier self, that nervous wreck who was convinced everything would go wrong.

Backstage, the celebration continues. It's my third school talent show, but the first with an after-party. Where were these superfans last year when I nailed that high note from *Les Mis*? Half of Annondale High wait with flowers and compliments, bursting to congratulate Haley, Beth, or their gender-bending backup dancers already mythologized as the *Riverboat Queens*.

"I swear, it was like I blacked out up there. What just happened? That was insane!"

"They were going *crazy*."

"Dude. Little Davis. Your dance solo? In the heels?! People lost their goddamn minds!"

"It was the most epic performance in the history of epic performances. You guys killed it!"

"How did you keep it a surprise?"

"Those dresses, though. Yo, Joe, you got some *titties*!"

"You better take that off or you're about to get yourself a boyfriend."

"Mark, *girrrl*, you honestly slayed."

I turn to the groupie formerly known as Jia from chemistry class. "Hey, have you seen John?"

She responds with theatrical pizzazz like she's impersonating something she's heard on TV. "Yasss, Queen!"

"You have? Amazing." I exhale, then raise my eyebrows impatiently. "Where?"

"Oh. No. Not actually. I've just always wanted to say that."

I scan through the crowd, searching. *Where is he?* I even put my heels back on to get a better view. Behind me, two seniors sneak shots from a silver flask, not realizing that the greenroom mirror reflects every swig into the teacher-infested hallway.

"Out, out, out," Mr. Wagner shouts as he shuffles them away. "If you were not *in* the show, you can wait for people in the Hall of Fame hallway. We have got to clear this area. I do not get paid to be your little chaperone."

With a collective moan, the rowdy crowd thins. I get trapped in a circle of sophomore girls complimenting my legs.

"You look better in a dress than half the actual girls in our grade."

"Wait, did you shave?"

"No, his leg hair's just really light."

"I'd honestly murder someone to have your legs."

Finally, I see him. John.

He's celebrating with Damien and Joe, who have actually *added* makeup since I last saw them. He must not have been able to find me through the crowd.

I get excited, in advance, for the hug. His arms, the squeeze.

It's not like it's some big accomplishment, like I need some grand validation from him. We nailed some simple choreo.

But I don't know—maybe I'm so happy because I thought it'd be so horrible? Maybe everything truly awesome starts with the possibility of tragedy? Maybe I just want a kiss.

I get closer and hear him hyping up Damien and Joe. "I didn't think it was humanly possible to wear a shorter skirt than that powder-puff game. Dudes, y'all killed it."

I'm ecstatic just to see him—my boyfriend!—on what's quickly becoming the happiest night of my life.

He turns.

The hallway and everyone in it disappear. He's always had that effect on me. The room could be full of shirtless firefighters and loose cash and I wouldn't notice anything but John.

He sees me. Finally, he sees me.

I smile as I float up on my tiptoes, so high my borrowed heels lift off the ground.

His eyes talk first.

He leans away slightly. Looks me up and down.

Slowly, I take off my wig, hold it by my side.

The stringy synthetic hair scrapes the linoleum floor as I tug at my too-short dress.

I wait for him to say something—anything.

"You gonna change?"

Junior Year

October

(Six Months After the Talent Show)

Spiraling

The bottle spins on flattened carpet, and I'd rather be anywhere but here.

I had to come—I haven't left my house for anything other than ACT prep in over a month—but right now I'd rather be graphing a parabola in the public library instead of sitting on dusty concrete watching a contraband Heineken play matchmaker to a bunch of horny teenagers.

The great mystery of my life right now is how I can be sitting in a circle of friends, shoulder to shoulder with this intimate collection of comrades deliberately selected out of seven and a half billion alternatives, my *friends*, these people I share my weekends and secrets and stolen vodka with . . . and feel completely alone.

Which one of these is not like the others?

The one with the broken heart.

My parents sold me a lie. They told me I was special, and here I sit, suffering from the most unspecial ailment of them all: a generic, run-of-the-mill broken heart.

I cross the circle to switch spots with Shanna and sit cross-legged on a skewed rectangle of uninstalled beige carpet. It's somehow less comfortable than the concrete. Someone makes a joke and I laugh loudly, perfectly.

In tonight's fantasy production of *Normal*, playing the role of "Me," is me.

My family has an unspoken motto: Problems aren't problems until other people know about them.

By that construct, my life has no problems at all.

Shanna calls everyone to attention as she steals a yellow pillow from Reid Meyers's lap to make her rusted water-pipe backrest a little more luxurious. "First of all, everyone shut up. And second of all, for the couple of idiots who don't remember the history of this party, Throwback Night was invented by Mark Davis in ninth grade, so *obviously* he gets the first spin."

I hop up and dramatically take a few quick bows. "Well, my invention is useless to me now. What am I supposed to do with this?" I point at the green bottle glittering expectantly under buzzing tubes of fluorescent light. Everyone laughs. Being gay is pretty okay, but it presents some complications during coed spin the bottle.

"Yo, what happens at Throwback Night *stays* at Throwback Night," Reid Meyers says with a seductive wink.

Reid Meyers is like the guy who plays gay guys in Hollywood movies: handsome, happy, and heterosexual.

"No, no. I'm gonna go start an LGBTQ game of spin the bottle, which will just be me in the corner spinning in circles, drinking alone."

Standing strong against a cacophony of counterarguments, I swat my hands at my friends and hustle toward the folding table at the bottom of the stairs. It's decorated to evoke the vibe of a middle school dance, seasonal plastic tablecloth and all. As I add a little more spike to my punch, I call back, "Shanna, it's all yours. I'll come back for truth or dare to make all of Reid's dreams come true."

I make a vodka-Dr Pepper and chase it with a Kroger-brand frosted sugar cookie. It tastes like a birthday cake iced with hand sanitizer. I shake my head and push through.

To call Throwback Night my invention is a bit of an exaggeration. It was just—when we got to high school, we were suddenly too cool to play all these games that I actually thought were amazing: truth or dare, suck and blow, chicken or go, etc. So one night, just like every other night in Annondale, Michigan, there was absolutely *nothing* to do, so I offered a suggestion: Let's find that old white bedsheet we used to hang on clothespins to create a make-out section in the middle of Lisa Sonshine's basement and play all those games that taught us how transactional sex and love could be. It was an instant hit. Wrapped in the warm excuse of nostalgia, we were permitted to be silly preteens again. A tradition was born.

So, you see, I haven't always been this sad sack of over-indulged emotions. There was a time when I liked parties so much, I even started them!

I might be the first person in the world to have peaked at thirteen.

But tonight, I am happy. I am Moving On. My older brother told me *only an active heart can heal*—yes, that's actually how he talks—and I think maybe this drink will get things pumping. Though, my older brother also told me that alcohol doesn't really fix your mood, it just amplifies it. Happy + Drunk = Happier; Sad + Drunk = Sadder.

The crazy part is that *I* dumped *John*, technically.

But only because I knew I was about to get dumped.

Dumped + Drunk = Dumped-er.

Suddenly, Joe Thomas is holding my shoulder. Muscle-y Joe Thomas. *When did he get here?* We've been friends forever, but he's more of a group friend, not a one-on-one friend. And now his giant hand, wide enough to palm a basketball, strong enough to pop it, is squeezing my shoulder while he stages a drunken debate with himself regarding the merits of two potential starting wide receivers, I think for the Lions. He even uses his phone to retrieve receiver statistics when he needs quantitative support for his increasingly passionate yet still uncontested opinion.

His brown eyes look golden in the glow of his phone.

His hand feels so strong.

My T-shirt is worn thin in strategically fashionable locations, so when muscle-y Joe Thomas squeezes my shoulder and the lean muscles of his tan forearms pulse with determined conviction, it feels like there's nothing at all between his strong hand and my naked skin.

Truth or dare, Joe?

No. Oh my God. No. That's stupid. I'm just lonely. One hundred percent stupid. I don't even . . . *no*. Think about something else. Make another drink? No, even stupider. Just think about something else. Something other than his hand. His bulging fore-arm pulsing as his strong hand warms my cold sh—*No*. Something else.

Something like . . . when my dad found out how much this fashionably tattered T-shirt cost, he made me mow the lawn seven times to pay him back. And each of the seven times he made me wear the same old Hanes T-shirt that my mom uses as a clean-ing rag. "Next time you want a ratty old T-shirt, make your own. Your credit card is for *emergencies*, young man."

The T-shirt's super cute, though. And while I have no idea why Joe Thomas is now talking about "*fucking field goal kickers*," I have successfully averted a boner.

Huzzah! I can still do something right.

"When did you become best friends with Joe Thomas?" Crys-tal asks as she drags me away from Joe's TED Talk to the busted yellow couch in the corner where Damien's drinking something that looks like radioactive Kool-Aid.

"Drink this." Damien hands me his cup. "You need to get your swagger back."

"I never had swagger."

"That's part of your swagger."

"Well then, consider it back."

Crystal and I have been friends since sixth grade. She's gor-geous but dresses so no one notices. Damien noticed, though, and tried to date her at the start of high school. She told him she could never, in good conscience, hook up with someone who went to a Writing Winning College Essays seminar as a *freshman*. He was friend-zoned and then became friends with me. I knew it was strategic, but he was funny and always understood the chemistry homework, so I was cool with the arrangement.

Crystal collapses onto the couch and takes Damien's drink. "Do you ever feel like you're watching yourself?" she asks.

When neither of us gets it, she elaborates, "Like you're separate from yourself, and just watching your life from afar."

Damien takes the drink back from Crystal. "I don't think we do the same drugs anymore."

"It's not drugs, *Damien*." She says his name like an insult and looks up at the beige ceiling tiles. "Like, we're inside." She pauses for clarity, talks philosophically. "My body is here, talking, laughing, drinking your disgusting drink. But my actual soul is, like, outside, watching us from the bushes, thinking, 'Humans are so weird.'"

The ceiling fan wobbles as it spins.

"Your soul sounds kind of creepy," Damien reflects. "Wait, actually—is it sober?" He exaggeratedly looks out the basement window. "Can your soul drive us home?"

Crystal shouts an exasperated exhale up to the ceiling fan, rolls her eyes at the collective ignorance of all humanity, and melts into the couch cushion. On her descent to the unvacuumed rug, she grabs a skinny strip of paper (which I painstakingly cut) from a giant plastic Pistons cup. "Would you rather," she reads with bored resignation, "be a bird or a snake?"

I suppose when it first started, I got some sort of sick satisfaction from the heartbreak—*Think of all the songs I could relate to!*—but now I just want to be happy again, and I don't know how. I pray to

any God who'll listen, any God willing to descend into this basement of adolescent sin, that He grant just one more miracle. I don't
need bread and I've got my own wine, but if He could just turn
this muddy puddle of a person into something other than nothing, I promise I'll never sin again. I'll go to Youth Bible Study on
Wednesdays, I'll finish my SAT flash cards, and I'll drink nothing
stronger than the grape juice at the center of the communion trays.

SAT SENTENCE COMPLETION PRACTICE

*Choose the answer choice that contains the word or words that best com-
plete the sentence.*

1. Forgive me, Father, for I stole my father's vodka, and
   that's what started this party to begin with—this
   _____ party that I don't even want to be at
   anymore.
   A) debauched
   B) debilitating
   C) debased
   D) debasement

2. Forgive me, Father, for I know not where to go. I'm too
   _____ to drive and too _____ to have
   any fun.
   A) drunk; sober
   B) smashed; crushed
   C) blotto; blue
   D) fucked up; fucked up

3. Forgive me, Father, for I know not how I got here. I used
   to be so __________ .

   A) happy

   B) happy

   C) happy

   D) happy

✧ ✧ ✧

My mixed drinks aren't making me feel any less lonely, so I find a shot glass.

It parts the clouds inside my chest and starts spreading sunshine, everywhere, warming my heart and wrapping its rays around every single rib, going up to my shoulders and down through my arms, down to my elbows and fingers, and warming the pit of my stomach, spreading sunbeams down, down, even down there, through every inch of my thighs and my knees and my shins, through my calves until it massages my feet with warm rays of everything's-going-to-be-okay.

It feels so good I take two more.

And then one more.

I laugh at someone's joke. I don't even know what the joke is; I just laugh at approximately the same volume as everyone else. "Stop. I can't. I can't deal," I say through a smile as wide as 18 Mile Road, the main road that my brother will have to take to come pick me up now that I'm drinking. My brother, who, in addition to being perfect, doesn't have to fake his own happiness.

I take another shot. It tastes like nail polish remover and wet grass and pulls the ceiling down lower. The room, closing in. A villainous trap in the suburban version of Indiana Jones.

I've gotta get out of here.

I move to leave, when Jeff White barrels toward me. "We're trying to convince Haley to come," he explains. "Quick! Look cool," he art-directs as he points his phone at my face. "Is that you looking cool? Man, I get why Beckett had to dump you."

I dumped *him*, I want to shout. But who cares?

He sends the picture and bobbles his head, waiting for a response. Impatient, he pushes his best friend, Spurling, into an empty stool. "Trampoliiine time," he shouts.

"If my neighbors see you, I'll chop off your balls!" Lisa yells.

"You're obsessed with my balls."

"Not much to be obsessed with."

I watch Jeff fly up the stairs and, before my brain even processes what I'm looking at, before I can pray for an alien abduction or a spontaneous combustion, before I have time to start pretending like I'm having the time of my life, I see him.

Or, not him, yet, but I see his faded gray Chuck Taylors with the extra-long laces, double wrapped around the back, and I know it's him.

Why is he here? I didn't think he'd be here. That's the whole reason I'm here. Why would he come here? This is my party. I *invented* this party. It's *my* party and I can cry if I want to, but I really, really, *really* don't want to, so *why is he here?*

And why are mine the first eyes he sees?

Entropy

I'm staring at the stairs as he steps down.

It probably looks like I've been staring at the stairs all night, just waiting for him.

Him.

Him who's apparently been using the month since our breakup to get even hotter.

To John's credit, he let enough time go by for me to believe our decline had nothing to do with the talent show. When I delicately mentioned that it felt like we were growing apart, he had his shoelaces tied before I even finished the sentence. "Yeah. You think we should break up?"

I was shocked. "I'm not saying we should break up; I'm just wondering why you're distant."

John, it turns out, just didn't feel that connection anymore.

For God's sake, I get more explanation when I get partial credit on a physics quiz.

But I know why. I do. He gave it away even before the talent show: Halloween our freshman year. See—all I ever wanted to do in my *entire life* was wear a couples' costume with my boyfriend, and I finally had a boyfriend. I was so proud of my suggestion, too, because John has all these big muscles, and I was giggly, skinny, and in love.

"What if you were Popeye and I was Olive Oyl?"

He didn't even look at me when he answered. "Dude, Mark. If I wanted to date a girl, I'd date a girl. Plus, isn't that cartoon a hundred years old?"

I don't even think he meant it to be that deep, but I think the answer's in there. It's not a sin for guys to like guys. I think we've all moved past that. The only homophobic people left are people you wouldn't want to hang out with anyway. But for a guy to act like a girl? Well, that's where we draw the line. When Damien and Joe do it, everyone knows it's a joke. But me? A little too close to home. John's a "you wouldn't even know he was gay" kind of gay (Annondale's favorite kind), and he couldn't risk it all for a boyfriend in a dress.

That said, it's been a month. It shouldn't still be so hard.

But you can waste a lot of life wishing for what shouldn't be. This is what things are: hard.

And I'm still staring at the stairs.

His hair is shaggier than normal, and he walks over with a nonchalance I wish I could clone.

He slaps backs, bumps chests, and tosses out nicknames like T-shirts at a basketball halftime show. His shirtsleeves are tight enough to reveal the outline of his almond-shaped shoulder muscles, and short enough so you can see his biceps bulge with every hello. Veins like tributaries flow down his forearms, his hands. Those hands. That smile.

I have a question, but I don't want to ask it.

Have your eyes always been this green?

His pupils are like tiny backyard trampolines. I lie down on them.

Trampoline. *Polypropylene.* A thermoplastic polymer ($(C_3H_6)_n$) used in a wide variety of applications, including backpacks and trampoline mats.

I rest in the dark polypropylene of his unfocused gaze.

No. No. No polypropylene. No trampolines.

But I can't escape. His eyes are not windows, they're like little black holes that suck my soul.

"As an object [such as a sixteen-year-old homosexual] enters a black hole; the temperature increases and raises the **entropy level**—a measure of an object's internal disorder—until the object disappears and is lost forever."

I snap alert just before I'm lost forever.

John raises his eyebrows. I feel some combination of stupid and drunk, and before I do anything dumber, I turn to Joe Thomas and ask him a question about field goal kickers.

Inexcusably, John joins our conversation. "Whaddup, Joe?"

Jeff bounces back downstairs and shouts a loud hello to John, jumping on his back as Joe pours three shots, for Jeff, Joe, and John.

Inexplicably, I speak: "It's a *'J'-Partyyy*!"

I regret the words before they're even in the air. I sound like a bad Bar Mitzvah DJ. I clarify, in case my dazzling sense of humor was lost on the crowd: "Ya know, J-Party. *JeffJoeJohn.*"

"Uh, yeah, we got it, Mark Party," Jeff says dismissively as they raise three red Solo cups to cheers.

"To Life."

"To Love."

"To Lax!"

I just stand there ruminating on what ridiculous version of myself thought it'd be a good idea to shout *J-Party*.

His chest muscles get bigger during lacrosse season. They make upside-down parabolas through his white T-shirt. His laugh has always been so generous, but still earnest, so validating for whoever gets it. Every decibel, every ounce, every inch of John reminds me how inevitable it all was.

My brain starts swimming. Words move in slow motion. *Shit.* I do the test my brother told me about, and . . . the ceiling is, indeed, spinning.

I put down my cup and muster the courage to finally escape this prison of macho chitchat.

I turn back. He's watching me walk away.

God, it would have been so much cooler if I hadn't looked back.

He fist-bumps Joe and Jeff and floats over to me.

"Where you running away to?" He raises his hands with playful confusion.

"Away from *you*." I don't feel like playing.

"Am I that bad?" He smiles. "You look cute."

"What's the goal here?"

"What goal, Mark? We're talking."

"This is *my* party," I say, as the party disappears and the whole world becomes just John.

"Mark, we gotta be able to see each other." He puts his hand on my shoulder. I brush it off. "This isn't *you*, all angry."

"I'm not angry," I say angrily.

"You look good. Have you been having fun? Playing spin the bottle?"

"With who? Who would I spin the bottle on? Or whatever the right preposition is . . . for that."

"You're the only drunk person who thinks about prepositions."

"*For whom the bottle spins*," I say, with poetic overenunciation.

"Nerd." He laughs. "You still in th—"

"Seriously, I cannot chitchat you right now." I exhale, exhausted, into the ceiling. It spins.

He laughs his perfect friggin' laugh. "You can't *chitchat me*?"

"Leave me alone. I'm not doing well, grammatically, at the moment . . . ," I plead. "I can't chitchat *with* you."

"What'd Eric always say? 'Buzzed Good, Drunk Bad.'"

"Drunk Good, *You* Bad."

"How is Eric? Up at Northwes—"

"*I can't.* I'm sorry. We used to spend every second together. My grandma knows you don't like lettuce on your tacos! And now we're 'chitchatting'?" My eyelids feel heavy. "I just wanted one night. One night. It's bad enough that everything reminds me of you. I'd rather not have *you* . . . remind me of . . . you."

"That doesn't even make sense." His perfect friggin' Netflix rom-com laugh.

"It does make sense, actually," I say defensively. "It's a syllogism . . . or something. You know, like 'quitters never win.'" My hand gestures get broader. "Solipsistic."

"All right. No need to queen out, Princess Thesaurus."

"You know, my fucking luck that the most homophobic kid at school is the only other gay one."

"Oh my God."

"But you know what, don't even worry about it . . . because *my* eggs aren't in *your* basket anymore!"

"What are you talking about?" He's holding in a laugh the way you do at church.

"It's *your* loss, because *alllll my eggs* . . ." I make a dramatic swirling motion with my arms. ". . . are in my *owwn* basket now."

In my head it's a very profound conclusion, up there with the great anthems for single ladies, so I storm away triumphantly, walking steadily to prove I have life all figured out. I walk so steadily that when I bump into the folding table holding all the snacks and drinks, I barely flinch as it all comes crashing down around me. The crunch of plastic cookie containers, the thud of glass vodka bottles, and the rustle of the ninety-nine-cent fall-foliage table-cloth unite in a chorus of my embarrassment as the entire socially relevant population of Annondale High School looks over with collective pity.

"God, he's a mess," someone whispers as I focus on saving the last of the Absolut before too much more spills out. Joe Thomas magnanimously helps me scoop up potato chips and put them back in the napkin-lined basket.

"Touchdown," I say to Joe as we're both crouched down cleaning up. He, appropriately, looks at me confused. There's nothing victorious about this moment. And then I shout, slur, into the depressing, deafening silence. "It's okay . . . 's okay. It's just, a new game. For Throwback Night. It's called Seven Minutes in Hell. And I just won."

Constellations

Hey, are you around?

Yeah buddddddy

Can you come pick me up?

Would be an honor and a privilege.
Where you at?

Hell.

What are the cross streets

18 mile and coodge

*coolidge

Oak river nbrhhd

Hold up

617 Chester

Leaving now

I wait for my brother on the curb, as far from the house as possible without lying in the road. The streetlights from the highway cast a faint glow on the otherwise pitch-black neighborhood. The street is silent except for a faint bass beat coming from Lisa's basement. The houses are so dark they look dead.

I lie back on the grass and look up at the stars, but I can't even find the Big Dipper.

Whatever. Constellations are bullshit, anyway. Is there anything more insulting to the stars than forcing them into constellations? The beautiful, vital chaos of the universe and we think it'd be better to say it looks like a spoon.

Eric's navy-blue Jeep crunches over the curb.

"Dire times at Annondale High?" he asks as he turns down the music and I flop into the front seat.

"High times in dire Annondale."

"Holy word slur, Batman. Drink much? Where's your car?"

"I'm Robin. I'll get it tomorrow."

"What was the original plan?"

"Didn't have one."

"Failure to plan is planning to—"

"Don't talk like a fortune cookie."

"Well, if I'm driving to the complete other side of town"—he reverses into Lisa's neighbor's driveway to turn toward the main road—"*and* taking on the risk of you puking all over my car, the least you can do is humor me with what the hell happened tonight."

"I'm an idiot."

"Know thyself."

"You're an idiot."

"Anger is fear turned outward."

"Gahhhh! You really have one for everything. Fine. I was having fun. I made my drinks too strong."

"Were *you* making them? Or were you taking them from someone else?"

"No! I was making them, like you taught me. But I was a bad influence on myself." He turns out of the neighborhood into the bright lights of Coolidge Road. "I just wanted to have fun. And just as I was about to *start* having fun, like, I *literally* had a delicious sugar cookie from Kroger with the sprinkles and the frosting that's like a whole entire *pancake* of frosting, this delicious cookie, *in my hand*, and my whole night is about to get perfect when—"

"John shows up," he finishes my thought, then turns toward me as we wait at a red light. "Did you guys talk?"

"About the same shit. How I'm a queen. And emotional."

"Are you kidding me? He said that? In the middle of a party?"

"Definitely. I think so. I can't really remember. Not really. But something like that. Definitely said *queen*. I think."

"Buuud." He holds it like a half note and sings it to the sky. "You don't need to get so drunk! Yeah, some people need to get drunk, because it's the only way they can have fun. But you're fun, just regular. You don't need to hit it so hard."

"I'm not fun."

"Well, I know it's hard to believe right now, in the thick of it, but this will pass, and there will be a time in your life when you look back on it all and think, 'Fuck, I can't believe I spent so much energy on John Fucking Beckett.'"

"You just can't tell how hot he is because of your heterosexual eyes."

"You're a mess."

I shout to the empty road: "I'm a mess!"

"Can I tell you something?" His eyebrows move up to meet his short, decisively brown hair. Just brown. No further explanation needed. And when he does his hair in the morning, it stays that way all day. Meanwhile his dirty-blond little brother has to keep a can of hairspray in his backpack because by fourth period it looks like he had lunch on a Jet Ski.

"Tell me anything! It can't possibly be worse than the sad fact that I am of the privileged point one percent of gay children in America who have a hot gay guy at their school and I went and messed it all up by being too gay for the gay guy." My syllables string together like a floppy noodle.

"You should seriously consider not talking anymore tonight."

"*Youuu* seriouslytalker . . ."

"He's not the guy for you."

"Oh my God, I called him a J-Party."

"He's not the guy for you."

"I'm a prisoner of your car!"

"Listen to me. You don't want to hear it, but he's not. A *Lax Bro*? Come on, Mark."

"That's a stereotype."

"I'm just saying. He's a solid guy, but not for you." He grips the steering wheel firmly. His arms are strong, like mine should be. He takes his right hand off and taps my head. "And I think somewhere in that wet little brain of yours, you get that."

"*Your* brain is wet." I swipe his hand away and look out the window.

"And you want to know the truth? The bigger truth? Little bro, every *good* relationship makes you wanna be *more* of yourself. Not less."

"You're a fortune cookie with a driver's license."

"Shut up, queen. I'm also a fortune cookie who holds the fate of your junior year in my hands. One word to Mom and Dad about the reason I had to pick you up and the only place you'll be going on the weekends is church." I swing to hit him but hit the ceiling light instead. He pushes my hand back to my lap. "And I'm not talking shit, but bud, *good* relationships make you want to be so fully fucking activated, so fully *you*, that even the parts that you thought were broken they somehow teach you to love. You're not out there wondering if you're too this, or too that. That person loves you *because* you're too this and too that. Wants you to be *more* too this and too that."

"I'll believe it when I see it."

"You're sixteen. You'll see it. Just because it ended doesn't mean it was this big failure. Plus, you had a decently healthy, year-plus relationship in *high school*. That's pretty fuckin' good."

"Only because he didn't have any other options."

He swats me on the back of the head, with much better aim than I had. "This pity party is not cute. And it's not you."

"I want Taco Bell."

All the King's Men

Monday morning, I walk into our rooster-themed kitchen and find my mom stirring the Crock-Pot. "Mom, can you sign this permission slip for the choir trip?" She puts the rooster ladle on the rooster spoon rest and wipes her hands on the rooster towel, but Dad gets to me first.

"Overnight field trip, huh, bud?" he says, revving up. "Better not get into any funny business in"—he pauses to read the location—"*Springhill Suites by Marriott Midland*."

This is why I always give things like this to my mom.

"Dad, it's choir. And it's *Midland*. Come on, I'm gonna be late."

He starts scanning. "Yup . . . Yup . . . Lookin' good . . ." He reads painfully slowly. "You know your address, that's good. Way to go. Proving you're an adult with this penmanship. Great work. Remembered your mother's birthday. That's an A for genealogy!" With every word I roll my eyes. "Ah, nope." He starts scratching something out. "*House* phone for emergencies, bud. House phone for emergencies."

"Oh. Yeah," I say, and then laugh. "Can you imagine Mom in an emergency with her cell phone?"

Dad imitates a distressed Mom. "*Is it ringing? Or is that my alarm?*"

I join in, "*How do I get* the picture *from the* text message *to the* iPhoto?"

Mom takes off her rooster apron, giving us the Midwest Mom version of side-eye. "Nobody's having any emergency on any phone," she says, a little more seriously than she needs to. She defends her position as the last landline owner in America: "The house phone never runs out of batteries."

"Mom, we're joking. It's for a friggin' field trip."

"Don't say *friggin'* to your mother."

Signed permission slip in hand, I drag my backpack through the wet grass of our front yard and return to a far more important task: praying that my cookie-table-tumble is not the Monday morning headline.

"Hello to the luckiest dude in Annondale." Damien pulls me backward by my backpack to catch up to me in the hallway. "After you left, Reid Meyers accidentally swallowed chewing tobacco, and just as he was going in to kiss Beth Dorsey, he puked all over the trampoline."

"And Beth Dorsey," Crystal adds. Then she gets stern. "You could have said *goodbye*."

"I had to escape."

Damien hops ahead, spins to face us. "While you were outside, did you happen to see Crystal's soul peeking from the bushes?"

She hits him in the arm. "It makes sense if you actually *think about it.*"

"I have to conserve every bit of thinking for physics at the moment."

"Right. Those of us in the slow-kid classes have plenty of brain left to think about life. You know, you really have a *way*, Damien." Crystal rolls her eyes and Damien winces apologetically.

Crystal is a genius, but she turns off at school. Damien is brilliant but most of his success comes from anxiety: *If I actually believed in myself, I might never study.* I'm an idiot insanely motivated by a GPA competition against an older brother who graduated with a 3.97.

"Hey, drunk-o," Haley shouts without stopping as we merge into the intersection of the main stairwell. "Friday," she calls, slapping me on the back as the two-minute warning bell buzzes us into a hustle. "You better be fucking fierce."

This Friday: Haley Stewart's Annual Halloween Shit Show.

Damien tilts his head. "I think for Haley, school is just the boring part in between parties."

He looks at Crystal as she turns right instead of left, to the admin offices rather than the English hallway. "Where are you going?"

"A meeting with Mrs. Pointer," she answers, almost falling asleep at the thought of our overinvolved guidance counselor.

"What about?"

"I'm sure she's just gonna tell me what a great job I'm doing. Maybe ask me to set up a mentoring program."

"Crystal's Wisdom for Wayward Freshmen," I add, matching her sarcasm.

Damien looks like my mom worrying about house phones. "Well, good luck." He squeezes her arm, then, before parting ways, he calls back to me. "For Haley's, you in for firefighters?"

"What are we, twelve?"

"*Sexy* firefighters, bro."

"What does that even mean?"

"Well, you have to decide by tonight. Skinner's buying helmets."

Olive Oyl drama aside, John and I eventually developed a reputation for cute couples' costumes. Freshman year, I was one half of Mario and Luigi (even though I wanted to be Princess Peach). Sophomore year, I was one half of Batman and Robin (even though I wanted to be Catwoman).

This year, I'm one half of nothing.

And any third grader with a calculator knows that one half of nothing is nothing.

My phone vibrates.

Reminder: Today is the day
You promised

"Phone away, Mr. Davis," yells assistant principal Dr. Cook, whose sole purpose in life seems to be preventing students from checking text messages between classes.

Last night, as Eric and I were FaceTiming our way through Pep Talk #932, I promised him I would "crush this Monday." I had been whining that it felt like John was that one Jenga block holding the whole tower together, and without him, I was just a toppled pile of Jenga blocks. Eric indulged my stupid metaphor but told me I had it wrong. "You'll see. Your Jenga tower's about to reach the *sky* now."

I sneak a peek when I know Dr. Cook is gone.

Stack those blocks bud

I send him a gif of Humpty-Dumpty, after the fall.

"One more time and it's mine," Dr. Cook yells.

This man can chameleon himself into beige brick.

I don't really like talking about my problems with anyone, even Damien and Crystal. I don't know, I feel like it's my job to fix things, and it's not right to bum anyone out with them. However, with my brother, I don't mind. Plus, he *lives* to help people. Has been that way forever. When we were little kids, Eric had this epiphany: He was home sick and saw this therapist on daytime TV giving "tough love" advice to all these families, and he realized, the same way you study for math tests, you can *study* life: "Learning life makes more sense than learning SOH-CAH-fucking-TOA." So to Eric, happiness is no different than a standardized test. Difficult, maybe, but if you study hard enough, memorize the right formulas, you can crack it.

I put my phone away and search the basement of my soul for something resembling confidence. I turn into the more subdued English hallway and—

Bam.

Despite the fact that I'd designed a path around school specifically to avoid him . . .

He's in a group, walking from the end of the hall toward me. Laughing.

Be chill, I think. *Just say hi. Chitchat. Chill chitchat.*

Long tubes of fluorescent light outline a path straight from me to him.

I smile.

Inhale.

Walk normal.

He sees me.

People *do* get back together . . .

Without slowing his stride, he gives me a head nod.

A head nod.

We dated for two years.

It hurts more than if he had punched me in the face.

I nod back, but too late. I nod to empty air.

I can feel him walking away, like he's playing tug-of-war against my lungs. It gets tighter and tighter with every step until I can barely breathe, and maybe it's because Haley Stewart told me to be fucking fierce or because my dorm-room Dalai Lama actually sometimes knows what he's talking about, or maybe it's because I'm just *so sick of being sad*, but I decide, once and for all, that I will be the Humpty-Dumpty who puts himself back together again.

✧ ✧ ✧

I hype myself up all day and FaceTime Eric immediately after school.

"No, a great *fall*," I explain from the back stairwell. "The stuff with John hurt. I had a 'great fall.' But now Humpty-Dumpty's about to have a great *fall*!" I dramatically overenunciate. "Get it? A wonderful autumn!" My voice echoes down the white stairs as a streak of sunlight streams in through the narrow windows. My shoes squeak on the rubber floor.

His face is framed by red and orange leaves as he pauses in front of a gothic building and a blur of students passes behind him. "You know I support you in everything you do, but you gotta drop the Humpty-Dumpty metaphor."

"*Drop* Humpty-Dumpty? *Again?* Has he not fallen enou—"

Eric hangs up, and when the screen goes black, I notice the time. Musical rehearsal starts in three minutes and I'm about a mile away. I'm supposed to be *in* costume by 2:40 because it's only a week until dress rehearsals and if the costumes don't fit, then Mrs. Mould needs to know *today*.

I sprint through the math hallway and try not to think of all the calculus homework I have. I run outside, taking a shortcut through the expansion classrooms that make our school look like a trailer park. My cheeks feel flush as I rush back in and round the corner past Mrs. Pointer's office and remember that I need to email those animal shelter volunteer forms *tomorrow* so I don't come across as "one-dimensional" on college applications. I whoosh past the tuba lockers, where band kids suck face at 7:00 a.m., and finally make it to the stage with just enough breath to say hello to the diligent freshmen already head to toe in three-piece tuxedos.

Normally we do a fall play and a spring musical, but last year's fall play was this *insanely* depressing Arthur Miller play, *All My Sons*, and the whole city is still recovering. So Mr. Wagner said, "Goodbye, drama, and *Hello, Dolly!*" (his exact words).

Surrounded by giddy waiters and fake champagne, I take a deep inhale of sawdust and spray paint and grab the tux marked *Mark*.

In the greenroom, I hurl my cheap jeans, hand-me-down flannel, and overstuffed JanSport into the back corner and float into my costume. The wide, structured shoulders of the suit jacket make me feel sturdy and strong. I clip on my bow tie with a satisfying snap. My breathing returns to normal as I trace my hand over the slippery satin of the lapel. In the mirror, I smile. My life might suck, but in this tux, I am a rich old man who makes his own decisions.

"Pardon me," I say regally, as I step over the sophomore stagehand taping down a power cord.

I emerge from the wings, and the lighting director shouts, "Jim, let's bring house to half and test full stage lights with the follow spot for end of act one."

In an instant, every light beams white like the gates of heaven, just in time for my entrance.

Mr. Wagner whispers in awed reverence, "Simone."

I turn and get almost nauseous with jealousy.

Rendered powerless by the beauty of her dress, Mr. Wagner drops his director's folder onto the gray carpet of the orchestra section and repeats the only word he can find. "Simone."

He uses an armrest on the front row to hop onto the stage. Closer, he delicately lifts the tulle of her skirt, fluffs the fluff of her shoulder pads, then steps back, speechless, for a quieter, "Simone."

It's red like the sunset and puffy like a cloud.

Poofy in the sleeves and perfect in the waist.

Tight and glittery on top, big and billowy on bottom.

It's the kind of dress that can stop a heart.

It's the kind of dress that can steal a scene.

It's the kind of dress that can make a teenage homosexual in a stupid tuxedo wonder why girls get to have all the fun.

Mrs. Mould's dyed red hair is wrapped in a messy bun, barely held together by a No. 2 pencil. Beside me, she whispers like she's got a dirty secret, "Halloween City."

I stare.

It feels less like seeing something for the first time and more like remembering. As Mrs. Mould details her search for the perfect evening gown, a memory from a decade ago floods my mind.

Eric and I were on spinny bar stools in Herschel's Diner, splitting a double-decker piece of vanilla cake with vanilla frosting and rainbow sprinkles, feeling like grown-ups because Mom let us eat our dessert at the bar. The bell on top of the front door chimed and we turned to the entrance—mostly just to test the spin of our stools.

In walked a little girl, about my age, wearing the dress that will forever occupy a place in my memory. I forget people's names, I never remember my locker combination, and I couldn't even tell you where we went for spring break last year—but I will never forget this dress. At seven years old, I saw the dress that taught my baby gay heart how to beat.

Two adults waited with her. I suppose they were her parents, but the dress was so refined and she carried herself with such dignity I wouldn't have been surprised to find out that they were her royal guards. I tried not to stare, but it was like a chandelier hanging in a garage. Sequins circled the bodice. The purple fabric glistened in the flickering fluorescent lights. The tulle almost—but not quite—touched the floor, and the puffy sleeves crinkled *hello*.

And Simone Morrison's princess dress is identical, except in red.

Mrs. Mould goes on. "Who's got the budget for a gown?" she tells Mr. Wagner as she takes in the red dress from every angle. "And me and my little sewing machine certainly can't do what we used to, so I called everyone—dance studios, vintage shops. Even called Rose Theater up in Chelsea because they did *My Fair Lady* last year, plenty of evening gowns in *My Fair Lady*, and Ray still works there, so I called him up, but they had nothin' but day dresses left. Well, of course this is an evening scene. Can't wear a day dress to a dinner. And then—I was only there because my grandbaby can't get enough *Frozen*. Needed a new Elsa wig, of all things. Never in a million years. Can you believe it? Twenty-nine ninety-nine. Of course it's a little over the top, but my goodness, it's supposed to be an *old* dress, after all, and if we cut off these poofy princess sleeves, put a little draping in the front, throw on some white gloves and a feather headpiece, well, from row L they'll think they're looking at Carol Channing herself. Or at least Barbra! Can you believe it? Halloween City!"

She takes one last look with an awestruck smile and then turns her eagle eye on me.

She tugs hard on the back of my vest, yanks the hem of the

jacket, pulls out the shoulders, grips my waistband, and tugs, harder, at the vest. "We have to take it in more," she says, like it's my fault.

But it's okay—I'm hardly even here.

In my head, I'm halfway to Halloween City.

Excited and Scared

I take the stairs two at a time and text Mom rehearsal's running late.

I speed to the Maple Mini Mall before I have time to change my mind.

As I tornado through the revolving door, *everything* clicks. Halloween. Catwoman. Herschel's Diner. *Rollin' on the riverrrr.* Floating in the talent show. Princess Peach. *You gonna change?* Heck yeah! Change right into—

"Where are the girl costumes?" I hurriedly ask a half-vacant employee.

He flops his hand like he's swatting at the world's slowest fly. "Girl costumes is like half the store, man."

"Right, I'll just browse. Sorry!"

Never before have I been filled with such certainty. I know what I'm looking for and I know that I'll find it. I know, on a cellular level, that the universe would not bring me to this looted Halloween superstore just to punch me in the gut with some logistical complication like, "Yes, but not in purple."

Imagine! Once I thought happiness was so complicated, only to find out that it's not even a question.

It's a dress.

I find it easily. I knew I would.

I grab it quickly, barely even checking the size chart. This could all be a dream, and I have to buy it before I wake up.

Sure, my parents will hate it (sophomore year talent show reviews—Mom: "We loved the song you sang *last* year, honey"; Dad: "Not exactly something for a father to see."), but that's why God invented lying!

In line, the clear plastic dress bag gets foggy in my sweaty hands. I feel giddy. And scared. Like when you're driving to a party with a water bottle full of vodka under your passenger seat.

The man behind me bumps my back scrounging in the checkout display for a candy bar. I turn around and—

Shit.

Jeff Miller. Reid Meyers. Kevin Wolfe. Walking. To this line.

I freeze. Then duck. Then stand regular because ducking looks way more ridiculous than standing. I give the cashier an apologetic facial expression, like someone who just realized he forgot to get party streamers, and abandon the checkout line. I inch around a wide orange cart, hopefully before half the varsity lacrosse team sees me holding a dress.

My heart beats louder than Halloween City's spooky Spotify playlist as I sidestep over to the outermost aisle and take refuge behind a giant wall of tombstones.

I close my eyes, breathe, and join the dead.

"If you're trying to steal something, it's smarter to go *out* of the store."

A steady voice comes from behind a bin of goblin body parts.

I stay still but turn my head, stuttering, "Oh, no, I'm just . . ." I look down at the costume like it's no more consequential than a bag of avocados, flip the bag around to hide the picture on the front. "I forgot something."

He matches my whisper. "Who are you hiding from?"

It would be impossible to feel any dumber.

The guy who's not buying my bullshit is Ezra Ambrose. We have English together, but already I think this is the most we've ever talked. I stand up straight and collect my dignity from the sticky linoleum of Halloween City.

"I'm not hiding from anyone," I say, too defensively. "I was just trying to see if they had any more of these . . . skeleton arms. For my costume."

"And what will you be donning this Halloween, Mr. Davis?"

I fidget with the dress and reflexively hide it behind my back. "I don't know. Trying to figure that out. Last minute, I guess." I try to change the subject. "What are *you* going as?"

"'What I'm going as' is really a subordinate line of inquiry, given I'm not going anywhere." He enunciates every syllable, speaks with an almost regal monotone somewhere between serious and sarcastic. He's taller than I remember.

I awkwardly laugh. "So, then, what are you doing in Halloween City?"

"My mother has been unexpectedly struck by the holiday

spirit, so she sent me to buy lawn decorations," he explains, holding up the box of a ten-foot-tall dancing air puppet, the kind that wave their arms outside a car wash, but this one is white like a ghost. "It's strategic," he confides. "I'm hopeful if I make it tacky enough, she'll take me off the party-planning committee." He angles his head down. Very short stubble outlines his sharp jaw.

His eyes look like they have a secret, and I don't know why I'm nervous. "Oh, I do the same kind of thing." I shift weight and tighten my grip on the dress bag, "Don't tell my mom that I'm secretly, like, an amazing vacuumer."

As I continue strangling the life out of this poor tulle, I nod to a second box in his hands. "What's that one?"

He turns it to reveal a fog machine.

"Oh, super cool," I respond like a nerdy eight-year-old.

"Indeed." He keeps the formality in his tone. "And after Halloween, I can turn my basement into Annondale's first gay club."

I laugh, awkwardly, and wonder where all the words I once knew have disappeared to.

"It's crazy we've never really met before," I say, just for something to say.

"Yeah, *crazy*," he accentuates, mocking me with a playful smirk.

When I look a little hurt by the teasing, he does a small, very unexpected, rather bizarre arm flail, like a deflating dancing air puppet.

I smile, bashfully, and we meet eyes. I try to look away.

I can't.

I continue. "I just meant because . . ."

He lifts his eyebrows, lingers in the blank space. "We're both . . ."

I roll my eyes with a smile.

"We're both . . . ," he repeats, drawing out the words with playful suspense, forcing me to fill in what we both know we both are.

". . . in Mrs. Parsons's English class," I finish, with the tone of a reprimanding nun.

He takes the smallest of steps closer to me. "It's always great to meet another guy who . . ." He pauses seductively. ". . . is in Mrs. Parsons's English class."

We hold eye contact, for somewhere between a second and an entire lifetime.

"I should probably pay." He breaks us out of wherever we just were. "Every minute my front lawn goes without this frantic air puppet is a missed opportunity." He steps forward, casually, but then peeks his head out the aisle, looking left, then right, then left again, theatrically scanning the checkout area like a diligent Secret Service Agent. He turns back before walking ahead. "The coast is clear, Princess."

Through a broad smile, he makes it sound like a compliment.

"I'll see you tomorrow . . ." He takes a small step, walking backward so we don't have to stop looking at each other.

I finish for him, ". . . in Mrs. Parsons's English class."

A Crush

"**W**hy are you dressed up?" Damien asks, looking up from the flash cards on his phone as we meet each other in the cafeteria after our before-school meetings (Him: Student Government, Me: Students Against Drunk Driving, Both: Just for College Applications).

"I'm not dressed up." I self-consciously rub my khakis.

"And your hair is different."

"It is not," I say, too defensively.

Damien, annoyed, taps his phone. "What the fuck does 'vociferously' mean?"

Crystal joins with a tire-sized bagel from the school store. She looks at me.

"Why are you dressed up?" she asks.

"I'm not dressed up!"

She tears off a chunk of her bagel. "Why are you so mad about being dressed up?"

"I'm not dressed up."

"You're wearing dress pants," Damien says.

"They're . . . *casual* dress pants."

Of course it's customary to talk to your best friends about your new crush, but given recent history it just seems a little *off* to suddenly say, "I know I've been crying about a guy for a month, but last night I stood in the orange glow of the Halloween City sign and realized I was in love, madly, deeply in love, so this morning I spent forty-five minutes picking out an outfit, but then changed outfits because I thought my outfit looked like an outfit I spent too much time picking out, but then changed back because the second outfit was wrinkled and that seemed to make the 'I'm not trying too hard' point a little too *vociferously*."

"Where are you going?" Damien asks Crystal as she, again, turns away from the English hallway and toward the admin offices.

"What can I say, Mrs. Pointer's obsessed with me."

"And why shouldn't she be?" I rub her shoulder.

"Is everything okay?" Damien asks.

"It's stupid. I'm changing English classes, so they're just figuring out where there's space."

"Why are you changing English classes?"

"You always ask the most *fascinating* questions, Damien," she says, gazing at the ceiling like it's a planetarium. She skips ahead. "Everything's fine! You look cute, Mark!"

"I look *normal*!" I protest.

We split. Damien goes to calculus, Crystal goes to Mrs. Pointer's, and I go to think about why my insides feel upside down.

✧ ✧ ✧

In Mrs. Parsons's English class, I get there early and try to sit normal.

How do I normally sit?

As all the early-arrivers arrange our Post-It-flagged study packets, Mrs. Parsons tells us that today will be fun. "A breath of fresh air from the pressures of practice exams."

If you think people are excited to hear this, then you don't know nerds. These are the same kids who went to summer camp for AP Bio—no fresh air till admission emails.

Ezra enters.

I pretend to be reviewing my notes from yesterday's class, without a care in the world.

My stomach seems to be somewhere in my throat.

The loud buzz of the tardy bell startles no one.

Mrs. Parsons pauses for dramatic effect, her nest of gray hair nodding with the wind of the ceiling fan as she plays with the chunky beads of her green necklace. She leans back against her desk with a sly smile, quite proud of herself for all the suspense. "Put all that away," she says. "We're going to do something a little different today."

Our essays are getting "robotic," apparently. Too transparently "test-prepped" (says the woman who makes us take a prep test twice a week). "The difference between a 'four' and a 'five' is often *emotion* and *humanity*, which must be established in the introductory paragraph." The freckle on the back of Ezra's neck seems to have cast some sort of spell on me. "Your intro must be attention-grabbing and memorable," Mrs. Parsons continues. "It needs to shake the lapels of the AP grader and shout, '*This* is going

to be a great essay within your pile of boring, mediocre essays.'"
How have I ignored this person for two years and now a freckle
feels like soft porn? "So we're going to do a day of *rapid introductions*. You'll get three sample prompts. For each, you'll write
an introduction paragraph." It's right where the smooth arch of
his shoulder muscle slopes into his well-trimmed dark hair. "To
reinforce the theme, I'd like you to work on the assignment with
someone you don't know very well. Introductions over introductions!" I can't stop staring.

Mrs. Parsons beams like she's just let us out for Field Day. The
class stands. Everyone awkwardly scans for prospective partners.
I sit statue still. I don't even blink. I don't even think I remember
how to blink. The white SMART Board blurs in my dry eyes.

Marcus Heller, who I definitely don't know very well, unless
you count the time his mom drove me home from show choir auditions in seventh grade, walks over to me. I try to mask my disap-
pointment.

But he strides past to Tiffany Mayo.

And in all the suspense, I hadn't even noticed Ezra approach-
ing from the side.

"It's fate," he says with a sly smile.

My brain says *stand* but my legs say *blergerderfamrksdjfa*.

"Totally." I finally start functioning. "And since we already
made our introduction last night, it'll give us more time for the
assignment!" Okay, *barely* functioning.

It's loud in the classroom, and Mrs. Parsons said we could
spread out, so Ezra leads us through the doorframe into the hall.
The way his jeans fit, the way his shirt drapes, the way his shoulders

slope into his arms—it's all just *correct*, without trying too hard. Like a sentence without adverbs.

Clearly, he has no interest in filling the silence, so I do. "How was the rest of your night?" I nod to a spot on the floor, against some lockers, where we could sit.

"Anticlimactic," he responds as he adjusts himself on the gray industrial carpet and leans back against the lockers. "How'd your princess dress fit?" He tilts his head and smiles.

It takes me off guard—I think he wanted it to—but I smile back. "I don't think you'd be able to concentrate on the assignment if I told you."

He playfully rolls his eyes. "A princess for one night and he's already self-obsessed."

"Shut up," I say, desperate for a better response so we could just flirty banter forever, innuendo until we die.

"Wait," I say, remembering, "we didn't get the assignment sheet." I quickly stand, then realize something else. "You don't even have a pen."

Ezra blushes, just barely, and bashfully holds up a TI-84 Plus. "But I do, inexplicably, have my calculator." The awkward sight of it is more reassuring than a hug from my grandma. He's nervous, too. *He's nervous, too!*

I hustle inside, grab an extra pen, give myself a pep talk—*getagripgayboy*—and take an assignment sheet as Mrs. Parsons watches over me disapprovingly.

"A *little* fun, Mr. Davis, but it's an assignment that should still be taken seriously."

I return, ashamed, into the hallway.

Ezra looks at the paper. "What kind of a sick woman calls the following *fun*." He reads, "'Write an essay—**introduction only**—analyzing the rhetorical choices former Vice President Spiro Agnew made in the below 1969 televised address to the nation.'"

If tiny spelunkers climbed into my brain right now, all they would see is a neon 69.

Get it together! Focus on Spiro Agnew.

I look over Ezra's shoulder at the sheet and realize all the prompts are just as boring.

"What if . . ."—I start proposing the world's nerdiest rebellion—"we did the introductions as homework, and used this time for, like . . ."

"*In-tro-duc-tions*." Ezra uses a comically deep voice and lifts his eyebrows seductively.

"No," I admonish. "Well, yes. But no."

With a hop, he heads down the hall. "Adventure?" He walks the way he sits, with this effortless refined posture that makes you certain he always knows which fork to use.

I stomp behind like a frazzled hall monitor. "I don't think she meant we could *go* anywhere. She didn't give us hall passes or anything."

The metal door of the back stairwell slams behind us as I trail him up the steps.

"You're Mark Davis," he calls back without slowing down, "you're untouchable at this school and it's adorable and implausible that you don't know that."

"Maybe I'm looking out for *your* best interest. I might go free, but you"—I look at his black shirt, black jeans—"you're already dressed like a ne'er-do-well."

Who says ne'er-do-well?

"I'm invisible. I could strip naked and self-immolate and it wouldn't make the school paper."

We hurry ahead until he turns and wordlessly unlocks the door of the yearbook office, leading me through.

"You're on yearbook?" I ask, in a convincing imitation of my *mother*.

We stand between two locked doors in a dark passageway full of spare computer monitors and expensive cameras, and it instantly becomes very apparent that we're alone. He flicks a switch and the electricity turns on. Bright lights buzz above and a whole system of equipment hums. A spotlight shines on a news anchor desk with a green screen backdrop.

I hustle behind the desk and channel my inner anchor. "*We're live from the third floor, just moments after Ezra Ambrose self-immil . . . self-emula . . .*" I stutter, then abruptly end. "*Over to you, Bob.*" I hang my head in shame.

His short black hair forms a sharp arch over his dark eyebrows. "Stick to singing, slugger."

I blush and hope he can't tell.

"What do you do? Other than yearbook?" I ask, spinning on my news-anchor stool, around and around, feeling giddy with rebellion. "I never see you around."

"I try my best never to be '*around*,'" he says, dripping in condescension for no apparent reason.

"Okay, geez. 'Not around.' Noted." I make a literal note in my notebook, and then press ahead. "Well, are you about? Below? Within? Where *is* Ezra Ambrose?" I ask, impersonating a pushy journalist. He smiles. Encouraged, I keep going. "Be careful, I could go on forever. I remember the whole list of prepositions. Are you between? Beneath? Above? Atop?"

All oxygen leaves the room and his eyes widen instantly. "Did you just ask if I'm a t—"

"You *know* I didn't!" My jaw drops to the floor. "You know I did not ask that, you absolutely know that." I blush so hard you could light a cigarette off my cheeks.

His long-sleeve T-shirt drapes over his arms and I can see the outline of his biceps—the lean muscles of weekend yoga and organic vegetables, not the bulky mass of free weights and protein shakes.

I pull myself together and turn the page in my notebook for a fresh start. "We have to do the assignment."

"Things were just getting good!"

"Things were just getting very bad!"

"What do *you* do besides singing? And plays? And playing dress-up?" He teases with a smile.

"Please stop talking about that."

"Oh, come on," he teases again, but I don't smile. "You're serious," he says, sitting up straight. "I'm sorry." It sounds like he means it. He reassures me, casually, "It's a Halloween costume. Even local news anchors dress in drag for Halloween. You're not exactly spearheading the second Stonewall."

"I know . . ."

"And even if it—Men are allowed to wear dresses."

"It's not even my first time in drag," I say, sounding like a kindergartner trying to prove he's not afraid of the big-kid slide. "But, anyway, it's not my Halloween costume. It was just . . . something I had to get . . . Simone Morrison . . . for the play. For this ball scene." I make up the lie on the spot, but it's pretty good. And necessary.

Last night as I sat on my bed, grasping my $31.79 prettypretty princess dress, I had a rather obvious realization: The people I was hiding from in Halloween City *are the same people who'll be at the party*.

Also, the boy who wears dresses is the one girls want to go shopping with. The sexy firefighter is the one guys want to date.

"For Halloween, I'm doing, like, a group costume thing," I tell Ezra.

"Of course you are," he says, again condescending.

"What does that mean?"

"The holy 'group costume.'" He holds his hands up like he's waiting for communion. "An archetypal collaboration for the teens who chug beer in basements and always throw parties when their parents are out of town."

"I'm starting to figure out why you're not around."

"I'm more interested in being atop."

"Well, it *starts* by being around." I shut him down.

"Then invite me to your Halloween party."

"Doesn't sound like you'd have very much fun."

"Will *you*?"

The *you* has weight to it. I give him the strongest side-eye I can muster. "Of course I will," I say, annoyed at the implication. I remind him, because it seems like he forgot, "You don't know me."

The sexual tension deflates like a farting balloon.

Ezra waits. "If you'll permit a reset," he says delicately. "What is your group costume?"

I feel like an idiot saying it out loud.

I delay as long as possible.

"Firefighters."

The fluorescent light buzzes above us.

"I can tell you want to make fun of it."

He nods with noticeable restraint. "A very noble profession."

"*Sexy* firefighters."

"Well, that goes without saying." He puts his hands up. "Who else is in your squadron?"

"Just my friends. Damien Cole, Jeff Miller, Joe Thomas—"

"Joe Thomas"—he speaks like a snobby college professor and I wait for the insult—"Joe Thomas would *not* be an ugly firefighter."

It's unexpected, and it's like a pressure valve being released after ten minutes of stressful flirting (plus five years of being friends with this stupidly hot guy that I can't admit is hot because I'm friends with him). I laugh and it feels like splitting a secret. "Oh my God, he could be on a box of underwear," I confess rapidly, leaning forward.

I quickly tone it down. "But he's also, like, really nice."

"I'll bet he is," Ezra says, unconvinced.

"You know, you can be a little pretentious."

Behind Ezra's stool, the black screen of the blank teleprompter reflects my worried face. I meant it playfully. It sounded mean.

"I'm probably just trying to impress you," he admits.

I fidget with the ends of my shirtsleeves. "Well, it was working until you made fun of people who throw parties when their parents are out of town." I spin, a little, then back. "Who *doesn't* throw parties when their parents are out of town? If your parents go out of town and you don't throw a party, are you even alive?"

He takes the tone of an *aha*. "*That's* why I feel so dead inside," he deadpans, then lifts his eyebrows with an accusation. "You *are* a bit of a stereotype, though."

"Of *what*?"

"A blond teenage Midwesterner chugging beer in a basement."

"I'm in *musicals*," I counter.

"A blond teenage Midwesterner chugging beer in a basement singing *Hello, Dolly*."

"Wearing a princess dress for Halloween."

"I thought it wasn't your Halloween costume?" he responds knowingly.

"It isn't! I was joking."

He looks in my eyes and suddenly I feel naked.

"Anyways, who says 'Midwesterner.' We're literally in Michigan. What else would we be?"

He shrugs.

"You're a 'Midwesterner,' too."

"I'm from Portland."

"Oh, well, then I bet you're a *Portland* stereotype." I search my brain but come up short. "It's not fair. I don't know anything about Portland." A stack of old yearbooks looks lonely in the corner. "Maybe everyone in Portland is grumpy, horny, pretentious, and alone."

He cracks up.

Like, really, really laughs.

He looks at me like he just flipped to the back of his textbook and I'm the unexpected answer to a practice problem he thought he understood.

The five-minute bell buzzes over his exhale. He holds up the assignment sheet, blank where our first paragraphs are supposed to be.

"Mark Davis, I think we're going to have to find a time to finish our introductions."

Attention-Grabbing and Memorable

When I get home, I think very hard about how a normal person would tell his parents in a normal way that he is going to a classmate's house to work on a normal English assignment.

"I'm in here, honey," my mom calls from her room.

Normally, when I get home from musical rehearsal, she greets me at the door with her favorite questions: how school went, how much homework I have, whether I handed in my rhetorical analysis essay on Spiro Agnew. But tonight she's in her room packing a suitcase.

"What are you packing for?" I ask, confused.

"We're actually going to go visit your brother," she says, a little too brightly.

"Huh? You're going to visit Eric? Today? It's Tuesday."

"Yeah, just for a quick visit," she says, as if they do last-minute trips like this all the time. "It's been a while, and we haven't been up there since he moved in, and it'd just be good to see him." Her casualness sounds forced.

"But . . . why wouldn't you go on Friday? For the weekend? Are you missing school tomorrow?"

"Probably will just miss the rest of this week, but it's no biggie. And Dad isn't too busy at work, so it was a good time." She rubs my shoulder as she heads into the bathroom to get her toiletries.

"Okay . . . ," I say skeptically. But I also don't really know what I'm skeptical about. "I wish I could come. But I can't miss school; it's kind of a big week."

"No, of course not, honey. We'll plan the next trip further in advance. This was just kind of spontaneous." Now I know something is up, because my mom is about as spontaneous as a memorized monologue. The woman puts *grocery shopping* on the calendar.

"Spontaneously going to see Eric?" I ask.

"Yes. I think he's a little more homesick than he expected."

"Eric Davis? Eric Jonathan Davis, who hasn't experienced a negative emotion since that one time he cried coming out of your womb?"

"Don't talk about my *womb*, honey. But yes, Eric Jonathan Davis is a little homesick. We'll just be gone until Friday. Saturday at the latest." She pats my shoulder again. "Don't overthink it."

An instruction that has never once successfully prevented someone from overthinking it. But my worry has nowhere to go, like a trapped fly in the mason jar of my overanxious mind, bouncing against outlandish theories like Eric has some rare disease or my parents are getting divorced—but Eric's never looked healthier, and the only thing I've ever heard my parents argue about is whether ketchup should be refrigerated.

> Are you homesick?

I shoot off the text on the way to my car. I'd briefly considered inviting Ezra over to my house, in the spirit of *if your parents go out of town and you don't have people over, are you even alive*, but then I also remembered a related commandment, which is: If two people of compatible sexual orientations are alone together in a house with no parents, they have to hook up. And that seemed like a lot of pressure to put on a relationship that began twenty-four hours ago in a Halloween superstore. So I put the key in the ignition and pray that Ezra's parents are home.

I wave to Mr. Martell, who's mowing his lawn for probably the third time this week. My dad calls front yards the "shoes of the house," because you can tell a lot about a man just by how he keeps his front yard. And people *will* talk shit. You should have heard my mom when our new across-the-street neighbors went a month without deadheading their petunias.

I turn onto the main road and follow Google's directions to Ezra's house. *You're just doing homework*, I remind myself. *You met him yesterday and you are just doing homework*.

His neighborhood has a fancy sign at the front announcing itself—CRESTWOOD HEIGHTS—and you can immediately tell everyone pays a service to mow their lawn. My neighborhood has a name, but the only way you'd find out about it is if you were invited to the annual Pine Meadows Memorial Day Potluck. I suddenly start to wonder, What if I'm not good enough for a guy who lives in a neighborhood where all the mailboxes are in little brick castles? His mailbox is nicer than my hou—*You're just doing homework*, I interrupt my own manic monologue. *You met him yesterday and you are just doing homework*.

On the sloped street in front of Ezra's dark brick house, I park.

My phone vibrates.

I tell mom I'm homesick because it makes her feel special
You know moms. They need to feel NEEDED.
Plus they wanna see the campus before it gets freeeeezing

While I'm still a bit skeptical, I have to start practicing hellos in my head, and scenario plan different hellos depending on who answers the door.

My phone vibrates again.

Slurpee Sluesday?

Shit. Slurpee Sluesday is a tradition that started in seventh grade after Crystal's first-ever trip to the principal's office because, for an English assignment on alliterations, she handed in a piece of paper that said: "sloppy sluts slurp slurpees on sluesdays."

We've been getting Slurpees on Tuesdays ever since.

But I *completely* forgot.

Shit im so sorry!
I have an English paper.

And also maybe sort of a date?

Gah! So much to tell you.

I'll call you after.

I put my phone away and walk up Ezra's driveway.

The house has the tower of a castle with the quirky brickwork of a cottage, and it's so intimately interwoven with the hill it sits on it's hard to even tell where the hill stops and the house begins. You could Google-Street-View every suburb in the entire world and not see another house like Ezra's.

I run my hands along the tops of well-trimmed bushes.

I quickly put my hands in my pockets because it's probably rude to touch people's well-trimmed bushes.

Hey, I practice in my head. *Hi. Oh, hi. Hello.*

Ezra's mom answers the door. She's polite, friendly, and her asymmetrical black dress makes it clear this is a woman who has better things to do than small talk with a sixteen-year-old.

From the fluffy white couch of his fluffy white living room, Ezra holds up a *printed* final copy of our group assignment.

"You already finished it?" I talk quietly, like at a library.

"I had a feeling you were going to be distracting, and I couldn't risk it."

I glance at his mom and wonder if we're really going to flirt in front of a mom.

"Well, then what are we gonna do?" I ask, heading toward him.

"First human ever to be upset that someone finished his homework."

"Ezra, I have a client call starting in five," his mom calls from the silver kitchen, "so why don't you finish your homework upstairs?"

Ezra hops up and leads me to a stone staircase. I whisper, "First parent ever to tell two flirting teenagers to go to the bedroom." I instantly regret making it all so obvious.

"You're *flirting* with me?" He runs up the stairs, aghast. "I thought you were here for homework." He holds the paper close to his chest and makes a face of lost innocence.

I become keenly aware that I still have my shoes on. No one told me I should take them off, but it *feels* like a house where people take their shoes off. But it'd also be so random to just take your shoes off in the middle of the upstairs hallway. I keep them on, but walk delicately.

His bedroom looks empty on purpose, as if posters on the wall would be entirely too *obvious*, and it's so clean that I'm not convinced anyone lives here.

"So," I ask, "how did you make Spiro Agnew 'attention-grabbing and memorable'?"

We make eye contact as he hands me the assignment sheet.

We both hold the paper, both hold the eye contact, frozen in a moment, together.

And I wonder why this feeling makes me so afraid.

✧ ✧ ✧

"*I saw the best minds of my generation destroyed by madness.*" The YouTube video plays on his laptop, an old recording of an old poem. Sitting against the headboard of his queen-size bed, shoes finally off, I'm frozen, nervous the slightest lean will make me look like a sloppy slut who slurps Slurpees on Sluesdays. "*Angelheaded hipsters burning for the ancient heavenly connec—*"

Ezra talks over the video. "We can't listen to it all now. But it's your homework."

"Like I need more homework," I joke, surprised I can still form sentences. "Where'd you even find this?"

"Remember we read *In Cold Blood* for Mrs. Parsons? Well, I looked up Truman Capote. He was gay!" Ezra says, excited. "But unfortunately, that was the last book he wrote, and according to Wikipedia he died a sad alcoholic," Ezra adds. "Anyway, Truman Capote was enemies with this other writer, William S. Burroughs, also gay—or maybe bi—who once *cut his finger off* because of a guy. And William S. Burroughs was friends with Allen Ginsberg—*also* gay!—who wrote this poem that we're listening to now." He pauses. We listen. "*. . . or drank turpentine in Paradise Alley, death, or purgatoried their torsos night after night . . .*" Our shoulders touch and it feels like fire. "*. . . with dreams, with drugs, with waking nightmares—*"

"Oh, and William S. Burroughs and Allen Ginsberg were friends with Jack Kerouac, who wrote *On The Road*," which we read last year, "and *he* was maybe bisexual! Or at least experimented. Who knows? Everyone was everything!" His knee knocks into mine. Our toes touch.

"That is the most highbrow YouTube black hole I've ever heard of," I say with a smile. "And the gayest."

"They never tell us the good stuff in school."

I have a song lyric in my head, and I don't want to say it, but I think if I don't let it out I'd be like a tea kettle that just explodes because the spout didn't open. "They say his name in *Rent*," I say bashfully, well aware that quoting '90s musicals is probably not the sexiest move. "'*Ginsberg*.'" I say it with just the slightest melody, not wanting to queen out *too* much, and using every ounce of self-restraint I have to not bust out *GinsbergDylanCunninghamAnd-Cage! LennyBruce! LangstonHughes! ToTheStage!* doing different voices for the different cast members.

"Well, you fill me in on queer musicals and I'll fill you in on queer literary rivalries." He turns the volume down on his computer, takes it off his lap. "Together, we'll conquer the world."

"I'm pretty obsessed with musicals," I say, like a confession. Or maybe a test. I look in his eyes for a reaction. "I guess that's a stereotype, too."

"I regretted that the second I said it," he responds quickly, looking grateful for the chance to apologize. "I *do* think you're different than them."

"They are different from each other!"

He hurries to his point. "What I meant to say was, I'm probably just jealous of your Halloween party."

Our shoulders press against each other, firmer.

Kiss him. No, I can't, it's too soon. *Kiss him.* I can't. *Kiss him!* Leave me alone!

"I'd invite you, but I wouldn't want to steal you away from your one true friend, that dancing air puppet." Our shoulders, closer, still, like our bodies have a gravitational pull. I babble,

"Which I thought I'd see in your front yard. Mom and Dad veto it?"

He laughs. "Just Mom."

"Dad was on your side?"

"No, I mean, *just* Mom," he says. "Broken home."

I feel bad instantly, and I can't tell if his matter-of-fact tone means it's no big deal or that it's really heavy.

"Oh man. I'm sorry."

"Man," he says, mocking me with a small smile, "it's okay." His shoulder stays against mine, and he leans. "Some homes are better off broken."

I look too concerned about it. My face shows too much emotion. "Damien's parents are divorced," I say, sounding very close to the type of person who randomly tells you about their gay cousin after you tell them that you're gay. "We don't have to talk about it if you don't want to."

He taps my foot with his. "You seem to be the one having difficulty."

I laugh at myself. "Oh. Yeah, sorry. I mean, it's not a big deal. Everyone's parents are divorced."

"Except yours."

"Well, no. Right. But maybe someday!" I respond with an absurd cheerfulness.

My heart beats so aggressively I'm convinced he can feel it through our shoulders. I look straight ahead and swallow.

"Come with me on Halloween," I say quietly.

He angles his head. Our chins almost touch. "Are you inviting me on a date?"

"Maybe." My knee, his thigh, our chins touch. "Are you gonna say yes?"

"That depends," he answers. My veins tingle, and my mouth is so dry. He asks, "Are you going to be dressed like a firefighter?"

The duvet cover rustles. "I don't know . . . maybe something more"—I swallow—"'attention-grabbing and memorable.'"

Our mouths are so close I can feel his breath. He lifts his eyebrows. "Spiro Agnew?"

"Shut up," I tell him through a quiet laugh.

"I'd be honored."

His kiss starts softly, like the opening sentence of a perfect introduction, or the first line of an old poem. In the background, an urgent poet pushes us on: ". . . *the cosmos instinctively vibrated at their feet . . .*" His kiss. His kiss.

Doomed

The next morning I can't think of anything except his kiss.

In history we're learning about a coup d'état: a sudden, violent overthrow of an existing government by a small group.

His kiss *coup d'état*-ed my whole brain.

Our lips fit like puzzle pieces, his mouth soft but strong, everything, perfect.

Mr. Erickson drones on, "Now, this can all sound like some out-of-touch intellectual exercise, studying violent overthrows from the 1500s, but modern governments would be well served to study the precursors to a coup d'état. There are some common patterns that indicate an overthrow is on the horizon, and as we all know, those who forget history . . ."

". . . *are doomed to repeat it*," the class parrots.

I write the words in my notebook. *Those who forget history are doomed to repeat it.*

I obviously don't need to write that down, but sometimes I just mindlessly take notes and worry about what's important later.

The words taunt me. They change the ecosystem of the room.

Hastily squeezed in below the bottom line, they grow to take up the entire page.

How could I be so stupid? So nearsighted?

This is not the first coup d'état staged by a kiss.

And those who forget history are doomed to repeat it.

9TH-GRADE HISTORY LESSON: THE *FIRST* FIRST KISS

In the suburb of Annondale, Michigan, it's customary for select upperclassmen and a few handpicked underclassmen to attend the annual Miller Homecoming After-Party. The tradition began seven years and two Millers ago, due to the Miller parents' unflagging belief in the sweetest sentence any teenager can hear: *Well, they're going to drink anyway, so I'd rather have them do it under my roof.*

I was invited because I was one of two freshman guys on homecoming court. An astonishing accomplishment, if you consider that I collected novelty erasers as a kid and have been known to ask math teachers for extra practice problems. But being in musicals probably won me the theater/orchestra/band bloc, being gay probably got me the "gay best friend" vote, and being Eric's little brother probably got me the rest. Eric Davis's little brother *had* to be cool.

Proving them wrong, I was sitting alone on a cold

bench in a poolside garden full of trampled perennials and a toppled-over gnome.

John and I didn't really know each other yet, but we'd met two weeks earlier because he was the other freshman guy on homecoming court. He swaggered over. "A king on his throne!" he shouted. "Now that you're royalty, you don't let anyone else talk to you?"

My heart was racing like crazy because, as I've mentioned approximately seventy-five thousand times, he's hot. "I guess I can make an exception for fellow royalty."

"We really sound disgusting right now."

The second he said "we," I was his.

"We are literally the worst," I confirmed. "But you started it. I was just being agreeable."

"You having fun? Who'd you come with? I'm a little outta my league at parties like this."

"You seem to be doing just fine."

"Oh yeah? You been checkin' me out?"

"God, no. Don't be ridiculous. I just mean, you're talking to a *king* right now. So what could be better?"

He put his hand on my thigh, and the sun started shining at eleven o'clock at night.

"I can't think of a single thing."

We chitchatted a little more. Then, from the bottom edge of the pool, some senior shouted, "*Cops!*"

I froze, devoting all my energy to a panic attack flashing forward to all the colleges I wouldn't get into because of my freshman-year jail time for minor-flirting-in-a-garden-with-a-slightly-drunk-lacrosse-player.

John grabbed my wrist. "Come on!" he shouted, astounded by my deer-in-headlights reflexes.

The dumb drunk kids ran into the house. The dumber drunk kids ran to their cars. The smart ones—which now included me and John—just ran. No middle-aged cop wants to chase some all-state midfielder through the woods.

When we got far enough out of sight, John stopped and hid, standing stiff behind a tree. I pulled out my phone to send a text to Spurling.

"No," John whisper-shouted. "They'll be looking for screens. Keep your phone away. Got-ta *hide*." He was a little more drunk than I'd thought. And a lot more adorable.

I laughed. He shushed me. I held my breath as I tip-toed to join him behind his tree. But then I breathed out way louder than I would have if I'd just breathed normally to begin with.

"Let's go. I think my friend Spurling's having people over."

"Shhh." He turned, put his back against the tree, his front toward me. "Did you have fun?" he asked. "Who'd you come with?"

"You already asked that."

"Fine." He pushed me, playfully but unexpectedly, so I fell ass-first to the ground. I felt the dampness from the leaves move through my boxer briefs as my once-cute outfit turned into muddy bootcamp fatigues. "Time to go home." He extended his hand to lift me up.

"No. You don't get to be the hero when you're the one who knocked me down." I got up on my own and led us out of the woods.

"I'm gonna have my work cut out with you, aren't I?"

We walked in the middle of the curvy subdivision street, with nothing but crickets and street-parked cars to keep us company. It was that very late early-morning hour when the darkness is so complete it feels like you're the only ones alive. The party seemed miles behind and the morning felt light-years away. And because we were so alive—our insides whirring with the freedom of a narrow escape, the buzz of foamy keg beer, and the unmatchable energy of unfulfilled hormones—we walked through the empty streets with cocky swagger, like we knew a secret the rest of the world was sleeping on.

Not a single house had anything other than a porch light lit. People were sleeping so deeply it felt like a dare. Or at least an opportunity: Everyone's asleep, do whatever you want.

I wanted a cigarette.

That week I had been auditioning a new personality. High school had just started and I was nervous that all the singing, studying, and church stuff would severely constrain my social possibilities. I needed an edge. But pot made me paranoid and my mom had successfully convinced me that a single puff from a vape pen would kill me instantly. So I turned to something that at least had the decency to kill me slowly. It was disgusting, but I had no choice. I did like the almost vintage quality of it: I smoked in black and white.

I pulled out a cigarette from an Altoids tin in my front left pocket. The rough wheel of the lighter scratched my thumb as I cupped my free hand over the flame, puffing rapidly so it took the light.

He took a step toward me, took the cigarette.

"You smoke?" he asked.

"Not really. Just at parties." I eyed my now-broken cigarette in his giant hand. "You steal?"

"Not really. Just from smokers." He pushed me forward and then walked behind me, with both arms wrapped over my shoulders, hands clasped at my chest. "Come on. At least vape."

"Anything that needs a charger is not cool."

"So an iPhone isn't cool?"

"The *least* cool! Are you kidding me? Useful, but *so* not cool."

"You have a lot of opinions."

"I think about things a lot. My brother says I'm in my head too much." It sounded *so colossally unsexy* as I said it, but his chest was pressing against my back, and I could feel his heartbeat through my wet T-shirt and his fingers were drumming on my stomach, and I was lucky I could walk let alone flirt.

He spoke right into my ear. "What would you say if I told you I don't want you to smoke?"

"I'd say thanks for the feedback." I elbowed him off my back and, again, pulled out my Altoids tin.

"I just hate kissing smokers."

I barely looked at him as I started lighting my second-to-last cigarette. "You kiss a lot of smokers?"

The soft soles of his tennis shoes barely made a sound as he took a step closer.

"So far just the one."

He moved my hands away from my mouth, leaned forward and kissed me. Wrapped his arms around my waist and kissed me.

My Altoids tin clanked on the pavement. I kissed the way you kiss when you don't want someone to know it's your first kiss. Too much tongue, too much bobbing my head side to side. But it didn't matter. He was in charge. Every heartbeat felt like a trampoline bounce shaking my entire head, throat, chest, legs, house, woods . . . it beat so hard it shook my toes and it shook the trees that still had a few leaves left to fall.

My body moved with no instruction. My hand cupped his square jaw. I wanted to memorize his back muscles, every inch of his arms.

Before this kiss, being gay was a theory. Like all little boys who get erections during Axe body spray commercials, I was pretty confident in the theory, and I was more or less "out," but still. This kiss made Me make sense.

An identity, a personhood, sealed with a kiss.

As first period winds down, I close my history notebook.

It shouts at me anyway.

Those who forget history are doomed to repeat it.

Defeating a Coup D'état

Ezra stands above my backpack as I adjust my folders so everything fits the way it's supposed to. "That was brutal," he says of our most recent practice AP test.

"Analyzing the merits of globalization when I've only ever left Annondale to go to my grandma's house? Yes, brutal." *Stop*, I think. *Stop whatever this is and wherever it's going.*

"I'm worried about you." He hesitates and lightly kicks the legs of my desk. "I promise I was not *meaning* to see it, but, as you were fastidiously rearranging your folders, I noticed the grade you received on the most recent calculus exam," he says in a troubled tone.

I zip my backpack and respond with no more flirtation than if I were talking to Mrs. Parsons. "And what about that worries you?"

He puts his hand on my shoulder, presses down, but it feels like being lifted and I need this to stop. "I'm worried you're studying too much," he says with a small smile. A first kiss is fun, but the last kiss is awful, and I'm just getting out of the last awful, and *those who forget history*—I need this to stop.

We walk into the hallway. "That is a valid concern." I can't go back there. Not again. Not now. "Hey, but speaking of "—I step a little farther away, create some distance between us—"I just got hit with an insane amount of history reading."

He smiles. "I've heard the call, and I believe it's incumbent upon me to distract you." He speaks extra regally, like a knight before a maiden. *Yes, but how long until it starts hurting?*

"Well, pray tell"—the only regal thing I could think of—"I don't know if you've heard, but 'junior year is the most important year.'"

"You know, that sounds familiar." He adjusts his backpack strap, asks me a question but talks to the carpet. "Who do you have? Erickson?"

"Unfortunately."

"Well, same!" He perks up. "Study buddy?"

"I wish. I can hardly understand it even with my undivided attention, let alone a cute guy to distract me."

"I promise the utmost focus and productivity."

"I've been fooled by that before."

"We got a perfect score!"

"*You* got a perfect score."

He leans against the railing of the crowded main stairwell. "Understood. Well, tonight we'll divide and conquer. And we'll regroup tomorrow, strategize our next decisive engagement."

"Yeah, for sure," I respond.

He reads my eyes and doesn't hug me goodbye. "Okay. Great."

✧ ✧ ✧

The next day I tell Ezra, "Tonight's worse than last night." A theater meeting, a ton of calc. "But soon!"

The next day he doesn't ask to cash in our rain check.

The day after that we hardly say hi.

He forgets about Halloween.

By Monday, it's almost like we'd never met at all.

Boo

The plastic red firefighter hat is too small for my head. I'd widened it by cutting a line through the back, and the slit grows bigger as the party gets louder. It slices into my skull, and my whole head feels like a paper cut.

But I have to keep it on, otherwise I'm just an idiot in pocketless red pants, a pit-stained white T-shirt, and Jeff Miller's dad's black suspenders. I don't know what to do with my hands—have I always had hands?—and the pants are so tight they make my stomach feel pudgy.

Everyone else in my group looks perfect. It was Reid Meyers's idea: "Sexy firefighters, like on a fucking calendar." There are twelve of us. Damien even wrote *January* on his abs.

Crystal, mocking us (and everyone), is dressed as a sexy potato.

"What the fuck's a sexy potato?" Reid Meyers asks her.

"Don't you ever just look at a potato, Reid," Crystal says, under three giant body pillows duct-taped around her torso, two burlap sacks over the top and bottom, held up by an oversized red bikini, "and think"—Crystal starts gyrating against a banister and talking like a porn star—"oh, baby, look at that potato—oh, sexy potato, you're making me so, so . . ." Reid looks terrified and walks away. Crystal looks at me with *mission-accomplished* eyes.

With every new person I feel more alone, and somewhere inside the locked trunk of a secondhand Jeep parked in front of Haley Stewart's house on the last dirt road in Annondale, a purple princess dress with puffy sleeves glitters for no one.

Junior Year

November

The Best Bad Photocopy

"**Y**ou unfuck your life the opposite way you fucked it!" Eric shouts at the ceiling, shouldering me against the wall as he hogs my entire bed. "Same road! Just turn around."

I try to knock him off the bed so I can be left alone with my bad decisions.

I'd explained to Eric why I had to ghost Ezra, and for the first time in his life he was almost speechless. "Are you gonna spend the rest of your life in hiding because you broke up with John Beckett? *Don't let the fear of tomorrow steal the joy of*—no, you know what?" He stopped. "I'm not even wasting good advice on you. You're the dumbest nerd I know."

Eric dodges my kick, leaps up, and lands on top of me.

"Ahh, fuuuuu . . . Ahhh, get off-ah!" I shout. He feels like a burlap sack of metal tools, all sharp edges and unforgiving elbows. I kick him away but it's impossible. Even liberated from the demands of high school athletics, he still lifts weights like he's in prison.

"Duke! Come 'ere, Duke!" Eric calls. "Come on! Up here,

boy." Our golden retriever—absolutely losing his mind because he's been *invited* to jump on furniture—flies up and starts wrestling and biting at anything that moves. My head gets trapped under his tail, and suddenly I'm in a car wash made of dog hair. Eric keeps hitting me, alternating fists like the WWE action figures with the Power Punch button.

"I could kill you right now," I shout, muffled under my own pillow.

"You couldn't live without me!"

I hit him with the pillow. "I'd like to give it a try."

"Mark! MAAAAARK!" Dad shouts from downstairs. "For God's sake, Mark! You gonna wake up before dinner?"

I turn to Eric. "Oh my God, it's ten in the morning on a *vacation day*. What the hell? Can he say one thing that's not annoying?"

"Chill, bud. He's just doin' his job."

"Can *you* say one thing that's not annoying?"

Soap bubbles slip down the driveway, and I wish I could go with them.

Why? I had made the wrong decision with Ezra. I think on some level I knew it was wrong, but I also thought it was necessary, and now I just feel like an idiot. A lonely idiot.

As I finish drying my dad's car, he calls from the front porch, still in his slippers. "Hurry up, son. Those leaves aren't gonna blow themselves."

In an unprecedented display of self-restraint, I don't even *mumble* anything about blowing yourself.

The leaf blower sounds like an angry vacuum cleaner, and I rest in the solitude of a boring chore.

Eric barrels out, carrying the rake and three giant leaf bags that look like pumpkins.

This is my brother: all the makings of an epic ego (in the Annondale Athletics Hall of Fame for *two* different sports, started going to high school for math in seventh grade), yet he genuinely likes helping other people more than he likes helping himself. And he always knows what people need. Not just me, and not just with yard work. He has this superpower: He can look at you, see inside your heart, find that thing you so deeply *wish* were true about yourself, and find a way to make you believe it is.

If I didn't love him so much, I'd hate him.

I turn off the leaf blower and switch to raking.

Case in point: Mr. Sullivan, our dumpy grumpy driver's ed teacher who has a meltdown if you go one millimeter per hour above the speed limit because *the speed limit is not a suggestion, it is a MAXIMUM*! Well, one day Mom and I were picking Eric up from driver's ed, and as class was ending, Eric said to the teacher, "I bet you learned to drive slow because you had to give the ladies more time to check you out."

You should have seen Mr. Sullivan. In his coffee-stained tie with his beer belly hanging over his baggy khakis, he smiled, almost to himself, and in that moment, he was as seventeen as he ever was. Handsome, happy, and had all of life to look forward to.

That's what Eric can do.

When I started driver's ed, Mr. Sullivan asked me how Eric was doing—wistfully, too, like an old girlfriend.

Which is probably the most annoying part about it all. For about 99 percent of the world, I'm just "Eric's little brother." And sometimes I feel like nothing more than a flawed photocopy of my older brother. Close to the original, but like, 20 percent less good, a bit duller, some big ugly ink splotch in the upper-right corner.

But I am happy to have help with the yard work.

Gradually, the leaves form satisfying piles: oranges, browns, and yellows in sun-splashed mounds that shout *all messes can be restored*. I tie up the pumpkin bags and step on the sidewalk to take in the splendor of the spotless yard—moments ago a disaster, now not a leaf left unraked. Duke sprints over with delirious congratulations, wagging his tail so frantically he might take flight. We half hug, half wrestle, and I rub his belly where the fur is almost white. He rolls over and smiles at the sun.

All messes can be restored.

"Now *that's* a good son," my dad admires from the front porch. I stand back up, with just a little bit of pride. "He's home from college takin' on bonus work just to make his brother's life easier."

You're kidding me.

I just did the entire friggin'—whatever. A person could go crazy trying to get equitable parental attention when your competition is Eric Davis. I just keep my mouth shut, be grateful for the help, and be the best bad photocopy I can be.

"What's your most embarrassing moment?" Damien asks, leaning forward so far into his laptop it just might suck him in.

"That's stupid," I reply. "No college essay is going to ask about your 'most embarrassing moment.'"

We're using our Thanksgiving vacation to "get caught up on college stuff." Hunched over his dining room table, Damien points to a downloaded PDF full of sample personal narrative prompts. "It's on the list."

"Well then, the list is stupid. No college essay is gonna ask that."

"I don't know." He tilts his head. "College essays are some nosy motherfuckers."

Crystal mimics a professor voice, "'*What's the biggest obstacle you've overcome?*'" and then mocks confrontation, pulls up like she's about to fight. "What's the biggest obstacle *you've* overcome, Marquette University?"

I laugh and pile on. "Remember in eighth grade when Mrs. Ferrante made us write a personal poem about the last time we *cried?*"

"In iambic pentameter!" Crystal shouts. "Eighth-grade trauma in iambic pentameter." She echoes Damien's point: "Nosy. Mother. Fuckers. All of them. For real, *guidance counselors?* 'Crystal, honey, can I steal you for a minute?'" Crystal pantomimes a big bite of a giant salad (Mrs. Pointer, at seemingly all hours of the day, is eating a giant salad). "'Have you ever had thoughts about suicide?'"

Crystal pauses with wide eyes. "Does *this thought count?*"

We crack up, but Damien stops us laughing. "We're practicing personal narratives." He nudges. "They're supposed to be nosy. Come on. 'What's your most embarrassing moment?' Show, don't tell." He repeats the mantra he learned in the Writing Winning College Essays seminar he has now attended three years in a row.

"Well, one time I crashed into a folding table full of orange pop and cheap vodka because I was trying to get drunk enough to not care about my ex-boyfriend, but instead I got so drunk I cared *only* about my ex-boyfriend."

"You're in!" Crystal shouts. "Welcome to Lawrence Tech University!"

"Come on, take it seriously."

"Okay. Most embarrassing moment." I consider it. "Here we go."

Crystal interrupts before I start. "You farted during a moment of silence."

I practically snap my neck to stare her down. "*That. Was Jeff. Miller.*"

She lays out the facts. "Seventh grade. School assembly. Remembering the lives lost of Barnes Middle School alumni. You farted during a moment of silence."

"I—We've covered this. It was Jeff—" I shake my head and change tactics. "Whoever smelt it dealt it."

"You're both gonna be living in your parents' basements and going to Annondale Community College if you don't shut up and focus on the prompt!"

"Okay." I sit up, really think about it, and then remember. "Okay, got it. Once, at my grandma's house, I saw this old-timey picture of some random dude, like, the hottest dude who ever lived. Long Tarzan hair, fucking Captain America face, and I was just *staring* at it thinking to myself, holy shit this guy is *hot*. And then my grandma comes over and says, 'Isn't that a lovely picture of your father!'" Damien throws his pen against the wall. "I was traumatized. Didn't jack off for a month."

"You're in!" Crystal shouts. "Welcome to Grand Valley State University!"

Damien stands up in revolt. "In addition to being the *most disgusting thing I've ever heard in my entire life*, it's not even delivering on the prompt. It's not 'embarrassing.'"

"Name something more embarrassing."

"No one else knew about it!"

"Some of the most embarrassing things happen just in my own head."

"Crystal, you go." Damien can't even look at me.

"Well . . . ," Crystal says introspectively, almost to herself. She shifts in her seat, and something about her eyes looks serious.

"You don't have to say something *actually* embarrassing. This isn't even a realistic prompt," I reassure her.

"Well, this is pretty embarrassing," she says, pulling her hair back behind her shoulders, then pulling one side forward again. "And I have been *trying* to tell you," she says to me, "but you've been busy on dates, or stuff you don't even tell me about. And you"—she talks to the table but means Damien—"have been busy with your fucking panic attacks." She motions to his very distressed face. "But . . ." She pauses like she has an announcement. "I'm sort of transferring to Driggs in the new semester. Or maybe a little before."

"What?" I ask, in genuine shock. Driggs is a "nontraditional" community high school, barely a step up from a prison high school, and if you're not messed up before you go, you become messed up while you're there. DJ Farley was sent to Driggs freshman year because he put an acid tab in Mr. Carson's coffee cup. I personally think, if you really wanted to punish a kid like DJ, you'd sentence him to a week of studying with Damien, not a lifetime of swirling around with kids who do the same drugs he does. Apparently, Mr. Carson still has acid flashbacks, and not a single person at Annondale High has seen DJ Farley since he got sent to Driggs.

"Why?" Damien asks, also in shock.

"'Academic performance.'" She pronounces it like a crime.

"That's bullshit." I don't know what to say.

"It's a policy, or something," she says with strained casualness. Her eyes pool with water, but she wipes them quickly and stiffens up. "Maybe it'll be better. And then after I can live in my parents' basement and go to Annondale Community College."

"I didn't mean that," Damien apologizes.

She talks like she doesn't need the pity. "Layla Yousef goes to Driggs and she says it's way better. It's like, focused. And there's less bullshit. Nobody pretends their life purpose is coordinate geometry."

I just don't get it. "What's the point of having two nerd best friends if you don't use us to study?" I ask.

"You were busy," Crystal says again. And something about it stings.

Crystal and I met the summer between fifth and sixth grade, at an "incoming students Barnes Middle School mixer." Being bad at sports was really a death knell for my social life as an elementary schooler, and I've never been the type of person who can just go up to a group of people and say hi, so I was standing alone, in the corner, by the chips and pop.

She was standing in a group: three girls who were somehow already stylish, two guys who looked like they'd been six feet tall since second grade, a short dude who seemed like he'd already done jail time, and Crystal. She had on baggy jeans, and her hair looked like she cut it herself with safety scissors.

She came over to get a chip. A single chip.

"Is that your mom?" she asked, motioning to the woman serving punch behind me who kept giving me aggressively encouraging eyes that screamed *Go make friends*.

"No." I shook my head defensively and didn't even look at the crazy punch-bowl woman.

I'd heard of Crystal. Rumor mills start buzzing before you start middle school, about who are the hot guys, cool girls, and popular groups from other elementary schools. Unless she'd read the reviews of the Linden Elementary School production of *Pirates of Penzance*, I was pretty certain she'd never heard of me.

Me standing alone became increasingly awkward. "I'm just waiting for my friend," I lied.

"No you're not," she said with no hesitation but friendly eyes. The first of so many surprises.

"You're right," I admitted, shifting weight to my other side. "Actually, I'm just trying to choke to death on one of these sprinkles"—I motioned to the leaf-shaped Kroger-brand cookie I was holding—"because I think that's the only way my mom would let me leave before this stupid mixer is over." I pointed back to the crazy punch-bowl woman who was, in fact, my mother.

She laughed and looked me right in the eyes. "You're weird," she said, and it sounded like a compliment. "You went to Linden?"

"Yeah, but Barnes next year."

"Well, duh. We all go to Barnes next year. This is a Barnes Middle School mixer."

"Oh. Yeah." I tried to laugh it off but inside felt like a trapped toad. "*Duh.*"

"Well. I have to go." She pointed back to her friends. "But I'm Crystal. What's your name?"

"Mark. Davis."

"Cool. Well, nice to meet you, Mark Davis." She stuck out her hand for a firm handshake.

The next day I got an email to my school email address: "hey this is crystal from the mixer (duh) emails are so random but I don't have ur number. i was thinking we should be MIXING so if u didn't die from sprinkle suffocating u should come to Shanna's Friday."

I told my mom, and she looked as happy as when Eric won the 400-meter dash and an "America & Me" essay competition on the same day. And after that afternoon, my life was completely different. It sounds dramatic, but it really was. And I've never stopped being grateful to be Crystal's friend. If this friendship isn't a miracle, then I don't need one. Jesus turned water into wine, sure, but Crystal made middle school fun. *That's* some fucking omnipotence.

And not only was I too busy to help her, I was too busy to even notice she needed it.

The clicks from the turn signal sound as loud as a siren.

"I'm so sorry, Crystal," I finally say as I drive her home from Damien's house.

"I'm not *dying*, Mark." She laughs. "I'm going to Driggs."

"It's just bullshit. A bad grade in geometry shouldn't mess up your whole life."

"If you're trying to make me feel worse, then you're nailing it."

"I'm sorry," I say, and can't find the right words to say next.

Rochester Road is busy. She fiddles with the button that rolls up her window, pulling it up, up, again and again even though her window is already up.

"Driggs would fuck up *your* life," she says quietly. "This is my life."

Her house is on the main road, and I always get nervous turning into her driveway.

The turn signal clicks.

Crystal exhales. "It's just really fucking impossible to get grades to go *up*." Her eyes pool with water. "You try your literal fucking hardest and your thing goes up, like, point one points. And they could give a shit. It's like they want to get rid of you."

I desperately want to cheer her up. She means so much to me and—I turn.

"Maybe it *will* be good," I say as we bump over the curb. "Maybe it really will, like Layla said."

"Yeah," she responds, flat, "it'll be grand."

It hurts, seeing her like this. Seeing her so affected. I guess I always felt, somehow, that Crystal lived above the silly considerations of high school, as if she existed on a different plane than the rest of us, where parents and pop quizzes and stupid high school bullshit didn't touch her. "When do you switch?"

"Basically already switched. Start at Driggs after Thanksgiving."

"We should have done something for your last day," I say, surprised.

"It's not a birthday party, Mark." I still don't know what to say.

And I'm filled with this sense that Crystal could use a friend very different than me. I don't know who, but—someone who notices things. Someone who gets it, without it having to be explained. And now it's too late and I still don't know what to say.

She looks out the window, where a blue recycling bin has been tipped over by the wind. "Remember in middle school when you asked me what I wanted to be when I grew up?"

"Yeah." I look back at her. "And you said, 'The first lady garbageman in Annondale.'"

"Then you wrote a whole-ass play about it." She smiles. "With a theme song. Sung to a dumpster."

In her driveway, I put the car in park. "'*They may call you trash, but baby, just maybe: Trash is treasure.*'"

She laughs, a little, and looks at the glove compartment. "So I guess there's already been a ton of lady garbagemen in Annondale," she says, sad. "I like, called them. The Annondale Department of Sanitation." The wind slaps the screen door against her house. "I still have that play, though."

I stare at the steering wheel as if it will tell me what to say. I wait too long.

I finally realize, "Okay, why are we acting like this is some big goodbye?"

"I know!" She exhales, relieved. "I mean, we don't even have any *classes* together."

"It's not even going to be that different."

"You're still gonna see me fourteen times a day," she says, and pulls the door handle. "So I'm gonna leave." She gets out, quickly, and turns around, speaking through the open door. "And I'm not even gonna say goodbye." She spins her head away and slams the door.

"Neither am I!" I shout, just as it shuts. "You're not gonna get a goodbye outta me."

My shout bounces off the shut doors. She doesn't look back.

On the walk up her driveway, she wipes her eyes with a shirt-sleeve and I wish I was a better friend.

Unfucking My Life

I want to go back to the beginning of the year, back to Throwback Night, and focus less on John and more on Crystal. Tell her that *yes*, of course sometimes I feel like I'm just watching my life, *of course* sometimes my life feels like a movie that I have no control over and hardly even a part in, and of course being with you, really being *with* you, is more important than being sad about John.

But I can't go back. All I can do is at least make the movie of my life one I could bear to watch.

Tonight at dinner, Mom makes an easy chicken thing because tomorrow's Thanksgiving. Eric regales us with stories of brilliant professors, impossible midterms, and a decades-long civil war between North and South Campus. He assures Mom he's spending more time in the library than at parties hosted by Greek letters, but when he provides way too much detail on a "semiformal" at the Shedd Aquarium where an older Kappa Sig threw a bottle of Ketel One in the beluga whale tank, Mom interrupts.

"Mark, tell your brother about Praise Band."

I just sit there, forgetting that my commitment to being present and living fully might apply with my family, as well.

"You been quiet tonight, bud," Eric says between chews. "What's up? Over there fantasizing about Mr. Donegal again?"

Mr. Donegal was Eric's fourth-grade teacher and still the hottest person I've ever seen in real life. When I was in second grade, I started bawling at the dinner table because Mom wouldn't let me invite Mr. Donegal for Thanksgiving.

The plus side of that meltdown was I never really had to come out to my family.

"Donnelly was a good basketball coach," Dad says. "He really made you a player, Mark."

"What? We were talking about Mr. *Donegal*. But even—what are you talking about, basketball?"

"You had potential. If you would've stuck with it."

"I *sucked* at basketball."

"You didn't 'suck,' Mark," Mom corrects (because of my language, not my basketball ability).

"Who cares if I did? It might surprise this family to find out that basketball plays a very small part in most adult lives."

"Probably about as much as calculus," Dad hits back.

"You want me to drop out of calculus so I can focus on basketball?"

"Nobody's dropping out," Mom says, more concerned than she needs to be.

"What are we even talking about?" I shout, dumbfounded.

Mom leaves the table and heads to the kitchen, taking as many plates as she can carry. "Mark, tell your brother about Praise Band."

I laugh. "I would *love* to."

Mom continues clearing the table, and eventually we all help. Well, no, Dad just sits there like the Sultan of Suburbia, but Eric and I help. "Praise Band is good. Lots of singing. Very little dribbling. And I sometimes give the sermons now, which is beyond weird."

"The *sermon* sermon?" Eric asks as he puts the ketchup away.

"And they're wonderful," Mom adds.

"Yeah. Like, quoting from the Bible and stuff, giving people a lesson to carry through the day. I don't know, it doesn't really matter. People only go to the contemporary service for the music."

"Honey, that's not true."

Eric adds, "And people only go to church at all for the gossip and cookies."

"*Now* you're sounding like a college boy," Dad cuts in. "Fifty grand a year to get you to stop believing in God."

"Hey, speaking of cookies," Eric segues. "Do we have ice cream?"

"Sure do," Mom says, proud. "You didn't answer my email about what flavors you wanted, but there are three of your favorites in there. Be sure to leave some mint chip for your father."

"Hey, Mark," Dad calls, "under that ice cream should be a bottle of Stoli. Bring that back over here with a couple of glasses."

"*Absolutely* not," Mom shouts, out of nowhere. I've never heard Mom shout, not even at Duke. Not even close. "Joe, absolutely not."

"I'm not having any," I say, just assuming I'm the one getting in trouble.

Dad answers in a consoling voice. "This isn't a frat party,

Carol. A little sip with his family. This is the kind of thing that *stops* kids from going too far."

I'm still confused at the abrupt turn dessert has taken, but I perk up. Perhaps I'll get to have some Stoli at this not-frat-party.

"Put it away." Her voice shakes.

I put the bottle back.

Mom opens the freezer and pulls the bottle back out. She walks to the garage and we hear the thud of glass hitting plastic as she drops the fifth in the recycling bin.

She walks back in the kitchen, her voice like a strained impersonation of her voice. "Mark, you've been wanting to watch that new Netflix show. Maybe that would be nice for you three?"

Eric's lying on two-and-a-half couch cushions and I'm squished against the right side. Mom and Dad are already upstairs, but we're still watching CBS, some random detective show. Neither of us takes the initiative to switch to Netflix.

"It *is* kind of nuts," Eric says during a commercial, "that we have school assemblies for basketball. We should have school assemblies for, like, math tests when you think about it."

There is obviously plenty I could contribute on the topic of the absurd prominence we give sports in high school (high *school*), but at the moment I can't think about anything except Mom.

Finally, I say something.

"That was crazy."

"What?" he asks, staring blankly at the TV.

"*What?*" I sit up. "Mom freaking out. Have you ever seen her yell?"

"I don't know," he downplays. "She didn't really yell. I think she's just sick of all the drinking."

"Who's drinking? Dad has literally had that bottle in the freezer for a year. And the last time I drank was half a wine cooler at Haley Stewart's Halloween Party."

"Mark, it's not funny."

"Who said it was funny?"

"It was probably me, talking about those dumb college parties." He looks over and kicks me, softly. "We're all adjusting." I kick him back. "Now quit overanalyzing our mom. What's going on in *your* life? Where're Damien and Crystal? Why are you home on the night before Thanksgiving?"

"Both visiting family, why are *you* home?"

"Honestly, a vacation for me is *not* going out."

"I can see why Mom's freaking out."

"Don't change the subject."

My eyes go back to CBS, some commercial for toilet paper. I watch.

And I'm so sick of *watching*.

I start, tentatively, "Maybe it's time to unfuck my life."

"Huh?"

"Maybe tonight's the night," I say with inexplicable resolve, "we unfuck my life."

He laughs. "And how are we doing that?"

"I don't know." I deflate.

He jumps up, starts pacing, as excited as Duke when Mom grabs his leash. "Well, let's figure it out!"

I lay out the facts of the case. "I ended it with Ezra before it could even start."

"Then start it!"

"Exactly!"

"Why shouldn't it be so easy!"

I try not to sound like a buzzkill. "Well, I think I sort of irreparably damaged it."

"How do you know?"

"He doesn't even look at me in Parsons's class."

"But you don't *know*."

"I have a feeling."

"Did you have a feeling that you should end it?"

"Yeah . . ."

"Well, then we've proven your feelings can't be trusted."

"Exactly!" I almost fly off the couch, giddy with what feels like a real crack in the case.

He grabs my phone from the coffee table and hands it to me.

"Call him."

"You're insane, no one *calls* anyone."

"Then text him."

Our last text was a month ago. It just sits there, oblivious.

What if he's forgotten all about that . . . hardly even a kiss.

I stare at his name. My thumb refuses to move. My phone feels heavier than a brick.

"Let's go," Eric says, urgent but matter-of-fact.

"Go where?"

"To Ezra's." He's already got the keys in his hand.

"That's even weirder than calling."

"You like this guy?"

"I think so."

"Then be weird."

Eric drives. I regret it more with every power line we pass.

"I should at least text him that I'm coming."

"Sure."

"Or maybe it's more romantic as a surprise."

"That's a good point."

"Help me!"

"It's more romantic as a surprise."

"He's going to think I'm crazy."

"Well, right now he thinks you're an asshole, so crazy might be an upgrade."

The hedges in front of Ezra's house are so thick you can't even tell if the living room light is on.

"Don't drive up the driveway," I tell Eric. "Just stop. I'll walk up."

On the sloped street in front of Ezra's dark brick house, Eric parks. The random tower and the quirky brickwork make the house look almost haunted. The path from his driveway to his front door isn't sidewalk cement, it's cobblestones. I walk unsteadily, dodging tree branches and overgrown bushes a long time past flowering. My breathing gets heavy and I stare at the sharp corner of his front porch, thinking at some point a plan will click.

I keep staring, but no plan clicks.

I hear actual crickets.

I give up.

This is stupid.

I'll look crazy.

I already do.

I turn around, start back through the branches and the bushes, when suddenly a sliver of light shines on the prickly leaves to my left.

"Mark?" His voice sounds just as confused as it should be.

I turn too quickly, talk too cheerily. "Ezra!"

"Hey," he says, not returning my exclamation point.

"Well, I was just—Happy Thanksgiving!"

"Happy Thanksgiving." He's not getting any less confused.

I stumble over the cobblestones and finally step on the porch. "I was just talking to my brother, actually, and we"—my arms feel alien and very long—"well, that doesn't matter, I just wanted to come over and see . . ." I take a breath. He's in a white T-shirt and clean gray sweatpants. His eyes narrow as he waits for me to start making sense. He stiffens his left leg to block his little white dog from escaping. No plan clicks.

"Ezra, I'm really sorry."

Now or Never

It feels like even his house is judging me. It shines behind him, white tile, white couches, bright lights, and no sound. Not even background dialogue from a bad sitcom can save me from the silence.

He leans against the doorframe. It's cold, but he doesn't invite me in. "Sorry, for what?"

I start to steady. "I'm sorry for the way things went." Words tumble out, unplanned and unorganized. "I really liked you, and then I just got scared, I guess. I don't know, I had kind of a bad summer, and I got scared. I know it's not an excuse. Just—there is no excuse. It was dumb. I was dumb."

"To say nothing of your Halloween costume." He doesn't smile.

I stare at the white tile where his dog used to be. Even the dog got bored of my bullshit. "You saw?"

"Pictures, posts, etcetera." The door is still only halfway open.

"Yeah." I shuffle nervously and wrap my jacket tighter. "I think you're an amazing guy, and I feel stupid for messing it up. But I'm good now and I was wondering if you'd let me try again?"

He says nothing.

A gust of cold air rustles a pine tree and the needles scratch the gutter above my head.

My heart freezes. The silence feels like failure.

Finally: "Is that so?" He sounds confrontational. "You're 'good' now?"

I respond meekly, "Yeah."

He just stands there, long enough for me to wonder if I should leave.

Then, with a decisive tone, he fills the emptiness. "I think I deserve to be wooed."

"Wooed?" I arch my eyebrows, eager but confused.

"Yes. I'm contemplating your really-quite-awful . . . *was* that an apology? And I think, for me to take you seriously as a human being who can function in a two-way relationship, I think I deserve to be wooed."

"Oh. Well, yeah. Of course. I could woo you."

"Go for it."

"Now? You want me to woo you now?"

His eyes say *now or never.*

"Shit. Yes! Well, not 'shit' about the wooing. You do deserve that, actually. Okay. I just, I'm not very good on my feet. Can I . . . come back? Or, like, woo you later this week?"

"Later?" he asks, appalled.

It *has* been a month.

"Friday!" I beg. "You're staying in town for Thanksgiving, right? Friday. At six? Prepare to be wooed!"

As soon as he closes the door, I run down his driveway with a facial expression that looks like champagne.

Eric knows before I even say a word. "Lil' bro, you did it!"

"Shhh," I plead. "He's still right there." I point through the tall bushes to what moments ago looked like the Tower of Terror but now glistens like the Magic Kingdom. I tell Eric everything, word for word, as he weaves confidently through the winding streets of Ezra's sprawling neighborhood.

"It's not like we're together," I downplay. "But there's the possibility for a chance."

He pats my back, way too much like a dad. "I'm proud of you, bud."

"All I did was freak out on a guy's front porch. No reason to be 'proud.'" I shake off his hand, then look out the window, proud.

Turning onto the main road, Eric accelerates and raises an invisible glass. "To the 'possibility for a chance!'" We pantomime a toast, I turn the music up, and he drives fast.

The bright lights of empty mini-mall parking lots whizz by, and it feels more like a runway than a road. Through our rearview mirror, I watch the only other car turn into its neighborhood, and suddenly my insides feel like sky. Grounded sky, if that makes sense. The way phones held up at a concert look like stars. My mistakes feel stupid but manageable. What's next feels like nothing to worry about. And maybe it will all burst as soon as we get home, or maybe I'll come up with a thousand new reasons to be scared. But for this moment, I feel free.

Eric comes back to the basement with the bottle of Stoli.

"She just tossed it in the recycling bin. Didn't even dump it. Tossed it in, bottle cap still on." He shakes his head in delighted disbelief. "God, she is so pure."

"Eric, she will *kill* us. Did you hear her? She will *murder* us. She will be in the *Annondale Gazette* as the Mother Who Murdered Her Children."

"Take your shoes off and put your coat on," he says decisively as he tiptoes back upstairs. "It's time to celebrate."

Eric turns the basement doorknob, slower than the last turn on a locker lock. He shuffles ahead on soft socks, to not squeak the floor. I hover inches behind, holding my breath. Slowly, he opens the laundry room door. Even slower, the door into the garage. I hold my shoes in my hand and daintily step onto the cold cement.

We are sneaking out.

Inside the odor of motor oil and dead leaves, I lace up. Eric raises his eyebrows with grave importance, pointing to the side door in the garage, the final frontier, a notoriously squeaky exit route that's all but rusted shut.

We side-shuffle between hanging shovels and our parents' cars. Crouched down in front of the door, he strategizes. "Opening it slowly will kill us. That squeak would wake the Emersons.

You turn the knob; I ram it with my shoulder. One thud, no squeak. On three."

I grab the knob and turn, but my hand just slips off.

I turn it more. It still doesn't budge.

Throw my weight into it, it—

It budges too much. It spins a full 180 as soon as it unsticks, and I fly to the left, where the top of my head slams into a sharp corner of thick wood and I look up and watch breathlessly as a fifty-pound folding table totters on two bent nails, one wobble away from crashing down, ricocheting off the lawn mower and onto Dad's leased Ford Explorer. I hold tight to the doorknob as a folding table decides whether or not to ruin my life.

"*Three!*" Eric linebackers into the door and it thuds so quickly it doesn't even squeak. We tumble onto the wet grass and my chest convulses in laughter. He covers my mouth so I don't laugh awake the entire neighborhood. He squeezes his eyes and rolls on the ground in a wheezing, uncontrollable fit. I bear hug my own chest to try to get a grip, and soon—silence.

Nothing but an arc of light from the open door. We listen, wait for the sound of Mom's slippers on the steps, or Duke galloping into the foyer.

After what feels like an hour and a half, Eric stands. I start to close the door, but Eric reprimands, "How do you think we're going to get back in?"

We walk casually on the sidewalk, just two responsible, adult-age humans out for a late-night stroll.

Then I realize something.

I reach into my pocket for my phone.

My full voice sounds booming because of all the whispering. "Eric, it's ten p.m."

I notice a light on in the Emersons' living room.

Their *living* room.

His jaw drops with an exaggerated exhale, and he flops his head up to the sky. "Ten! P! M!" He spins into the street and we both start laughing, unrestrained.

"We could've just walked out the front door."

"It felt so late!"

"Imagine how suspicious we look sneaking out *before* curfew," I say. "Basically a neon sign that says we're doing something illegal."

"Well then"—he pats the base of his backpack—"we better start doing something illegal."

Behind our old elementary school, stray grass blades stick to my wet tennis shoes as I hoist myself up on the monkey bars. Eric lounges on a half-moon jungle gym, his feet hooked under a rung at the bottom and his back bent in such a way that his head just crosses over the half circle's co-vertex. Just as the whole playground starts to spin, I give myself a pat on the back for remembering my ACT math words even when I'm drunk.

Eric extends the almost empty bottle of Stoli toward me.

"Are you *kidding* me?" I push it away. "Not a friggin' chance. I'll puke."

"'s a forest," he says, spreading his arms out like a frontier explorer. "You can puke."

He takes a drink that's got to be at least three drinks.

"I have to *woo* him!" I shout. "How do you *woo* someone?"

"*Wooooooo*," Eric howls at the moonless sky.

"Google it," I command. "Google *woo*."

"*You* Google *woo*."

"Google it!"

"Ya know, in my day we had to woo without Google."

"You are two years older than me."

"Well, still. You decide! Don't internet it."

"I'll internet it if I want to internet it." I pull out my phone, and before the screen even lights up I drop it in the mud. I reach for it—but fall instead.

"Oh, you're *drunk* drunk," Eric says, proud, swinging off the jungle gym to help me up.

But standing up makes him unsteady (even though *he* once lectured *me* about never drinking too much while sitting down because then it all hits you when you stand up). He wobbles on one leg, hopping and leaning farther and farther until finally he falls into the muddier mud right next to me. As he slow-mo crashes down, he heroically holds up the Stoli, not spilling a drop.

He rewards himself with a celebratory swig.

I watch in awe as my brother chugs vodka like it's Gatorade. "How do you not need a chaser?" I ask as I wipe my dirty phone on my dirty jeans and Google "how to woo."

It autofills, ". . . a man." Google knows what's up.

Eric steals my phone and clicks the first link. "'Nine Ways to Woo Your Man,'" he reads. "Okay, okay. 'Number one: Dress up.'" He laughs. "Oooooh, what are you gonna wearrr for Ezraaaa?"

"A dress!" I shout, before I have time to censor myself.

"Now *that* is a plan."

"I was kidding."

"Please. We share a bathroom. You think I never saw you wearing a towel like a ball gown?"

I hammer-punch him in the gut. He slaps mud on my face, and it feels cold against my cheek.

"You should wear whatever the fuck you want. You should wear a towel ball gown to Winter Ball if you want to."

"Back to the topic." I use my muddy hands to turn his head back to the phone screen, which is now locked because we wasted so much time on his self-help seminar. I lean over his shoulder and unlock it with my face.

He continues scrolling. "Boring . . . boring . . . Ooh! 'Number seven: Bake something!'"

"Shut up, it does not say that."

"It does." He shows proof. "Better ask Mom for her cinnamon roll recipe."

"Find a gay one. Google *woo* but add *gay*."

"Okay, okay!" he shouts, sitting up as he gets more excited. I sit up, too, and rest my chin on his shoulder to see the screen in real-time. "'Twelve Ways to Woo a Guy on Your First Date,'" he reads, "from Pride dot-com!" He's so proud of himself. Suddenly, he looks shocked. "No way! 'Number four,'" he reads, barely getting it out through his laughter. "'Come with condoms!'"

"Google!" I say, scandalized.

Eric turns to me with glassy eyes. "You are using condoms, right?"

"I am not having this conversation."

"The rate of STIs among—"

"Trust me, I'm safe!" I insist.

"Only dates with 'Miss Michigan' lately?" he teases, and holds up his right hand, driving home the punch line of our state's stupidest jack-off joke. "Or *Mister* Michigan."

"That doesn't even make sense." I pick up a glob of mud and toss it into the sky. It cannonballs down and, instead of landing on Eric, plops onto me. I just let it sit on my forehead, then ask something I've always wondered. "Hey, did Mom and Dad ever talk to you about birds and the bees?"

"You kidding me? Dad wouldn't *stop* talking about it. Sat me down. Woulda been pissed if I *wasn't* having sex." His words overlap, like his brain is zigzagging on the highway. "Gave me condoms even. Which, according to Pride-dot-co—"

"I *knew* it!" I shout.

"What? Whad he say to youu, about . . . the *bees* and the bees?" He giggles at his relentless cleverness.

I wipe the mud off my forehead and slap it onto his cheek. He just laughs lazily, and lets it sit there. "They didn't say anything. Not one thing." I sound angrier than I want to. "I think they're cool with me being gay as long as they don't have to picture it."

"Ah, come on, bud," he says, reassuring. "They've been champs about everything."

I shoot up. "What the fuck is *everything*?"

He takes another giant glug. "You're a mean drunk." The teasing calms me down. With a flick of his wrist, he hurls the empty Stoli bottle up up up to the sky, where it spins and spins and little tiny vodka droplets fall like drizzle.

He looks back at my phone, "'Number five . . .'" But then, with an exaggerated boomerang-style windup, he hurls my phone far, far away. My eyes widen as I watch this very expensive Frisbee soar through the flat black sky.

Time stands still.

My phone suspends midair.

I hold my breath.

"*Fuck* number five," Eric shouts as my jaw drops to the dirt and my phone skids on the tough rubber mat of the big-kids' playground. "Fuck Google. Fuck phones."

"Eric, you psycho!" I jump up and run to my phone.

"Fuck the whole worl wibe web. WhirlWhyWeb. World. Wide. Web."

I pick my phone up like it's an injured bird. With compassionate eyes, I press the side button.

"*Thank God*," I say, even though I'm not sure if He wants to be involved. Regardless, the screen lights up.

"You have to be your*self*, bud. Fuck these lists. Be yourself. You're amazing"—he taps, hard, on my sternum—"in *here*. You know? Fuck these lists."

Just as I rev up to push him in the mud for almost breaking my phone, Eric leans over and, right in the puddle where I used to be sitting, pukes.

✧ ✧ ✧

Eric being so drunk somehow sobers me up.

It was so fun and then *so* not.

He, however, is still having a blast.

His arm is over my shoulder and his feet are barely moving, definitely not walking. His entire weight is against me, and for most of the walk I am literally dragging him.

But he's still having fun, still laughing, even still strategizing about how to woo Ezra.

"Be your*self*, Mark! Cuz you'rrre awesome and iloveyou!" He stops us in the street, where in the last thirty minutes we've gone about seven feet. "No, Mark." He places both hands on my cheeks, turns my face to meet his, and stares with great importance. "I really fucking love you."

He's loud and I'm annoyed and he's bigger than me, so it's pretty impossible for me to be the sheepdog.

"Gimme your phone," he says, stopping in the middle of the road and stealing it from my pocket. He swipes around, gets excited, presses a button, and puts his mouth right up to the speaker. "Ladies and gentlemen, this is to record, for all of human history, how much I fucking love my brother." He takes a deep inhale, rounding out his random voice memo. "And with that, good night!"

Pleased with himself, he smiles and spins into the street, so unsteadily he starts to fall. I grab him by the jacket just in time.

"All right, Eric, if you can *spin*, you can walk," I whisper-shout like an angry mom as I snatch my phone back. "See. Just do that again, except instead of going in a circle, go in a line. F—Eric! *Pleeease*. Just six more houses."

It gets worse as we get closer. By the time I see the open side door of our garage, I'm so over it I don't even care if we get caught.

We seem to have entered a new phase, and he's barely responding. This man could give a college lecture on tricks that prevent shit like this from happening—look at the ceiling, touch your finger to your nose, always pour your own drinks—yet he lost the ability to form sentences four houses ago.

I shimmy him through the garage, trying to make sure he falls into steady objects like cars and not hanging objects like shovels.

"You have to be super, super quiet when we go inside. Okay?"

I open the door to the laundry room, then the door to the foyer. His shoes squeak on the tile and his arm slams against the door, the door slams against the wall, the wall shakes the grandfather clock, the grandfather clock chimes, and I hear Duke scratching at my parents' bedroom door.

The soft thud of Mom's slippers will be next. Going upstairs will be impossible.

I piggyback him down the basement stairs, but we stumble out of control and almost crash into Mom's scrapbooking station.

I sit him up on the futon, sit next to him, look at the ceiling, and exhale an exhausted sigh.

I turn over and look at him.

His eyes are half-open, not asleep and not awake.

Suddenly, I'm nervous about something way scarier than getting caught.

"Eric. Just let me know you're okay. Okay?" I slap him lightly on the cheek, like they do on doctor shows.

He starts leaning. His neck is floppy like a wet noodle, and his head almost hits the wooden futon arm, but I grab a pillow just in time.

I untie the muddy laces on his shoes, slip them off one at a time.

"Just try—sorry, Eric. Just try to keep your leg still," I whisper. "Come on, bud." He kicks, which for some reason I find reassuring. "We'll just get these off and then you can sleep."

I turn on the TV, put it on the Netflix options screen, to make it look like he fell asleep while watching a show.

He mumbles something I don't understand, and I stare, not knowing what to do, how to help.

"Okay, Eric. It's fine. It's fine. Let's just—up we go. Let's just get your shirt off so it doesn't smell like shit in the morning." It's muddy, and messy from the puke. "Here we go." I get him halfway vertical so I can slip his shirt over his arms.

He's asleep, but even his sleep looks different.

I go upstairs to get his blanket.

Mom's waiting for me at the top of the stairs. "Hi, honey," she says, "Did you have a good night? Did you boys go somewhere?"

Maybe the craziest part about all of this is it's not even past curfew.

I stay a safe distance away and imitate the chipperness I had less than an hour ago. "Yeah, we randomly went to the school and played on the swings. Just stupid stuff. We're gonna watch a movie now, get cozy!"

"I'm so glad you're getting time together," she says. "You know there's that soft blanket in the games closet, too," she says as she watches me drag Eric's comforter from his bed.

"This is perfect. Night, Mom! I love you."

He doesn't look good.

I should tell Mom and Dad.

But he's just drunk.

I should lighten up.

His breathing is weird.

He could throw up again.

People choke on their vomit.

You read about it in health class.

I Google some stuff, but Google convinces me he's already dead, so I put my phone away.

I compromise with myself.

I won't tell Mom and Dad.

But I'll watch him.

I take the lid off the short white garbage can in the basement. I move it next to him. I lift his head off the pillow and scoot underneath him. I put his head in my lap. It's a bizarre setup, but it makes sense in my head. If I fall asleep, I'll feel his puke, and I'll wake up before he chokes.

I should just tell Mom and Dad.

I'm probably overreacting. Probably one kid in 1973 choked

on his own vomit and they've been using that story in health class ever since.

He's on his side.

I'm right here.

This is just what people do. Reid Meyers puked on Beth Dorsey and everybody lived to tell the tale.

I rub his shoulder and talk, just so I stay awake.

"Tomorrow's Thanksgiving," I say to Eric, just random babbling like when you're testing sound levels on a microphone. "We'll sleep late. Mom'll make cinnamon rolls. We'll watch the parade." The water heater gurgles in the storage room. "You *know* Dad'll make us say what we're thankful for, so you better start thinking of it now. And I don't care how hungover you are, you're helping me with the Christmas decorations." His breathing seems fine. Everything seems fine. "What do you think your ornament'll be this year? Probably something Northwestern-y. Mine'll probably be . . . I don't know, actually. Maybe a clay figurine of a gay kid crying about his boyfriend." I laugh. "What a dumb year." I exhale into the nothing of the basement. "Beat you on the ACT, though." I rub his shoulder. Bop it, really lightly, and take a long inhale. "The internet says you'll pee any minute now." I look down at his head. "Don't you fucking dare."

Thanksgiving

I rub my eyes and groan. I'm hungover and there's no sign of
Eric.

I hear footsteps upstairs and slowly make my way to the
kitchen.

"Well, look who decided to wake up," Dad says with a spatula
in his hand.

"Dad was gonna send Duke down at seven, but I blockaded the
door," Eric replies with a huge smile. "And!"—he spins dramatically
from the stove over to me—"I guarded the biggest cinnamon roll
just for you. My favorite brother."

"Did you sleep well, honey?" Mom walks over, rubs my
shoulder. "You boys haven't slept in the basement since you were
little kids. Makes me all fuzzy inside, everyone back at home." She
walks back to check on a casserole.

The heat from the open oven door makes the kitchen feel like
hell.

The Thanksgiving smells make me nauseous. Doughy sweet
potatoes sit in blocks of butter, globs of Cheez Whiz are plunked

on frozen broccoli, chunky gravy waits by a raw turkey, just sitting dead on the counter. A loud slurp comes from the kitchen corner as my mom shakes a can of jellied cranberry and it all glops out, ridges still visible.

I sit at the table. Eventually, the scent transitions back to whatever it normally is. Every house has a very specific smell, but you grow immune to the one you live in. It's kind of terrifying, when you think about it, that you're oblivious to the most obvious things in your life.

In front of me, Eric places a fancy-occasions dinner plate with a cinnamon roll the size of a steering wheel. Frosting drips off the plate and he says thank you with his eyes. I say nothing with mine, afraid I'll overdo the expression and give us away. Instead, I stare at the blue flowers weaving around the border of my parents' wedding china and play along. Last night never happened.

As I listen to the condensed milk glugging out of the can, I can't take it. I go to the bathroom and stare at my reflection long enough for it to feel like a separate person. *What the fuck*, I whisper to myself. It's not shocking that Eric doesn't have a hangover—he's built different, never even needed braces. But he couldn't walk. He needed help *walking*. Does he need help walking at school? I flush the toilet to pretend like I'm peeing. He needed help.

Dishing up my turkey, I decide it had to have been just one weird night. One weird night. We were sharing a bottle, I remember as I take a bite of sweet potatoes. I hardly drank anything. He probably thought I drank half the bottle. I take seconds of cheesy broccoli casserole. So he probably didn't even realize how much he was drinking. By the time I get to pumpkin pie, it hits me: We weren't measuring our drinks. I add a second spoonful of Cool Whip. This is why you always measure your drinks!

"Mark, don't think you're gettin' away with not telling us what you're thankful for." Dad smiles big, and playfully tousles my hair as he makes his way back to the table with a cup of coffee.

"I'm thankful for Mr. Donnelly. And all he taught me about basketball."

His smile drops, and I instantly hate myself for saying that. Sometimes I really hate myself.

I close the door to the storage room, where Eric and I have been sent to get the Christmas decorations.

I have to say something.

"Ummmmmm?"

He tugs the string to turn on the exposed light bulb and smiles. "You're my hero."

"Uhhh—*yeah.*"

He moves an old tent and a pair of ski boots out of the way so we can get to the storage bins.

"I mean. Eric. You were *gone*. Gone gone."

He grabs the far end of a long box with fake tree branches popping out of it. "Did we at least figure out how you were gonna woo Ezra?" I pick up my end and he apologizes, in his way. "I love you more than Dad loves cheesy broccoli casserole."

I smile. I am officially blowing it out of proportion. People drink. People sometimes get too drunk. I myself once puked at Winter Ball. Why am I acting like a mom?

We maneuver the long box around the storage room door and onto the basement stairs. I walk backward and up the stairs. "You should have been measuring your drinks, though," I tell Eric.

He looks up at me. "The student has become the master."

He nods his head and keeps us moving.

Every year, Mom gives us a new ornament, something that celebrates a hobby or commemorates an accomplishment: the flat wooden Boy Scout teddy bear for my first year of Scouts, the clay soccer player for the year Eric made varsity.

Mom narrates as we hang up ornaments from years past. "Oh, and that one"—she motions to a carton of eggnog with a bluebird coming out of it—"that one"—she can hardly get the words out she's laughing so hard—"I found at Cracker Barrel, and it was that same year your father found you"—she nods to Eric—"hiding in your closet . . . chugging an *entire carton of eggnog.*" We all know the story but crack up anyway. As the song changes on the Christmas playlist, the only sound in our family room is my family laughing.

In the shadow of our well-trimmed tree, Dad swings his recliner back to get a little momentum. "Wait, can't open this year's ornaments without—gotta get these lights! Mark"—he turns to me—"see if you can reach the female end of that extension cord there." Dad motions under the tree for me to grab the receiving end of the short white extension cord twisted around the tree stand.

He doesn't mean anything by it, "the female end," that's just how he's always talked to us about extension cords. And electrical connectors. Modem cables. Pipes. Bolts. Even LEGOs. Male end into female end. The only way it works.

I yell at him every year, and every year he tells me he didn't invent the English language. A ritual as predictable as eggnog. But this year I just do it. Grab the male end from my dad, the female end from under the tree, and plug them together.

New Me: a good friend, a good brother, and a good son. The Holy Trinity.

"*Now* it's Christmas!" Mom beams as she steps back to take in the radiance of our tree. A lifetime of ornaments sparkles in the white light.

"The only reason you like Thanksgiving is because it's the first night of Christmas!" Eric jokes.

"Well, no. Now I like Thanksgiving because it means our whole family is back together." She smiles and hands my brother a small red box. "All right, Eric," she says with uncontainable glee. "Time for your ornament!" He goes first because he's the oldest.

"Actually, I think Mark should have the honor this year. Switch things up a little bit." His words drip in double meaning.

I unwrap my ornament: a plastic, glittery guitar, to commemorate Praise Band.

I pretend to play it and everyone laughs.

And Eric unwraps his: a purple sphere as delicate as a light bulb, with the Northwestern wildcat roaring out from a big white *N*. It looks so fragile hanging on the tree, like one brush with a fake pinecone could shatter it into a million little pieces.

Herschel's Diner

The very next night, Ezra looks at me with a mischievous smile that makes me forget everything I'd been overanalyzing about Eric. He spins on a bar stool at Herschel's Diner, head tilted down, perfect eyes peeping perfectly under the sharp arch of his dark hair.

His smile is small, but wide enough to show his dimples.

His arms are lean, but strong enough to press against the short sleeves of his logo-less black T-shirt.

"Don't declare victory yet," he says, reading my mind.

I wanted to whisk him away to an island off the coast of Guatemala and live off pineapples and tongue kisses, but since I have a midnight curfew and no passport, I had to settle for Herschel's Diner.

"Isn't it stunning?" I direct his eyes to the spinning dessert case—the brightly lit, six-foot-tall temple of high-glycemic perfection intentionally placed right at the front just to torture small children who are about to endure an entire dinner of parental chit-chat before they can even begin arguing over whether to get the Oreo one or the one with the rainbow sprinkles.

"It's almost child abuse that your parents would only let you get one dessert as a whole family." With nothing but a few ketchup-drenched french fries left on his plate, Ezra hops off his bar stool and strides to the cakes, positioning himself so close you wouldn't be able to slide a dinner receipt between his nose and the perfectly Windexed glass.

"*I know!*" I follow. "But we wouldn't actually argue. Eric would just pretend he wanted chocolate more than sprinkles, and then whisper in my ear what I should say to convince him. 'Okay, now tell me that, since Dad likes chocolate, he'd take a smaller bite of the sprinkles.'"

Ezra elbows me lightly in the ribs as we both bend down to look at the rotating assortment. "Well, you're in the real world now, and we're getting the strawberry tart and you're gonna like it!" The waitress steps behind the counter, puts an order pad back in her apron and rests a serving tray by her side. Ezra points to a heavily glazed lump of fruit in a brittle beige crust.

"You're *kidding* me. A tart?"

"A tart." He stands firm.

"Deal-breaker."

"Fine, I'll take it to-go."

"I drove."

"Linda," he asks our waitress as she cuts out our tart slice, "you'd drive me home if this self-centered man hasn't learned his lesson yet, right?"

"Honey, I'd drive you to Oklahoma to get you away from a self-centered man." Ezra turns, so proud of himself. She goes on,

"But that kid's family's been comin' here for twenty years and his dad tips twenty-five percent. Hope you got comfortable shoes."

Ezra shakes his fists at the sky. "*Argh*! The un-usurp-able royal family of Annondale."

The bell on top of the front door chimes as a mom, dad, and daughter walk in. The adorable little girl looks like she dressed herself: knee-high rainbow socks, pink light-up shoes, and a travel-soccer-team jersey tucked into a purple tutu.

Suddenly, I can't stop thinking about the last time I was in Herschel's and saw a little girl in a pretty dress.

I hesitate to share it. It makes sense, to tell him—this whole date is fueled by nostalgia—but it seems risky. It's too early. It's too weird. Too much.

I do battle with the stiff crust of the slippery strawberry tart.

"Seem to be enjoying yourself for someone who 'hates fruity desserts.'"

I speak delicately. "Okay, speaking of fruity . . ."

His eyes light up; he does a full 360 on his bar stool and grabs my knees when he gets back. "*Go on . . .*"

I laugh. "I think you're on a sugar high."

"Don't change the subject; tell me your fruity story," he play-fully demands.

"Well, it's related to what I was buying when we met," I start tentatively. And I tell him all about the purple princess dress with puffy sleeves. I try to stay cool, but talking about it gets me excited, and I can't help but tell him how the sequins glittered in the fluo-rescent lights and how the sleeves poofed like cumulus clouds and even how the tulle grazed my leg when she walked past our bar stools, and just when I think he's going to get up and leave upon realizing he's splitting a tart with a crazy fruit, he asks me what color her shoes were.

"Pink gel!" I shout, way too loud for the six o'clock crowd.

And if someone in fifty years were to ask me when I fell in love, I'd say: on a Herschel's bar stool while I blabbed about a dress and he asked me what color her shoes were.

Outside the Binary

"**A** guy from school is coming over later to work on this group project we have for English," I say to my parents during dinner Sunday night, trying to not sound like "a guy" is a guy I've spent the entire weekend dreaming about kissing.

"And who is your partner?"

At first I hear *partner* wrong. I hear it like, "life partner." *Play-itcool, Mark, playitcool.*

"Oh, well, it's not really a group—it's more just, homework, I guess." *Ohmygod.* "His name's Ezra. Didn't really know him before English this year, so it's good to . . . get to know someone."

Play it cool!

"Sounds great, son. Been a while since we had a new face around here," my dad says. "Ezraaa," he chants. "Cool name. Is that one of those names that can be for a boy or a girl?"

Kill me.

"Yeah, it is kinda cool," I say casually. "Uhhh, I think it's just a boy name? But I'm not sure."

"I'll have to ask Mr. Ezraaa."

Please, God, kill me now.

Ezra gets to my house around 7:00 p.m. I desperately want to shepherd him upstairs before my parents intercept us, but I also need to act casual. Slightly conflicting goals. When the doorbell rings, I burst—*nonchalantly* burst—from my homework spot at the dining room table. I hurdle over the living room coffee table, dodge the floral couch that nobody ever sits on, and land panting in the foyer. But my dad gets there before me.

He opens the door and I nervously fidget with the bottom of my sweatshirt. But in a nonchalant way.

"You must be Ezra!" Dad booms, as Duke spins in excitement. They both love a new audience.

"You must be Mr. Davis. Nice to meet you, sir." Ezra extends his hand, and I can instantly tell he gives good parent.

"Ezra." My dad enthusiastically shakes his hand. "Firm handshake. Very good. Come on in." The screen door swings closed as Ezra steps into the foyer and takes off his shoes. "Now, we were talking at dinner. Can that name be for a girl, too, or is it just a boy's name?"

If I had a tranquilizer gun, I would shoot my father.

"Mr. Davis, are you asking if my name goes both ways?" Ezra gamely replies, with a sly smile.

A laugh bursts out of my dad like a cannonball. "Hah! We got a live one, Mark."

My mom joins us, sounding like a gentle island breeze compared to the rolling thunder of my father. "Hi, Ezra. I'm Mrs. Davis."

"Pleasure to meet you, Mrs. Davis. You have a lovely home."

My dad picks up. "Dear, we were just talking about his name. It's a nice name! Maybe for a boy or a girl?"

"Well, I believe it's a *Jewish* name. Is that right, Ezra?"

Things are getting dangerously reminiscent of that time my great-grandpa asked William Yang how long he had been in America—William Yang who grew up two houses down from us.

"Correct you are, Mrs. Davis. From the Bible, in fact. It means 'helper.' And correct *you* are, Mr. Davis. Although I've only met boy Ezras, I'm sure there are some modern women out there named Ezra, and perhaps even some Ezras living outside the binary."

I jump in immediately before my dad has the chance to ask what "outside the binary" means. "Well, we should probably get started on our homework."

"You don't want to work in the dining room, honey?" my mom says as we head upstairs.

"No, we'll go to my room so you and Dad can watch TV."

Ezra smiles as we head upstairs.

When we get to my room, everything suddenly makes me self-conscious—the baseball-themed wallpaper unchanged since elementary school, the cheap white desk handed down from Eric, the granny dresser that now seems to take up half the room, and the stupid soccer ball pillow that isn't even comfortable. I'm so familiar with these things I'd stopped looking at them and now that I look at them, they look ridiculous.

"Sorry, I haven't remodeled in about ten years."

He scans the room diligently, takes a lap like he's the food inspector at my summer catering job. He examines the shelves above my desk, a tiered temple of self-esteem full of singing trophies and musical theater medals. Just seeing him so close to my bed makes my entire body tingle.

He turns to me, my soccer ball pillow in his left hand and a drama plaque in his right. "This curious combination of theatrics and machismo would be *perfect* for an introductory paragraph about you."

My door opens from the outside. "Let's just keep this open so it doesn't get too stuffy in here for you boys," my mom says.

I turn to Ezra. "My mom's onto you."

He shrugs his shoulders and smiles.

"I actually hate soccer." I put the pillow back. "Now, come on, this homework isn't gonna do itself," I say, instantly obliterating any sexual energy with a convincing imitation of my father. "You can use the desk. I'll sit here." I sit on the edge of my bed. My bed. I'm on my bed. He's next to my bed.

"Ah yes. A diligent taskmaster. No time for idle conversation." He doesn't sit at the desk, but steps closer to my bed.

"Oh, no, I didn't mean to, like, rush us. I just meant, well . . ." I blush and white-knuckle my bedpost. "We can finish our work, and then if there's time left over, hang out. Or whatever." Bed bed bed bed bed.

He hops to the right and grabs a framed picture of the Praise Band. "Who are these perfectly diverse people?"

My heart is now beating somewhere on the ceiling and I tell him I'm in a band for church.

"What's a band for church?" He lights up at the prospect of unpacking this.

"We sing rock songs about Jesus." I laugh to make sure he doesn't think I take it too seriously. "It's cool. Well, as cool as you can be in church."

"What's your band called?"

"You'll make fun of it."

"What is it?"

"The pastor came up with it so we couldn't argue."

He arches his dark eyebrows.

"'Find Your Faith.'"

He impersonates a radio announcer: "*You're now listening to the smooth sounds of Find Your Faith.*"

"I wanted us to be called the Bible Thumpers, but Carmen"—I point to the piano player in the picture—"said it was maybe sacrilegious."

"Are you religious?"

"Well, religious enough to be in a church band." I scoot over and take the picture frame, placing it back down. "But not, like, a crazy God freak or something."

"Of course not," he reassures me. "But you believe in God?"

"Well . . ." I hesitate. I feel like this is heavier than we should be getting on a third . . . whatever-this-is. But I don't want to seem stiff. I also don't think I've ever been asked this question. Is that possible? I've gone to church every Sunday for sixteen years, and not a single person has asked me if I believe in God? "Yeah, I believe in God."

"Are you sure?" Ezra asks playfully.

"Yes." I steady myself. "I believe in God."

"But what about calculus homework?"

"What about *English homework*!" I shout, waving my unopened laptop.

He just smiles. "You're cute when you're flustered."

✧ ✧ ✧

Ezra holds up a bright blue trophy with a silver microphone on top of it.

"I don't mean to intimidate you," I tease, "but I did win the seventh-grade talent show."

"Annondale royalty!" Ezra beams.

"You know, it was actually horrible," I remember. "Do you know Bryan Patchett? Well, as I was holding my big-finish-final-note, he shouted '*Fairy*' at the top of his lungs."

"What *decade* was this?" Ezra jokes as he puts the trophy back in its rightful place. "It appears you got the last laugh."

"Yeah, I mean, it was so dumb. And even—at that point I kind of knew I *was* a fairy. I just wish I would have told people before Bryan Patchett did." I suddenly get self-conscious about what a random story I'm telling. "Anyway, doesn't matter, my brother gave me a pep talk and sent some giant football player to scare Bryan Patchett." I desperately search for a smooth segue away from Bryan Patchett. "So . . . what was your first homophobia?"

I think I'd prefer to have been born a bush.

He laughs. Thank God. "Still waiting for it," he says. "It's actually mandatory to be queer in Portland. The mayor has quotas." He concludes the room tour by lying on my bed. He looks up at the ceiling, "The only person upset about me being gay was my mom."

"Oh," I say, visibly shook. The wheels on my desk chair rattle as I adjust my seat, instantly sorry I brought up something heavy.

He turns his head to look at me. "Don't worry, she's very

progressive politically," he says reassuringly, "she just thinks, for myriad reasons, a person should do whatever they possibly can to avoid the company of men."

My shoulders relax, relieved by the joke. "She's not wrong," I say, gripping the padded base of my chair.

He has brown eyes, so dark the iris almost blends with the pupil, and when you look in them, trying to decipher where the edges are, trying to see if maybe they'll tell you how, in the last ten minutes, the entire universe has shrunk down to the size of this boy, my bed, and me—well, then you get lost. And then you find yourself perhaps staring too long into his eyes.

"At this exact moment"—he looks confidently into my awkward eyes—"I'm glad I ignored her advice." On my bed, he slowly rolls to his side, leans on his elbow, props his head in his hand, and his eyes say *come join me*.

"When did your parents get divorced?" I ask, wondering if they give out bright blue trophies for the *world's most incompetent flirter*.

He bounces my soccer ball pillow against the wall behind him. "Well, end of sophomore year, my mother caught my father in flagrante delicto with someone who was, most assuredly, not my mother." He speaks matter-of-factly, without the lilting cadence of his previous sentence poems. "My mother has a client in Annondale, and Annondale has the decency to be two thousand four hundred miles away from the 'lying fucking bastard' formerly known as my father. So we moved."

I fidget, adding, "Wow, that's a really big move." The silence gets longer. I scratch my leg even though it doesn't itch. "Hopefully the move at least was kind of fun. Always thought that'd be cool, like, a moving truck and everything."

It is, I think, a ridiculously stupid thing to say.

"Yes, we ate beef jerky and sang country music with the windows down."

I contort my face in apology. "Yeah, it probably wasn't fun."

"*Your* parents were exceedingly delightful. I bet"—he switches back to a chipper tone—"your mom does the housework and your dad the yard work. When you were a kid, she read you bedtime stories and he threw the ball with you. They both love you very much, and all that matters is that you try your hardest."

I push him over to the far side of my bed so I can lie down. "*I* do the yard work," I correct. Our arms press against each other, fit perfectly, everything—down to our knuckles—touching.

I turn my head and he turns his, and our lips are so close I can feel his breath in my mouth.

My door is still open. *Damn it.* My door is still open. *Why didn't you close it before you got on the bed?* I try to remember how Matilda from those Roald Dahl books moved stuff with her mind. *Door. Close!* Or was that Hermione? Roald Dahl was racist, I read. Antisemitic, I think. They found these old letters. And then J. K. Rowl—*Oh my God, just close the fucking door.*

"So let me get this straight," I say, as I awkwardly stand back up and try to remember how to walk. "You moved here sophomore year." I turn the knob gently, so it doesn't make the click. I walk back. But when I get back, it doesn't feel right. It feels like I broke something. I don't know where to sit, or lie, or whatever, convinced that by now he'd probably rather make out with racist Roald Dahl.

I sit against the headboard, too stiff. Like a parent about to read a bedtime story. "Why did we wait until junior year to meet?"

He grabs my ankle and pulls me down toward him. "I noticed you on my first day."

I laugh and nudge him with my shoulder, squeezing him against the wall. "Why didn't you say hi?"

"If memory serves, you were otherwise engaged." He nudges me back. He continues, getting even closer, "Plus, you always seemed to be in a group."

Our eyes, eye to eye. Our noses, nose to nose.

"Well, you should have said hi," I whisper.

His arm slides under my lower back, my bare skin feels his bare arm, and my entire body feels like a puddle that's had a power cord drop into it. The fabric of our pants swishes against each other, and my mind swims in my brain. I shudder when the bed creaks. He slides us down onto the carpet, where it doesn't creak. My elbows burn. Space collapses and time expands, and his tongue is strong and in charge. I lean so far into our kiss that our heads bump against the hard wood of my bedpost, but we don't stop. It hurts, but we don't stop. Shirts on but still, my ribs feel his, our chins fit, feet, hands can't decide. I open my eyes just to prove that it's real. Everything over and under, more, disordered but perfect, a jumbled mass of colliding boy parts that sing in unison proving once and for all just how much God loves gays.

And despite what my dad believes about extension cords, it turns out two male ends can come together and make electricity.

He squeezes me, firm but so gentle, and says, simply, "Hi."

Lunch

I think about him all morning, but I don't see Ezra again until lunch the next day.

He's eating alone. Not in a sad way, but in a self-contained way. Like a majestic moose.

"You were wrong, you know." I walk up to him without sitting down.

He looks up from his lunch. "Oh yeah?"

"My dad did the bedtime stories. And he didn't read them. He made them up." I'm still standing. "He had all these characters . . . the main one was Mr. Giraffe. And Mr. Giraffe would come pick me up and we'd go on an adventure to visit Mr. Elephant and Mrs. Peacock, and everyone else in the jungle, and when we were done, we'd go to this empty field and he'd guide me through a meditation. Very hippie for a Midwest stereotype."

"Well then," he says, without skipping a beat, "I was right, more generally."

"And how's that?"

"That you're different than them." He gazes left, then right.

"Oh my God, *they* are different than *each other*," I emphasize, laughing underneath the loud chaos of the cafeteria. "Eat lunch with me and you'll see."

"Merging lunch tables," he says, sounding more condescending than flirtatious. "The ultimate symbol of high school romance!"

I look down at the empty seats surrounding him. "No disrespect, but there's not much to merge."

"Oh, I'm terribly sorry for the misunderstanding." He raises his eyebrows. "This seat is actually for Mrs. Peacock—she's just picking up her chicken tenders. Almost cannibalistic, if you ask me."

Grateful to be back on flirty ground, I playfully grab his lunch tray. "Come on! Come meet my friends."

"No disrespect, but I'd rather not."

I taunt him with his own submarine sandwich.

"I have to do some reading for physics," he says, serious.

"Come on, you've got to eat." Still holding his tray, I turn to walk down the lunchroom toward Damien, Jeff, Haley, and everyone.

"I'd rather not." He reaches across the table and grabs the edge of the tray. I lose my grip and the tray tilts, and a full cup of Sprite—with no lid because we're saving the turtles—teeters but doesn't topple, saved by the fluffy white bread of his turkey sub.

"Oh my God, that was almost a disaster, I'm so sorr—" I quickly place his tray back on the table. Stray strips of iceberg lettuce float in a shallow puddle of Sprite. I delicately move his single brown napkin to clean up the debris. "Saved by the sub."

I smile. He doesn't.

Ezra slides the tray back to his side.

"Let me buy you a new one."

"It's fine."

"I'm so sorr—"

"It's fine." He unzips his backpack and pulls out his physics book, angles his eyes up to me but keeps his head down. "I better . . ."

"Yeah. Of course. Sorry. Okay. Well, I'll talk to you—" I turn and walk away.

Damien looks over to Ezra as I sit down and unload my sack lunch. "That the guy you were telling me about?"

"Yeah."

He nods his head studiously and steals one of my pretzels. "Seems to be going well."

I take a deep exhale. "Do you think there's such thing as a personality transplant?" I ask. "Like, go to a doctor and have them give you a whole new personality."

He looks back to Ezra. "I think your boy's in my physics class."

I tap a carrot stick on top of the table. "Did you do the reading?" I ask.

"Didn't have any," he says in between bites. "Sub today."

I look over at Ezra, not really looking at his open physics book.

"So wait, like, a butt lift," Damien reflects, "but for your personality?"

My phone vibrates.

Okay Layla Yousef was on something it's not awesome

I'm grateful for someone else's problems to distract me from my own. I try to cheer her up, so maybe one of us can have a good Monday.

It will be! You're just ACCLIMATING

I'm just DROPPING OUT
Trash.

Treasure.

I bet if you pull your grades up you can come back!
It wasn't just grades

I type something. *?? What else was it?* Delete it. Focus on the positive. Be a good friend.

Well, that's in the past now!
Are there any clubs or anything you can join?

CLUBS?!!!????!
Have we MET?

I type something. Delete it. Wonder if a personality transplant would make me a better texter.

k talk to you later the mathletes are having a lunch meeting
tell mrs pointer I say hi

The Choice

"**E**very relationship has a 'thing,' bud." A blue beanbag chair and a light-wood desk blur by as Eric settles in front of the off-white brick of his dorm room wall, now so familiar after months of almost daily FaceTimes. "So the guy doesn't want to sit with your friends at lunch? If all else is gravy, keep skatin'."

I get a weird visual of ice-skating on a frozen pool of gravy. "I've never even *heard* of a couple that doesn't sit together at lunch. It'd be like, I don't know, if Mom and Dad lived in different houses."

Eric turns off a desk lamp, too bright in his eyes. "It's possible—and I'm just puttin' this out there, I don't know for sure—but it's possible you will reach a point in your life when—"

"I know," I interrupt him. "*When I realize there are bigger things than where you sit in the cafeteria*, I get it. But I just want to know *why*."

"If he wants you to know why, he'll tell you." He focuses his gaze. "Give it time. You can choose to focus on the one thing that's wrong, *or* you can choose to focus on the nine hundred fifty thousand things that are right. Yesterday you talked for twenty minutes about how you like the way he leans against the lockers."

I gaze longingly out my window. "He leans great."

"It's a choice, bud. Happiness is a choice."

"*Namaste!*" his roommate, a Santa-Claus-sized guy with dark red hair, shouts like an angry football coach, leaning so far into the screen he blocks out the wall.

Eric messes up his roommate's already unruly red hair and pushes his face out of frame, continues, "You think Mom likes *everything* about Dad?"

"I'd really prefer if we stopped using Mom and Dad as the relationship analogy."

"It's not a problem unless you make it a problem," he concludes. "Keep on skatin', bud."

When November gets cold like winter, Ezra and I go to Stony Creek, this giant nature reserve, with Duke and Ezra's dog, Buster.

He gives me a kiss after I put the car in park.

I'm distracted, and I accidentally let Duke out of the back seat without his leash on.

Thankfully, Duke likes people more than freedom, so with the whole world in front of him, he just runs to Ezra and asks to be pet.

Buster is a fluffy white dog that is impossible to see under the first snow of the season. And he has an *exact* replica of Ezra's personality. Duke is bouncing all around, so happy to be outside, but Buster is acting so above-it-all, like playing outside is such a stereotypical dog thing to do.

We crack up about that. Ezra calls it a "predictable but delight-ful alignment."

I hit him with a snowball and call him a nerd.

The lake is almost frozen, and I keep on skating.

Junior Year

December

Ho Ho Ho

Eric hops into my room the Thursday before Annondale High's holiday break and stands above two textbooks spread open on the gray carpet.

I've been nervous all day, anticipating this moment.

"Lucky those things aren't graded on a brother curve," he says to me, then reaches down with a giant smile. "Ezraaa"—he holds the *a* like a half note—"at last." Eric gives Ezra some sort of massively heterosexual handshake backslap, then beams. "Half the reason I wanted to come home for this Christmas party was to meet the dude who's turned my little brother into a life-size heart-eyes emoji."

Ezra returns the flattery as he stands up. "Mark can barely open a math book without mentioning his perfect older brother, so the pleasure, indeed, is mine."

I shuffle anxiously in the corner. Two separate worlds suddenly becoming a Venn diagram.

It turns out they have plenty to talk about. Namely, my deficiencies. It's barely three minutes into their introduction and they're cracking up over how I repeat myself when I'm nervous, how I run lines in the bathroom, and how the only time I get truly angry is if somebody yells at Duke. But I'd be lying if I said it didn't make me very happy to see the two most important people in my life laughing about how I drive like a grandma.

"It's worth it, by the way," Eric says, motioning to our open and ignored physics books. "All this AP shit. Frees up your college schedule to take way more interesting classes."

"So what interesting classes are you taking?" I ask.

"Ah, I'm staying too long, fuckin' up your studying." He turns away.

"Please, *God*, fuck up our studying," Ezra begs.

"All right." Eric happily relents, settles into my desk chair while Ezra and I sit, backs against the wall, on my bed. Ezra leans into me, and we listen like kids at Bible school.

"Actually, I couldn't come up earlier this week because I was trapped in the library trying to write a paper on this philosopher named Foucault." Instantly, I'm enchanted by the premise of writing a paper somewhere other than my dining room table. "Ezra, you know this dude?"

"No," Ezra says. There's a first for everything.

"Oh, this guy's the real deal. For one, he would definitely *not* approve of all my little quotes, making progress seem so simple. Dude doesn't even believe in progress. Some of these philosophers don't even believe in *time*! What's to believe in?"

Ezra scoots closer to me. Eric continues, "Anyway, the paper is on *The History of Sexuality*—how we've come to view sexuality as core to our *essence*, who we are. But actually, that's just a social construct designed to make us easier to control. How 'bout that?

Back in the day there were all these dudes who were gay, or bi, or whatever we would call it now, but because it wasn't this huge *thing* tied to the core of their essence, they just went about their business without needing to define it for society." Eric concludes, proud, "Ya know, this was a long time ago, but your generation seems to be headed in that direction."

"Eric, you're two years older than us."

He laughs. "You know what I mean."

"We want to go to college," Ezra moans. "We don't even talk about gay sex in sex ed!"

"Did you know that?" I look at Eric. "Like, *literally* the only time Mr. Manderfield said the word *homosexual* was in the STD section."

Ezra adds. "And not an *L*, *B*, *T*, or *Q* in sight."

"My boy Foucault would say that's because school is an institution as much about discipline and control as it is about education." He hops up. "And speaking of school, recess is over. Keep studying that physics, fellas. Crush the APs. Make room for more interesting classes."

"Can we go to college *tomorrow*?" I interrupt our reading, still kind of giddy that my brother just tried to impress my boyfriend with his firm grasp on the History of Butt Stuff.

"Foucault!" Ezra tastes the name in his mouth like ice cream.

"Physics." I plop the word out like sludge.

"Seems hard, though."

"College?"

"Yeah. Draining."

"I guess."

"Your brother looked tired."

"If that's tired, then I hope I'm exhausted for this physics test."

"I don't mean it as a bad thing. I just mean, he looked a little tired. He was up late writing a paper." He looks up from the book. "Human beings get tired."

I'm getting annoyed but don't want to be. "Okay, we have to focus or we're not gonna have enough science credits to even go to college."

"You really do live in a planetarium of protected perfection."

I point to the bright blue text of the summary quiz. "'*A disk is initially rotating clockwise around a fixed axis with angular speed ω_0 . . .*'"

The physics test is merciless but by 4:00 p.m. the next day, it's a distant memory. Because: the Davis Family Christmas Party. Far and away the biggest event on the Pine Meadows social calendar. Even older college kids who make my brother look like a lightweight wake up early to make it back to Michigan in time for Honey Baked Ham. The cheesy potatoes are on a folding table in the garage, pop's plopped in the snow outside, the beer's on ice in the laundry room sink, and my dad makes everyone within spitting distance of the legal drinking age do a Jäger-bomb with him in the kitchen.

Yes, even our "no alcohol" rule gets a holiday.

Every corner of our house holds a Christmas vignette that Norman Rockwell would be proud of. Ivy weaves up the banister behind an electronic Santa who waves "Ho Ho Ho." High school sweethearts reunite under the mistletoe over cups of virgin eggnog as a fifth grader and her flute squeak out an apologetically off-key "Deck the Halls."

Please come! It's been FOREVER.

Seeing Crystal would be a true Christmas miracle. Damien, who's already at his family's in Ohio, hasn't seen her either. She probably has a billion new friends and doesn't have time for desperate texts from the lonely fifth grader she saved from the punch bowl. When she first transferred to Driggs, we texted a ton, but somehow we've lost our flow. It's like, when you make a joke but have to explain it. I try to be chipper whenever we text, but end up sounding like my mother.

My mother who is currently decked out in a home-sewn Christmas sweater that you better not call ugly. Real bells jingle from faux-suede antlers as she beckons. "Everyone to the living room. We're starting the carols."

"Carol loves the carols!" Mr. Stevens shouts, because somebody has to.

We used to carol around the neighborhood until someone had the now-obvious aha that caroling for all the neighbors who weren't invited to the neighborhood Christmas party was sort of pouring salt in ye olde yuletide wound. *Happy Holidays, Mrs. Perry. Here's all the fun you could be having if your husband didn't talk about drywall all the time.*

"All the boys on the couch," my mom yells, but she doesn't need to because we're headed there anyway. All the boys always sit on the couch. It's a tradition that started when all the boys could fit in car seats. Now it's a hilarious photo op as we try to defy the dimensions of three saggy floral cushions and squeeze in eight grown men. Ezra watches lovingly, hiding behind a potted plant as I edge an arm in between Eric and Hansen McCabe.

"I don't think so." My dad gets up, grabs Ezra under the armpits, and *literally* throws him onto the couch. He lands somewhere between me and McCabe's plate of mini cheesecakes, disrupting the delicate physics of our already overstuffed couch. Eric grabs on to Ezra's arm, but it's too late. Half of us tumble over the right arm of the couch, and the other half slip down by the coffee table. Mrs. D'Angelo heroically saves two cups of eggnog from spilling all over the cream carpet, and Duke spins like a souped-up dreidel trying to decide whether he wants to steal a Christmas cookie or wrestle with Eric.

Squished between the couch and the pink armchair that currently holds a hysterically laughing Mrs. Foster, Ezra and I land in a position very close to cuddling.

As the laughter fades and people start cleaning up the broken candy canes and stray slices of Honey Baked Ham, Ezra squeezes me from behind and whispers in my ear, "Leave it to the Jewish kid to ruin Christmas."

The warm air against my ear melts my insides. I turn my head urgently. "If you don't stop whispering, I'm going to get hard in front of half my neighborhood."

My mom calls everyone to attention. Nothing drops a boner like your own mother. "Okay, one last thing," she says with a proud smile.

I stand up, whine, knowing where this is going. "No, Mom! I don't want to this year. I'm getting too old for this."

"Mark, don't talk back to your mother," Mr. Stevens playfully reprimands from the dining room table.

"Come on, Mark!" Mrs. Washington chimes in. "It's like living in the neighborhood of a celebrity. We have to hear you sing!"

After some half-hearted protestations, I agree.

Sally McCourt used to accompany me on piano, but couldn't make it back from her college in Virginia, so this year I sing "O Holy Night" a cappella.

The room goes silent. Mr. DeWolfe waves his lighter in the air. Even the middle schoolers come back from the basement.

My favorite place in the world isn't a place at all. It's an open-throat vowel anywhere between D-flat and F-sharp, held for at least a whole note. But if I had my way, I'd hold it until New Year's Eve.

My dad dramatically falls on his knees as I sing "*FALL on your knees.*" So, instead of singing *O hear the angel's voices* I sing, sternly, with double vibrato, staring down at him like a musical theater villain, "*Don't JOKE while I am SINNNNNGINNNG.*" Everyone laughs.

While I crescendo to the big finish, standing between the attention-hog known as my father (who's now nursing a knee injury) and the waving lighter of my old T-ball coach, my brother wraps his arm around my boyfriend, and they look at me with eyes that say forever.

If sound is a wave, as Ezra and I learned in physics, and so is light, then so, it feels, is love.

✦ ✦ ✦

Mom's in a good mood all the next day, fielding phone call after phone call (*"Honestly, Carol. It was the best one yet."*) as we all pack for Rockford. We're leaving first thing tomorrow morning. To Grandmother's house we go.

"We're leaving *at* seven, Eric. Not *around* seven—*at* seven," Dad shouts from the dinner table as Eric grabs his coat to go out. "That means bags packed and all of you in the car *at* seven. It doesn't mean waking up at seven, it means—"

"I know what it means, Pop." Eric comes over and puts his hand on Dad's shoulder. "I'll be in the car, ready to rock and roll, tomorrow morning, December 23rd, at seven a.m." He tousles the little hair that Dad has left and heads over to Mom, who's cleaning up in the kitchen, to give her a kiss on the cheek. "I'll even do you one better," he says as he grabs his car keys from the key rack above the house phone. "I'll be in the car with your Starbucks order at six fifty-five."

"I'll believe it when I see it," Dad says.

"Coconut milk cappuccino for me, please," I shout from the couch as Netflix autoplays the next episode of this documentary on a California cult who all died by suicide in order to board a UFO.

"Mark, honey, maybe we can put something a little more pleasant on?" Mom calls from the kitchen.

"But think how pleasant our lives will look relative to this. Compared to 'cult leader suicide pact,' Aunt Debbie won't seem so bad."

"Great strategy, bro," Eric shouts. "All right, I'm off. I won't be late."

"You better not be," Dad says, stern. "You know your mom stays up."

"Just going to say hi to some people. I'll probably be back before you fall asleep in your recliner."

Which is around 9:30. But Eric's not back by then.

He's not back when I let Duke out one last time at 10:00.

He's not back when I finish episode six and go to bed, either, which is around midnight.

The walls in our house are paper-thin. I wake up in the middle of the night to my mom saying, in a frantic whisper, "He's not answering, either. We have to do something."

I sit up in my bed and check my phone. 3:14 a.m.

"Like what, dear? Call a search party? File a missing person's report? He's probably just passed out at some friend's house."

"We shouldn't have let him go out."

I hear my parents' door open. I'm just in my boxers, but I get up to see what's going on.

"Go back to bed, honey," my mom says gently, as I peek through my bedroom door. "We're still waiting for your brother. He'll be home any minute."

God, what an idiot.

I'm still half-asleep, though, so I obediently go back to bed.

Until, a couple hours later, the house phone wakes me up.

The ring shakes the house. No one calls the house phone except Grandma, so it sounds more alarming than if a rooster were crowing in the middle of the foyer.

"Hello?" my mom answers, worry already in her voice. "Oh God. Yes, I will."

Her voice hangs in the air.

"Oh God, Eric, what happened?"

No No No

She speaks with an angry mix of relief and confusion. "Your father and I are on the way; you can explain in the car."

It's only ten minutes before my alarm is set to go off, so I hustle to get into my car clothes, while straining to eavesdrop on their conversation.

I hear the phone beep off. "He's in jail. Our son is in jail," Mom says, dumbfounded. "Our son is in jail." It's as if the truth of it is hitting her as she says it.

"Oh Jesus. For what? Where?" Dad is pissed. He has none of Mom's worry in his tone. Just pure pissed.

"Royal Oak. Our son is in jail in Royal Oak." She still can't believe it. "I told him he could explain when we got in the car."

"I cannot be*lieve* this." Dad hits something, hard, maybe the headboard. "This is ridiculous! Jail?"

Mom says nothing.

"What are we gonna do?" Dad shouts.

"Start by picking him up, I suppose." She sounds like she's in shock.

"And then what? Drive to Rockford?" The closet door slams shut.

"No, we can't go to Rockford." She pauses, takes it in. "I'll call my mom."

"And tell her what? That Eric got arrested, so we're canceling Christmas?"

"Dear, we can't pick up Eric from jail and then drive to Rockford."

"Let's talk about it in the car."

I'm standing in my door dressed for the trip when they walk out. "What's going on?" I ask.

"Your brother is just in a little bit of a situation," Mom says, in a strenuously calm tone. "I'm sure everything's fine. We'll be back soon. There are bagels in the freezer, and just—"

"*Ho-Ho-Hooo-Merry-Christmas,*" shouts the motion-detector Santa in our foyer.

"Oh, shut that thing—" Dad kicks it.

"Be by your phone," Mom finishes.

I don't think the house has ever been as quiet as it is in the second after they shut the door. As I look at the toppled-over motion-detector Santa, his white cotton ball beard slumping on the cold cream tile, I don't think any house has ever been this quiet.

When they get back, it feels like I'm trespassing in someone else's house.

Eric's in a haze and hardly acknowledges my existence.

Every conversation sounds like something I shouldn't hear.

If problems aren't problems until other people know about them—then this Christmas, I'm "other people."

From the dining room I hear, "I don't know how many more ways I can say I'm sorry."

"Well, you're gonna have to think of a couple more," Dad shouts. "Maybe you can start by calling your grandmother and apologizing to her."

"You're not calling Grandma," Mom intercepts quietly. "She's worried enough as it is."

"I am sorry. I'm sorry. I don't mean to get upset, because I know I really, really, really messed up. And I hate that this is affecting Christmas."

"*Affecting* Christmas!" Dad laughs. "Yeah, I'll say, Eric."

"I'm sorry. It was an awful night and a horrible mistake and I feel horrible."

"You've gotta think of something better than that."

It's bad. It's really bad. Part of me wants to eavesdrop and piece together everything, and part of me wants to hide, just close my eyes until the bad part is over. I don't like hearing them fight. I don't like hearing Eric use this voice that I've never heard him use before. It's everywhere and it's bad.

"Did you watch another one of those silly movies?" my mom used to say consolingly, when I'd walk into their bedroom with my blankie dragging behind me.

"Not silly, Mom. *Scary*." Eric loved scary movies, and I used to try to be tough.

"Just close your eyes, honey," she'd say, so comforting, "that scary stuff doesn't happen in real life."

I go to the basement and close my eyes.

But I hear them through the ceiling. "Eric, when is this going to stop?"

"Now. It's going to stop now. Really. This is it."

"That's what you said last time. And here we are again."

"I know. I know."

"What are we going to do?"

"I just . . . This was a bad night. One bad night."

"There have been a lot of 'one bad nights.'"

The night at Thanksgiving. The spontaneous visits to Evanston. Part of me is scared: How many "one bad nights"? But part of me believes him. Parents are *always* dramatic.

"I think I should just go back to school," I hear Eric say through the ceiling. "My friends have a house. I can crash there 'til the dorms open."

"That's ridiculous. It's already five o'clock. Tomorrow is Christmas Eve. We're staying together."

"Well, I'm not signing anything."

"Eric, please. If you're not going to stop for yourself, stop for us."

"This is what your mom and me have decided, and if you're not okay with it, then no more Northwestern. You'll move back home and go to Annondale Community College until you start living more responsibly."

"Fine. You know what? Fine. I'll sign your paper. This is ridiculous, though. I'm not a child. And you know what? Moving back home? Right now, this drinking shit isn't affecting anything. It's completely isolated. I have a three point nine GPA. But I'll sign anything. I'll sign something saying 'if this happens again, you have to cut off your left foot.' Because it's not going to happen again."

I don't want to listen anymore. I don't want to hear this.

"But for the record," Eric reiterates, in a steady, self-contained tone, "this is stupid. School is the one thing that's going well. And that's what you want to take from me? Because if you take school away, then drinking actually will fuck up my life. You'll be creating the future you're most afraid of."

They don't say anything.

It's mean, the way he says it.

He's so good at pinpointing what someone cares most about. It's Eric's superpower. For her afternoon coffee, Mom will pull the Northwestern mug out of the dishwasher and wash it by hand, even if there are a hundred clean mugs in the cupboard. Dad basically bought out the entire Northwestern gift shop. *"As if I need to give this place any more of my money."* This is the first time I've heard him use his superpower this way.

I hear his footsteps go upstairs.

Mom and Dad stay in the kitchen.

"I just don't want him going back there."

"It's not *there*, dear. It's him."

Eric used to tell me that there are three types of kids you can be. You can be a *good kid* and that's a really easy life with your parents, but it might get you teased at school. You can be a *bad kid*, and that's a really fun life at school, but it gets you messed up with your parents. The key is to be a good kid who does bad things. The captain of the football team who smokes a little pot on the weekend. The National Honor Society president who sometimes steals Smirnoff from his parents' liquor cabinet. Good kids who do bad things. "But that's the hardest life to pull off," he would tell me. "You gotta be street smart *and* book smart." And he would say, "In that life, your GPA is your right bower. Got it, little bro? Your GPA trumps anything they've got to say."

I come upstairs.

No one's there.

I think about checking Eric's room, but he probably doesn't want to talk anymore.

I think about going to Mom and Dad, but it feels like picking a side. It's always been Eric and Me vs. Mom and Dad, and he's *always* had my back when Mom and Dad were punishing me, no matter how right Mom and Dad were.

So I just stand in the middle of the kitchen.

Duke walks over, slower than normal, nudges my hand with his nose and looks up at me with pleading eyes.

No matter how much family drama, you've still got to walk the dog.

I open the drawer under the house phone and find a pen and Post-It note. *Took Duke to Stony Creek. Text if you want me to pick up anything for dinner.*

It'll be nice to get out of the house. To get out of the entire neighborhood. To just *be*, but not here. And then maybe they'll resolve it, have the conversation they've been holding in, that final conversation they don't want me to hear.

I hustle through the foyer.

"*Ho-Ho-Hoooo-Merrrry-Christmas*," shouts the relentless electric Santa.

Duke, oblivious, spins in excitement as I grab his leash. He leaps into the van like he already knows where we're going. The back seats are still down from where our suitcases used to be, so Duke luxuriates in the open space. The captain chairs in the middle row look like tombstones.

Stony Creek is empty except for a few ducks too stubborn to fly south. The ducks don't quack and the trees are too bare to catch the wind, so the only sound is the potato-chip crunch of my heavy winter boots as they hit the snow, and even that is inconsistent, the path so well-trodden most sections have no more give than slippery cement. The trail turns from birch trees to open field, and Duke chases after a deer in the distance. I let him.

The snow stays still. The lake is frozen at the edges.

I don't decide to scream, I just do.

Nothing happens. Not even an echo.

Alone, I thought I might finally *feel* something. Fear? Concern? Anger? Sadness? I reach for emotions like a rock climber reaching for a ledge, but there's nothing to grab on to.

Parents always overreact. That's what they do. Sarah Lawson got *three* MIPs ("Minor in Possession") her senior year and there was a rumor she got arrested in college because they found horse tranquilizers in her dorm room. But her dad knew the dean, so she didn't go to jail. Well, Sarah Lawson lives in Chicago now and works in a skyscraper and lives in a building where there's someone whose *job* it is just to open the door. Mrs. D'Angelo told me at the Christmas party. It's called a doorman. Sarah Lawson got three MIPs and now she has a husband, a dog, and a doorman.

My phone rings, and it scares the crap out of me. Duke barks at the ring and a manic family of ducks starts flapping and honking like crazy while I struggle to get my glove off and answer the phone.

"Hey, babe!" I fake happiness.

"It's so good to hear your voice," Ezra says. "I'm driving otherwise I'd FaceTime! Are you at your grandma's yet?"

I don't know where to start. What to say. I want to say everything, but everything is maybe nothing because I don't know anything. I want to say how scared I am. I want to tell him how I wish someone would tell me what's going on. I want to talk through things with *someone*, even someone who knows less than I do, and I want to say how weird it feels for me to be the one worrying.

Instead, I say nothing. "In a park with Duke, actually." Not a lie, technically.

He responds cheerily, "A perfect way to stretch out the legs after a long car ride. What's on the agenda for tonight?"

Eric once taught me the secret to lying. Don't *invent*. Use true details, even if they're not true for you in that moment. It prevents you from going over the top with it.

"Tonight it's my cousin Lizzy's birthday dinner. Family tradition: lasagna."

"Homemade lasagna." Ezra beams. "Delicious."

"You give us too much credit," I correct. "It's just Stouffer's."

"Homemade Stouffer's!"

Before every lie, there is a moment. A moment when you

consider it. *Should I?* And in that moment, I think about my brother, and how much shit he's going through at home, and it feels like the truth would be a betrayal—to take his pile of shit and spread it around.

I tell Ezra my aunt is calling. "I probably need to pick up the pop for tonight."

It frightens me, almost. How naturally I lie.

I put my phone back in my pocket and bend down to rub Duke's belly. "Good boy, Duke." I pat him on the side. "Go get 'em!" He runs ahead. The ducks retreat. The sound of breaking branches and the panting of a blazing golden blur gradually fades away.

Alone, under a sky so cloudy it looks like one never-ending gray, I want to cry. I kick a frozen patch of dirt, barely visible under the trampled snow, and hurry myself up: *Feel something.* But all the parts of me are in conflict, yanking from emotion to conflicting emotion like one of Duke's rope toys, and I don't know what to feel.

I look up at the sky, flat and gray, and just feel empty.

Family Dinner

The pizza's lukewarm, but no one takes the initiative to heat it up. We sit around the table. The muted TV plays a football game.

"Do you eat in the dining hall on Sundays, too?" Mom asks Eric. "Or is that more of a weekday thing?"

Dad takes a pepperoni off his pizza and you can hear the cheese becoming unstuck.

"No, we eat in the dining hall on Sundays—those of us with the full-week plan."

I try to scoot my chair as quietly as possible to give Duke more room, but the chair legs scrape the floor.

"Sometimes we all pitch in for snacks for the dorm," Eric adds. "I use that WildCash." Dad's fork taps on his plate. "Thanks for adding that."

Under the table, Duke groans in his sleep.

"Do you have a nice class this year, Mom?" Eric asks a question I've never heard anyone in our family ask, ever.

"Oh, very nice." The ice machine in the refrigerator makes a gurgling noise. "Seems like the kids get smarter every year."

"That's nice you're makin' the most out of that meal plan, son," Dad adds. His knife scrapes the plate. He's cutting his pizza?

"Mark"—he turns to me—"you think you'll have a solo again at the spring concert?"

Could I shout? *Let's just talk about it!*

Could I turn to Eric and scream? *Tell me what's actually going on!*

Could I grab my dad? *How many "one bad nights"?*

My mom? Could I hold her hand and ask her why her eyes look so sad?

Could I stand on the table and shake the chandelier and not stop yelling until everyone stopped pretending?

Or, perhaps, I could take Crystal's advice and send my soul to the bushes. Divide myself and send the true part away, far, far away, so only the shell has to endure this dinner.

Could I ask the questions I want answers to? Could I do what's almost obvious and just, *my God*, just tell the truth to the people I love and ask for it back from the people who love me?

Could I?

I speak delicately, like everyone else, and tell them yes, I hope I will have a solo at the spring concert.

Finally

"I'm heading back tomorrow, bud." Eric stands behind the couch, looking vacantly at the basement TV playing the final episode of my Netflix documentary. Pretty grim when a cult suicide show is the bright spot of winter break.

I look up at him from the couch. "Oh. Before New Year's?"

"Yeah. Bunch of school stuff to do." His hands rest on the back of the futon.

Two and a half years isn't that huge of an age gap, when you think about it. But it was once. Huge. Uncrossable. And our relationship dynamic seems frozen at the age when he taught me how to tie my shoes.

"Cool," I say. "I'm sure it's good to get a head start on everything. Have you picked a major yet?"

"Landed on philosophy. Job prospects be damned." He cracks a half smile.

"That sounds kind of awesome. Like nothing we learn in high school."

"For sure," he replies, from somewhere very far away.

"It's crazy you have to decide so soon."

"The first dress rehearsal for life . . . is life."

"You're a philosopher already," I say, more subdued than I wanted to sound.

Eric fills the silence. "So. What about you?" He scoots my feet over so he can curl up on the other side of the futon. "You and Ezra good? Our boy fully wooed?"

I sit up. "Yeah, we're good. He's awesome, actually."

"My little bro's in love."

He says it so normal. How can he be so normal?

There's this quote people post online sometimes, something like, "A good friend bails you out of jail. A best friend is by your side in the cell." Eric is my best friend. I know that's corny to say because he's my brother, but he's my best friend. Always has been. I'm blowing this all out of proportion. I try to act normal. "I really like him." But still, everything is stilted and shallow in a way that feels like I'm not talking to my brother or my best friend, and it's my fault, because Eric is trying, but I can't figure out how to act normal.

"Tell me more about Ezra! Way better than Beckett, right?"

"I mean, Jesus, why would you bring up John?" I respond, instantly angry for reasons I don't understand.

"Dumb comparison, sorry—I." He looks at me. Stops trying. "You don't have to get so defensive."

"Got it, thanks." It's like my body has been so desperate for a clear emotion, flailing for something to grab on to, and now that it's been introduced to anger, it doesn't let go. I reply, so sarcastically it makes me sick, "You're right. This Christmas would have been perfect if I weren't so defensive."

Eric doesn't hit back.

He's tired.

For the first time in history, I win.

He stares at the TV, and so do I, as if a paused Netflix screen might tell us what to say.

Barely audible, a sniffle.

I turn to look at my brother.

Tears silently stream down his face. His eyes are closed, trying to gather strength, or just hide. When he sees me looking, he smiles, laughs at himself while lifting his eyebrows, as if to say, *I can't believe I'm crying any more than you can.*

He takes a breath to talk, but no words come out. He exhales like a laugh, points to the tears, shrugs. Barely audible, another sniffle.

I stare, paralyzed. And then finally I scoot over on the futon and, tentatively, put my arm around my brother. Just for a second, he lets his head rest on my chest. His chin might shake if it weren't so clenched. His entire body looks like it wants to cry, and every muscle fiber tenses to make sure it doesn't.

I look down at his brown hair and try to tell him it's okay to—

"Ooof," he says, sitting back up abruptly. I can feel tears through my T-shirt. He laughs at himself, like a person who just woke up from an unexpected nap, and wipes his eyes with his shirtsleeve.

Then he makes a joke of it and theatrically wipes his eyes with *my* shirtsleeve.

He looks at me with an embarrassed smile and bloodshot eyes. "Weird Christmas, eh?"

The basement stays so still.

"Eric, are you—" I start, tears forming in my eyes now, too.

He purses his lips and shakes his head no.

But did he know what question I was asking? *Eric, are you okay?* That's what I was asking. Does he just not want me to ask? I arch my eyebrows in confusion. He still shakes his head no. But does he know what question I was asking?

I clarify, quietly, insistent and articulate. "Are you okay?"

He shakes his head no.

His eyes, blacker now than they are blue, blink.

"Of course I am, bud," he says, arching his eyebrows and forcing his mouth into a smile. He takes a deep breath in through his nose, his chest rising with the inhale, and pushes a deep, audible breath out through his mouth. He clenches his teeth and looks back at me. "Of course I am!" He laughs a little and nudges me with his shoulder. There are still tears in his eyes, waiting to fall.

We're so close he barely has to move to wrap his arm around me. He keeps wrapping and puts me in a headlock, my head on his chest, messes my hair with his other hand.

"Gahhh." He exhales a playful wrestling grunt. "Now, tell me about Ezra," he asks.

And I do.

Because it just seems like a nice thing I could do for my brother.

The End

The doorbell rings.

It's 8:00, but everyone seems to be asleep.

I run upstairs to answer the door, catching my breath as I look through the peephole.

"*Ho-Ho-Hooo-Merrry-Chr—*"

If this Santa doesn't learn to shut the f—

I unplug it.

Standing on the front porch, looking toward the street, balancing a wicker basket wrapped in cellophane and topped with a big red bow, is Ezra.

I unlock the door. Open it.

"I thought you were in Rockford for Christmas."

"I thought you were in California for Christmas."

"I'm Jewish. Hanukkah is over."

"Oh, well, come in. Come in!" I stall, trying to think of something. "We just got home a second ago. Everyone's exhausted." That part is true. "Long car ride."

He stays on the porch.

"I thought you were staying until New Year's."

"We were, yeah." I shuffle nervously, still holding the door open. "Come in, it's freezing."

"Why didn't you call me?"

"I just . . . it's been a weird . . . we just got home. I was gonna call you tomorrow." I try so hard to sound casual. He stands so still. "Trust me, you want nothing to do with me after a seven-hour drive." I chuckle. The outside air is so cold.

"Why don't I believe you?"

"Ezra. Come inside." He looks serious. Hurt. My insides flailing, I try desperately to keep it light. "What's the basket?"

"How was Lizzy's lasagna?" He's angry.

I don't know what to say. "It was good. Ezra, come in."

He puts the wicker basket on the porch and turns toward the driveway. "Merry Christmas," he mumbles over his shoulder. His words condense in the cold air, trailing behind like a speech bubble in a comic strip.

I run after him. "I swear, if you just let me explain."

He turns around quickly. "This doesn't work, Mark. You doing something bad and then delivering some heroic monologue to take it back. I don't want a monologue. I want a boyfriend who doesn't lie to me." He turns to his car.

"Please, Ezra. Can I just explain? I did lie and that's awful but—" I look back at my house. It looks so simple from the outside.

He interrupts me. "To be honest, I don't really care. And I don't really feel like doing this."

He's standing so far away he might as well be in another suburb.

"I'm so sorry, an—"

"You're not sorry," he concludes, as decisive as the click of a lock. He turns back around, one more thing to add. "You're sorry you got caught. You're sorry you can't pretend everything's perfect if your boyfriend is mad at you."

Maybe because he says it like it's something he's been waiting to say, but it spirals me into anger and I'm too tired to fight it. "Trust me, Ezra, everything is *really* far from perfect, and if you actually just let me explain instead of jumping down my—"

"I would have cared about your explanation if you hadn't *lied* to me," he says, loud. I suddenly become very aware we're arguing on the front lawn. "A liar will always lie again."

"Oh my *God*, Ezra"—I exhale to the gray sky, matching his anger—"I'm not a liar. I lied about—"

"Please pause while I pull up Dictionary dot-com for you."

"Just let me *explain*." I forget about restraint and shout. It doesn't feel like I'm having a fight. It feels like a fight is having me—just building on itself, snowballing, becoming so much different than it started.

He impersonates my voice, higher than his own. "'*I lied to you, but I'm good now,*'" he says, reminding me of my previous bad apology on his front porch.

"Ezra, I swear, please—I didn't lie. I just didn't tell the truth."

He turns away, again, and calls back with a quiet rage, "You sound really stupid right now."

"Stupid?" My eyes widen, and I'm not nervous anymore, just pissed. "You can be such an asshole, you know that, Ezra?"

"Swear words are for simple minds," he says as he's unlocking his car door.

"*Such* an asshole."

He turns around. "Congratulations for turning *me* into the bad guy instead of focusing on your own shit."

"I thought swear words were for simple minds."

"You bring out the simplest in me."

"Oh my God"—I toss up my hands—"how am I with someone who's so pretentious?"

"You might not be."

My stomach drops.

Ezra pauses, but then keeps going. "How am *I* with someone who's a *liar*?"

"You do it, too." I hit back. "Why don't you sit next to me at lunch, Ezra? Because of your *physics* reading?" I arch my eyebrows and step closer to him.

"How long have you been holding on to that one?" He steps away from his car, and we're face-to-face.

"As long as it takes for you to actually give me an answer! So while you're on Dictionary dot-com, you should also look up lying by omission."

"Oooh, three-syllable insult. You get that from your ACT flash cards?"

"Fuck. You. How many syllables is that?" I turn toward the door.

He runs, fast, uncharacteristically sloppy, to block me from getting to the porch. He stands between me and my house. "You have an incredible ability to make this about me," he says. "Why don't I *sit with you at lunch*?" He's dripping in condescension. "What, am I in some sort of teen movie from hell?" He starts getting really mad, but at the same time regains his composure, his polish, his diction. "Sincere apologies if I don't feel like spending the only free twenty-seven minutes I have all day being made to feel like shit by the ruling class of Annondale High, individuals who will all invariably reach the apotheosis of their existence somewhere between a Grand Slam at Denny's and a hand job in the prom parking lot."

"Apothee-*Asshole!*" My scream echoes off the maroon bricks around my front door. The porch light is on a timer, and it clicks on. Something about the light, seeing the light, snaps me out of this hostility tailspin where whoever shouts the loudest wins. I look at Ezra, the porch light outlining his clenched jaw, and suddenly, like remembering the right answer the second after you hand in a test, I remember every reason I love him.

I turn to Ezra, speak, so much softer. "Who makes you feel like shit?"

He's still staring right at me, and responds with cold sarcasm. "Why? Will your big brother get a football player to beat him up for me?"

It hurts.

It's over.

Final knockout.

"Jesus, Ezra," I whisper.

I stare at the sharp corner of my front porch and wonder if this is really the end.

Outlining a stack of firewood, there's a pile of old snow, icy at the edges.

I lied. We fought, he won, but I lied first. I look at the cracks in the ice, take a deep breath, and talk, softly, finally. "We didn't go to

Rockford." I swallow. "When I called you, I lied." The cold suddenly hits me. "Everything I said on the phone was one hundred percent a lie. And I am very, sorry." My breath shakes, and I speak quietly. "We didn't go to Rockford." I look at my house, the window by my dad's home office. It all looks so simple from out here. "I'm sorry, can we get in your car?"

The short walk to his car makes me feel even worse. He's still mad, and I think, for some reason, my need to change location is exactly what he hates about me.

The car doors close and echo in the silent interior. I look at him, but he talks first.

"I didn't mean what I said about your brother. I really—I don't even know what I was—"

I interrupt him. "I'm sorry. I'm the one who needs to be sorry," I say again, softly, slowly. Then I speak like each word is its own sentence: "We didn't go to Rockford because the night before we were supposed to leave my brother got arrested."

"Oh. Fuck," Ezra says. "I'm sorry."

"No, you're—" My eyes well up, but crying feels manipulative. I take a breath and keep talking. "You were mad, because of what I did. Umm . . ." I try to find the right words. "He drank too much. And I think he does that a lot." My breath catches and my chin shakes and I can't help but actually cry. "I didn't tell you because I didn't know how"—I swallow, sniffle, and talk, steadier—"and maybe because I didn't want you to know how not perfect my *planetarium of*"—I can't remember the phrase—"whatever, really is. Or so you wouldn't find out that my brother really is all these things you hate about Annondale." I lift my eyebrows and a tear refuses to stay put. "Guess he peaked in high school." I wipe my eyes and laugh, pointing at my face. "And now, I'm crying to get away with lying."

He takes a beat and looks at my watery eyes. Ezra never fills his silences with *ummm*.

"That's awful, Mark. I'm so sorry. And in addition to being so sorry for those stupid insults I hurled at you and your brother," he says diplomatically, "I'm sorry that you and your family are dealing with all this." He continues, compassionately but still cold, "And I'm sorry I didn't seem like a person you could tell."

"No, *I'm* sorry." I squeeze the armrest on the passenger-side door. "*I* am sorry! I'm the one who is sorry, and I'm also sorry that I'm making *you* feel like you need to apologize. I'm sorry. *I* lied and *I* am sorry." I don't know. "I—" I look out at the grass on our front lawn. The shoes of the house. "I don't want you to think my family is messed up."

"Every family's messed up."

I feel defensive. *We're not messed up*, I want to say. *It was one bad night*. But instead, I just tell him. Everything. Even Thanksgiving. And just when I start to think that maybe this is the right thing to do—maybe problems do get lighter if you share them—I see Eric peek out of his bedroom window and I feel awful. Like I just talked shit about the guy who's been guarding my life with his for sixteen years.

"I'm sorry your family's going through this."

We're not going through anything, I want to say.

I speak firm, and talk straight to him. "But the conclusion of all of this *still* has to be that *I* am the one who is sorry. And I'm sorry I'm not a better boyfriend. Because—" I look at the glove compartment and begin to talk, but before the words are even out, I regret them. It feels too soon. Or not the right time. Or manipulative, like tears, to get away with lying. Or even desperate, for feeling so much, so quickly. Or too close to the moment when I thought he hated me. Too close to the moment when I shouted "fuck you." It's barely a whisper in the middle of our first fight, not at all how I fantasized about saying *I love you*.

In the rearview mirror, the D'Angelos' black lab pulls on her leash.

The first dress rehearsal for life . . . is life. What bullshit. You get a rough draft for an English essay, but you have to get life right on the first try? Why shouldn't everyone have a few different lives, see what works out, and then go back to the beginning and do it perfectly? *Okay, cut! Let's take it from the top of page Tuesday, but this time tell your boyfriend about your brother and save "I love you" for next year.*

In the transparent brown of his eyes, I can see flecks of gold.

He never fills his silences with *ummm*.

Junior Year

January

An Angel

The room is dark except for neon guns hanging from the wall. The neck of his white undershirt glows in the black light as he unexpectedly veers left and grabs a red LazerQuest vest.

"I love you," Ezra says with a sinister smile. "And your ass is mine."

"We can't be on opposite teams!" I protest from inside my blue LazerQuest vest, which he helped me buckle.

"Did you know that Haley Stewart volunteers at my aunt's synagogue every other Saturday?" he tells me as he pulls his shoulder strap to make it tighter. "And that Jeff Miller *recreationally* reads Kurt Vonnegut?"

I smile. "Slow down, you're gonna like these people more than I do."

As the rowdy crowd for Shanna's birthday party buckles into their glowing army gear, Ezra gives me a small kiss.

In perhaps the greatest plot twist of my entire life, our argument made things *better*. Ezra and I yelled, said things we didn't mean—but also a lot of things we did. Once it was out there, we could sort it out.

For his end of the bargain, Ezra offered to eat lunch with my friends twice a week. "I suppose I can at least scratch at the surface to uncover what lies beneath," he laid out a compromise from his fluffy white couch. "But if I'm even once made to feel 'less than' because my value system doesn't revolve around who can chug a—"

I kissed him before he could get to the pretentious part.

The laser professionals push us inside and I hustle to a hiding place.

Up a steep and very narrow stairway, I find myself in a protected tower fit for Rapunzel, and in the chaotic quiet of the Annondale LazerQuest, I imagine I'm a princess in need of protecting. A delicate maiden trapped in a castle whose strong boyfriend defends her honor—to say nothing of her beautiful, bountiful, flowing blond hair.

My vest vibrates and shakes me back to reality. "You're *dead*, Davis," Spurling shouts as he blazes by. I slide against the cold plastic of a fake rock and wonder why my fantasies have such outdated gender roles.

Ezra's so good at laser tag I almost ask for his NRA card.

Suddenly, Joe Thomas. Muscle-y Joe Thomas. "Mark"—he points to the screens, now flashing our scores—"you MajorDavis?" I nod. Ezra ogles. Joe slaps my shoulder, firm. "You're last place out of everyone."

Indeed. Negative points. Taken out yet again by fantasies of becoming a princess.

When Joe Thomas gets out of earshot, I tease Ezra, "Could you *be* more obvious?"

"Obvious about what?" he pretends. "Oh, was that . . . Joe? Thompson? Tomlin?" He smiles, then grabs my arm and looks to the very top score. "Wait, hmm, who could ZapGod be? Maybe one of those eleven-year-olds from the Saint Anastasia youth group?" He smiles, proud.

After our fight, my end of the bargain was much simpler and more absolute: No lying. Ever.

"In the moment, I overreacted," Ezra told me from his fluffy white couch. "There are about a thousand things I wish I could take back."

"A million for me," I admitted.

"And it's *possible* that my mother might have drilled into me, maybe too ardently, the need to be wary of a man's lies." His eyes glimmered through arched eyebrows. "*That said*," he continued. "You cannot lie. Ever. Never, ever again."

"I promise."

"Never," he repeated.

"Ever," I promised.

I don't know, maybe you have to come close to losing someone to realize how much you love them. "Henceforth, a zero tolerance policy vis-à-vis lying."

Underneath the laser tag scoreboard, Damien shoulders into Ezra. "Yo, ZapGod, you're a fucking *sniper*." He explodes with energy, overcaffeinated and on cloud nine thousand after beating his highest SAT practice score on the real January SAT. "I had a *killer* hiding spot behind that neon rock bridge thing, and here comes

ZapGod makin' SEAL Team Six look sloppy," he says as he leads us toward the bar, just a couple steps away. "Man, this place is heaven."

Damien is the reason Ezra stopped counting how many days a week we were eating lunch with my friends. They like each other, even when I'm not around. Which is great, but also—*don't have fun without me!*

We're still here! Come meet us!

I look at the text before I press send. I miss Crystal pretty much every day. I know Damien does, too. He thinks maybe it's just easier for her to fully commit to her new school if she's not hanging on to her old friends . . .

"Crystal?" Damien asks as he watches me delete the text.

I nod. "Hey—do you think we did something?"

He hands the bartender a very fake ID. "I think we *didn't* do something."

I stare at my phone. He's right. If we would have noticed, before. Or if we would have done something her *first* day of Driggs. If I would have *made sure* we had Slurpee Sluesday her very first week. But we didn't, or I didn't, and now I don't know what to say, and every day that passes, it seems harder and harder to say anything. It's like a weight that gets heavier the longer you don't pick it up, so then when you try . . .

She called once, before the holiday break. But I fucked it up. I made a joke ("*Who calls someone?*") but it came out wrong. We kept talking, but I sounded less like a friend and more like that random uncle you have to talk to when your mom hands you the phone on Christmas. "*So how's school?*"

I steal the first sip of Damien's beer.

"Kid, I gotta see your ID if you're gonna—"

"Sorry!" I apologize to the bartender, and hustle away before anyone else in the Davis family gets arrested.

"It used to be called Sadie Hawkins, actually." Eric gives me a history lesson mere minutes before he leaves with Dad to go to court. *Court!* In Royal Oak. My brother is going to *court* and he's talking to me about Sadie Hawkins. "And the tradition was that it was the one dance when the girl would ask the guy. I don't know when— before I started—they changed it just to 'Winter Ball.'"

He grabs his coat, Dad waits by the door, and Mom makes herself busy. The moment is tense, but in general, by some miracle, the whole family is back to normal. Last night I even heard Dad say, "This will be a good excuse for us to explore Royal Oak." A good excuse to explore Royal Oak! *Court!*

Credit where credit is due, Eric's a master.

I ignore all of my history reading and wrestle with my new obsession: how to ask Ezra to the formal formerly known as Sadie Hawkins.

Because, well, in case this wasn't abundantly clear . . . I'm the girl.

Now, I actually *hate* when straight people—*heteronormative, out-of-touch* straight people—look at a gay couple and assume one is the guy and the other is the girl. We're both guys, that's the whole point!

That said . . . I'm the girl.

I don't even mean it the way people would probably *think* that I mean it, not to mention the world doesn't even really think in these girl/boy terms anymore.

However, in my head, I'm the girl.

And that's about all I know about that.

"Hey, bud." My dad gently knocks on my door. I look at my history book before turning to him. They're already back from court (*court!*) and I haven't even read three pages.

Seeing him in the doorway makes me realize I don't think Dad has ever once come into my room. He's more a "scream-from-the-bottom-of-the-stairs-and-tell-you-to-come-to-him" kind of guy.

"Hey, Dad. How's it goin'?"

"This weekend you're ridin' solo, huh, bud?" he says, very conversationally. He and Mom are driving Eric back to Northwestern, and they're going to stay at Grandma's for the weekend. A belated Merry Christmas. I have a life-altering Spanish test on Monday, and even though Eric says, "There are bigger things in life than a Spanish test," I'm pretty sure he's just trying to distract me from our GPA competition.

"No parties, I know," I say, looking back to a stack of textbooks. "I have a ton of work, so it's not even really possible."

"Yeah," he says, "that goes without saying." My dad always

talks slow, but tonight there's a commercial break between every syllable. "Well, I was thinkin', son. Twenty-four hours in the day, even *you* can't study for all of 'em." He pauses. "So, you know, they do that *Broadway in Detroit* thing every now and again." He stands next to my bed and looks like he might even sit down, but stays standing. "We went to a couple, that's right. Now, I'm no expert on this kinda thing, but one of the guys at work had what you'd call season tickets, or that *equivalent*, for plays—or anything, really—that comes to the Fisher Theatre, and there's a play called *Waitressing* comin' there now—it was on Broadway, just a little bit ago—and he can't use 'em for one reason or another, and it's one of those nonrefundable kinda deals. And I thought right away, Oh that might be something kind of fun for you and Ezra, the two of you to do together."

My eyes widen. "Wait, really? Dad, that's so—" and before my face gets too recently-crowned-Miss-America, my dad dives into *very* specific driving directions.

"Your little phone's gonna tell you to take I-75, but listen, that construction's gonna add at least fifteen minutes, so what you're gonna do is hop onto Woodward from 16 Mile," he starts, and borrows my pen to draw a physical map—a *physical* map!—on the back of my history homework. "It's a straight shot to Grand."

Satisfied, he turns to leave.

He pauses in the door, though. Looks back to my desk like a worried baseball coach.

"And son, now, we . . . you and I"—he swallows—"haven't really . . . talked, *too* much"—he takes a step forward, but then a bigger step back—"about"—he taps his fingers on my dresser and shifts weight onto his other foot—"about you and Ezra's *relationship*." He takes another breath. "But I'd say . . . to *you*"—another breath—"well, really, nothing different than what my dad said to me." He stares at the carpet. "And that is"—he turns to the side, mumbles quickly—"well, that's not really gonna work here."

He looks at my bed and scratches his arm.

My dad resumes, but kind of apologetically. "I had this all sorted out in my head, but I'll be damned." He steadies himself. "Listen"—he points his finger at me—"you're a smart kid, son. So just be smart, all the way through."

I tell him I will, I promise. And I tell him thank you.

He nods his head, looking—confused? Disappointed? Relieved?

He turns and walks out the door.

Bees and the bees.

Then he yells from the bottom of the stairs, "And when you get to Grand, you park where it says *Official Fisher Theatre Parking*. Everywhere else you're gonna get scammed or stolen and if you get your car stolen, you're not gettin' another one."

I pick Ezra up around 5:00 p.m. on Saturday, both of us in cute little blazers. I send a picture to my parents to show them how wholesome it all is right before we drive to dinner. The most notable thing about the restaurant is that I spent approximately ninety-seven hours picking it. I read every Yelp review of every restaurant within a ten-mile radius of the Fisher Theatre, and then corroborated Yelp reviews with *Free Press* reviews, verified with Google reviews, then quadruple-checked with Tripadvisor ratings. I spent so much time finding the perfect restaurant I was almost too late to get a reservation.

But it's perfect. Loud enough to feel cool, but not so loud that we can't hear each other. Expensive enough to feel fancy, but not so expensive that I'll get in trouble with my dad. Nice enough to feel romantic, but not so nice that it looks like I'm trying too hard. As I look around at the modern brass light fixtures, the exposed brick wall, the cool college-age couple next to us, our tattooed waitress, and Ezra's happy face, I think: ninety-seven hours well spent.

And now—to the theater!

The first time I ever walked into the Fisher Theatre, it felt like life was finally rising to the occasion. *Oh, yes, Mr. Davis, we apologize for the mix-up. Follow me.* This *is where you belong.*

Ceilings sparkle, staircases greet us like trumpets, and women wear fur with intention. Marble columns frame the hallway. Men wear suits that have never been worn to a parent/teacher conference. The red carpet looks like the Oscars, but fancier, because if you look deep enough, you'll see little flecks of gold.

"When was the last time you were here?" Ezra asks as we bathe in the grandeur. I tell him, in way too much detail, how much I liked *Les Misérables.* And then *Chicago.* And then *Rent.* And then *Next to Normal. Phantom of the Opera. Matilda. Hedwig and the Angry Inch.* And then I make a joke because I'm self-conscious about how much I'm queening out about musicals. "They could sing my chemistry book, and as long as it had a swelling chorus, I'd be in heaven."

Ezra imitates a cheesy performer, singing with hyperactive vibrato to the chandelier:

"*So-di-um Chlorrr-ide!*"

Most musicals have an "I Want" song, that lays out, early in the show, what the main character wishes for, or wants. In *Hamilton* it's "My Shot." He wants to start a movement that lands him in the history books. *Pippin* has a famous "I Want" song that I sing for auditions sometimes: "Corner of the Sky." He wants to find where his spirit can run free. For non-musical-theater nerds, Disney movies have them, too, like *Little Mermaid*: "Part of Your World." She wants to be where the people are, she wants to see, wants to see them dancing.

On the plush red carpet of the Fisher Theatre, I realize that even though I never *really* had the courage to sing my "I Want" song, I got what I wished for anyway. I am on a date with a cute boy talking about musicals.

"What's your *favorite*, though?"

I pause, as if it's not a question that I consider fifty times a day, countlessly reordering my Top 5, and even feeling bad for the ones that fall off the list, as if being in my Top 5 is some kind of achievement that Lin-Manuel Miranda would be concerned about.

"*Rent*," I answer. "It's probably lame. And it's old. But it's younger than my second favorite, which is *Les Mis*. But older than my third favorite, *Spring Awakening*." Ohmygodshutup. "Well, whatever, I just love it." We inch through a few underdressed forty-year-olds whose baggy jeans are disrupting my Fisher Theatre fantasy.

He sings: "*It was my lucky day today on Avenue A.*"

"You know it!" I stop us in the middle of the aisle as he channels my favorite character (Angel!) from my favorite musical. "I truly could not love you more."

He smiles, proud, like a kindergartner coming home with a check-plus. "I listened to it after you mentioned it on our first date," he says, blushing just a little.

"Us sitting on your bed doing English homework was *not* a date."

"Me trying to *woo* you with my knowledge of fifties beat poetry was *definitely* a date."

I look in his eyes, backlit by the shimmering edges of the balcony boxes. "Well, it worked."

He corrects me, smiling as the usher hands us our playbill. "Eventually."

The soft suede of our theater seats feels luxurious as we fold them down and sit.

"Isn't Angel awesome?" I say, then laugh at what a musical theater nerd I'm being.

"The awesomest."

"You know what I think is the *most* awesome?" He laughs at me, but with love, so I keep going. "Is, like, she's not ashamed. She's different—nonconforming, ya know?" I never know what words to use for her. "But she loves herself, and it's not about that. She's nonconforming but it's not *about* that." I don't think I'm expressing myself right. I try. "So many queer plotlines are just about how shitty it is to be queer, you know? At least at the start. And I so remember seeing *Rent* for the first time, with my dad, of all people, and the actor playing Angel was, or referred to himself as, 'he' in his bio. And then Angel is Angel, right? So I was just, like, *waiting* for the plotline where Angel has to process her shame or has to learn to love her nonconforming self or has to come out to her dad or maybe there'll even be, like, a Mrs. Doubtfire moment where they all find out the *truth*. I was dumb, but you know what I mean? But it was never about that. She just loved herself. And everybody else loved her." We knock into the seat divider, and he wraps his forearm under mine. "It sounds so stupid when I say it out loud, but at the time it was, like, revolutionary. She was different and that wasn't her plotline."

I start to feel myself almost crying, so I smile to stop things from getting too heavy. "And I *need* to go to 'Avenue A' someday."

Suddenly I worry, "Is it real? Is it a real street? Avenue A?"

He pulls out his phone. "You haven't Googled it?"

"If it's not a real street, I think I would die. My entire awakening rests on the existence of this street. No—I don't even want you to look it up." I steal his phone. "I wouldn't be able to take it."

He wrestles it back from me and leans so far into the aisle I can't reach him. I watch him urgently type "Avenue A" into the Chrome browser bar . . .

The Wi-Fi in the Fisher Theatre is slow.

"It's probably not real! It's probably some made-up street and my entire life is a lie."

My heart races and I'm legitimately nervous.

"Avenue A!" he shouts triumphantly, and an old man in front of us turns around, unamused.

"Wait, really?"

"It even has its own Wikipedia page!"

"A *street* with a Wikipedia page?!" I grab his phone again. "I bet there's not a single street in Michigan that has a Wikipedia page."

"Eight Mile definitely has a Wikipedia page."

"Gah! It's too slow . . ." I hand him his phone back.

"We'll go there someday. Together. To Avenue A," Ezra says, so matter-of-factly, leaning into me, bumping against the seat divider—*My God, I could take a sledgehammer to this seat divider.*

We take a breath, together. The ceiling is so high it feels more like a golden sky.

"What time is it? Do we have time? I'm gonna get us drinks. And snacks." I remember that my dream date definitely involves reaching into a bag of candy at the same time and giggling as you finger-wrestle over who gets more Skittles.

"I'll come with."

"No, you guard our seats! Don't move a muscle." I step over him. "You want anything special?"

"Surprise me."

As I'm waiting in line for drinks, I think a little bit more about *Rent.* Avenue A. How it's possible that someday we really will go there together. And it'll be happier and more beautiful because once I didn't believe it existed. Maybe beauty always starts with pain? The soil breaks. The mother screams. The boy assumes life will always hurt. But then happiness comes, unseen, like air. The breath before the song.

"How did you get this?" Ezra asks after he takes a sip of his souvenir cup of Diet Coke and realizes there's vodka in it.

"I found a bartender who looked gay and I flirted with him," I say with a wink.

"Just in case he's still watching . . ." Ezra leans over and kisses me. "Where's yours?"

At the sound of our kiss, the man in front of us snaps his head around and gives us side-eye.

After he turns around, I whisper to Ezra, "Straight people get to kiss in public without ever feeling like they're taking a stand."

Ezra whispers an admission of guilt. "I did scream 'Avenue A' at the top of my lungs. His side-eye isn't wholly unearned."

I smile. For the first time in my entire life, I want to skip seeing a musical—just fast-forward to the part where we're alone in my house. The lights dim. Our fingers interlace. Ezra squeezes my hand, and the first song starts.

Waitress is good.

I think.

Actually, I have no idea.

All show, I'm thinking about what I should do with my hands, if I'm eating more than my share of the candy, if I should try to start footsie. By intermission I joke with Ezra that I have no idea what's going on.

"It's not exactly Foucault," he teases as we stand in the majestic, crowded lobby.

"You're a distracting seat partner."

"Oh, you're telling me. Have you seen yourself in that blazer? I'm shocked I can even stand up right now."

The second half is good, and the 11 o'clock number is *incredible*, and we talk about it the whole ride home. We drive through the bright city streets of Detroit, past old mansions and refurbished museums and through some gritty city streets a long way from the renaissance. The excitement of downtown gives way to the monotony of the highway, but tonight, everything seems lit up extra bright.

"I was tearing up, but you were *sobbing*," Ezra teases.

"I was not sobbing." I hit him on the shoulder.

"You were sobbing before the show even started." He turns my hit into a hug. "*It was my lucky day today on Avenue A.*"

He leans over and honks the car horn. "Woo-hoo your parents aren't home!"

I laugh. "I thought you didn't like people who threw parties when their parents weren't home?"

"That's only because I wasn't invited!" he shouts through laughter.

"What time do you have to be home?"

"*Never*, just gun it!" He pumps his fist almost through the windshield.

I smile and take the car to at least five above the speed limit. But then slow down instantly, and he laughs. "Your brother was right; you *do* drive like a grandma."

We get to my house and I feel drunk.

My pop had no vodka, but I'm positive I'm at least buzzed.

Ezra stands in front of the unwound grandfather clock and screams so loud it echoes in the foyer. "Woo-hoooo!"

"Ezra!" I reprimand.

"Don't you go to keg parties at Shanna Miller's house? What's with this 'best behavior' business?" He tiptoes across the wide white tiles. "Do you mind if I corrupt you?"

The kiss is hot. Beyond. And kissing somewhere other than a bedroom or a basement feels as scandalous as toking a bong in the middle of gym class. "I was more corrupt before I met you." He pulls me back into the kiss.

I think he's a little bit drunk off of that *one* drink, and his low tolerance makes him doubly adorable.

He abruptly pulls away and lights up with an idea. "Can we steal beers?"

Hearing Ezra Ambrose ask what, on any other night, he would label a *woefully quotidian teenage question*—is perhaps the sexiest thing I've seen in my entire life.

I know for a fact there's an open case of Coors Light in the storage room, still left over from the Christmas party. Does beer go bad? We're technically still an "alcohol-free home," but in the face-off between morality and frugality, my parents just couldn't bring themselves to throw away ten cans of perfectly good beer.

"I'll be right back." I hustle downstairs.

My insides feel like the first day of summer vacation. I can't wait anymore. I've been thinking for a week about the perfect non-prom-posal-y way to ask him, and I've come up with nothing and maybe it's the musical or all this talk of Avenue A or all the kisses that were building up when we were separated by that homophobic armrest, but I'm just gonna do it now!

His eyes light up when I return, and he hops out of my dad's recliner.

He tries to grab the beer from me. "Wait wait wait." I stop him. I bend down on one knee and hold the can of Coors like an engagement ring. "Ezra Ambrose." I taste each syllable as it leaves my mouth. "I thought junior year was going to be the worst, and you turned it into by far the best. And I love you so much it feels illegal. Will you go to Winter Ball with me?"

He jokingly rolls his eyes. "Oh God, a *Winter Ball promposal*?! I really have become everything I revile."

I hit his leg and make him help me up. "It could have been a flash mob." I crack open the can. "Shut up and drink your beer."

He tilts his head back, and I reach above and pour half the can into his mouth like a fountain. He swallows some, but most of it foams out, overflows all over the beige linoleum of my kitchen floor. He chokes as he hurtles forward, takes off his beer-soaked blazer, and tosses it at my face. "Shut up and do my laundry!"

He grabs the can and chugs the rest. Clenches his eyes shut and then moans, "It's warm." He looks at his white button-down, now soaked in beer, and takes it off. A little patch of chest hair, right between his pecs. Drops his shirt to the floor, where it soaks up even more beer.

My heart beats in my throat and electricity courses through my veins. Everything—the little indentation at the bottom of his neck, the stray hairs in between his eyebrows, the wrinkly skin where his fingers bend, that small bit of fuzz in the middle of his chest—it's enough to drive me completely crazy.

"You haven't answered my question."

"Winter Ball?" He steps closer to me, speaks slowly. "I don't have anything to wear." Looks to his blazer on the ground. "You ruined my one good blazer."

"You can borrow my tux."

I can feel the heat from his chest.

"But then what would you wear?"

He grabs me by the hip bones, pulls me closer.

"Come upstairs."

I haven't even touched it since Halloween, stuffed it in a dark corner of my closet and an even darker corner of my memory. But tonight, no guardians at home, a guardian Angel on my mind, and a sticky boyfriend by my side, it's time to share what I really want to wear to Winter Ball. What I've dreamed of wearing to a ball ever since, on a swiveling maroon bar stool in Herschel's Diner, I discovered a new level on the metronome of my heartbeat. And as I reach to the back of my closet, more than excited I'm just angry that I waited this long.

It just seems, sometime not long after you're born, you're given this life. Beginning to end, your entire story. And your job is to just fit into it. And it's the same life, for everyone. It's as if they just look at you, no matter who you are, and say, *Hey kid, here's my life. Now it's your turn to live it.* And they put you in a little baseball outfit before you can walk. And then *you* put you in a fucking firefighter costume because it's just, like, way more complicated to try to live a different life. And even if you're gay, you just have to live that same life. Because if you don't, well, your entire story becomes about the dress. Your plotline gets devoured by a dress. Even though it's just, like, what felt right for your life.

Inside an unmarked white gift box inside a bright orange shopping bag sparkling underneath a carefully folded semitransparent film of off-white tissue paper lies purple fabric shinier than a new car, tulle as fulfilling as the final clue in an unsolved mystery, and sequins more triumphant than the final high note in the greatest "I Want" song ever sung.

"... *the purple princess dress with the puffy sleeves!*" Ezra bursts out, too impatient to wait for me to get to the punch line. He stands and takes the box as I hold up the dress and take in its glory.

The purple fabric glistens in the glow of my floor lamp. The sleeves crinkle hello as I hold it up by the puffs; it drapes elegantly, almost touching the floor, full and alive even without a body inside.

"More taffeta than an entire Disney Princess Parade." Ezra beams. "You will *undoubtedly* be the belle of the ball."

I drop the dress to the ground and kiss him and kiss him and kiss him. Like kisses have been building up all night. When I'm done kissing him, I kiss him again.

He pulls back with a smile and looks at the dress on the floor. "That's no way to treat a lady." He picks it back up and points his eyes to the full-length mirror on the back of my door.

He takes off my shirt for me; the narrow neck hole squeezes my cheeks, scrapes my ears, messes my hair.

He smooths my part, stares into my eyes, and tosses my T-shirt to the bed.

He unbuttons my pants, unzips, while still staring into my eyes. My heart beats; I become my heartbeat.

He gets down on one knee to slip off my pants, sliding his hands from my waist to my toes.

He looks up, on his knees, face inches from my underwear, and raises his eyebrows. "I would like to nominate myself for the Presidential Medal of Self-Restraint."

He holds open the unzipped neck of the dress.

I hold one foot in the air, like Cinderella in Old Navy boxer briefs.

The slippery fabric tickles my thighs.

The sequins scratch my stomach.

The tulle itches on my shoulders.

And it feels incredible.

He guides me by my waist and walks us over to the door, shut tight out of habit.

Along the walk, he gives little neck kisses with each step.

Through the full-length mirror, he looks me in the eyes, and I hold on tight to a reflected piece of evidence that it just might be possible for someone, one person, to see the whole Me and not want to return parts of it for a refund.

In the arms of Ezra, I grip the shiny fabric of my purple princess dress with puffy sleeves and smile a smile I didn't even know I had.

In one superhuman backward bound, he lands on my bed.

"Get over here, Princess," he calls as he plops his warm beer on my nightstand and tosses the soccer ball pillow to the floor. I walk daintily on the balls of my feet. In my head, I'm in the perfect pair of heels. The slippery fabric swishes with each step. Static from the tulle makes my leg hairs stand up. Ezra lies back on his elbows, his neck stretches to watch me, and he bites his bottom lip.

Under the too-bright light of my childhood bedroom, as tulle pools around us like rings around a planet, my boyfriend kisses me. And for the briefest moment before I kiss him back, I look at my life. *My* life. And under a costume I bought to look like a princess, inside, I feel like a queen.

Just Me and My Brother

I drive Ezra home, and I wish he lived farther away so our night could last closer to forever.

He walks up his bush-lined driveway, ever so slightly unsteady, and he blows a kiss back to my car. I pull away, almost dizzy. I get nervous that driving giddy might be close to driving drunk.

I call Eric before I even back out of the driveway.

Mom and Dad are in Rockford by now, and it's a Saturday, so Eric'll probably be out with friends, or maybe taking it easy due to his recent court date (!), but either way I don't care. I need to talk to my brother.

"*Whaddup, little bro*?" Eric shouts. It's loud wherever he is, and I can tell by his double dose of enthusiasm that he's definitely not taking it easy.

"I know you're out, so I'll be fast, but I just asked Ezra to Winter Ball!" I give a bashful smile.

"Brother!" Eric shouts back. "*This* is the greatest news in the history of *news*!" He's doing that drunk thing where you emphasize random syllables.

"Eric, it's just Winter Ball."

"This is amazing! AMAzing amazing! Can you FaceTime?"

"No, I'm driving."

"Pull over. We gotta FaceTime. This is huge."

Cars whizz by, too fast. It startles me each time. I should have pulled into a side street, but I thought he'd start the FaceTime faster.

The screen's blurry at first, but it adjusts to reveal a crowded frat room, movie posters on the wall, probably twenty people overflowing off a futon.

Eric shouts. "*Lil' bud*, can you *hear me*?"

"Yes!" I laugh.

"Okay, everyone. Ready?!"

Everyone looks happy to be included.

"One-two-th—"

Before he finishes three, a chorus of disorderly voices strive for something like drunken unison. Some say "CON-GRA-TU-LA-TIONS" and some say "MARK" and others laugh their way through "ERIC'S LITTLE BROTHER."

"Thank you." I blush.

"God, I fucking love that kid," Eric says to the group. "All right, private party now. Out, out out out," he playfully yells. It's fun seeing his life, his new friends.

When he's alone again, he gets close to the screen, earnest. "I'm happy for you, bud."

I laugh as I roll my eyes. "Eric, it's just *Winter Ball*!"

"Yeah, *fuck* Winter Ball," he says, aggressive. But then just as instantly, he's gentle, placing each word like it's a bead on a prayer necklace. "But what's cool is you're in love. That's the ticket. Love is the ticket."

"Yeah, hey . . ." I nervously laugh. A white car speeds past my driver's-side rearview window, going too fast, and I check to make sure my lights are still on. ". . . have you done the finger to the nose test in the last hour, dear brother of mine?"

"BRILLIANT!" he shouts. "Fuck. You're smart. Here goes!"

He uses the hand that's holding the iPhone to execute one of his foolproof Buzzed Good, Drunk Bad tests. The screen blurs past a blue beanbag chair, an open door, a gray wall as he extends his elbow and swings his arm parallel to the ground. In one hazy swoop he swings it back to his nose. *Smack.* The screen goes black as it slams against his forehead. A loud crash. His phone falls to the floor and everything spins until it stops, pointing up at the ceiling.

"Eric! Eric!" I shout, instantly worried. "Is someone—" I try to shout loud enough for someone else at the party to hear. "Eric! Someone!" Gradually, the phone stumbles up, jerking around as it shows what might be a broken table, a few spilled cups of beer, and something that looks like muddy fruit punch.

"Bro." Eric comes back on the screen with messed-up hair and an unfazed smile. "Little bro, you have any idea how much I fucking love you? I love you so much. Coolest fucking kid to ever live in Annondale. I love you, brother. You know that, right?"

I exhale. Smile and shake my head. "Of course I know. I love you, too."

He looks into the FaceTime camera as he stands up. "You in a car? Are you driving? That's not safe, bro. No texting and driving. No FaceTi—"

"I'm not driving. I stopped, remember?"

"Yeah. Yeahyeahyeahyeah. Safety first, brother."

Someone shouts off-screen, "Oh my God, what the fuck did you do to my room?" The guy laughs and Eric runs into the hall.

His eyes look extra blue against the navy-blue walls. "Okay. Okay. I love you, bro. We're all going to Winter Ball. Okay?"

"All of us," I say sarcastically.

"Yeah. Yeah. Sweitzer. And I got this girl Ashlie. We'll all come. I'm comin'. Know why?" He focuses back on me and sing-songs, proudly: "'*We will do everything together . . .*'"

It's the first line from our favorite book.

"'. . . *just me and my little brother,*'" I sing-song back.

He smiles at how quickly I get the reference. This Little Critter book Mom would read to us when we were kids. We were convinced they wrote it just for us.

"*We will do everything together*, like goin' to Winn-terball," he adds.

"Okay, Eric. This little critter's gotta drive home."

"Love you, little bro. Drive safe. No texting."

"Love you, too."

"Love you *more*, though."

"Okay, you win. You love me more." I smile and press end. He always wins.

A Prince(ss) Prepares for a Ball

On January 21st, Damien and I make a reservation at P.F. Chang's for January 27th.

Winter Ball!

And guess who he's bringing?

"She didn't even like that stuff when she went here," he protested as he processed my new bold personality.

"She and Ezra can bond over their mutual misery."

"She'll think I'm asking her *out* out."

"It's just Winter Ball."

He thought about it. "It's just Winter Ball . . ."

The next day I got a text from Crystal.

Don't you think it'll be awkward?

Winter Ball is always awkward.

I miss you a lot actually.

I miss you so much I could puke.

Wait didn't you puke last Winter Ball?

Yeah in the girls bathroom.

See?

Winter Ball is always awkward.

I make a reservation at P.F. Chang's.
Party of Four.

January 22nd

On January 22nd, Eric tells me P.F. Chang's is a chain restaurant. It almost breaks my heart. I thought it was . . . doesn't matter. Bigger things to think about.

My parents.

Vis-à-vis my potential *attire*, I'm 99 percent positive my parents will freak the fuck out.

They've been cool about everything. Never even made it feel like being gay was something they had to learn to be cool with. But I catch little glimmers of uncool. My dad after the talent show. Little jokes I overhear about the musicals and the makeup I have to wear for plays. Once Duke humped another boy dog at a dog park and my dad made some dumb joke about "Oh God, it runs in the family." Just little glimmers that maybe "no conflict" doesn't mean "totally fine."

But on the whole, I think the dress itself they could sort of learn to live with.

What they would *hate* is the attention.

Attention is good if it gets you in the athletics hall of fame. But

Annondale is not exactly Avenue A, and I think they'd be beyond freaked out by the attention. Boys who wear dresses to formals go viral on the internet. I can't even *imagine* something my Midwest mom would like less than a son who goes viral on the internet.

So they'd be fine, just so long as I could nonconform from the comfort of our living room.

January 23rd

On January 23rd, I make a plan to tell Ezra the bad news. I even preplan a little joke to soften the blow: *Ezra, I don't have the balls to wear a ball gown.* I mean, imagine sitting at P.F. Chang's in a purple princess dress with puffy sleeves? Plus, it's more a costume than a dress.

"You excited for your gown?" Ezra whispers in English.

"I'm excited to see *you* in a tux!" I evade.

When I get home, my mom is holding up Eric's old tuxedo. "Honey, you've *got* to try this on." She's been trying to get me to try it on for a week. "If it needs to be taken in, there won't be any *time.*"

January 24th

The ring shakes the house.

Really late in the night on January 23rd, so technically January 24th, I wake up to an early-morning call to the house phone. We all wake up.

"Hello?" my mom answers.

Worry is already in her voice because it's so late in the night. And the only reason we still have a house phone is for emergencies. She doesn't even sound tired or groggy. Just worried.

"Yes, this is her." Her voice trembles.

I sit up in bed.

"Yes"—her voice breaks—"that's our son."

She's already crying. There's no lead up to the cry. It's like the tears were ready, waiting. It's hardly been any time—*some of these philosophers don't even believe in*—whoever's on the phone couldn't have even said anything. But it's like she knew what they were going to say from the first ring—*House phone for emergencies, Mark. The house phone never runs out of batt*—like there's only ever one reason someone gets a phone call in the middle of the night.

"No . . . no," she says quietly.

I walk quickly. In just my boxers.

"NOOOOOO!"

It starts out high, almost like a shriek, and then reaches low into her soul, feeding off every pain she's ever felt, every fear she's ever had, until it's no longer her pain but all pain. The pain of the entire world in a single scream.

Through the blinds I see the bedroom lights go on across the street.

My dad is saying "No," over and over.

"No, no, no," in a high whimper, like a hurt animal. He's curled up, into himself, on his side. He's leaning toward the phone. The covers are off and he's naked except for a pair of underwear. His arms are wrapped around his knees and he's crying harder than my mom, but quieter. You only hear it on the inhales.

I'm still standing at the door.

I never go into my parents' room without them saying come in.

Come on in, honey. She always says it sweet like a lullaby.

She can't say it now though—*come on in, honey, did you watch another one of those silly*—she can't say anything. I just stand there at the end—*just close your eyes and try to go t*—and she cries and Dad cries and she tries to pick up the phone to talk to the phone but she can't talk but the phone talks there's something the phone needs to say but no one can talk—*don't worry that scary stuff doesn't happen in real li*—

I watch.

It doesn't feel real. It can't be real.

I just watch.

The phone talks. Muffled sounds like it's underwater. I step. So carefully, over the threshold of the open doorframe. No *come on in, honey*. Underwater. Slow zombie walking. Watching zombies talking underwater.

I don't say anything. Or touch anything. A movie. *That scary stuff doesn't happen in real life.* It's not real. It can't be real. If you say nothing . . . if you touch nothing . . . a movie. I remember to blink. You'll wake up soon. Blink. Just watch. *Nobody's having any emergency on any phone.* Just watch.

From the nightstand, the phone talks.

I can't talk.

If I say nothing . . .

"Mrs. Davis? Mrs. Davis?"

Softly, but yelling. Sympathetic yelling. Underwater yelling. Urgent underwater yelling. *"Mrs. Davis? Mrs. Davis?"* The fabric on the nightstand is pink with flowers that are even pinker. It's all wrong. The room gets dark and the carpet gets cold but the nightstand stays pink. It's a bad movie. A wrong movie.

"Mrs. Davis?" the phone says.

"Mrs. Davis?"

I'm holding it by my ear. The house phone is so light.

If I say something, the movie ends.

Don't break it.

Don't break the movie.

Say nothing, the nightmare . . . It's not real.

"**H**ello?" I say delicately.

"Yes, hello. To whom am I speaking? Is this Mr. Davis?"

The phone talks. A woman talks on the phone to me. To me
she's not delicate enough
she's breaking it

"Is this Mr. Davis?"

"Umm . . ." I forget to swallow. But then I do. "Yes."

I can hear the woman breathe. "I'm so very sorry for your loss."

Oh God. She broke it. She broke it.

My lower lip starts shaking and I never knew that crying starts in your chest.

"I'm so, so very sorry for your loss."

I heave forward with my mouth open, and everything shakes. The room shakes, and the phone shakes in my hand, and they're something different than tears.

I have to tell Eric. I have to call Eric. He can help. He'll fix it. Let me talk to Eric.

My shoulders cry.

And cry.

I have to talk to the phone.

"Thank you," I say, barely out loud.

I don't know why I say that. *Thank you.* I had to say something.

Sorry for your loss. No. NoNoNonono. Nobody's lost. Nobody's gone. Don't be sorry. Nobody's having any emergency on any phone. Just close your eyes, honey. Come on in. Just lie in your bed and close your eyes. Did you watch another one of those silly movies?

I look at my parents. I touch my cheeks and my arms and my neck and my chest and my face and my legs and my lips and it's all real and my cheeks are wet and real and oh god the oh god the room shakes.

"Mr. Davis, I'm just going to give you a few details, and then everything else can wait until tomorrow."

A few details.

"The body is . . ."

The body?

Eric's body.

"Northwestern Memorial . . ."

Purple.

Shaking. Crying.

Purple coffee.

"Acute alcohol . . ."

A cute alcohol. Little pink flowers.

Alcohol with all three angles less than 90°.

I look up from the phone and see myself standing in the dresser mirror.

I go silent at the sight.

In the corner of the mirror, my mother cries.

I feel nervous. Nauseous, suddenly.

The cordless house phone falls on the cream carpet, beeping, beeping because I didn't hang up, as I run to the bathroom and hurl my body over the toilet to throw up.

But nothing comes out. I heave and heave, but nothing comes up. I feel numb. I slowly stand and wipe my face with a navy-blue towel. The towel feels soft in my hand, and I stare, dazed, until the little loops of yarn go blurry in the fog. I wipe around my mouth, like a mother to a baby, even though there is nothing to wipe, and I am not a mother or a baby.

In the distance I hear my father. "He should have been *home*," he screams, from somewhere miles away.

I turn and I see myself in the mirror. Another mirror. My face red from crying. *You again*. My body tired from crying. How long have I been crying? My mouth open, eyes lost, my reflection fills me with rage. *You*. I hit myself. I hate myself. Me. Still here. I reach above the sink and hit myself in the mirror over and over with the bottom of my fist. The mirror's so hard. I keep hitting. I put one knee on the counter so I can get closer, and then I punch, properly, my nose—again—begging the mirror to break—*just fucking break*.

"Just. Die," I whisper through clenched teeth as blood drips down from my knuckles like tears.

A streak of blood stays on the mirror. I look up into the unlit ceiling light and turn my back to my reflection. My hands shake and my head hurts. I lean against the wall and the towel bar sticks into my chest. My forehead is pressed flat. My head hurts, like a headache that hurts your whole body. I slam it against the wall, my forehead. Slam it again. The wall shakes but doesn't break. Nothing breaks. Slam it again. A framed prayer falls off the wall *and the serenity to know* thumps on the bath mat and lands wire side up on the tile made of tiny squares. It doesn't break. On the wall, a bent nail, exposed, looks naked and alone.

My mom runs into the bathroom. She pulls me out like it's on fire. The whole house is on fire. We're all on fire. We have to get out of here.

"We have to go!" I shout, not knowing what I mean. I pull a towel with me as she pulls me out of the bathroom.

"Sit down. Sit down," she whispers to me, but I'm already sitting. Leaning against the bathroom doorframe, knees curled into my chest. She sits, too, with her back to the phone, leaning into me, and takes my head into her neck, rubs my hair. "Sit down. Sit down," she keeps saying, quieter each time, rubbing my hair, my shoulder, her chest, bumping into each other, holding each other as we cry.

She wraps a bath towel around me like a blanket.

She sits, and we cry.

No

There is no morning, no night, no time.

Some of these philosophers don't even believe in time.

The coffee maker beeps three times. The sun comes up. No one turns on the TV.

I grab the plastic rod that twists open the blinds and twist it so far it breaks.

I stand at my window and shout Fuck You to the sun. Except the words don't come out.

"F—"

Just dry crying.

Ricochet in circles.

Ezra? But I can't talk. It's impossible. Everything.

Alone, I try to say a word. A test. Any word. Just to be sure I still can.

I look at my physics book. My tongue is heavy and fat and fills my entire mouth. Touches the roof, the cheeks, the bottom, like a mouth full of raw steak. *Physics.*

I wet my lips and put my lower lip under my top teeth to start.

"Ph—"

My teeth start shaking.

I bite my lip and cry.

We can just go back. There's got to be a way to reverse this. A retake. Rewind. A mistake in rehearsal. A flubbed scene. The director needs to stop us and say, *Just a little mix-up. Let's take it from the top of page Tuesday and run the day again.* There's got to be a way to go back; it can't be this instant. Nothing is this instant. It takes a week to get a driver's license. Nothing is this fast. What kind of world do we live in where you can die faster than you can get a fucking driver's license?

There has to be something we can do. Someone we can call. There weren't enough warnings. We didn't get enough time. Let's just take it from the top of page Tuesday. We'll do the day again. We have to do the day again. We can't give up. There has to be something we can do, he's our brother, there has to be something we can do, someone we can call, there has to be a way back, a way to reverse this, I'm just asking for a day.

Nightmares without sleep. The ceiling wobbles and the floor falls out and my teeth, on fire, fall into my hand. With my fingers I feel inside my lips, under my gums—could those really be? Toothless I'm falling, drowning, with spiders and they're on fire. "*. . . with dreams, with drugs, with waking nightmares—*" A shadowy figure at the bottom of the well shouts like my father yelling on the phone.

"I need names. I need names of who was at that party. Who

dropped him off? This is—Don't tell me what you can't tell me. God*damn* it, maybe if you actually did your job, my son—Don't you *dare* tell me to calm down!"

I try coffee for the first time and it tastes like tin foil.

My neighbor comes over and makes breakfast.

Get out of my house, I want to shout. I go back to my room.

GET OUT OF MY HOUSE.

I go downstairs. There's cereal still on the counter, flavors we've never had before, and cold scrambled eggs on the stove.

I go downstairs and there's lunch by the breakfast.

My dad's on the phone.

Some things are obvious but unexpected. When it happens out of state, you have to ship the body home.

I go downstairs, and I want to say *No thank you*, but every time I try to say a word, I start crying. She asks again.

"You want me to heat it up for you, Mark?" Mrs. D'Angelo asks.

I shake my head and run back up to my room.

The body.

The body.

We will do everything together.

Just me and my big brother.

My mom can't talk, except when she prays.

She wouldn't have been praying out loud if she knew I was up here.

She asks a question, but no one answers.

I guess God doesn't talk to people anymore.

He used to. He'd come right down and talk to people. Noah. Ezekiel. Samuel. Abraham.

The Lord would speak to Moses face-to-face, as a man speaks with his friend.

But my mom asks a question and no one answers.

No

Dad says, "Dad?"

Reality bends into itself. Time is a circle. Dad says *Dad*. I stare at my ceiling.

"Yeah, idiot. Boppa is Dad's dad," Eric told me once.

"No he's not!" It seemed impossible. Boppa was Boppa. And Dad was the dad.

"Then who's Dad's dad?" He paused as I considered it. He tried a different way. "Like how we're Mom and Dad's sons. But each other's brothers. Everybody's a bunch of things."

"Dad, yeah, it's Joe." He takes a breath. "Is Mom there? No, both—both of you . . . Yeah, that'd be good." He waits. "Hi, Mom. Hi . . . Well, there's no easy—Mom and Dad, Eric died. I know . . . I know.

"An accident up at school, with alcohol." Breath. "They took him to the hospital, but he had just had too much."

He uses the exact same words every time. Same tone. The tone when you're saying a line over and over just so you can memorize it for the play. You're not trying to get the feeling right, you're just trying to memorize it. It's not even words to you anymore, just syllables that go in a specific order.

"An accident up at school, with alcohol." Breath. "They took him to the hospital, but he had just had too much."

"An accident up at school, with alcohol." Breath. "They took him to the hospital, but he had just had too much."

You can't change the line. You just have to say it the way it was written.

There's so much to do, even right away.

It seems mean for there to be so much to do.

People to call, forms to fill out, places to go, places to call.

Death means over. How could there be so much to do?

"He sure was, Deb. We can . . . That's right, when you get here . . . She's—well, she's doin' the best she can . . . No, that's all right. I'll call her. Thanks, sis. I love you, too."

Every person he calls says they can call the other people. But he calls everyone. Our aunt. Our other aunt. Each of our three uncles. Mom's side, too.

I suddenly realize it's not "our" anymore.

Our aunt. Our uncle.

There's no more "our."

"Joe, you just let me know—You just tell me if you want me to make any of those phone calls, all right?" Mrs. D'Angelo says as she cleans up the lunch no one ate.

What's the past tense of "our"?

The doorbell rings.

Mrs. DeWolfe holds a casserole.

"If you're not gonna eat it now," she tells me, "just put the oven on warm, all right, Mark? It's already cooked, just keep it warmed up for your mom. Tent the tin foil so the cheese doesn't stick. You can call me if you need anything—anything at all."

I try to say *thank you*, but I start crying. I just shake my head up and down, quickly.

"You're a strong boy, Mark. You're a strong family."

A Word

"**M**ark, honey," my mom says, barely loud enough to hear, "let's go downstairs, have some dinner."

I try to say *okay*, but I can't.

I stand up, and she waves for me to come toward her, in the door.

"I need you to know—I love you *very* much," she says through tears inside the hug. "And I am so, so . . ." She can't talk but refuses to stop. "I love you so much."

Downstairs she does not eat. I don't want to, either. She tells me a little food will be good.

"Three more bites," she says, like when I was so little. "Three more bites."

"We did all we could," Dad says, in a strained whisper.

"*That's not true!*" Mom screams.

I put my hands over my ears.

A glass breaks.

"Get it out of the house!"

A bottle breaks.

"Get it all out of the house. Get it ouuuut!" my mom screams.

Neighbors are over, but she still screams.

Another bottle breaks.

"Get. It. Out." She screams from the pit of her soul.

"And if you need it, you can leave, too!"

It's still light out. The screen door cannot slam.

From my bedroom window, I watch him walk away.

There's broken glass in the family room. Mrs. D'Angelo is cleaning up. The walls are wet with brown alcohol.

I walk over to her.

It's finally dark out.

I've been trying to talk all day, but I can't. Even in the moments when I stop crying—when I go numb instead of crying—I take an inhale to make a word, and it starts all over again.

I try to ask, *Will you call Ezra for me, please?*

But all I can do is hand her my phone.

Ezra's contact is open on the screen. She looks at me and takes my phone.

"Do you want me to call him?"

I nod.

"Tell him, too?"

I nod.

I'm standing close enough to hear the ring.

I hear Ezra through the phone. He's loud, cheery, and regal. "*And just when I was convinced you were going to ghost me* again!"

"Ezra, right?" Mrs. D'Angelo asks. He shifts tone abruptly, says *Yes* like a question. "Ezra, I'm with Mark. We're all here at the Davis's. I'm afraid I have some sad news." She takes a breath. "Mark's older brother passed away last night. Eric. Late last night."

She turns to me, shields the bottom of the phone with her hand, speaks quietly just to me. "Do you want to see him, Mark? Do you want me to tell him to come over?"

She talks into the phone again. "Mark's here at home, with his family. He—he'd like to see you."

Sophomore year, I went with my family to Washington, D.C.

I remember Eric and I being amazed by this one picture in the National Geographic Museum. They had all these nature pictures, blown up huge, and one was of a Hawaiian island after this huge volcanic explosion. It was all black. The whole land was just black, black, black. The trees were charred; the streets were covered in dried lava, soot, I don't even know. And in this sea of blackness, there was a shiny, lime-green little bird flying around. Searching to see if there was anything alive, I suppose.

Ezra stands on my porch like a lime-green bird.

We say nothing. I try, but still can't.

He lies next to me on my bed. It's small for two people. He doesn't ask any questions. He doesn't tell me I'm strong or say he's sorry. He just holds me.

He's there when I wake up, sometime late in the night. It's dark out. I turn over, gently so I don't wake him. I look at his eyelashes, his eyebrows, his lips.

His eyelids slowly open, and I look in his eyes.

It's barely a word, more like an exhale, but with watery eyes, I say, "Hi."

A Day

The sun shines, and it seems impossible that it's a school day.

It's just another day.

"Come on back after school," my mom says to Ezra, leaving no room for discussion.

The house gets silent.

My dad picks Grandma up from the airport—she comes down from Illinois. Up from Illinois. My mom waits at home, waits in the living room, on the floral couch under the front porch window. I've never seen anyone sit on that couch except during the Christmas Party. *All the boys on the couch.* But it's the closest to the front door, so that's where my mom waits for her mom.

The airport trip, there and back, takes two hours. She sits on that couch for all two hours. And when my mom sees her mom . . . it's not a hug. They become a single person. And when Grandma whispers to my mom—"A mother should never have to bury her child"—it's like the night of the phone call all over again, maybe even worse.

It sounds less like a scream from a person, and more like a person inside a scream.

People say the sun shines, but the sun does not shine. The sun *is* its shining. A ball inside the shine. A mother inside her scream. A house inside the ring. A son inside the pain.

And outside, the sun does not shine.

Another Day

S omeone posted something online and someone tagged me in the comments and I clicked on the notification and I wondered if it was possible to blow up the entire internet.

I turned my phone off.

No more people.

"You're really steppin' up, bud. I'm proud of you," my dad says the night after I do some stuff at the funeral home. "Ezra, you, too. Mrs. Davis and I—we're very thankful."

I can't believe there is so much to do. And so many people, everywhere.

Mom spends all her time with Grandma, so Dad makes sure everyone has everything they need. "Comin' right up," he'd told his sister's new boyfriend when the guy asked if we had any lemonade. Me and him spent forty-five minutes trying to find the plastic pitcher Mom makes lemonade in. We looked everywhere. "It has a red top," my dad kept saying, over and over. "It has a red top!" When we finally found the pitcher in the storage room, Dad chucked it at my chest and said, "Piss in it before you give it to him."

I laughed. I couldn't help it. And then Dad did, too. And both of us looked like we felt kind of guilty for laughing, but we couldn't stop. It just—it really took us forever to find that fucking pitcher. And what kind of dickhead asks for *lemonade*.

I went upstairs and told the guy we didn't have any. Even though we did.

I don't know—it just felt like something nice I could do for my dad.

A Funeral

Inside the doorframe, Mr. Doug looks apologetically at four toppled-over wooden train cars, the kind where the cars connect to each other with rounded magnets. "They were supposed to clean this up." He shakes his head, disappointed, and crouches down. He's Grandma's age, but limber like a kid. He snags up a yellow, then a blue, then a green wooden train car. The wheels wobble as he cradles them in his left arm and reaches under the chair for the front one with the black choo-choo part. A glowing cartoon Jesus watches over him with outstretched arms.

"It's all yours," he says, as my family and extended family shuffle inside the "big-kids' playroom." The church nursery's next door. I used to get so sad when they'd send Eric here and me there. But when I *finally* got big enough? No kid's ever been as big as I was the day I graduated to the big-kids' playroom.

Mr. Doug looks again at the train set in his arms. "I don't even know why these are in here."

My aunts and mom set their purses down on the miniature chairs. Everything's miniature. The wooden hooks where we used to hang our winter coats are almost at my knees. When did this room get so small?

"This'll be perfect," my uncle Nick says, then bends down and takes the clip-on tie from my little cousin Joey's hand. "We're gonna leave this on, okay, big guy? Today's gonna be a big-guy day."

Mr. Doug was the first adult who ever told me to call him by his first name. But I couldn't do it. Every time I went to call him "Doug," my brain stopped short and demanded a "Mr." in front of it. So we compromised.

"And feel free to leave anything you want in here. Donna'll lock it up during the service," Mr. Doug says. "Pastor Rick'll probably come by a little after eleven to bring you into the sanctuary." He politely shuffles to the door.

The room is crowded. I'm stuck in the doorframe. I try to step out of his way.

He gets to the door and pauses. Places his hand on my shoulder.

Mr. Doug's gaze has always felt so personal, almost like a pinkie-swear. He looked at us kids like he was one of us. Like he, too, couldn't believe that we all had to be in this bizarre world with all these incomprehensible adults. His hand is more fragile than I remember, and he squeezes the soft part of my neck that wraps from my collarbone to my shoulder blade. I used to have to look up so high to see him.

Mr. Doug nods his head and keeps his hand on my shoulder.

In my cartoon Bible, my favorite picture was of this desperate, crouching man in dirty white robes who was glowing because Jesus touched his forehead.

But I don't glow. My breath catches on itself. My back arches down because the cry needs my whole body. A miniature chair comes under me and I sit, wider than the seat, heaving with each inhale, my hands on my knees and then my elbows on my knees, and it feels like I'm suffocating, and—*It's okay, it's okay, Mark, it's okay*—so many hands, and I try to stop, but something about trying to stop makes it even worse—*There's no law says we have to start right at eleven*—I cry and move my head up, try to see if maybe looking at the ceiling or something helps, and suddenly—no one except my mom.

The Saturday before my first Sunday in the big-kids' room, I was terrified. We still had bunk beds, and Eric sat on top of my covers in the bottom bunk as I pressed a soft stuffed elephant to my cheek. "You know how when you cry in the little-kids' room, Miss Lisa will go get Mom?" Eric was trying to prepare me for the brutal ascendance from Young Worshipper to Junior Disciple. "Well, Mrs. Myrtle just watches kids cry. Sometimes even locks the crying kids in the bathroom. Cuz you can't cry in the big-kids' room."

I did cry in the big-kids' room. That first day, even Eric couldn't quiet me.

I look at my mom. Her eyes, raw sadness. Her face full of something like fear. A sense of understanding spreads inside me, gradually, like a drop of food coloring in a glass of water.

My dad, next to her, holding me, too, their weak son who will always be weak and will always need taking care of and they'll never be allowed to just be sad. As they rub my shoulders and hug me, tight but somehow distant, I feel something deeper than sorrow. Guilt. What kind of monster steals strength from the weak? Like some reverse Jesus who takes bread from the poor and kicks the lame man just trying to walk.

I can't need so much anymore. I won't need so much anymore.

I press my lips together, curl them into each other, pressing tightly to stop the trembling.

"I'm okay."

Just outside the door in a wide white robe, Pastor Rick waits patiently. "In your time," he says.

Through the empty hallway on the way to a crowded sanctuary, we walk to my brother's funeral.

Alone

I'd read online that some people, in order to get through the funeral, take a Xanax or a Klonopin. I didn't have anything like that, so before we left the house, I drank ZzzQuil from the bottle and took three melatonin. I figured it probably won't make me feel different but at least it might make me feel less.

It just makes everything foggy. They usher us to the door I've only ever seen Pastor Rick come out of, the door behind the pulpit. As we walk, it feels like backstage. Everything that has such dignity and meaning when they bring it out—a Bible, the offering trays, the candles—is plopped on the counter like a Crate & Barrel catalog. I stare at a bottle of red wine by the communion trays. *The blood of Christ, given for you. The blood of Christ, given for you. The blood of Christ—*

It's just a regular bottle of wine, like you could buy at John's Party Store.

Ezra holds my hand as I look out into the congregation. The first person I see is the vague outline of Beth Dorsey.

It feels so . . . *random*, to be making eye contact with Beth

Dorsey. I feel bad for her, instantly, as she struggles to figure out what to do with her eyes. Then Jeff Miller, in the row behind her. Then a girl who was in my brother's homecoming group senior year. And John. The neighborhood girl who once watched Duke when we went to Rockford. Back to John.

I unfocus my eyes to turn all the people into a blurry pile.

The organ plays. An arm turns me forward. Eric hated this fucking organ. Eric. I feel in my pocket for the notes I hope not to need. My eulogy even has an "attention-grabbing intro," three key points, a conclusion, like a proper speech.

"When you're up there, don't look at your family, just look out at the clock and talk to God," Mr. Doug told me when he walked with us to the back door.

"Mark." Dad steadies my right hand fiddling with the note-cards in my pocket. He whispers underneath the song none of us are pretending to sing, "You don't have to do it, big guy."

Ezra squeezes my left hand and looks at me with eyes that agree.

But they're wrong. I have to. People need to know.

They need to know that he wasn't a bad kid.

He was a good kid who just had a bad night, but he wasn't a bad kid.

He was a kid who did amazing things like on my very first day of high school when I was so nervous because I didn't have lunch with any of my close friends and I thought that would just cement me as a loser for the rest of my life, the First Loser in the Davis Family, he . . . What did he do? I can't remember. What did he do?

I try to start from the beginning. *From me and my family, I just want to thank everyone for being here.* What's next? *My brother . . .* No. What's next? The words float around in my head, but they refuse to form sentences, and I try to start again but I can't even remember the first line now—"it's always good to start by thanking everyone for coming to help celebrate the life of your loved one"—and I look back at the crowded congregation, and I feel Ezra's hand on my thigh and my dad's hand around my notecards, and I look at my little cousin trying to take off his clip-on tie and my aunt and uncle and my aunt and Boppa and Pastor Rick. *The Blood of Christ, given for you The Blood of Christ, given for you The Blood of Chri* and I feel my mom's arm over my dad and onto my shoulder *just look at the clock and talk to God* and I look backward at the blurry pile of a million people who came together to honor the life of my loved one and I feel—completely—alone.

A Party Sub

I never gave a eulogy for my brother.

Pastor Rick gestured for me to come to the pulpit.

I wasn't even crying, but my brain was misfiring, like it broke down in the big-kids' room, and when it got put back together, someone put the parts in the wrong places.

Stand, my brain said.

But my legs did nothing.

Maybe that melatonin hit harder than I thought.

It's just as well. The eulogy was full of lies:

"And if Eric is listening from up there, and I know he is . . ."

I know he is? Wouldn't that be nice, to know something.

I have a theory now that nobody believes in heaven. Not even the pastor. Because think about it: If people *actually* believed in heaven, in their heart of hearts, in their quiet moments, a funeral would be a fucking rave. People would be dancing and toasting, and the visitation would make Club Chaos look like the library. Plus, everyone would be so *jealous* of the dead guy, especially if the dead guy died young, because it'd be like, shit, Eric Davis found a way to fast-track it to transcendent bliss. Lucky son of a bitch.

"He's in a better place," Mr. Lahr tells me at the reception after the funeral.

Then why are you fucking crying? I want to shout. I want to pin him against the wall by his parent/teacher conference tie and shout, *If you actually believe that, then why are you fucking crying? Explain it to me. Explain it! And why are you crying in front of me? You don't think I've seen enough people fucking crying for one lifetime? Get the f—*

But I don't shout anything. In our kitchen in front of a sliced-up party sub, I just nod my head and let Mr. Lahr say something that makes him feel good about my dead brother.

I feel a tug on the sleeve of my suit jacket, and I think I might actually scream.

I turn.

She's holding a Slurpee, her eyes, so instantly comforting, her dark red lipstick. No words because she knows there are none. And even if there were, she knows I wouldn't want them.

Crystal.

With nothing left to cry, I rest in her eyes.

She knows, too, somehow she knows that right now, every touch feels like the edge of a saw. So we don't even hug, she just wordlessly leads me upstairs.

Damien's waiting in my room. Dark suit, unbuttoned at the top, holding a blue Gatorade. He knows, too.

Crystal leaves and returns with Ezra.

He knows, too.

We sit on the edge of my bed.

No one touches me. No one talks. The four of us, we just *be*.

During days and days of calls and forms and handshakes and hugs and "sorrys" and "so sorrys" and "so very sorrys," I have so often wanted to scream:

Can we just *be*?

Someone has died.

Can we just—*be*.

On the edge of my bed, the four of us, we—*be*.

The Slurpee tastes disgusting.

"I mixed too many flavors," Crystal explains, unprompted.

"It's perfect."

With every sip, each breath feels a little less like a blade.

A tear falls, but it feels like emptying out.

This is what friends are, I guess. The people who know when to save you from the other people.

In too much pain to even hurt, I fall back to rest, close my eyes, and pray for sleep.

Grief Counseling

Maybe a week or a month or an hour later, I complain to Damien before leaving for my grief counselor. A guy my mom found. "Three sessions," Mom said delicately. "If you hate it after three, you can stop."

Damien hands me a cookie from one of the countless tins of baked goods we have in the kitchen. My mom is sleeping and my dad is at the hardware store with my uncle getting something to fix the birdbath. My dad's on a fixing rampage, fixing things that have been broken since before I was born.

"Maybe all this means I'm already at stage four: depression. Even before my first grief counseling session."

"Look at you, man." Damien somehow gets me to smile. "AP Stages of Grief."

There's a white noise machine in the waiting room so you can't hear the other patients crying.

"Sit wherever you want," he says when I get in his office.

I look at a little couch, where most people probably sit. I look at a fluffy armchair, right by the box of Kleenexes.

I look behind him and see his desk chair—a black ergonomic office chair with a mesh back, adjustable armrests, and lumbar support. I raise my eyebrows for permission.

"Wherever you're comfortable," he says.

I take the desk chair.

I'm not one of your little patients, Dr. Amato.

He asks me a couple questions, but I don't answer, so he changes strategy and starts talking.

He tells me that none of this is my fault.

He tells me that when someone dies of a disease like alcoholism or addiction, there can be more complicated emotions than if someone were to die of, say, cancer. And he hopes this will be a safe space to process those emotions.

He wasn't an alcoholic, I want to scream.

I nod my head and say, "Thank you," because I'm nervous he thinks I'm a jerk, which I am because of the desk chair thing, but I actually am just really trying not to cry.

He asks me how I'm feeling, and *mad* is all I can think of, but I know that "mad" is on that ladder of grief thing, and I think it's just stupid that I'd be exactly what Google said I would be, but after an exhausting amount of silence, I finally just say it.

"Mad."

"Who are you mad at?"

"Oh my God." I roll my eyes.

"None of this is to make you uncomfortable. I just want to explore that anger a bit deeper. In your time."

The clock ticks in the background, and I can still hear the white noise machine through the wall and the electric desktop fountain from the lobby that drip-drip-drips with the tick-tick-tick.

"I don't know."

He just tilts his head.

Everyone! I want to scream. Everyone. Who *wouldn't* I be mad at?

You. You don't know anything about my brother.

Me, for not doing something. After Thanksgiving. After Christmas. After everything.

And everyone else.

We had a visitation, obviously. And a lot of people showed up, which felt good. But as the brother, honestly, anywhere I went in the room, it was like I was death itself. Conversations stopped, faces looked sad and scared. I hated it, and it was all these emotions about how to act or how to respond to people on top of whatever mix of emotions about my brother being dead, and I just wanted to take a Vicodin and disappear for a month.

I went behind this room-divider thing, into a little den-like place in the funeral home where my family could store our bags and stuff, and I just chilled there for a bit, in between my mom's and my aunt's purses. And I played with my aunt's cigarettes. 100s. Like a baby, I just took the pack and played with them, up and down, up and down. And I overheard these two guys that were in Eric's year talking outside the room-divider thing. They obviously didn't know I was in there. They're these Michigan redneck–type guys. The ones who chew tobacco and ride snowmobiles in the winter and four-wheelers in the summer and drink Mountain

Dew in the morning and talk with this sort of southern drawl that doesn't make any sense because we're from Michigan.

"Yeah, man, gotta get suited up for tomorrow."

"You got a suit and all that?"

"Yeah, I got my go-to funeral suit."

"I got a tie for interviews and shit, but I think I gotta borrow a jacket from my stepdad."

"Nah, man, just a tie'll be fine."

They were way bigger than me, but I swear in that moment I could have killed them. I could have strangled both of them at the same time and beaten them up and strung them over their fucking snowmobiles and doused them in Mountain Dew and sent them over a cliff. Your *go-to funeral suit?* And honestly, *this* is what you're talking about? My brother's dead and you're within twenty feet of my mom talking about *dress code?*

Everything about death is so generic. Eric was the most special person in the entire world and everything about death is so generic. What people say to you, all the steps of the reception and the funeral and the number you call for the certificate, and what the pastor says and what the casket looks like and the tombstone and all this stuff that's the same for every person who dies.

Sorry for your loss.

I can only imagine what you're feeling.

My prayers are with you and your family.

All these things that you could literally copy and paste for *any* dead person. I know people have to say something, and I know it's awkward, but whatever, figure it out. Say something special. Say something more special than *sorry for your loss*, because he wasn't some hundred-year-old man who died from a long brave battle and death was really a blessing; he was nineteen, and one day he was alive and perfect and the next day he was dead, so you need to say more than just sorry for your fucking loss.

"Tell me about your brother," he says after I don't say anything besides *I don't know*. "What was he like?"

I stare at the pointy corner of a patterned rug, right where it overlaps with parallel strips of blond wood. I stare long enough for it to go hazy and all the colors to blend together. My jaw gets shaky and my eyes get blurry and I press my lips together, tight.

I shake my head.

He waits for me to talk, but I don't.

"What we'll do in our work together over the next few months—"

"Three sessions," I cut him off.

"What we'll do if we work together is learn how to memorialize your brother by holding on to and celebrating the joy of his life, not holding on to the pain of his death."

But this makes me mad all over again. Not because it's not true. God, I hope it's true. But it just sounds like something he's said ten thousand times to ten thousand people who come in and sit in his big comfy chair and cry into his Soothing Aloe Kleenexes.

He asks me to "unpack my anger."

"I haven't actually been that angry. I just didn't know what to say."

"What have you been feeling?"

"I know you're just trying to get me to go through the ladder of grief."

"Stages, actually."

His abrupt correction takes me off guard. "Huh?"

"You're likely referring to the five *stages* of grief. Denial. Anger. Bargaining. Acceptance." He looks up at the ceiling, pensively. "I missed one."

I look at him in disbelief. "Aren't you a grief counselor?"

He looks in my eyes. "Which one did I miss?"

"Depression."

"Oh. Thank you. What would we do without depression?"

"You'd probably have no patients."

He angles his head down; his eyes lighten. Maybe he wants to smile but he doesn't.

"Where'd you learn about the stages of grief?"

"Everybody knows about those."

"Not everybody has them memorized."

"Google does."

"What motivated you to Google them?"

I look at him, and all around the room, to the Kleenexes, and the couch, and the wall of books about feelings, and decide his question is too obvious to answer.

"It's a strange setup, isn't it?" he admits. "Talking to a stranger about your feelings."

Obviously.

"I promise it's less strange if you talk."

Eric would know how to handle this guy, but I can't figure it out, how to get out of this.

"What'd you have for breakfast?"

"Are you trying to be funny?"

"Not at all."

"A Nature Valley granola bar that got crumbs all over my car. You know what makes me mad? People who ask questions about me. Anyone who asks *me* how *I'm* feeling."

He nods his head. The anger feeds on itself.

"My brother is *dead* and you're asking about *me?*" I'm getting too loud. "I know people ask because they're trying to be nice. Well, you ask because it's your job. But seriously? The other day in friggin' *Kroger*, this lady who I haven't seen since she brought orange slices to my elementary school soccer games asked me how I'm feeling. And how my *mom* is feeling. In the middle of Kroger. And it's the one millionth time I'd been there that day because for some reason I don't write the list down, I just try to remember it in my head like an idiot, not to mention I've never even been the one to do the grocery shopping, so already it's weird, and then this lady who I don't even know puts her hand on my shoulder in the middle of the *sandwich-bags aisle* and asks me how my mom, who just buried her dead son, is feeling. Guess!"

I inhale and he nods his head, waits. I talk quieter.

"There should be a book about '*Tips on How to Talk to the Recently Bereaved in a Way That Doesn't Make Them Want to Suffocate Themselves with a Sandwich Bag.*' And it'd say: 'Give them a hug and tell them something special about whoever died.' Answering questions is exhausting."

He nods his head, waits.

I stiffen.

"He wasn't an alcoholic."

"Say more about that." He nods his head, waits. And all this nodding and waiting is making me even madder.

"He wasn't an alcoholic. So you shouldn't have said that thing at the beginning. Okay? He wasn't an alcoholic."

"Tell me more about what you think about that word, 'alcoholic.'"

"Say it."

"Pardon me?"

"You said he was, at the beginning—Say my brother wasn't an alcoholic."

Eric had my back. Always. And I'm not gonna sit in this depressing room while Dr. Nobody in his baggy khakis makes my brother sound like some sad alcoholic. He just. Had a bad. Night.

He speaks in a voice as calm as his try-hard zen fountain. "I said alcoholism is a disease. I certainly would never diagnose someone whom I did not have direct experience treating. All death is challenging, but deaths resulting from drugs or alcohol can be a very specific challenge." He's choosing his words carefully. "Tell me more about your reaction to the word 'alcoholic.'"

I realize in that moment that I'm bigger than him. Taller. Probably stronger. I stand up. I want to leave. I want to hit him. Of course everything makes me mad and now him most of all.

"He just had a bad night." I stay, standing, speaking to the wall.

"Tell me more about that night."

I shake with the collected rage of weeks of Mountain Dew rednecks and pity-eyed casseroles and *I bet God has big plans for him up in heaven* and billboards on the freeway that keep trying to sell chicken nuggets even though someone has died. Someone has died and you're talking about a Limited Time Offer on 20-Piece Chicken McNuggets.

I rest my forehead on the wall, and it reminds me of the night, which reminds me of my mom. How sad she'd be if I wouldn't even do three sessions.

There's only one person I ever wanted help from, and that person is dead, and this guy is not second on the list. But three sessions. For my mom.

"I'm sorry."

"No need to apologize." He sets his pen on his lap and adjusts the buttons on his cardigan. "You have to be careful, though—I'm tougher than I look."

It's about the exact opposite of what I thought he would say. I don't want to, but I smile.

"Will life ever stop sucking?"

He looks at me, looking for the right thing to say, scanning his memory for the therapist school chapter on this.

"I don't think so," he answers.

My face contorts to communicate, *What am I here for, then?*

His posture is so still. "I can't imagine a world where the pain you're feeling right now will go away completely. And it would be irresponsible to suggest otherwise. You lost a brother, a bond, and that's unfair, and sucks very, very much. Grief doesn't *proceed* in stages, contrary to what Google told you. It bounces around, your brain almost like a pinball machine, lighting up whatever emotion the grief happens to hit. And I don't think your pinball will ever completely stop hitting sadness, and anger. But it might hit them less consistently, and with less force. We might be able to get your ball to leave this awful corner, where it's just bouncing *sadness-anger-sadness-anger-sadness-anger-sadness-anger*. We might, if you do the work."

Maybe it's just as generic as everything everyone says—"grief is like a pinball machine"—but I'd never heard it before. Or maybe my mom told him that I'm obsessed with completing my schoolwork, so if he tricked me into thinking this was sort of like an assignment, then I'd follow along. Or maybe there's something in his eyes that tells me he's on my side.

"I loved him so much." I focus on a single strand of light blue yarn in the patterned rug, and tears collect but refuse to fall. "The mad, I don't even really care about that. But—sometimes I'll go a few seconds without thinking about him. Which is a miracle on its own. And then I'll realize he's not here. Like, not *physically* here. And for the briefest fraction of a millisecond, I'll think he's just away at college. And he'll come back for Easter. Or when classes end in June. He'll come back when his internship is over in August. Or he'll surprise Mom for her birthday in September. And then when I remember he's dead . . . it's like he dies all over again."

I feel a single tear outline my nose, and the office air makes the wet trail cold.

"Makes me want to blow up my pinball machine."

He tilts his head and nods, slightly. He doesn't say *I know how you feel*, and he doesn't tell me *God never gives you more than you can handle*.

He just nods his head, like someone who is on my side.

A Step

I had my song picked for the spring musical audition, even memorized it. But I was too sad to sing it.

Two days after I turned away between the doors, Mr. Wagner called me into his office and told me it's not too late.

My big plan was that the spring musical was going to be the thing that got me "back on my feet." That's what I said to myself, those exact words. I think I even said it to Damien.

And then I couldn't even walk through the doors.

School is weird, mainly because it's normal.

Normal except people are over-the-top nice. Joanna Zhang bumped into me at the lunchroom condiments station and apologized as if she had just run over my dog.

And normal except I suck at it. Can't focus. Damien lets me borrow his notes for the classes we have together. Time passes, somehow.

I *hate* when people talk about it, but I also hate that not everyone is talking about it. I feel like the whole world should be doing nothing other than talking about my brother. But if someone comes up to me and tries to talk about my brother, I want to douse myself in lighter fluid and run into an acolyte candle.

And I just—I still can't believe I never gave a eulogy for my brother.

I call Ezra during a rare moment when he's not at my house. As the FaceTime screen rings, reflecting my face back to me, I try desperately not to think about Eric. So many FaceTimes.

"You know what I just realized," I say as Ezra and his navy-blue comforter join the screen. "I missed Winter Ball."

"Correction: Winter Ball missed you."

"How do you know?"

"Touché. You're correct. I did not attend. But any function without you has a noticeable absence, I know that much."

"People are too nice to me nowadays. You're supposed to be treating me like a regular human. That was our deal."

"When is your retake for the Spanish midterm?" he asks. I missed most of February classes. Somehow, it's March. Some of these philosophers don't even believe in time. "That midterm will most assuredly treat you like a regular human."

"I wish. Señorita Lopez is just using my current average as my midterm grade. The rigors of foreign language won't even dare to humble the boy with the dead brother."

I shouldn't have said "dead brother." It's too dark, even for Ezra. I try to move past it.

"Maybe you could humble me?" It sounds *way* more sexual than I was anticipating. But, ya know what, it wouldn't be the worst thing . . .

"I have absolutely no idea what that entails"—his cheeks look flush—"but I'm quite literally up to the challenge."

"I don't know what it means, either," I backtrack. "Actually, I do. I need to get out of this house. I need to go somewhere other than Kroger. I need to have dinner with someone other than my aunt Debbie."

"Tomorrow! Don't think one more thought about it. I'll take it from here. I'll pick you up at seven."

"I love you."

"Where are you off to tonight?" my mom asks as she enters my room.

"Ezra invited me over. I don't know. I think we're just gonna chill at his place for a bit."

"That sounds fun. He's such a nice boy."

"Yeah, he's awesome." It's weird because in a lot of ways we're going through the same thing, but I don't know how to talk to my mom yet. I know Eric was my brother, but before he was my brother he was her son, and when I talk to my mom, I get why people are so scared to talk to me. I don't know what to say or how to act. I don't want it to look like I'm moving on.

"I'm glad you're going out. It's good to get out. We can't stay in this house forever."

"No, we can't," I say. Both of us are crying but pretending we're not.

My tears don't fall so much as march, solemnly, like a funeral procession, down my cheek.

"What are you going to wear?" she asks.

"Uh . . ." I laugh a little bit and gesture to the shirt I'm wearing, a green gingham shirt, Old Navy, I think. "This . . . ?" I look over to her for approval. My mom has never really taken an interest in my fashion choices before.

"Oh, I think we can do better than that. That looks like something you'd spend the whole day in," she says as she walks from the door to my closet. She starts sifting through my clothes, briefly pausing on each shirt to examine it. "I've always liked how this shirt brings out your eyes." She holds up a solid royal-blue button-down. She's definitely crying, but talking like she isn't.

"Yeah, that would be good." I wipe my nose and my cheek, where a few tears have collected. "Uh. What do you think about shorts? Change these?" I motion to my navy shorts. It's almost spring and it's finally warm.

"Maybe the khakis. Some nice khakis." She knows where I keep them, so she goes to her favorite pair. "Men always look better in pants. You know, you and your father both look so handsome in khakis."

"Yeah." I turn my head to collect myself a little bit. "I like that."

"Good. Well, you change. And be sure to let us know when you're headed out." She talks slowly, softly, like a bedtime story.

"I won't be late. I'll be back before you go to bed."

"You know your curfew. No need to rush home."

"Yeah, yeah." My breath is shaky. I move to close the door.

"And Mark?"

I have one hand on my door, but it's still open. I try to perk up. "Yeah?"

Her voice is so soft. Fragile. But it has the tone of a lesson. "About the outfits . . . you know, guys like to know you put in that effort. Not too much, not like they're all you think about, but that you went the extra mile to look good for them."

"Right." My voice breaks and my lower lip quivers. Somehow, she says a million things by saying that one thing. She says everything I've been too scared to say, and puts us back on a path. To where, I don't know, but a path to somewhere. I take a shaky breath. "I'll remember that, Mom. Thanks."

I keep waiting for my brain to stop believing in God.

It'd be logical, I think. And a lot of my least favorite stuff to hear comes from God people. How God needed another angel, or this whole category of stuff that makes it sound like God intentionally took Eric because of some bigger plan.

But I don't stop believing in God. I don't know.

Maybe, however long ago, he set the world up with certain rules. And maybe the world isn't going exactly how he wanted it to go. Maybe that even bums him out sometimes. But he can't change the rules in the middle of the game. And I don't know. It makes me like God even more, for some reason. That he's not as powerful as he thought he was gonna be. That he wanted to make this perfect world, but it didn't turn out exactly the way he wanted. I get that. And it makes me talk to him even more.

But I talk to him differently.

I'd say there's only one thing I've really learned during about a million months of being sad. It's that . . . you shouldn't pray for outside stuff, but you should pray for inside stuff.

Whenever I prayed for Eric to come back, which I did an embarrassing number of times, or when I prayed for my mom to get happier, or when I prayed for people to magically understand how to talk to me in a way that didn't piss me off—none of that came true, and I'd just get more upset. But when I prayed for inside stuff, it sort of worked. When I prayed for the courage to get through the day, or the humility to let myself cry, or the compassion to be there for my dad—those things came true. Those things happened. So now, when I pray, I just ask for inside stuff.

They say things get better with time. But I don't think that's true. It hurts just as much today as it did when it first happened. Things don't get better. You get better. Better at dealing with the things that stay bad.

When Ezra picks me up, he's wearing a tuxedo.

"Oh my God, I'm changing immediately! You didn't tell me there was a dress code," I say before the door is even fully open.

"You look perfect. I won't allow you to change a single fiber. Not one button." He grabs my hand and walks me to his car. "Just think of me somewhere between your chauffeur and your gigolo." He grandly opens the passenger-side door.

"Well, good. Because my mom picked this out." I lift the top edges of my blue shirt.

"She's a fabulous stylist." He gently shuts my door.

"So . . . where are we going?" I click the seat belt as he gets back in.

"The answer will reveal itself in time. For now, just sit back, enjoy the ride, and take in the smooth sounds of forgotten R&B slow jams that live on exclusively through school dances DJ'ed by goateed divorcés."

In the background: "*All my life, I prayed for someone like you.*" I don't say much, and he doesn't, either. "*And I thank God, that I, that I finally found you.*"

Outside my house I feel fragile, like I'm one sharp turn away from shattering.

We talk about nothing much. He's nervous, too. He pulls up to an empty field in the middle of a wide square of houses, and he parks the car along the street. "Don't get out yet," he says, hustling over to my door.

"Mr. Davis." He opens my door with a grand gesture. "Welcome to Winter Ball."

The grassy field lights up like it's the first living thing I've seen in a month. Even though the grass is a little less lush in the field—the sprinklers from the houses don't reach all the way, so the green gradually becomes less vibrant toward the middle—it looks so alive. Through the big bay windows of the houses that frame the field, I can see families sitting down for dinner. Swing sets sit empty, all the kids have already been called in. Wooden playgrounds wait for tomorrow. Twilight throws oranges across the horizon and turns a few scattered clouds into a complicated mix of gray, purple, and red, but the sun lets the sky stay blue for a little while longer. Our shadows are long and they walk in front of us. Wherever we're going, they get there first.

The path is paved with rose petals that look like they were perhaps more orderly an hour ago. Some tumble in the wind, but enough lie dutifully to point the way toward a white gazebo. I've seen this gazebo before, hundreds of times. I pass it on the way to school. But I've never really looked at it. It's simple, wooden, all white with a white railing, gray shingles on its roof, and a little lighthouse-looking thing on top, also painted white. Eight sides. One opening, where the rose petals lead. Tonight, there are strings of Christmas lights wrapped around the banisters. A picnic basket waits in the middle.

"Ezra," I say, in awe, looking like the heart-eyes emoji he'd sent me a week ago. "You did all this? The roses? The Christmas lights?"

"*Ahem* . . . They are 'nondenominational celebration bulbs.'"

I laugh. "Whatever they are, I love them. I love it. I love . . ." I pause. "I love *you*."

"I'm glad."

I punch his shoulder.

"I love you, too," he says with a giant smile. "Here, let us walk, my lady." He takes my hand and leads me along the rose petal path.

"You know you're embodying every school dance stereotype you hate right now?" I smirk.

"Well, the other day when I was praying to our Lord and Savior Jesus Christ, he spoke to me, and told me to perhaps incorporate flexibility into my intellectual regimen."

"Jesus Saves . . . Winter Ball."

We follow our shadows up the single step of the gazebo. He

formally gestures for me to go first. Up close the paint chips away to reveal the wood underneath. Ezra had placed what looks like a brand-new flannel picnic blanket over the floor of the gazebo. A brand-new picnic basket waits in the corner next to folded hoodies, in case we get cold.

"Wait . . . whose gazebo is this?" I ask.

"Oh no! *Cops*! Run!"

I smile. "Seriously? To whom does this gazebo belong?"

"Gazebos fall under the Pocahontas Ordinance of 1617. No one owns them."

"'*You can own the earth and still*,'" I sing lightly, "'*all you'll own is earth untilllll . . .*'"

"That's the one." He takes a seat on the blanket.

"Seriously, whose gazebo is this? You know I'm way too much my mother's son to break the law."

"I know for a fact you used to get beer from Joe Thomas's older brother."

"God, you're on fire today."

"Also, following my religion research, aren't you not supposed to take God's name in vain?"

"We have a special arrangement."

"Well, to oblige my law-abiding Anne of Green Gables—the gazebo belongs to the Lawson family, and they've been informed by yours truly of our rendezvous."

"Who can resist the chance to cheer up the local sob story?"

"Don't be self-indulgent. I bribed them with cold hard cash."

I laugh. "What's the going rate for a gazebo with peeling paint within earshot of Rochester Road?"

"You'd be surprised. They knew the formal theme was Winter Garden, so they really upped their rates. Gazebo price gouging, if you ask me."

"I helped pick that theme!" I laugh again. Every time I laugh, it feels like I'm rediscovering something. "You like it?"

"Yes. I love it. Natural, yet refined. Plentiful, yet precious. I almost dressed like a sexy garden gnome in homage."

"Oh, that wouldn't have been fair! I'm innocent Anne of Green Gables over here, just trying to hold on to my virginity until marriage."

"If you've still got your virginity, then I've still got my baby teeth."

We are just two teenagers flirting in a field. We are a story that's been told a million times. Blissfully ordinary.

"Enough prelude! We have food and drinks. And of course, it being a *ball* and all"—he pulls out two plastic champagne flutes, each with a circular base that attaches separately. He pulls out the bottle of champagne, pops the cork ceremoniously, clicks the bases into place, and fills the glasses halfway, holding both glasses with one hand, the alcohol tilting toward the edge.

I watch the champagne pour. I watch the bubbles swirl up from the bottom. I watch the foam come dangerously close to the top. I watch this handsome man pour me a drink. This handsome man I love. I watch him have fun with alcohol.

What was Eric drinking the night he died?

Do toxicology reports just tell you that he was drunk, or do they also tell you what type of alcohol he was drinking?

Was he drinking champagne?

Probably not. It was a Tuesday night. But at the Christmas party his senior year, he drank champagne. He toasted with Mr. Stevens, and said something like, "Come, let us taste the stars!" And Mr. Stevens said something like, "Is that Shakespeare? You're too smart for this town, kid. Get outta here!" And Eric joked, "I'm doing the best I can." And then Mr. Stevens shouted to my dad, "Big-city dreams for this one."

I start crying.

Fuck.

Not now. No. Let me have one night.

I can't stop. I read this article on how to stop crying, and it said to press your tongue against the roof of your mouth and that will stop it, right away, guaranteed. But it doesn't work. *Fuck you, Google.* I press hard, like my tongue is holding a door closed, but it doesn't stop them.

"I guess it's a little early for me to be the lead in Netflix's next teen rom-com," I say.

"Oh god, I'm sorry." He looks it. And then he looks at the champagne. "I didn't think. I'm so sorry. God. Mark." And tears well up in his eyes, too. "I'm so sorry. I shouldn't have . . . I didn't think." He doesn't know what to say. His hands shake a little bit. No one ever knows what to say. "I'm sorry. We'll just . . . have the . . ."

And the tears are really coming now. I say through a clenched jaw, to myself, to my tears, to the universe. "No, no, *no!*" My cheeks shine with tears. "I'm fine," I say. I refuse to wipe my eyes because it feels like admitting defeat. Ezra doesn't know what to do, so he gently covers my hand, and with his other hand wipes some of my tears with his tuxedo sleeve.

"I'm all right," I say. And I laugh because I'm so obviously not. "Denial. Guess I'm back at stage one."

"Well, maybe that means you've run a full lap," Ezra says with compassion. "The starting line is the finish line, I suppose." He's working his way to a philosophical pronouncement, which I appreciate so much. "So it'd be impossible to tell, just by where someone is on the track . . ." He's speaking so delicately, not wanting to make light of anything, not knowing what to say. ". . . whether they've just won, or just begun."

Track. Four hundred meters. I wonder if anyone at Barnes Middle School has beaten Eric's record yet, or when they will—when his name will disappear from the record board.

Ezra continues, "And if it is, in fact, the beginning line . . ." He gets that comforting tone that everyone gets when they're dealing with *the bereaved*, exactly the tone I'd hoped to skip out on today. ". . . then I'm honored to be here with you. Beginning."

"Ezra, I'm so sorry," I say, but I can hardly meet his eyes. "This is the most wonderful, kind, *romantic* thing anyone's ever done for me. I'm so sorry and I know there's food and . . . I can't do this. You're amazing. Honestly. I think I loved you before I even liked you."

He laughs, slightly, with sad eyes, lips pursed together the same way I purse mine when I'm holding back the start of new tears.

"I just can't. I can't. I'm . . . dead. Inside. And I can only feel one thing. And if this"—I gesture to the gazebo, and the lights, and the sparkling twilight of my hometown—"if this doesn't do it." I shrug. "You deserve someone . . ." I'm looking him in the eyes as I take a shaky breath and look away, because I'm sick of people seeing me cry. ". . . less broken."

I can't stay.

I used to be mad at the world, but now I'm mad at myself. "I'm sorry," I say again as I get up to walk away. "I . . ." can't finish what I almost start. I walk out of the gazebo, into the open field, taking care to avoid the rose petal path. I pick a house that looks like no one is home, walk through their backyard, and get on the road.

Stage Zero, Again

I walk and walk and walk. No one walks along main roads in Michigan, so I look lost. It's eight o'clock, then nine, then ten. It gets cold as it gets dark. I want to turn around so many times and go back to the gazebo, but I don't. I wear my Grandpa's watch—the watch I had to fight Eric for. I pass the Walgreens. A second time.

I don't know why I want cigarettes.

Something that burns. Something that hurts. Something to do.

"I just need to see your ID," the Walgreens checkout clerk asks.

I feel for my wallet. "Oh, crap, I just ran out for cigs, I left my main wallet at home." My main wallet? What does that even mean?

"Sorry, man. I would, but, it's just that we have to scan the ID before the system'll let us sell it." The guy looks familiar, like maybe we'd gone to school together, or played soccer, or something. Short brown hair, spiked a little on top, long sideburns, a light tan line where Oakleys might go.

"No, I get it. No problem. Thanks anyway, man."

I walk out of the store and start back toward Rochester Road, but before I get there, the Walgreens attendant runs out through the sliding doors.

"Hey, wait up!" I turn around. "It's my break right now, actually. If you want . . . ?"

I stand in the dark. He extends a pack of cigarettes. Through the gates of the parting automatic doors, the light from the store beams behind him. He looks like an angel. The Renegade Angel of 18 Mile.

"Oh, yeah," I say, surprised. "Thanks, man. I really appreciate it." We walk over to the brick wall, between the dumpster and the back entrance. He flips open his pack and hands me a cigarette before he takes one for himself. He leans forward, cups his hand around his lighter to shield the flame from the wind. I take quick puffs to get it going.

He takes another out, taps the filter side on the back of his hand.

"Sorry to come into your store looking kind of like death," I say as he lights his cigarette.

"Ah, no problem. You should see the late-night crowd we get." He takes a puff. "You'd think in Annondale it'd be more polished, but man . . . we get some stragglers."

I laugh. "I bet. Even the suburbs can get pretty wild, I guess." I get light-headed and nauseous from the cigarette. I fill the silence. "You go to Annondale High?"

"Nah, Lakeside. Graduated last year, though. Just live on the other side of Rochester down there."

"Oh, sweet."

266 ✦ BECOMING A QUEEN

"Yeah, not too sweet, still with the moms and stepdad and all that. But workin' my way out."

"Nice. Well, good luck, man. I live just on the *other* side of Rochester. The Annondale High side, I guess." The smoke of our two cigarettes meets in the starless sky.

I take another puff. A car drives past on the highway. It isn't that late, but hardly any cars are out. We both follow the car with our eyes. Something to look at.

"Hey, you're Eric Davis's little brother, right?"

"Oh, yeah."

"I, uhh, I'm sorry, man. I was at the funeral. Got there late, though, ya know, so me and a couple buddies were in the way back, standin' up."

Our whole conversation is slow. Like watching a plane inch across the skyline.

"Oh, cool. Thanks for coming."

"You know, I'm sure you get a lotta this, but your bro really was a solid guy." He takes another drag and stares down at the glowing ember, rolling his cigarette between his index and middle finger, just watching the paper burn. "We played soccer against each other here and there through the years. Partied a bit together." A car pulls into the parking lot, just to turn around.

"He was hangin' out with one of my girls for a bit, ya know? Wish I'd known him better, but—was always kinda intimidated, to be honest, he was so smart and shit." He kicks a little rock against the dumpster and it bounces into the parking lot. Lights another cigarette.

"But yeah, most of the AHS guys, you know, feel all superior to Lakeside and shit. But your brother, man, he was cool," he says. "I don't mean to get you down or nothin', you're just tryin' to enjoy your night. But I just wanted you to know that."

He extends the pack again. "You want another one, too? I got a whole 'nother pack in there. Take as many as you want, some for the road, too, if you want. Sorry I couldn't sell you nothin' in there. They're just crackin' down on underage shit."

"Oh, no, I totally get it," I say. "Yeah, actually, I'll take another one." He pulls one out and hands it to me, and firms his lips around his cigarette to hold it steady so I can light mine from his again. I'm nauseous from the first as I start the second.

"Here, and you got this pocket here on this fresh blue shirt that was just *born* for holdin' cigs, man. Take the rest."

"Oh, you don't have to do that. Seriously."

"Man, they're yours. A gift from a friend of Eric's."

I imitate an announcement. "In lieu of flowers, the family requests cigarettes."

"Yeah, I could tell you're smart like he was. On that *In lieu of* shit." He laughs. "What's up with you? You a junior? Senior?"

"Junior."

"Bet you'll get into some smart-ass school like Eric, too."

"I'll do my best. Big shoes to fill."

"Yeah, man. Shit. I'm really sorry. Your family's goin' *through* it, I bet."

The stoplight changes to green at the empty intersection.

"Do you remember anything else?" I ask faintly. "About Eric, I mean."

His voice is strong. "Aw, yeah. I didn't wanna bring you down or nothin', but when I saw that was you, I was kinda pumped, cuz yeah, me and your brother, we were boys." He loosens up. "I mean, he was kinda boys with everybody, but we hung out. I got hundreds. Damn. We got into some crazy shit in middle school. Way too young for all that. It was easier then, ya know, to sneak booze and shit. John's Party Store give it to anybody."

"No scanning IDs there," I add.

"You're sure right about that. You are sure right about that. Man, where to even start . . ." He looks up and solidifies his thought. "Okay—once me and your brother were at this party, and I was nervous as fuck to ask this girl to be my girlfriend and all. You know how awkward that is, so young and shit. What's 'girlfriend' even mean? But yeah, he saw me all nervous and came over and gave me this little pep talk, like we were halftime with the Lions, talkin' 'bout, 'We only got this one life' and shit. This kid had *wisdom*. That's some *wisdom* for an eighth grader. And he handed me this water bottle, you know? I don't even know what was *in* that water bottle, but I can taste it to this day, I'll tell you that. Some mix of shit, probably. And he was like, 'Get your girl, man.' Pattin' me on the back. 'Get your girl.' The crazy thing is, I still fuck with that girl. All these years later. Who knows, ya know? If your bro hadn't had that tequila or whatever the fuck . . ." He laughs.

"Ah, I'm sorry," he says, when he notices a couple tears.

"Nah, don't sweat it." With my free hand, I point to my eyes. "Par for the course nowadays."

"As long as I'm not bummin' you out."

"Not at all. I like it. I really like it."

"Well, I could talk your ear off, man, once you get me goin'. Put a couple Coronas in me and we could be here *all night*. But yeah . . ." He shakes his head. "Like I said, if it were a different manager, I'da been able to hook you up, but this guy's *strict*. Gets his dick hard bustin' up stuff like that."

"All good."

"Speaking of my shit-ass manager . . . Gotta get back in there. But stay out here as long as you want, bro. Enjoy the finest moonlight views of Rochester Road." He says it like a late-night radio announcer.

"Actually, do you have a phone charger in there?"

"Yeah, for sure. You got an iPhone?"

I nod.

"We sell 'em, but come here real quick. I'll pop one open if you just need a little boost, so you don't gotta buy it or nothin'."

"Sweet. Yeah, thanks, man. I appreciate it." I follow him through the sliding doors, past the ATM in the vestibule, back inside.

While my phone charges, I browse under the blinding lights of the nail polish section.

"How many different ways can you say 'pink'?" he shouts. "Right?"

I laugh. "Hey, what was your name again?"

"Ah yeah, I don't think I properly introduced myself. Grant. Mitchell."

"Cool. Nice to meet you, Grant."

"Yeah, you too," he says. "Hey, looks like your phone's got a little juice now, if you wanna come behind and do your thing."

I go behind the counter. Send a text.

Hey. I'm at Walgreens. The one on Rochester & 18 mile. If you're
still awake, could you pick me up?

I unplug my phone and say goodbye to Grant. "Cool. Well,
thanks for everything, man. I really appreciate it. Sorry to be, like,
a morbid force in your evening."

"Fuck, man, you were the highlight of my evening."

I laugh. "Thanks. Shoulda seen me in my prime."

"Ah, your prime is so far aheada you, you can't even see it
yet."

As I'm about to leave, he calls back. "And seriously, if you
ever need anything. I mean, I can hook you up when I'm not workin', no problem. I got your back, too. For whatever. Eric was the
man," he concludes. "But ahhh"—he swats his hand down—"you
know that."

I go out and sit on the curb. It's close to the ground, so my chest
rests on my knees like a kid watching TV on the carpet.

After a few minutes, I stand to greet my ride.

"Sorry I ruined the ball," I say sheepishly, through Ezra's
open window.

"I don't care about fake Winter Ball," he says. "I care about
real you." He reaches over and opens the passenger door from the
inside.

I slide in. He's no longer in the tuxedo. Just black workout
pants and a white T-shirt.

"Have you been smoking?" he says disapprovingly.

"I may have had a couple hundred cigarettes with the Walgreens attendant next to the dumpster."

"And they say smoking has lost its glamour."

I speak nostalgically. "He was awesome, actually. He knew Eric. Had funny stories." Ezra starts driving toward the exit.

"So he was worth abandoning me in a field for?"

"I'm sorry!" I look at him with weary puppy dog eyes.

"It's fine. More chocolate-covered strawberries for me."

"Ah! There was chocolate? I would have stayed!"

We reach the edge of the parking lot, and he waits to turn onto Rochester Road. "So, Mr. Davis. Where to?"

"Well. Eventually, home. But still a little time before curfew so, yeah, turn left on Rochester and go through Long Lake."

We drive quietly.

"Turn left here. Yeah, just wind through the sub a bit." I point to a small house with yellow siding. "I lost my first tooth in that house," I say with quiet enthusiasm.

"And what was the going rate from the tooth fairy in those days?"

"I think I got a buck," I say, proud, my voice firming as the driveways click by. "But actually I had this whole plotline in my head, because my dad couldn't answer my question of how the tooth fairy makes all her money, so I got nervous that the tooth fairy was, like, really stretched thin, with all these expenses and no income. So I decided to leave the money under the pillow for her to take back the next night."

"Of course! Us fairies have to stick together."

I've been called a fairy quite a few times in my life, but never as a compliment. I smile. "That's right. Us fairies have to *stick together*!" I beat both my hands on the glove compartment, like a drum.

When I was growing up, the houses we are passing now seemed miles away. Riding to Mary Spagnola's house on my bike felt like taking a vacation. But they were really just a couple streets over.

"All right, now turn right, and then another right in the first driveway. And go to the back parking lot."

"Your elementary school?"

"Technically, it's the parking lot for a park *next* to my elementary school. But unofficially it's where couples go to make out after dances. Like Winter Ball."

"Oh, is that right?" he asks coyly.

"It is. I came here with Amber Rhodes after the St. Patrick's Day Dance in sixth grade." I grin. "Not to bring up exes or anything."

"We all have a past," he says lightheartedly as he puts the car in park. He exhales and relaxes into his seat, moving his hand to hold mine. "I'm so glad I finally landed one of the cool kids so he can show me where all the hot hetero make-out spots are."

"I'm not so cool anymore."

"Coolest person I've ever known."

I didn't know brown eyes could be so deep. It's like looking far into a forest, past the trees, into the darkness you don't understand but can't turn away from. In the parking lot next to my old elementary school, Ezra holds my hand with both of his, one on the bottom, palm facing my palm, one on top, slowly tracing the outline of my veins.

"I know you're new back here," I say. "But this is the part where you kiss me."

Senior Year

September

Waves

I never gave a eulogy for my brother.

The tulle of my purple princess dress pools around me as I stare into last year's physics book.

I'm relearning about waves.

"Grief comes in waves." That's what my grief counselor said today.

But he didn't specify: waves like physics or waves like ocean?

Probably ocean: Grief crashes into you when you're trying to have a nice day at the beach.

But *maybe* physics: Disturbances that transfer energy through matter or space with little or no associated mass transport (aka disturbances that you don't see coming). Plus, waves are everywhere. Light. Sound. Grief is everywhere.

I adjust the elastic strap around my shoulders, scratch the itchy sequins on my stomach, and get ready to crack this grief like a practice problem.

*"The wave **period** is the measure of time it takes for the wave cycle to complete.* (How long it takes me to cry?) *We usually measure the*

*wave period in seconds and represent it with the letter T. Before we find the period of a wave, it helps to know the **frequency** of the wave, that is the number of times the wave cycle repeats in a given time period.* (How many times I cry per day?) *Frequency (f) can be obtained by dividing the wave's velocity, usually symbolized by the letter v, by its wavelength.* (How hard I cry divided by how rapid my sobs are?) *Remember, we represent it with the Greek symbol: lambda."*

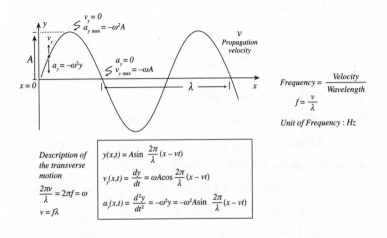

This isn't helping.

Grief is like waves: impossible to understand and kind of boring.

I get up to look at myself in the full-length mirror. I press the tulle down, smooth out the sequins. I'm not even smiling, but it's still pretty. It's just as pretty as it was when I bought it, and it doesn't need any help from me.

And it's stupid, I know, but it makes me happy—or whatever more complicated emotion now lives where *happy* used to. It makes me happy to know that something pretty survived.

Mom, Dad, Dr. Amato—they all think I'm crazy.

They don't say it, because they probably think saying it would make me even more crazy, but Dr. Amato's white noise machine isn't that loud. Behind gray walls they talk about "complicated grief" in tones that convey, in this context, *complicated* is not an adjective but a diagnosis.

One day, while wearing this princess dress, I stared at the ceiling for three hours.

They may have a point.

The lipstick did not join us without a fight.

"*I don't wanna go in there, it's so sad!*" the lipstick shouted in a high-pitched voice, like a cartoon squirrel, as I snuck it from the discarded makeup bin underneath my mom's sink.

"I know, neither do I," I replied, stern, eye to eye with where I thought the lipstick's eyes would be. "But life's tough, and you don't always get what you want. Plus, we've gotta help him. He's going crazy."

"*He's going crazy?*"

"He's going crazy!"

I looked at myself in the bathroom mirror, talking to a tube of lipstick. "See?"

Somewhere within driving distance of the Annondale Goodwill there's a guy with a thirty-one-inch waist wearing my brother's pants.

You know what would be crazier than going crazy? Not going crazy.

After dinner, I FaceTime Crystal and we stare at my ceiling.

"Have you ever heard of a second funeral?" I say to my upturned phone.

She says nothing but a quiet, confused "Hmmm."

I clarify. "Like, a do-over."

"You wanna do that *again*?"

"No, I just mean—the funeral happens way too right away. Eric's graduation party was a month and a half after he graduated. Take a beat, you know?"

"You can do whatever you fucking want. All the shit we do now was made up by someone. So make up new shit."

I think about it.

I just—I can't believe I never gave a eulogy for my brother.

"We have a chance to make everything turn out all right again. Turn our back on everything that went wrong." I distract myself by memorizing my audition monologue. It's a monologue about love, from a play called *Frankie and Johnny*.

The fall play is going to be *Our Town*. The *fall play* will get me back on my feet!

I have the full script, but I'm too afraid to read it. I just know someone's gonna die—someone always dies. The play we did my freshman year was *Macbeth*. About 95 percent of the people in that play die. My character walked into the final scene with a literal bloody head on a giant stick. The play we did my sophomore year was called *All My Sons*. It was by Arthur Miller and it was about a family that couldn't move on after one of the sons died. They blamed themselves. *I'm not kidding.* I played the brother. Seriously. Before her big monologue, the senior who was playing my mom would hide behind our fake house and rub Vicks VapoRub under her eyes. It was the only way she could get real tears.

I *will* do it. I have to do it. I attended the annual Annondale Theater Company info session and I didn't even cry once. I can do it.

Then it hits me. *We have a chance to make everything turn out all right again.*

I pull out the info sheet Mr. Wagner handed out.

We'll go into each in more detail on the following pages, but to give you an overview, **The Annondale Theater Company** has three main events every year:

- **The Fall Show** (this year: *Our Town*),
- **The Spring Show** (this year: *The Addams Family*), and
- **The ATC Talent Show** (where you have the opportunity to be you, and bring whatever talent you think can make the cut!!) *Tentative date: April 12th*

The talent show. The talent show!

They say that those who forget history are doomed to repeat it.

But they don't tell you which part to remember.

✧   ✧   ✧

"If you wanna do it, do it, bud," Eric told me as I agonized over the sophomore-year talent show. "Who cares what other people *might* say? Be yourself! Your full sequin-y self."

We were sitting in my bedroom and he was spinning himself around and around on my desk chair.

"That's easy for you to say when *your* 'self' is so fucking perfect."

"*My* 'self' just got grounded for half of senior year because I was too drunk at Spring Fling." He gave himself another spin.

"Yeah, but even when you get in trouble, it's in, like, a cool way. I'm gonna get in trouble for wearing a dress and it's not gonna be cool."

"You're not gonna get in *trouble*, bud. You're not doing anything wrong." He rolled from the chair to the bed, discombobulated and dizzy.

"Dad will hate it."

"So let him hate it."

"John will hate it."

"Then dump him."

"Dump John Beckett? Okay, while we're at it, why don't we throw the Hope Diamond back in the fucking ocean."

"I think you're getting historical treasures mixed up with the plot of *Titanic*."

"I've never even seen *Titanic*."

"The guy dies at the end."

"Which guy."

"The main guy."

"How does he die?"

"How do you *think* he dies, it's the *Ti—*"

"*Why are we talking about the* Titanic *right now?*" I shouted as I gripped the sharp sequins in my hand.

"Bud." He sat up against my headboard and reset us. "Does wearing the dress make you happy?"

I was nervous to answer. "Yes."

"Then *wear the dress!*"

"It's not that simple."

"Jesus. Damien and Joe fucking Thomas are gonna be in the *same dress*. You're way overthinking this."

"It's different for them."

"*Why?*"

"Because wearing the dress doesn't make them happy."

He looked at the dress in my hands.

I looked at the carpet.

Eric's shoes.

"Not in the same way it does me."

He nudged my chin up to look me earnestly in the eyes, and talked with tough love. "Well, don't come cryin' to me when we're eighty years old sitting in the retirement home and you're still holding on to that dress." He imitated the strained whisper of an old man, "*I just wish . . . I woulda worn tha dress!*"

"Shut up." I threw the dress and its sharp sequins right at Eric. It wrapped around his face like an octopus.

He smacked it to the ground with mock disgust. "Get your ball-sweat dress off my face." He stood, picked it up, and folded it, delicately, like a present, before placing it on my lap. He made sure I was looking at him before concluding, "Be. Your fucking. Self."

The talent show.

I don't know how. Or even really what (it can't be a *eulogy* eulogy; despite what Dr. Amato may believe, I'm not *that* crazy). But I know when: the talent show.

Something for my brother.

Basement

My head moves with his shoulder as Ezra leans forward to tell Netflix we're still watching. "I feel like I'm the worst companion, and the only reason you're staying with me is because there's some sort of rule: how long you have to wait after a tragedy to break up with someone."

"Close. I'm actually staying with you because I like all the casseroles people are still sending your mom."

"I knew it."

"But could you tell Mrs. Ross to use less corn in her tuna noodle?"

"I know! Why *so* much corn?"

"Government subsidies are destroying our casseroles." Ezra grabs my shoulders with both hands and plops me back down onto his lap. He looks down at my head, which feels like it might, at any minute, topple off my body and spin once and for all into oblivion.

"I love you, Mark." He leans into me and talks so close his breath warms my lips. "I love *you*. Happy you. Sad you. Corn-poop you."

"*Ew*! Oh, Ezra, *ew*, that's so gross." I scrunch up and curl into him like a hand around a branch.

"And I want to make you happy, without imposing upon you the obligation to be so."

I look up with my *translation, please?* facial expression.

"I'm not going anywhere."

You don't think you'll survive, but then you do. Somehow, you do. And you see him everywhere. Your dad's walk. Your mom's laugh. Your neighbor's wave. That's all Eric; he's in there. Eric would never go up to be an angel. That's so not his style, just sitting apart from everyone. No. He'd stay down here. Watch after us, and find some way to help from the inside.

Tonight, instead of a period, my boyfriend ends his sentence with a kiss.

And not in a gross incest-y way, but I know, in some way, my brother is in that kiss. Telling me it's okay. Telling me he's sorry and he didn't mean to, that he's not gone and he never will be, and that it will never be okay, but it's okay.

You're allowed to have fun.

Ezra kisses me gently at first, like a question I need to answer.

Don't fuck this up, lil' bud. This dude's hot for you. Don't fuck this up on account of me. You kidding me? I'll still be here when your little night of postpubescent adolescent passion is cum-*plete. Get out of your head and kiss him back.*

Ezra, I'm sure, can taste my tears.

I kiss him back.

And somewhere inside my head, a brother frozen at nineteen makes a joke about mouth-to-mouth. *That's one way to resuscitate yourself!*

Horace and Benjamin Plan a Party

He holds me from big spoon position on the wide beige couch of his basement and gives me a gentle squeeze.

"There's something important we need to talk about," Ezra whispers in my ear solemnly.

"What?" I say, nervous all of a sudden.

"What are we going to be for Halloween?"

"You scared me!" I elbow him in the ribs. "I don't know. I haven't really thought about it."

"You'd better start. It's only ten days away. And I finagled tickets to a raucous Halloween party."

I want to go. I desperately *want* to want to go.

"Technically, a gala," he continues. "Specifically, a *gay*-la." He smiles at himself. "Costumes mandatory. Hosted by Theater Absurd. *Absurdly* expensive, but apparently 'Metro-Detroit's number one Halloween Extravaganza.' I'm not sure how much competition it has, but regardless—a night like no other! In addition to costumes, you and I will also be going as 'Horace Burrows' and

'Benjamin Kelley,' respectively, the names on our fake IDs. We don't have to drink. We just had to be over twenty-one to attend."

"You rebel!"

"I just wanted to make sure we weren't stuck in this house passing out not-so-fun-sized Snickers with the reluctant suburbanite known as my mother."

I laugh, and he continues. "It's the kind of club where you can dance all night in a fog machine and kiss a twink in a bathtub full of bouncy balls. I watched a video from last year."

"I *am* a twink, aren't I?"

"Well then, meet me in the bathtub!"

"What are we waiting for, Horace? We need to go *now*."

"I'm Benjamin. You're Horace. Thank God we're studying."

"I have a sinking feeling this isn't what I'm supposed to be studying." I return to his question, but turn it around. "What do *you* want to be?"

He caresses my arm with his fingers, lightly, like a string, up to my shoulder and back again, around my stomach and back again.

He says, "Let's brainstorm."

"Which head are you thinking with right now, Mr. Ambrose?" I tease.

"A joke fit for the Solo cup crowd." He twists me by the shoulders and turns me around so we're face-to-face, asks, "What's the most *fabulous* thing you've *ever* wanted to be? Ever in your whole entire seventeen years on this revolving heavenly body?"

I perk up. "Well, we have to be a *couples'* costume! I don't even care what it is, just some sort of *couples'* costume."

"I like where your head's at," he says, as he reaches down and squeezes my . . .

"Get outta there! You said this is serious." I pause, thinking back to the last time I suggested wearing a dress on Halloween. "*Mark, if I wanted to date a girl, I'd date a girl.*" But then I hear another voice, a stronger voice, a told-you-so voice. *In good relationships, you're not worried about being* too *this or* too *that. The person actually wants you to be* more *this and* more *that.*

"Don't laugh. But do you remember, about ten thousand years ago, when we were juniors . . ."

He laughs.

"Yeah. Get it all out now, because if you laugh *after* I suggest it, I think I will die."

"Fine. No more laughing. Laughing ceased." He waves his hand in front of his face and flattens his expression.

I speak tentatively, with a devilish smile. "You know what I really want to wear?"

"What?"

I shout it like it's one word: "*Mypurpleprincessdresswiththepuffy-sleeves!*"

"I was *hoping* you were going to say that!"

"It's so *glamorous*! Honestly, it's the only thing in my house that doesn't . . ." Make me sad. But I don't want to say that word right now, so I stop myself. "Doesn't matter why. I love it."

"Well, my lady?" He extends his hand.

"But what would you be?"

"Prince Charming, of course."

I respond with a smile. "Stereotype."

Grief Counseling Session #34

Just when I think I'm almost healed, I slip backward. One step forward, ten steps back. Which puts me at grief stage: negative nine thousand and forty-two.

They say things get better with time.

They're wrong.

Because with time, he gets further away.

I wish I would have listened harder. I wish I would have memorized every sentence he ever said to me, written it down in a book the second after he said it, so I could replay it every day for the rest of my life. I wish I would have studied his face closer, memorized the freckles he got in the summer, so I wouldn't have to go back to pictures every time I feel my memory fading. I wish I would have taken more pictures. I wish I had more of everything.

It's been almost nine months—264 days—since I heard my brother's laugh. And I'm terrified that one day I won't be able to remember what it sounded like.

His laugh is an echo. And then an echo of an echo. And then an echo of an echo of an echo.

"Grief comes in waves," the PhD tells the seventeen-year-old who, just yesterday, almost nine months after his brother died, had a twenty-minute breakdown in the parking lot of Kroger because he saw a tiny movie poster ad on the front of a shopping cart for a dumb action movie that was the third in a trilogy of dumb action movies that his older brother loved.

"Grief comes in waves," the PhD tells the seventeen-year-old who, two weeks ago, almost nine months after his brother died, had sobbed through their sixty-minute session because he started to think his memory had catalogued Eric's laugh wrong, and then he started to wonder what if all his memories were a little bit off, and from here until forever he won't actually be remembering Eric, but he'll be remembering his *memories* of Eric.

"In deep, long-term relationships of interdependence, grief can be like a chronic condition that you and I learn to manage, together."

In a shocking plot twist, I actually like this analogy. It means I don't have to get rid of Eric.

And I like when Dr. Amato uses science-y words. It makes me feel like maybe someone somewhere has studied this and knows the way out.

A Princess and His Prince

"**I** feel like we hardly see Ezra anymore," my mom says as I finish grabbing my things to go, again, to Ezra's house, where we'll get ready for the Halloween part—sorry, Halloween *gala*.

I don't have the heart to tell her it's because our house still makes me sad, so I just speak in generalities. "I know! He says hello. It's just, his costume is really complicated, so it would have been hard to bring it all here."

I also don't tell my mom and dad that the party is in Detroit. And I definitely don't tell them what I'm wearing. I say we are going as "medieval people"—whatever that means. My dad's going through a lot, without also having to process his remaining son in a purple princess dress with puffy sleeves.

I wave to Mr. Martell raking his leaves as I drive through my neighborhood and revisit my plan to pay tribute to Eric at the talent show.

Ladies and gentlemen, please welcome to the stage . . . The MC stops midsentence and looks to the wings for confirmation. He looks too confused to even say it. . . . *Mark Davis performing a eulogy for his dead brother!*

Ezra opens the door before I even step on the porch. He's shirtless and he's already wearing his bright yellow Prince Charming pants.

"My prince!" I stare at that tuft of hair between his pecs and for a second forget my own name.

"*Excuse me*, my eyes are up here." And they are indeed. His face is painted with pale makeup and deathly dark circles around his eyes. "I had to do *something* Halloween-y." He reaches his free hand out across the porch. "Come here, my gutter-brained prince. We've gotta turn you into a pretty, pretty—"

"Is that our princess?" Ezra's mom calls down.

Ezra hustles me up the curved staircase to his mom's bedroom. She sits me down next to dozens of makeup brushes, color palettes, and fancy colored pencils arranged with intention like dental instruments.

It's all a lot more glamorous than the tube of lipstick I keep hidden in the hollow part of a basketball participation trophy.

Ms. Abramson looks at me (Abramson, *not* Ambrose: "That wasn't my last name even when I *was* married to that man"). Her hair's pulled up; a purple floral kimono flows over her light gray, almost white jeans. "Did you moisturize before coming over?"

"Umm . . . I don't think so," I answer, strangely nervous. I turn to Ezra. "Ezra, you're *sure* no one from school is going to be at this party?"

"Indubitably!" He bounces atop each syllable and playfully swoops around me. "Tonight is *As You Like It*." He calms my nerves with a throwback to junior-year English. "We shall leave the confining court behind and dance in the forest, switching genders like Rosalind into Ganymede, as we like it!"

I smile in awe.

"'*All the world's a stage*,' Mark," Ms. Abramson adds, "and if you ever doubted my son's undying devotion for you, I watched him memorize every gender-identity Shakespeare quote just for tonight."

"'*Come, you spirits that tend on mortal thoughts, unsex me here!*'" Ezra shouts as Ms. Abramson rubs cold moisturizer onto my skin. It feels strange but somehow comforting, someone else's hands.

"Now—we've just got to wait for your skin to soak that up before we put on a little primer." She pronounces each makeup term phonetically, like she's revealing the word on the back of a foreign language flash card. "I thought you'd at least have a basic understanding from YouTube, but we can start at square one."

Soon, a layer of foundation makes my face feel wet. A fluff of powder drowns me in mystery. A pillowy brush sweeps against my eyelids. The pad of blush is soft and reassuring, but then a sharp pencil scratches my lower lashes. "Look up, Mark. Look up." The torture chamber of the eyelash curler. I get flush with an abstract anxiety about everything. This is risky. Too public. Go back to your bedroom.

But somewhere inside my mind, a brother who always knew just what to say notices my nerves. *That Shakespeare-quoting boyfriend is onto something, bud. You're not doing anything they weren't doing in the 1600s.*

Ezra can't stop smiling. Ms. Abramson beams at her handi-work. "Are you ready to take a look?" she says, just as she poofs me with a loofah-sized bunny-tail of magic dust that makes me feel like I just came out of a genie lamp.

She steps out of the way.

The powder fog lifts, and I see myself in the mirror for the first time.

It's like staring into one of those backstage mirrors for movie stars, with the big round light bulbs all around the border. Ezra's house doesn't have a mirror like that, but that's how I feel on the inside—lit up. Like myself, but brighter.

"Oh my God," I say, surprised.

"You look so good, right?" Ms. Abramson calls back.

"I'm . . . *pretty*."

"Ugh, pretty girls are always so self-obsessed," Ezra teases as he moves to stand behind me.

His chin rests on my head and our eyes meet in the mirror. He wraps his arms around me and leans in for a kiss.

"Hey, don't mess up his makeup." Ms. Abramson pulls him away. "Or *her* makeup. Or *their* makeup."

"Indeed, Mark. Not only does the Ambrose/Abramson house-hold have more shades of blush than a Sephora, but we also proudly have on display all your pronoun options for the evening."

". . . or for-ever," Ms. Abramson corrects.

I smile into my smile and Ezra disobeys his mother, runs around my beauty stool, and steals a kiss.

"You see, Mark. Men cannot be trusted. This is exactly why I'm going to put this lipstick"——she holds up a silver tube——"and this lip gloss"——she holds up a pink tube——"in your purse for the evening. Just do little touch-ups throughout the night. Lipstick first, then lip gloss. Just a little, each time Prince Charming here starts acting like a horny teenager."

"God, Mom. '*Horny*?' Please! Not in front of a princess."

"I forgot how fabulous this dress is," Ezra says as I shake out my costume from my backpack. He gently cups the extravagant puff. "It's as if a pair of football shoulder pads and a cumulus cloud had a gayby and fed it only Easter candy and purple Kool-Aid." He shakes my shoulders. "Here." He lowers the neck of the dress so I can step inside.

It feels less like I step into it and more like it floats onto me.

Even the zipper just glides up gracefully. I can never zip the back when I wear it in my bedroom, but tonight it's like heaven itself is pulling a string.

Is it clinically insane to say that the dress looks happy to be out of the house?

As I hold a long blond wig in my hands, I don't know why I'm scared. I should be excited. I used to wrap towels around my head in the bathroom as a little kid and then pretend I was brushing my long blond Barbie hair. And now I get to have long blond Barbie hair. Why am I nervous? I laugh at myself in the mirror. "Okay, here goes," I shout to Ezra.

I lower my head, wiggle into the elastic net inside the wig.

Then, dramatically, flip back my hair like a slow-motion mermaid.

The long strands softly slap my back.

The synthetic hair settles into a perfect part.

My eyes adjust.

I see someone new in the mirror.

Someone other than Mark the Sad Boy.

It's Mark the . . .

Not-as-Pretty-as-He-Thought-He'd-Be-with-Long-Blond-Hair Girl.

I laugh into the mirror and then gasp at Ezra when he turns back around in full costume. His double-breasted white jacket is trimmed with gold rope, the fringe on his military shoulder pads dangles down his arms, and his ghoulishly painted face makes him look even more handsome—his cheekbones more stark, his eyes more striking.

My childhood fantasies might have overestimated how pretty I would be, but they drastically underestimated how in love.

He gets down on one knee and holds up a strappy sandal stiletto like it's Cinderella's slipper. That's what the box said, *strappy sandal*, even though they don't look like sandals at all. When we found them at Designer Shoe Warehouse—"*If you're new to heels, stick to open toe,*" some random website told me—I quietly turned to Ezra and asked with nervous eyes, "Don't you think fluffy feathers with the puffy sleeves is maybe going to be too much?" His smile settles it once and for all: In good relationships, you really don't have to worry about being too this or too that.

They *are* too much, which means they're perfect. I wobble

downstairs and we pose for the school formal picture we never got to take, his arm wrapped around my waist as we stand in front of his curved staircase.

A princess and his prince.

"Look how stunning we look," Ezra says as he shows me his phone.

"Ezra!" I look in awe, burst with glee. "How do you look *so* good so pale?" I beam, and then notice. "Wait, did you post it?"

"Indeed!"

"Wait, oh . . . can you not, actually?" I force out a smile.

"But you look incredible." He almost hops with enthusiasm.

"Ezra, I'm not kidding. Please take it down."

"Mark, why? It's perfect."

"I know, but it's just . . . This is online. You don't even care about that stuff. Just, please take it down."

"If we went as two shirtless gladiators, would you let me keep it up?"

"Ezra, I'm sorry, can we talk about it later? Every second it stays up is a second closer to my parents seeing it."

"So what if they do?"

"I just . . . it's not exactly the ideal time for me to be throwing new things out there. Can we . . . it's about to be a perfect night, so can we not spoil it with this?"

He deletes it. He doesn't look thrilled about it, but he deletes it. And as it disappears from the terrifyingly public stage of the World Wide Web, I give him a kiss that says *thank you* and *I'm sorry* and *I promise that's my last freak-out.*

In a ballroom as big as a football field, I dance with my Prince Charming.

The columns around the dance floor are splattered with blood. Bones hang from the gold-gilded ceiling like plastic stalactites. The chandelier above us looks straight from live-action *Beauty and the Beast*. We're technically in a temple, but it feels like a castle, and everywhere you spin, there twirls a dancing duo more glamorous than the last. Shirtless angels. Shirtless devils. Cleopatras and Egyptian princes. It's all so fancy, so city, so *adult*.

"We're gonna get arrested," I whisper to Ezra.

"Only if you can get arrested for being *fabulous*."

He spins me around and dips me on the dance floor.

I try to walk like a supermodel, but in my too-high heels, I waddle more like a penguin who's late for the bus.

The side rooms are full of spooky surprises, starting with a half-naked warlock stirring a bubbling cauldron. We skip his "Witch's Brew" and just wordlessly stare at the warlock's abs. They don't have abs at Winter Ball. We start walking to the next room, and then crack up when we both, at the same time, crane our necks trying to get another look at the abs.

"I wasn't looking. *You* were!" I giggle, then waddle ahead.

The next is a pitch-black room that feels like nothing at all. Just an empty black cube.

"Maybe it's on break, this one?" I suggest.

Then, out of nowhere, dozens of hands start grabbing at us

from every corner, like a very scary car wash, grabbing our ankles and our costumes and even my flowing blond wig.

"I'm pretty sure that disembodied arm just got to second base," Ezra shouts as we run like nervous kids to the next room, where a sexy dragon lady sits surrounded by glow-in-the-dark snakes that, between their fangs, hold tiny glasses of "Toxic Shot Therapy." The room after has a bunch of dead people that you're supposed to walk over to reach a keg pumped by a hunchback, and the room after has a terrifying baby doll spewing pea soup spiked with CBD oil.

Ezra turns to me: "Let's go find more abs."

He runs ahead, holding my hand, and I shout for him to slow down, but he just goes faster and we both go crashing to the ground. My *crinoline*, as Ms. Abramson called it (this giant underwear-dress made of concentric hula hoops), breaks my fall, but my wig flies off and soars through the air like a Hail Mary, rocketing through spooky cobwebs and nearly getting stuck in the sparkling chandeliers.

Finally, it lands—right on top of Ezra.

I can say with 1000 percent certainty that I have never in my entire life laughed as hard as when I make eye contact with my ghoulish Prince Charming as he wipes now-bloodstained strands of synthetic blond hair out of his blacked-out eyes.

Our laughing fit becomes a cuddle puddle in the middle of the dance floor.

Suddenly, a Black Swan and a White Swan extend their wings to help us up.

"Girl!" the Black Swan shouts as he starts helping me up.

"Girl!" the White Swan shouts, louder. "*Baby Drag Queen Lost Her Damn Wig*." He says it like a news headline.

"I know you are not out here livin' your full fish fantasy when your six-feet-under little *boy*friend here *draaags* your little bitty drag ass to the *floor*." They laugh almost as hard as we do.

"Was that a death drop or did you just drop dead?" White Swan asks.

"We saw it all. We saw it before you saw it. A premonition. I got two words for you, lil' princess: *Wig. Glue.*

"Yes, you are now attending the first class of Swan Lake Drag U. The first hit's free, but the rest'll cost you." He looks down at me, but I just look confused. "Awww, belle of the ball's just a toddler in a tiara."

Ezra and I can't stop cracking up long enough to say thank you to the Swans for helping us up. Just as we're about to pull it together, Ezra points to the stage, where a shirtless hunchback sings a love song to a bat.

"Look!" Ezra shouts. "*More abs!*"

I lose it all over again, falling back to the floor barely a second after White Swan finished straightening out my wig.

"Okay, Queen," White Swan says as he helps me up. "*Fi-shy!* Let them *have* it, mama!"

"Your waist's not even cinched and you're cinched for the gods. Giving me life and turning this party *out*, with your Dennis-the-Menace-Disney-Princess realness."

✧   ✧   ✧

The White Swan turns to us when we all duck off the dance floor to catch our breath. "We actually *hate* Halloween." Then the Black Swan continues, like they're two halves of the same brain. "It's like, fuck it. If you wanna dress like a sexy bunny rabbit, why do you have to wait for the societally approved day to do it?"

"Just dress like a sexy bunny rabbit!"

"*Hey! Happy Tuesday! I'm a sexy bunny rabbit!*"

"But we never let politics get in the way of a good party."

They both gesture, in unison, to an opulent chandelier with a dead body hanging from it.

"We're having a not-costumes costume party next weekend if you two want to join."

"Baby, they're *twelve*."

"Be a sexy bunny rabbit. Be whatever you want. Just don't be boring."

A *not-costumes costume party* is all I can think about for the next hour. Halloween is perfect. So perfect I need to invent a word better than perfect. So why not keep the costume on?

Yes, I think, maybe I could just live forever in this fantasy where I am a princess and my pale prince twirls me in a ballroom and two tall swans celebrate us in a foreign language. Where the goblins are sexy and the witches are stoned and not a single person asks me how my mom is doing. No one in the crowd looks at me with sad, sympathetic eyes, and none of them even know that they're supposed to feel bad for me. They just dance and call me pretty, even though I know for a fact that in this wig I sort of look like a horse.

I twirl, my dress spins, and as I feel the wind in my *crinoline*, it's the happiest I've been in a very long time.

Two terrifying clowns join me and Ezra on the dance floor. We dance and we jump and the clowns are way more wild than the Swans, and the taller more terrifying one starts grabbing my butt when suddenly, out of the corner of my eye, I—*is that possible?*—see a giant potato in a red bikini roly-poly-ing across the dance floor.

"Ezra." I stare, jaw dropped. "Is that a sexy potato?"

Horace and Benjamin Find a Sexy Potato

"**C**rystal!" I shout, and start running before the shout is even out, as fast as my strappy sandals can handle, over the dance floor and through the wolves, past muscular Red Riding Hoods and gyrating corpses and a group of guys who look like dead first ladies.

Out of breath, I put my hand on the shoulder of the sexy potato.

Before Crystal turns around, someone shakes me by my puffy sleeves, too vigorously, perhaps not aware that feathery stilettos are not the most stable foundation. I topple over, but just as suddenly, two strong arms cradle me steady, and I find that I've just fallen into the arms of a sexy firefighter.

"What is *happening*?" I shout as our burlap and tulle and elastic red suspenders mingle in a triumphant hug.

"Someone called me daddy!" Damien shouts as he looks back into the chaos of the dance floor.

"Someone is enjoying the attention." Crystal rolls her eyes.

"What are you guys even *doing* here?" I ask, and suddenly a thought hits me: They still go out, without me. Obviously. They leave the pathological griever at home and have fun.

But then an even more uncomfortable thought hits me: I still go out, without them. Leeching off their sympathy and then going to gay-las with my gay boyfriend.

Damien reaches behind me and grabs Ezra by his gold-trimmed shoulders. "Benjamin Kelley invited us," he says through a wide smile.

Ezra beams, proud. "How do you think I knew how to get fake IDs," Ezra asks, and the three of them huddle around each other and smile as a single unit.

I beam. "We haven't all four been togeth—" I cut myself off. *Since my brother's funeral* is not a thing to shout on a dance floor. Tonight is the inaugural Ball for the Happy Memories Only Club. Tonight is perfect, and I'm determined to keep it that way.

Damien slaps Ezra's ass like a football coach. "Now let's. Fucking. Dance!"

"I'm sorry!" Damien shouts over the crazy loud music.

"What?" Crystal shouts back.

"I'm sorry!" he shouts again.

A drunk dragon bumps into our dance circle.

Damien's drunker than the dragon, so he falls into Ezra.

My bloody prince holds him up.

"How am I the one in heels and you're the one falling over?" I tease Damien as I fluff my tulle.

"Have some." He pulls out a flask from inside one of Crystal's potato pillows, hands it to me.

"I'm good." I push it away. Not ready yet. Maybe never will be. Trying not to think about it.

"To who?" Crystal shouts back.

Damien leans forward, bisecting our dance circle. "I'm sorry to you!" The music is so loud.

"Huh?" She shakes her head.

"I'm *sorrrrrry*!" he shouts.

"You're *druuuuunk*!" she shouts.

"You can be drunk and sorry at the same time!" he shouts.

"Valid point," Ezra agrees.

"We are *out*!" I shout like a drunk aunt. "We are out! Together! Nobody's sorry!"

Damien's words blur together as he points to each of us, one by one, and recaps, "We're out. I'm sorry. You're hot." He falls into Ezra, gazes in his ghoulish royal eyes.

Crystal cracks up as she takes the flask away from him and puts it back under her potato boob. "Truth juice."

I nudge Ezra. "How do you feel about firefighters?"

"*Sexy* firefighters!" Damien clarifies as he manhandles his red suspenders. Everyone laughs. Damien scolds us. "A gentleman is free to sayyy 'nother gentleman is *hot*," he slurs. "Gentleman starts with *gentle*."

Ezra smiles, proud, leaning into me while asking Damien, "What are you sorry about?"

"Nobody's sorry about anything," I cut in. "Why are we not dancing anymore?" I motion for everyone to get moving.

"I'm sorry I wasn't a better friend," Damien shouts, right to

Crystal. The music is so loud. Damien's louder. "I could have been a better friend."

"It's fine." She brushes it off. "You're drunk."

"Yes: drunk. No: fine."

No one is dancing.

"I've wanted to say it forever," he continues. "I coulda been a better friend."

I interject, cheerily, "But look at us now!"

"I could have, too," Crystal says, like she's relieved to finally say it. Like she's instantly lighter, somehow.

Damien builds on his point. "I could have asked what's up more," he continues. "You know? Could have *really* asked."

"I could have answered," she yells, thoughtfully.

I fidget with the tulle of my ball gown, squeezing it in my fists.

"Well then, *what's up?*" Damien asks, testing the theory. "How's Driggs."

"Fine."

He gets closer, squeezes her pillows. "*What. Is. Up?*"

"Actually, no, it fucking sucks." She laughs. "I don't know. I have friends, so it's not that. But it's like, Layla Yousef was really fucking on something when she said it was better." Her laugh grows on itself. "I just didn't want to bugggg you guys!" She wiggles her pillows a bit, dancing silly but looking serious. "Plus, it just felt weird. Different, you know?"

"Yes!" It shoots out of Damien like a cannonball. "Like, *heyyy, how's schooool.*"

"Yeah, like you're my fucking *dad*." She cracks up. "Awkward!"

I laugh, too, but feel somehow excluded. I'm sorry, too, I want to shout. I am, really. Have been! But now it feels like I'd just be saying it because they said it. And it feels like the moment has passed, and the conversation is transitioning back to happy stuff. I can't just shout *I'm sorry* when they're now talking about happy stuff.

Crystal adjusts her giant red bikini and pulls me, Damien, and Ezra into a group hug. "I'm sorry!" she shouts like a celebration.

The DJ screams an announcement and someone blows an air horn.

"Well, I'm not sorry to you." Crystal points to Ezra, correcting herself. "I didn't do any fucking thing to you!" She says it with love, and keeps looking at him. "Oooh, I'm sorry I didn't notice your little chest hair before!" She rubs right between his shirt buttons. "Damien, you were right!"

"You didn't do anything to any of us!" I correct Crystal's earlier point.

"We're just being sorry right now, okay?" Damien puts his arm around me. "Let us be sorry." He taps me on the top of my wig.

A drunk dominatrix gets a buckle stuck in my tulle. "Oh, sorry." He awkwardly unhooks himself and walks away.

"WE'RE SORRY, TOO!" Damien screams back.

The drunk dominatrix has no idea what's going on.

Damien notices an outside patio. "Is it weird that I want a cigarette?"

"If *anyone* needs a cigarette . . ." Crystal watches him push through the crowd, when he suddenly turns back and grabs Ezra by his yellow prince jacket. Ezra lifts his eyebrows as he gets dragged to the smoking patio. "Just say no, Prince Charming!" Crystal shouts after him.

"Should I be worried?" I ask Crystal.

She leans deeper against me, the fabric of my fluffy sleeves flattening against her smooshed pillows. We walk off the dance floor as a single unit, and the room seems to quiet. I lean against the brick wall, grateful for a break.

"I love you," I say into the sudden silence, and it sounds like I'm sorry.

She looks deep into my eyes, holds my heart in her gaze.

"I love you, too, fuckin' weirdo." She smiles, and says it like a compliment.

"I'm sorry, too."

"Okay, Damien."

"I am. I just. I don't know. I feel bad about how, like, things aren't the same."

"It's not your *fault*. I'm the one who got kicked out of fucking school."

From outside, Damien waves us over with more energy than ever. "Come! Out!" he mouths, so close to the door his breath fogs the glass. I give him eyes that say, *In a second.*

I have an almost irresistible impulse to say something positive. *Well, we're not in school now; let's dance!* But I don't.

"Was it grades?" I ask.

"Grades didn't help."

I feel like I'm prying. But it also feels like she wants to talk. "It was so abrupt."

She plays with the strands of my synthetic hair, now bloody from Ezra's makeup.

"I might have called Mrs. Stabinsky a bitch," she reveals.

"What?" I can't help but laugh. "Why?"

Crystal smiles into her pillows. "Because she was being a bitch."

"Oh my God, Crystal." I look shocked.

"This is why I didn't tell you."

"Well—" I defend myself through a wide smile. "You can't call a teacher a bitch."

"That I have since learned," she says in a reflective tone.

"Well, what did she do?"

"Exactly!" she shouts, like I answered something rather than asked something. She playfully twists my wig around so the back part covers my eyes. "Did anybody ask what Mrs. Stabinsky called *me*?" I part the hair so I can see her. "What did *she* do. They can treat us however they want, and if we do *one* thing in response . . . Isn't it their *job* to teach us? Like, if we can't figure it out, it's not just our fault. I was honestly trying." Her voice gets small. "But once they think you're a bad kid, nothing you *ever* do . . ." She lets the thought trail off. "And then she called on me when she *knew* I didn't know the answer. She made me stand up in class and admit that I was a fucking idiot in front of everyone because I didn't know the answer." She twists my wig back to its normal position. "Not that I care."

I squeeze her shoulder, pull her closer. "You know what?" I ask.

"What?" She flattens the pillow around her legs. She looks angry all over again, but also a little embarrassed, like she's right back in that classroom.

"Mrs. Stabinsky's a *bitch*!" I scream it up to the spooky chandelier.

Crystal leans into me. "See, this is why they send the bad kids to Driggs." She squeezes my hand and smiles. "We corrupt the good ones."

"My life would suck without your corruption," I say, too serious.

Damien pounds on the window and screams even more emphatically.

"Speaking of corrupt," Crystal says. "Imagine Mrs. Stabinsky finds out Damien Cole gets drunker than Crystal Myers." She grabs my hand, helps me balance.

"Her brain would literally explode."

Crystal hustles over to a very chunky blood splatter on the wall. "Mrs. Stabinsky?" she shouts into the wall. "Is that *you*?!"

I walk over, laughing, but still too serious. "I love you."

As we lean against Mrs. Stabinsky's splattered brain, the party swells around us, and for a moment, we just *be*, together.

"So school isn't going great?" I ask.

"Okay, we don't have to talk about *all the awful things right in a row*." She breaks into a run and pulls me toward the patio. And as I trail behind her flapping bikini straps, I hear a voice, as clear as if he were standing next to me. "*Don't just stare into the void*," Eric told me once when I was having a stupidly hard time moving forward. "*Go out there and make something new.*"

New doesn't just happen to you, I think he meant. You've got to go out there and make it.

A giant bouncer dressed in all black stamps the inside of our wrists as a burst of cold air makes my leg hair tingle.

"Thanks for asking, by the way," Crystal says, almost a whisper.

Ezra grabs my hand and lifts it high into the Detroit night sky. "Give us a twirl, Princess." I step under. The music is loud enough to feel full blast even outside, and in the thin mist of other people's cigarettes, I twirl. My dress spins, and a potato in a bathing suit booty-bumps my boyfriend while a sexy firefighter grinds against a metal barricade.

I feel the wind in my *crinoline*, and it feels like something new.

Grief Counseling Session #37

"**W**alk me through the day he died."

"I really, really don't want to do that again."

"Walk me through what you remember, Mark. There *is* a productive way to reexamine the trauma of his death, but effective regrief therapy involves staying in the truth of the event."

I say nothing, just hold the piece of paper that derailed this regrief hellhole in the first place.

"What does all this Googling about alcohol poisoning accomplish, Mark?"

"It's not just *Googling*, I actually went to the library, okay? I just want to know what we could have done. I don't think that's actually a crazy impulse, to want to know what we could have done to save my brother's life. And you're a doctor, so I actually thought you'd think it was—" I unfold the photocopied chart of blood alcohol level. "I couldn't find the expanded one online, but the library had this one that was randomly published by the Wyoming government or something. But see"—I trace my fingers along the squares—"I don't know what his weight was on that day, exactly, but if it was between one sixty and one seventy, then he would've had . . . would've had to have had between eighteen to nineteen drinks to get to a .415 BAC. But on this chart, .41 is like, *right* at the edge of death. Underneath it, .39, is just called 'Legally Intoxicated, Criminal Penalties.' But then you get above .40 and it becomes 'Possible Coma or Death from Respiratory Paralysis.' So that means that if even *one* of his friends had asked him to walk them home, or if someone would have noticed that he was slurring his words. This other thing said that caffeine sort of, like, masks the warning signs. So maybe, if he would've had less caffeine that day. Maybe he had a Red Bull." I lean forward. "Or just think about. If I would have FaceTimed him around drink twelve, he might have been talking to me instead of drinking two of those drinks, and then he would have stopped drinking at sixteen or seventeen, which would have put him at .37 or .39, depending on how much he weighed, which is *below* the death line on the chart."

Dr. Amato says nothing.

"I know you think this is crazy."

"It's not crazy, Mark."

"Well, okay, I know you don't like that word. But I'm just trying to prove to you how *close* it was. Point-four-one is the lowest end of the death part of that chart. It's *right* where the colors turn red. *Just* on the other side of it, like, .39 and below—which is basically one drink different, for someone around one hundred sixty pounds—is orange, not red, and that's just, ya know, the medical color for crazy drunk. Not dead. So, it's not crazy. I'm just trying to show you how close it was."

"And what does that do for you, having that information?"

"It just, you know—it didn't necessarily have to happen. It was really close."

"But it did happen."

"Yeah, but it was really close to not happening."

Dr. Amato says nothing.

"I know you're not saying anything so that I just, like, sit here and let my own craziness wash over me. But it's helpful, okay? I don't know why, but there's a lot of stuff that's helpful even if we don't know why."

"I don't think it's helping you, Mark."

"I don't think you are, either."

Searching for the Swans

Party City looks like a Walmart going to a Lady Gaga concert. I push through the revolving door and the whole store smells like the inside of a rubber mask. "I bet if we lived on Avenue A, we wouldn't have to get our wigs at Party City."

"This reminds me of our first date," Ezra says with a wink as he holds up a clearance-sale banner telling us to *Make it a BOO-tiful Day!* "Something tells me this still won't sell."

"Stay focused," I tell him. "We need a dress your mom would be proud of—"

"—without exceeding the ten dollars your dad gave you for Noodles & Co."

"Nobody said it'd be easy."

"It will be easy." He smiles. "You, my princess, would look *boo-tiful* in a paper bag."

"Excuse me," I say bashfully, to a half-vacant employee restocking Thanksgiving-themed plastic silverware.

Ezra bursts forward to ask, "Do you have pretty, pretty princess dresses?"

"Huh?"

"Sorry." I pull Ezra back. "We're just wondering what aisle the girl costumes are in?"

"Oh, whatever we have left would be in aisle four," he says, with a floppy hand gesture that vaguely directs us to the middle of the store.

"We don't even know where they live," I remind Ezra. "We don't even know their names!" I have devoted half my life to figuring out how to contact the Swans. I even found some *Gay Detroit* blog and looked at *every* photo; I went to all the social media pages of all the gay bars in Ferndale, hoping for just one tagged Swan. Nothing.

"Well, we'll just throw our own *not-costumes costume* party. I'm certain Damien and Crystal will join us again."

I pull out my phone as we power walk to aisle four. Before I restart my search, I'm distracted by a post from our school newspaper. "Take a look at our annual roundup of AHS's spookiest, scariest, funniest, and even fiercest Halloween costumes. #AHSChariot #ColtsInCostume #AHSdoesitbest."

I walk with my head in my phone. It feels like scrolling back in time. Half the pictures are from the party I would have gone to any other year: Haley and Beth as ketchup and mustard, Norris and André as hot dogs. Of course John is in the roundup—all the lacrosse players went as dead lacrosse players. Then some sophomores as the cast of *Mean Girls*, two freshmen as Peter Pan and Tinkerbell, and . . .

"We don't have time for you to fall down an internet black hole," Ezra warns.

No.

DAN CLAY ✦ 317

Impossible.

I swipe back to the start of the pictures and then go again to the last one.

How?

"Hey, didn't you delete that picture?"

"What picture? Come on, get off your phone. Pretend Dr. Cook is here."

"From Halloween. Ezra, I know it's not a big deal to you, but it *is* a big deal to me. Okay?" I stop walking.

"What are you talking about?"

"I told you not to."

"Mark, what are you talking about?"

"It's the picture *you* took, and it's on *their* page, so unless Buster emailed it to them—" I can see my face in the reflective silver of one of the dozens of helium birthday balloons floating above us. I can see my angry face starting to yell at a boy who spends half his life trying to make me less sad.

I stop walking.

People tell you to "be yourself," but I count about a thousand different selves. And some of them are selfish and scared. There's the me who ghosts Ezra after a perfect first kiss and the me who picks the firefighter instead of the princess. There's the me who lies to Ezra at Christmas and the me who abandons DIY Winter Ball to smoke cigarettes behind the dumpster at Walgreens and the me who can turn a trip to Party City into something I have to apologize for.

"Sorry, sorry," I backtrack.

I take a breath, try to sort of explain.

With a giant smiling unicorn balloon floating above my head,

I tell him I get scared sometimes. Scared that *I'm* what's left for my parents. I tell him more about my dad. How disappointed he always looked after my soccer games, how his highest praise always went to Eric, always for sports stuff. That fucking talent show. And I tell him my dad's amazing, but that I think the more out-there gay stuff freaks him out. Mom, too, probably, in her own way. And then *I* get freaked out.

An older woman squeezes past us to pick out a mermaid birthday balloon and Ezra looks at me with the face of Dr. Amato.

People never talk about how selfish grief can feel. It's so consuming, and of course the people around you can't *say* anything. So I say something—*I'm sorry, I love you*—hand him a clear balloon with confetti inside, and ask him to race me to the girls' section.

Nothing's right. It's all too . . . *costumey*. Pocahontas and Princess Jasmine and Cleopatra and a sexy nurse. Captain Marvel, Little Bo Peep, Little Old Lady, and Sexy Referee.

"You know we don't *have* to get your dress at a costume store," Ezra says as he holds up an uninspiring adult Pikachu costume. "We could go to Nordstrom or something."

"I can't shop for a dress at Nordstrom's."

"Nord*strom*. No *s*."

I roll my eyes. "I can't shop for a dress at Nord*strom*."

"Why not?"

"I don't know, it's for . . . real girls. I'm more of a Party City girl."

"You could bring the party to Nordstrom."

"You can't even buy shoelaces at Nordstrom for ten dollars."

As I hold up a very wrong slutty cat costume, I start to see his point. But I don't know—there just seems something more extreme about wearing a dress that isn't considered a costume. It feels more like a *statement* if it's not sold in a bag that tells the world you're just messing around. *Don't worry, folks. This isn't a boy in a dress. It's a boy in a costume. Stand down!*

"Wait, Mark," Ezra shouts, crouched down in the corner of the aisle, reaching behind a braided "Rasta" wig. "Come look."

And there, stuffed into a see-through envelope no bigger than an iPad, gleaming like that green light must have glowed for Gatsby: the Adult Gatsby Flapper Costume.

Dark blue sequins striped with black velvet.

A matching sequined headband that glitters under the fluorescent lights.

Included: fishnet stockings (!) and a costume cigarette holder.

Laced with so much fringe it could get a job as that final spinny part of a Jax Kar Wash.

Ezra examines the price tag. "F. Scott Fitzgerald would be so pleased that his literary masterpiece is being used as an excuse to wear cheap fringe."

In line, I hide my screen from Ezra and immediately DM *The Chariot*.

I hate myself for doing it, but still have to do it.

Hey this is Mark Davis. I know this is random (and thank you for including us in your roundup!) but would you think I was totally crazy if I asked you to take down our picture? It's the last one.

It's just . . . I mean, I guess there's no other way to say this but I

don't want my dad to see me in a dress.

OMG! omgomg. I NEVER would have put it up

if I knew ur dad was homophobic like that.

I thought Lizzy asked u guys.

Or maybe she just screenshot.

No no—he's not homophobic. He's just . . .

I don't know, it'd just be simpler if you took it down.

I can't take your pic down without taking the whole

post down.

And it's getting a lot of likes. People really like it.

It's just . . . Could you repost without mine?

Oh I have an idea! Maybe I could block your dad?

I could block your mom, too. So she won't show him.

Or if they're divorced I won't block your mom.

(Sorry if they're divorced.)

And then there's the me who gets *The Chariot* to think my grieving parents are divorced homophobes.

I do us all a favor and put my phone away.

Two guys behind us in line hold sleeves of Solo cups. They're looking at me and Ezra the way you look at people when you don't want them to know that you're looking.

The taller one taps the shorter one on the arm and leans closer to his ear. "Nate, you sure you don't want to pick up a skirt before we go?"

They laugh, gently—more like an amused exhale. They look

no more dangerous than the guys I've been friends with since middle school. They probably have gay friends. They aren't even really laughing at me, per se. They're just laughing, simply, at the idea of a guy—a *real* guy, like Nate—dressing up like a girl.

I reach in my pocket for a piece of gum but then realize I'm already chewing one.

I move the dress from my left arm to my right and reach down to hold Ezra's hand. I lightly glide my thumb back and forth along Ezra's, tracing his thumb with mine.

Nate looks back, sees, and it feels like taking a stand.

Family

Every night, my family has the same routine, slipping into it like a pair of pajama pants. We eat dinner without the news on (no one really cares about current events anymore). Then, we eat bizarre flavors of ice cream. I think my mom has a hard time buying the flavors that Eric liked, and since Eric was pretty obsessed with ice cream, the only options left are things like Banana Caramel Cheesecake. Then, we watch sitcoms with generous laugh tracks and predictable plotlines. My parents used to like shows that tried to make you cry—hour-long dramas that were basically trauma porn. But I don't know . . . chefs probably don't come home and watch cooking shows.

I pass my dad the remote as he gets situated in his recliner.

You learn quickly that emptiness has weight. Even a spot as simple as the kitchen cupboards almost collapses under the weight of the emptiness. His favorite cup sits untouched for however many months it's been.

You learn quickly that silence screams. Every conversation has a hole that shouts louder than anyone's ever talked. Even a task as ordinary as hanging up your coat can sideswipe you with grief. I call them sadness land mines, and they're everywhere.

As I try to avoid them, I just wait.

Wait for my dad to say something about the Halloween picture.

Wait for him to find a wig.

Wait for me to make his life worse than it already is.

Or Something

I hold the dress up. It's a teal V-neck maxi dress with spaghetti straps and a high slit. It's beautiful and perfect and feels like holding a shooting star.

Through the mirror I see the TJ Maxx employee staring at me. Her eyebrows arch and her head retracts, like someone who's just tasted something disgusting, or an angry turtle.

"It's stunning," Ezra says too loud.

I give him my mom's patented *quiet down* eyes, say, hurriedly, "I don't think it'll fit, let's just go."

I can feel her still looking at me. Folding shirts and staring.

Crystal notices her, too, turns to me like she'd fight if we had to. "Who the fuck cares."

The fluorescent lights buzz above us.

I do.

Maybe if last year's lunchroom personality transplant had been successful, I wouldn't, but I care.

It's too real. A *real* dress? And I'm just consumed with a thought of, *What are you even doing?*

"Sorry, let's just go." The hangers squeak on the metal rod as I squeeze the maxi dress back in.

Damien strides over, arms extended, boldly displaying a very feminine flowery sundress. "Do you think this would look good on me?" he asks, full voice. The lady stares at him, too.

"Actually, yes, Damien." Crystal tugs at the edges. "I think it would really bring out your ears."

"Ezra," Damien calls, holding up a short black dress with silver sparkles on the sleeves. "Let me just get a peek how this might look on you." He holds it up as Ezra poses. "Just as I suspected!" Damien says, not loud but not quiet. "You do have the clavicle for it."

Crystal comes over with a Carhartt flannel from the men's department. "Yes? No?"

"Two thumbs *way* up," Damien says.

He turns back to me. "Okay, so—the flowery one for me, the black one for Ezra, the flannel for Crystal"—he grabs my dress back from the rack—"and the blue one for you."

"*Teal*," Ezra corrects.

"The *teal* one." He hands it to me. "Mark, how much money do you have?"

"Fifteen dollars," I say. He knows how much money I have.

Damien looks at the price tags. The angry turtle has long since moved on with her life. "Damn. Guess we only have enough for the teal one."

"But I . . . ," Crystal pleads, theatrically, as she puts her flannel back.

I roll my eyes, and with courage on loan from an invincible heterosexual, I take my teal dress to the checkout counter.

At home, I stand, beaming, in front of my full-length mirror.

"You're welcome," Damien says with pride.

"The world's first episode of *Straight Eye for the Queer Guy*," Ezra shouts.

"What a bitch," Crystal reflects.

"She was barely even looking at us," Damien downplays. "She probably just thought we were gonna steal."

"I bet she masturbates to conversion camp testimonials."

I stare at Crystal and laugh so hard I almost bust my maxi dress. "You are not right in the head."

Damien meets my eyes in the mirror. "What are you thinking, *mannn*?" There's weight to the question.

I inhale. "I'm thinking I kind of like wearing dresses"—I sit on my bed and bunch the long part in my hands—"*mannn*."

"Ya *think*?" Crystal says with a tone of obviousness that makes me feel like an idiot. But an idiot with a cute boyfriend and a very supportive costume department.

"Well, I don't know. I thought maybe it was a phase."

"Oh, the things I've thought were *phases*." Ezra smiles. "What are you thinking? Dresses for all occasions? For some? For fun?"

"I don't really *know*—but I don't think dresses for all. But yeah, dresses for fun. Or some. Ya know. Like, drag, or something."

"*Or something*," Ezra mimics. "Drag is for divas! No room for 'or something.'"

"You want more *diva*?" I shout, and throw my dress off my

body and on top of Ezra's head, and then I hit him with my fiercest death drop—jumping up and bending one knee back while pirouetting my arms in the air. However, I end up back-flopping into my desk and catching my hand on Damien's backpack strap, and his tombstone-sized physics book catapults through the air and body-slams my nose.

They look at me, lying on the floor, pretzel-twisted like the roughed-up loser in a game of full-contact Twister. "So, Diva," Crystal asks. "What's your name?"

"Oh, right," I say, suddenly nervous as I contemplate introducing this character to the outside world (where, I have no idea, but you can't be a drag queen from your bedroom).

"Something fabulous. Something fit for a queen." Ezra looks up and scans his mind for relevant references. He scans the room for clues, prompts, pausing on posters, medals, resting his eyes on old souvenirs. He looks so cute when he's thinking. "How about Angel? You love Angel. From Avenue A. Every day is *your* lucky day."

I laugh as I stand back up. It's perfect.

Except for one thing. "But Angel's Angel. I'm not Angel."

"Angel's Angel. Indeed," he says, a bit dejected but not deterred. "Something more original, something more *you*. What are you? You're wonderful. You're sweet. You're . . . you're . . . you're so kissable." He leans in and tests his theory. The kiss starts sweet and segues somewhere steamier. "You're distracting."

"Okay, lovebirds." Damien puts his physics book back in his bag.

"I like naming drag queens." I smile and pull myself into Ezra. "Let's name drag queens all day."

"Stay on task, dudes," Damien scolds. "What's your name? Brainstorm! Go."

Ezra takes the lead: "Queens . . . fierce . . . Trixie! Katya! . . . fabulous . . . divas. Britney. Whitney. Ariana! Rihanna. Umbrella-ella. *Please welcome to the stage: Ummm Brella!* MadonnaMariah-ChristinaSelenaCeline!"

"Hairy-anna Grande."

"Except you're the least hairy anna on the planet."

"Touché," I say.

"Touché! That's good. That's *good*." Ezra beams. "Touché . . . Touché Larue. *Please welcome to the stage*: Touché Laruuuuuuue."

"What does it even mean?"

Ezra, animated: "It means . . . innuendo. Wink-wink. Camp. Sontag. Look. Up on the stage. Is that a man? A woman? Why choose? Touché."

Damien, out of nowhere: "Mayaaaa Pinion!"

I laugh at the cumulative absurdity of our task.

I pause and take in my room, my mirror, my friends.

I look at Ezra, then back at Crystal and Damien.

I make a feeble suggestion. "What about Mark?"

"Mark?"

"Yeah."

"Mark the Drag Queen?"

"Yeah."

Ezra's skeptical. "Well, I don't know if it has enough . . . pizzazz." He switches into his dramatic announcer voice. 'Please welcome to the stage: Mark." It lands with a thud.

Damien tries, "Mark the Drag Queen."

"Yeah, it's dumb."

Ezra nudges my shoulder with his. "Needs more pizzazz, babe."

The tree outside my window sits perfectly still. There's no wind, so the leaves don't rustle, and the tree sits so still it looks like it's listening.

"Mark," Crystal repeats gently, sweetly, testing it in the protected air of my boyhood bedroom. The name bounces off my soccer ball pillow, bumps against the posters for all the musicals I wish I could have seen, ricochets between the gold-plated participation trophies for all the sports I never wanted to play, and finally sneaks out the window and whispers itself to the windless afternoon. The tree rustles, almost in agreement.

"I just think . . . it's me. I'm me. Mark. And so is she." I touch the dress.

"Mark." Ezra says it like a full sentence. Reassuring. Complete, on its own.

I smile.

Damien looks apprehensive. "Well, you'll have to bring a lot of pizzazz."

A Walk

Thanksgiving is impossible. Hanging up Eric's ornaments is . . . as sad as the saddest day. But you have advance warning for stuff like that. You can't really prepare yourself, but you do know it's coming. It's the random days that are the hardest, when the sadness steamrolls you out of nowhere.

I bought a bright yellow notebook to concept things out for the talent show eulogy. Song options. A monologue? Maybe a monologue. There are tons of monologues that would fit exactly. So I bought the notebook to keep track of different ideas.

But nothing's in it.

I spend all my free time thinking about it but have absolutely nothing to show for it. Just balls of crumpled college-ruled paper and a yellow notebook getting thinner by the day.

Some unremarkable night in mid-December, my dad turns on the TV and starts entering the numbers for *Wheel of Fortune*.

I take a few dry Golden Grahams from my bowl and settle into the me-sized indentation on the right couch cushion.

My mom starts putting her slippers on.

Suddenly, she stands up.

"Let's go for a walk," she declares triumphantly, as if she'd just suggested we pack our bags and fly to Disney World.

"You know what?" my dad booms. "That's a great idea. Grab your shoes, Mark. Let's go. Get Duke's leash, too. *C'mon, Duke. Go for a walk?*"

I feel like I'm missing something. Is *walk* a code word for something more interesting and I wasn't on the family memo?

My shoes are flung on the carpet in front of the ottoman.

The spot where Eric so often and so easily used to wrestle me into submission.

They're Adidas.

"*A-di-DUH*," Eric once shouted, with a thwack on the back of my head, when, after the busted-up Miller Post-Homecoming Party, I asked him if my track jacket smelled like smoke.

My shoes have laces.

Which he taught me how to tie.

"*. . . then cross the bunny ears over each other . . .*"

I grab my shoes and all the ski gear I'll need to go for a mid-December walk in Michigan and try to think of nothing, try to avoid picking up the unbearable weight of the emptiness. Because my parents and I are going for a walk!

And we're all very excited about it!

"The Roths' lights sure look nice," my mom admires as we pass the house three doors down.

"That all white is so elegant," Dad says. "A real classy family."

For a moment it feels like we might not make the turn around the block and just keep on walking until we reach the elementary school. And then keep walking until we hit the high school. And then maybe we'd start running, and we'd Forrest Gump it all the way to a place where nothing reminds us of Eric.

"So how you doin', with the waiting?" my mom asks, referring to my outstanding early-decision college application. Admission decisions are released in "mid-December," perhaps the most excruciatingly vague time line ever.

"Pretty good, I guess. I suppose nobody likes playing the waiting game." It was a phrase I'd picked up from her.

"But you've gotta do it," Dad says.

"Yup. Gotta do it."

People still ask—not as regularly, but they still ask: *How's your family doing?*

Before Eric died, they'd ask it like, *Hey, Mark, how's your family doin'?*

But now: *How's your family doing?* I guess truncating suffixes disrespects the dead.

The question seems impossible to answer, because it assumes one family, before and after.

The same family, altered.

But actually it feels like our family died with Eric, and what's emerging is not a variation of the old family, but a whole new group of people who have to define themselves and their relationships all over again. It feels like we're tentative actors rehearsing new roles. Mother. Father. Son. Not getting too big with the characters until we really learn our lines.

It's like in chemistry. If you remove an atom from a molecule, it doesn't become less of that molecule, it becomes a totally different molecule. If you take an oxygen atom away from hydrogen peroxide (H_2O_2), it doesn't become *less* hydrogen peroxide, it becomes water (H_2O). When Salt (NaCl) loses Chlorine (Cl), it doesn't become less salty. It just becomes a bunch of sodium (Na) lying around. "New compounds have few or none of the physical or chemical traits of the original elements. They have a new life of their own," said my chemistry book, unaware it was being profound.

The next day, after a couple scoops of Black Raspberry Dark Chocolate Brownie Delight ice cream, we take another walk. My dad asks Tyler Murphy to toss him the ball. Tyler Murphy tosses him the ball. My mom suggests that it's probably time for the Uptons to clean their garage. "But I think they repainted their door, so that looks nice," she adds, to even the scales after her savage suburban diss.

The next day, we walk to TCBY instead of having ice cream at home. It's cold, but we walk. We all get Shivers. The metal machine whirs as it blends the toppings. M&M's into vanilla for me, gummy bears into chocolate for Dad, *nothing* into vanilla for Mom.

"Mom, that's not even a Shiver."

She replies patiently, "Well, I like how they shake it up."

When they ring us up, my dad just stands there.

"You're buyin', right, Marky Mark?"

It's possibly one of his all-time favorite jokes, a true classic in the Joe Davis repertoire.

But it's not annoying tonight.

We take our Shivers with us on our walk. A family of three plus a hyper golden retriever walking with cups of ice cream in December.

We never used to go for walks.

And yes, the house still feels heavy.

But outside, the air is light.

Senior Year

January

Grief Counseling Session #7,459

"**I** actually have a question for you this time, because I can't figure it out. I've been doing research on memories, how to keep them fresh, but Google doesn't understand what I mean. I either get stuff about improving your memory—like, where you put your keys—or I get stuff about how to keep memories *alive*, metaphorically. Through memorials and baking their favorite cupcakes on their birthday. Stupid stuff like that. What I want is, like, the *science* of it. How to keep your memories of someone sharp."

"Tell me about a memory you want to keep sharp."

"Well, I don't really want to."

Dr. Amato says nothing.

"I have this theory. You're probably gonna think this is crazy, too, but you remember your pinball thing? This is my refrigerator theory. The refrigerator-during-a-power-outage theory. When the power goes out, you're not supposed to open the refrigerator door because you want to keep the cold air trapped in there as long as you can. The more you open the refrigerator door, the faster the food will spoil."

"So you think, the more you conjure memories of your brother, the faster they will fade?"

"Whenever you repeat stuff in that voice, it *does* sound crazy."

"I don't think it's crazy."

"It makes sense. It's like a photocopy machine. First, you photocopy the original. And then you photocopy the photocopy. And then you photocopy the photocopied photocopy. Each one gets worse." I pause. "I used to think I was like a bad photocopy of my brother."

"In what way?"

"No. That wasn't what I meant. I want to keep talking about the memory stuff."

"You are right, in a way, that memories are delicate things prone to adjustment based on what we do with them when we, as you say, pull them out of the refrigerator. But in fact, the latest research on *engrams*—the idea that memories leave a physical imprint on the brain—reveals that the more we dwell on a memory, or rehearse the specific events surrounding the memory, the *stronger* these neuronal connections become.

"But due to neuroplasticity, each time we revisit a memory, we essentially 'rewire' it. 'Reimprint' it. We don't put the same thing back in the refrigerator." He smiles. "The memory changes, for better or worse, based on how we recall it, and then it resets—or *reconsolidates*—stronger and more vividly with every recall. So, each time you bring up the memory of your brother's death and associate that memory with *blame*, it gets reconsolidated and more strongly connected with blame, each and every time. But if we bring the memory up without blame or anger, over time, those associations will start to slip away. Furthermore—and this is at the heart of why, in our sessions, we are working to 'relive' grief alongside more positive associations—there is a field of research related to memory substitution or redirection, if you will. People can redirect their consciousness toward an alternative memory by using two regions called the caudal prefrontal cortex and the mid-ventrolateral prefrontal cortex. The goal is, when you think of your brother, that you don't pull out the few *bad* memories. Rather, you hear 'brother' and your brain reaches for the good memories. The grief will never go away, but he can live on with you, through joy."

The zen fountain bubbles.

I tilt my head.

"Were you seriously not going to tell me any of this stuff if I hadn't mentioned the refrigerator thing?"

"Tell me something good about your brother."

"I need a narrower category."

"You can narrow it."

I think. "He just—I don't know. He had this way of fixing shit." I start laughing. "Okay, so one time this real asshole, Bryan Patchett—like King Asshole—I was singing at the seventh-grade talent show and just as I'm getting to my big finish, Bryan Patchett screams at the top of his lungs, *'Fairy!'*

"I was almost more upset about how upset it made me than I was about the actual name. Who cares, ya know? Nobody even liked Bryan Patchett. But Eric heard about it, and he sat me down that night, like a friggin' dad, and said the best way to get back at people like that was to just sing even bolder the next time. And actually, the very next night I was singing the national anthem at the boys' basketball game, and Eric said, 'Bud, you sing straight to Patchett and hold *freeee* like you're fucking Pavarotti.'

"I swear, I held that note until halftime."

Dr. Amato nods.

"I also heard Eric got this giant linebacker from the high school football team to show up at Bryan Patchett's house and scare the shit out of him. So, you know, he was thorough."

The rare sight of Dr. Amato's smile.

I fidget in my seat. "He said it way better than how I just paraphrased. I wish I would have written it all down."

Dr. Amato tilts his head. "You still can."

A Yellow Spiral Notebook

I write and I write and I write.

In the empty yellow spiral notebook that was supposed to house eulogy concepts, I write down everything I can ever remember Eric saying. I open the refrigerator and hurl out every conversation—words about love, friendship, focus, regret, confusion, confidence, happiness, hope, fun, reaching for wisdom even in his tips on how to tell if produce is ripe.

It's a sort of freedom, but as it builds, it becomes heavy. Like guilt. The notebook weighted with every word. The hard press of my pen pushes through, denting new pages, making them all stick together and crackle when they turn.

A symbol of his wisdom suddenly becomes a symbol of something else.

I flip through all the pages.

My God. If asked to document how *I* helped *him*—could Eric have even filled a Post-It note?

If I would have thought once about *giving* help instead of just *getting* it, would . . . could . . . he could be twenty.

He *told* me he was not okay.

I asked him, and he shook his head no, and he *told me* he was not okay.

And I did nothing.

I was sixteen when he died. He was nineteen.

I'm seventeen now.

He's still nineteen.

The doorbell rings.

"Mark, honey, Ezra's here!"

He could be twenty.

Ezra leans his backpack against my dresser and sits on the floor against my bed. "What'd you do today?"

I can't remember.

I stare into his backpack, full of light, bearable notebooks.

"Ground control to Major Mark?" Ezra says into my empty eyes.

The first thing my grief counselor ever said to me, with pitying eyes that made me so angry I wanted to scream, was: "It's not your fault."

It didn't even register at the time.

The only reason anyone ever says *It's not your fault* is when they know it really is.

Ezra pats the carpet next to him. "Mark, what's wrong?"

I want so badly for nothing to be wrong.

I want so badly to be the boyfriend that Ezra deserves.

I want so badly to be alone—alone with my sadness, alone with my *fault*.

"I'm sorry," I say into the carpet. "Just, a heavy day, for some reason."

He gently rubs his thumb against the back of my hand. "Tell me."

"Sorry. No. Nothing major. I just, well, I just started this note-book, because of Dr. Amato, with all these . . . lessons, I guess, that my brother taught me. It's an exercise. And so I was kind of, *in it*, when you came in. Sorry." I squeeze his hands. "I'm ready to pep up now!" I squeeze out a smile. My body squeezes out a tear.

Ezra wipes my tear and traces his fingers toward my lips. "Am I allowed to read any of it?"

"Sure, yeah . . . Yes. Of course." I pass him the yellow note-book. "Might as well make the whole world sad."

"The groom and groom both wore sadness," he announces, as he starts flipping through, reading slowly with watery eyes. He smiles at the parts I remember being funny. He nods at the parts I remember being deep. He reads a few parts out loud. "This is beau-tiful, Mark: 'It's not about how it looks, it's about how it feels.' *Amen*. 'Be gentle. Too much pressure and you'll damage the soft parts inside.' Your brother really was wise beyond his years."

"Yeah, he was. But that part was actually just how to tell if an avocado is ripe."

He punches me on the shoulder. "Well, there's a metaphor in there somewhere." He rolls his eyes, but then gets serious again. "These are really good, Mark. Better than any self-help book I've ever seen."

I smile, for real this time. "Literally Eric's biggest dream."

I turn to Ezra and let him in. "I never helped him. That's what

I was thinking about when you got here. And I know you'll say there's nothing I could have done and I get that that's true, but it's also true that . . . I never helped him. He needed my help and I never helped him." Ezra closes the notebook and rubs my shoulder.

Eric was obsessed with helping people. Turned helping people into a competitive sport. "There was a girl who came up to me at the visitation, in this reddish-brown sundress with yellow sunflowers on it," I tell Ezra, "which I *loved*, because funerals are depressing enough without all the black. Anyway, she grabbed my hands, both of them, and asked, 'Can I tell you a story about your brother?' It was the first good question I'd gotten all day. And she did. And I don't even remember what she said, something about, she had braces, in history class, and he made her feel special . . . something *nothing* like that, but it was something to her. He helped her. He helped everyone." Think of how many people, if Eric was still alive . . .

Is it too late to help him?

Could I help him help people?

I start crying and I am so. sick. of. crying. I just want to do *something* other than cry.

Could I help him help people?

"Okay, you didn't come over here to cry!" I look over to my closet. Our Narnia.

And it's not just Narnia for the pathologically bereaved. Ezra, bored with prince jackets, actually came up with his own drag character named Ezra Pound-town, who is a lady in a neon wig and an old gray mustache who reads poetry while chasing me around the room and trying to hump me.

If it's possible, I love Ezra Pound-town as much as I love Ezra.

Damien and Crystal, too. We made a video where we pretended to be filming a very serious PSA for the benefits of drag.

ME: *Hi, I'm Mark the Queen, and drag saved me from pathological bereavement.*

(giggles off-camera)

EZRA, in a British accent: *Hi, I'm Ezra Pound-town, and drag saved me from my crippling condescension.*

CRYSTAL, in oversized overalls and a mustache borrowed from Ezra Pound-town, with a thick redneck accent: *Hi, I'm Chris Till. I used to say whatever was on my mind. But drag taught me how to control my emotions. Oh, by the way, Mrs. Stabinsk—*

DAMIEN, in a blue body-con dress and a hot-pink wig accidentally on backward: *It's recording.* With a worried whisper he shoulders Chris Till out of view, tugs his dress, and, in his drag voice (a deep voice even lower than his own), continues: *Hi, I'm Foxy Fierceness, and drag saved me from . . .* he adjusts his dress again, visibly uncomfortable *. . . dude, what do drag queens do with their balls?*

The video is on my phone. And whenever I get too sad, which is still a lot, I watch it. And for forty-seven seconds I'm something similar to happy.

Ezra and I cuddle up and just watch random stuff on my laptop, eventually landing on some cringey self-help-y videos by some stupidly hot internet guy. The next video autoplays. "Why are we watching this?" Ezra moans. "We could make better videos with my wigs and your brother's produce-picking tips."

I imitate an "influencer" speaking into their phone. *"Hey, guyyyys. So, lately I've been getting a lot of questions about courage. You know, my opinion is, and there are gonna be a lot of haters out there who disagree, but my opinion is that having courage starts with being courageous."*

"That's actually quite a profound existentialist concept."

"Stop being ashamed of your shame and dance like you're already dead!"

He knocks my phone onto my bed and plops his head on my chest. "New outfit?" He hops to my closet and changes into the gray suit I wore for my confirmation, pairing it with a neon-yellow wig and a red pair of heels. He tosses me a tutu and a sequin tank top—two truly gold mine finds at the Annondale Goodwill.

The other day I was trying to think: *What will I say to my parents when they inevitably find all the girl clothes I hide in my closet?* Dresses piled up like contraband vodka.

And then I tried to answer the question even for myself: What *am* I doing?

I kind of have no idea.

I'm trapped in this head that overanalyzes

every

little

thing

but when it comes to drag, my brain's on spring break.

Maybe even my own neurons take pity on the poor kid. *He's had a rough go these past few months, fellas. Let's leave him alone when he's trying to figure out how to apply fake eyelashes.*

I don't know. It's kind of like being drunk, actually, but not. It shuts my brain up. It's an escape from the real world. And also, like being drunk, it makes everything, even just sitting around in my bedroom, a lot more fun.

I turn to Ezra in my fluffy tutu and grip the fabric like a happy maniac.

He takes my picture.

"Hey! If that goes into my family iCloud I'm screwed."

"It won't and you wouldn't be," he counters. "You're not doing anything *wrong*, Mark."

"Well, whatever. You know what I mean." I prance over to him. "At least let me see the picture."

He rolls onto the bed and playfully taunts, "No. It's my picture. You didn't want me to take it." He curls up against the wall with his phone clutched to his chest.

I jump on him and wrap my arms around, jockeying for the phone. "Well, you *did* take it, so now let me see it."

"You can't hide your drag and see it, too." He shields his phone from me. "It's my picture."

"It's my . . . body," I counter.

"Correction." He spins and wraps his arms around me in a combative cuddle. "It's *my* body."

In his distracted passion, I snatch the phone and run over against my door. "Ha ha," I gloat. "Crap. What's your passcode?"

"Get back over here, homo." He switches to a peaceful repose and scoots over so we can share the pillow. We nestle into each other as naturally as a teacup into its saucer.

He opens his phone.

It's just a picture. It's just a picture of me in a tutu and a sequin tank top.

I don't even have a wig on.

But I'm happy.

And it's not the picture of a person who's escaping.

Maybe more like the picture of a person who is *so fully fucking activated*. And happy. Simple, silly, happy, and *freeee*. I don't know a lot, but I know that Eric would love it.

"Okay, so maybe *Mark* wouldn't do it," I start.

"Do what?" Ezra asks.

"Stupid internet videos."

"Oh. Got it. We're talking about ourselves in the third person now, are we?"

I laugh, and continue, "Maybe *I* wouldn't do it . . . but maybe MARK would?!" I hop off the bed onto the floor. The setting sun reflects in my sequin tank top and shines a small spotlight on Ezra's cheek, just above the crest of his smile.

"Are you suggesting the world needs to meet Mark the Drag Queen?"

"Maybe?" I plop down, cross-legged on the carpet. "Yeah, no. That's dumb. That's even further from reality."

"Who wants to live in reality?" He kicks his legs in the air, heels high.

"*Not-fucking-ME*!" I shout.

I consider it. "Internet videos where I dress up in drag and share wisdom from my dead brother?" I hold up the notebook. "I can see the view count clicking up now . . ."

Ezra waits.

Sometimes I think he and Dr. Amato have secret meetings about the power of the pause.

"I could tell people what he told me." I fill the silence, then doubt. "But what do I know about making videos?"

"You could learn."

"But if I talked, would I use a boy voice or a girl voice?"

"Your voice."

"But what does *drag* even have to do with my *brother*?"

This one I can answer myself. Almost everything he ever told me was about being my full self, and I'm 100 percent positive he'd be delighted by how full my *self* has become.

Ezra presses on my eyes with his, like his stare is the thumb on a ripe avocado. "I bet he'd think, *Man, my dude really came up!*"

I smile. "That's so not how he talked."

"Then show me how he talked."

Downstairs, the microwave beeps over the TV's blare.

Somewhere inside my head, a brother frozen at nineteen reminds me how he talked. *Be yourself! Your full sequin-y self.*

I turn to Ezra. "He always wanted to help people."

It all connects. Helping Eric help people.

I could live forever with the guilt of never having helped Eric, play back the past and consider how I could have done things differently—watch myself go from 17 to 18 to 19 to 20 while he stays 19, 19, 19, 19—and have the past completely devour my future.

Or I could try. I could try to help him now.

Lessons from My Brother
#1

We name the account Lessons from My Brother.

It's not videos. The question of *How would I talk?* turns out to be insurmountable. It's just pictures, and Eric's words. And the first picture is me in a $16.99 silver sequin spaghetti strap dress. A curly blond wig falls over my yellow notebook, and on my wrist is a gaudy pearl bracelet borrowed from Crystal's grandma.

I write, too much for a caption, using lots of words to find the right ones:

> Hi. I'm Mark. I can hardly walk in heels, and my friend Crystal does my makeup, and hopefully I'm better at writing than I am at drag, but this isn't really about me. It's about my brother. My brother was my whole world, and, a year ago today, he died. He drank too much and he died. I don't really know who I'm writing this to, if anyone, but maybe some of you can understand: One person left and the whole world went missing.

So today I'm wearing a glittery dress because I want the sparkle to come back. Cheesy, I know. However, I think Eric would want that, too, because that's the kind of guy my brother was.

But as my English teacher told me when we were prepping our college application essays: *Show, Don't Tell.* It's hard to pick the right story. I feel like I'm trying to describe how sunny the sun is. So I'll just pick a random one.

As background, I suck at sports. I try to avoid them, but that's pretty hard to do where I'm from. Neighborhood sports leagues really are a special kind of hell for the unathletic. Maybe you get it. Imagine the premise: Every Saturday, we're going to gather up every person you've ever met in your entire life and they're going to watch you do something you suck at. Come on! If you suck at singing, it's not like you have to sing a solo in front of your entire neighborhood every weekend. And if you suck at school, no sweat. Graded papers are handed back *upside down* and standardized test scores are sent out in a *password-protected email*. But swinging a baseball bat is center fucking stage? I'm not saying I want kids to get bullied for more things, but just once I'd like to toss Clinton Doil in front of the whole school and make him spell *pendulum*.

Anyway, that's more of a rant, and my English teacher would definitely take points away for rambling. But actually, that rambling kind of relates to the thing Eric was so good at. I've always felt like my own brain was trying to destroy me. Telling me all the reasons I suck. And one miserable Saturday in third grade, in my Annondale Dodgers uniform, I missed a very easy and VERY IMPORTANT fly ball. I can still hear the disappointed groan from the audience ringing in my ears. My teammates wouldn't even look at me after the game.

We were in *third grade*.

I know now that it was stupid, but at the time, it was a very big deal. The biggest deal. And I always cared too much about stuff like that, what people thought about me, that kind of thing. Still do. So I was in my bedroom, still in my muddy uniform, crying. Eric came in and I told him why.

I always told him everything.

I was sobbing into my baseball glove. He lifted my chin, looked me straight in the eyes, with so much love.

"You are the worst baseball player I've ever seen in my life."

I threw my baseball glove at his head, but he persisted.

"You're like, comically bad. I mean, really, Mark. So, so bad. Sometimes I look at you out there and think, 'I don't think I could be that bad if I *tried*.'"

"You're not *helping*!" I punched him in the arm, and I couldn't help but laugh because it was the opposite of the pep talk I was expecting.

"But you know what?" He locked my arm so I couldn't hit him anymore. "There's *tons* of stuff you're good at. Math!" he shouted, like a revelation. "Reading! Singing!"

He looked around my room for more ideas. "Taking care of your erasers!" (I had a novelty eraser collection. Yes, that's a thing. It's like I was *trying* to get made fun of.) I rammed him with my shoulder.

He concluded decisively. "YOU don't suck. You just suck at baseball."

It's not even that great of advice, I guess. Like, better advice would be "Keep trying!" or "Practice makes perfect!" or "Never let 'em see you sweat!"

But it was great advice for me.

Because I did think I sucked. At, like, a cellular level. And after talking to Eric, I didn't.

His words always helped me, so I thought maybe they'd help you, too, whoever you are. And if you think you suck—well, maybe you do. But probably not at everything.

And if you've got a mean baseball crowd living inside your head, then I hope you can find a way to swap that out with something a little nicer. Something that sounds more like my brother. #LessonsFromMyBrother

I read the caption one more time.

"Lessons from my brother . . . ," I reflect. "Told in a sequin spaghetti strap dress." I look at the picture. "It doesn't make any sense."

"Name one thing on the internet that makes sense."

"It won't even fit as a caption. It's, like, a novel."

"Email it to Mrs. Parsons, she can edit it."

I nudge him with my shoulder.

I stare at my phone. "I don't want it to look like I'm doing it for the likes and stuff. That I'm using my dead brother to get likes."

"No one will think that."

"I don't even wanna know about likes."

"Who's to say you have to look at them?"

"And if some stranger calls me a gay-faced fruit salad, I don't wanna know about that."

"I'll manage the account. I'll only tell you the good things."

"Yeah, but then I'll wonder about the bad things."

"I liked it better when I was in charge."

"Well. There's a new king in town." I hop up and shimmy in my tutu. "And he's a queen."

Lessons from My Brother
#2

The picture is me in a purple princess dress with puffy sleeves. I'm not smiling, but my eyes are, and in my left hand is my notebook, and on top of the notebook, barely visible but there, is my favorite picture of Eric. I printed it out from my phone. We didn't have photo paper, so it's just on regular paper. He's holding a bag of Swedish Fish from the concession stand at the aquatic center, and he's sticking his tongue out at the camera. It's summer, so he has freckles around his nose that you could count if you zoomed in close.

And the caption says this:

Today I'm wearing a dress that makes me very happy, because I want to talk about happiness. Now, I'm potentially a top contender for the saddest person on the planet, at least lately, but I learned something from my brother. And to be honest it didn't make any sense at all when I first heard it, but I somehow filed it away and it's starting to make sense now.

One of my happiest memories has to do with this dress. We were at our family's favorite diner when a little girl walked in wearing a purple princess dress with puffy sleeves. I was instantly obsessed, and with pleading eyes I turned to my older brother and asked, "When am I going to be a girl?!"

Now, I don't think I actually wanted to be a girl. I just wanted to kiss boys and wear pretty dresses, and my seven-year-old mind thought only girls could do that. So I wanted to know when, if ever, I was going to get to be a girl.

And Eric just looked at me, shoved a giant bite of sprinkles cake into his mouth, and said, "Whenever you want."

I love you, Eric. And for any of you wondering when you can become what you dream of becoming: Whenever you want. #LessonsFromMyBrother

Lessons from My Brother
#7

*H*appy isn't the word for what it makes me. And I learn over posts three, four, five, and six that some emotions just don't have words.

The seventh picture is me in a fluffy tutu and a bright blue tank top that has metal studs like a bra outline. We got it at Hot Topic in the discount bin and it's all *a lot*. I'm looking in the camera trying to look tough, but I don't look tough. I look like a goofy kid trying to look tough. I don't have the long blond wig on. I have a short red pixie wig.

And the caption says this:

I've never been sad to be gay. Definitely not ashamed. I've always known, on some level, that it's a little bit fabulous. But I have been sad to be me—my kind of gay, or just my kind of person. Maybe a lot of us have heard stuff like this: You're too gay, too much, too silly, too loud, too shy, too this, too that, too you.

Well the only "too" I like is a tutu, so that's why I'm wearing this today. :-)

Once, I felt very, very low after a breakup. I came up with my own explanation of why I wasn't good enough for the guy, and I remember exactly what Eric told me: "Bud, good relationships make you want to be so fully *you* that even the parts that you thought were broken they somehow teach you to love. In good relationships, you're not wondering if you're *too* this, or *too* that. The person loves you *because* you're too this and too that and actually wants you to be *more* this and *more* that."

So I guess this post is for anyone who's considered toning it down.

Maybe turn it up.

Because if you can be yourself even when the rest of the world is trying to get you to be more like them, well, "That's the ticket, bud." #LessonsFromMyBrother

"Mark, you *have* to let me read you some of these comments. Or tell you *something*! It's insane, and you have no idea what's happening."

"I don't want to. I just want it to be . . . not about that. Just about Eric. I just want to say what he said and not think about what other people are saying."

"But Mark, it's *incred*—"

"No. Because then what if it stops being incredible? I don't want to stop."

"Suit yourself. I can't even read you one?"

I surrender, mainly because he's so cute when he's begging. "Okay, *one*."

"Victory! Triumph! Argh, the daunting task of finding the single best one." He scans through his phone, swiping his thumb up and up with great concentration. "Here we go, this is wonderful . . . Julez4994 says, 'Shut up, you gay-faced fruit salad.'"

I crack up. "You're a cyberbully."

He smiles. "I won't tell you anything, just like you said. But just know, something beautiful is happening."

Talent Show Sequel

"**D**o you ever stop to think, we started our drag queen careers on the same day." Damien puts his arm around my shoulder as we walk to third hour. He slaps a sign for talent show auditions in the hallway. "Talent show sequel? I still got my dress!"

"I do think I'm gonna do something," I tell him meekly. I haven't even told Ezra yet.

"Sing something?"

"Maybe. Yeah, I don't know." I think about telling him more, but it seems a little heavy for the science hallway. "Haven't really thought about it too much."

"You should sing, man. It's your thing," he says as he strolls off into the sunset of the science hallway. "People miss it."

I try not to be scared. Or at least not let the scared stop me. I try not to think about how, if a dress fucked up my life before, a dress can fuck up my life again. I try not to think about how so many people know that I'm sad. Or that now I can't really pretend to be normal.

And I try not to think that if they all know, then any minute, my parents will, too.

I try to focus on a message I got somewhere around the seventh post, from the girl in the reddish-brown sundress with yellow sunflowers.

> You probably won't remember me, and I hope it's OK I got your email from Beth (we worked at Baskin-Robbins together, forever ago!). We met at your brother's visitation. I rambled on and on about history class (sorry!) and how much your brother meant to me.
>
> I've been following your Lessons from My Brother since the very first post and I don't even really have the words to say how beautiful I think it is. I met your brother during a really tough time in my life. And I cry big ugly-cry tears just thinking how many people who might be going through a tough time, too, get to meet him now. . . . also I can't send you an email without saying this, and I hope it's not majorly creepy, but you look kind of insanely cute in a dress! Anyway, not to ramble on again (eek!), but you'll probably never know how many people you're helping. Just like Eric.

I'm sure people are making fun of me. Making fun of the glitter over group texts or asking John what it was like to date a *drag queen*. "Maybe you're straight after all, Beckett. You were dating a girl."

But they don't say it to me. And really, how could they? Tease the kid with the dead brother? Eric, still protecting me from beyond the grave.

Instead, they say it's beautiful. Or they'll ask what it's like to be famous on the internet, which I hate—makes me feel selfish all over again. Or they'll repeat my brother's words. Which I love. *I screenshot that. It really helped me.* And if they repeat Eric's words to me, for a second, I feel like he's still alive. Not in a crazy *"maybe he'll come home for Easter"* kind of way, but—still here.

So I buy half-off wigs and floor-length dresses and keep posting Lessons from My Brother.

And keep trying to think of something other than nothing for the talent show, now less than two months away.

School

I knew it would come, I just didn't know when.

I expected the worst, that's what I thought. But the reality is so much worse than anything my imagination could have come up with.

I'm in the library doing research for an argumentative speech I have to give next week. Two voices I don't recognize, younger, probably, whispering. But it's silent in the library, so I can hear them as well as if they were whispering to me.

"You're just jealous because he looks better in a dress than you do."

"Obviously it's cute and all. But sorry if I don't want to take advice from some dead guy. Like, this is horrible to say, but—is a kid who OD'ed really who you want to take life advice from?"

"Oh my God, you're literally going to hell."

"Bitch, you know I have no filter. I'm just saying."

I stare, motionless, at my computer.

12 Advantages and Disadvantages of Affirmative Action

The words blur. Everything looks like when you stare too long at the sun. Dark, blurry, bright splotches.

There are too many emotions to choose from, so my body settles on nothing.

AdvantAff and Disad12vantages of irmativeages Action

Sadness? Anger? At who?

I just . . .

Is it possible Eric didn't know anything at all?

"Sorry, just gotta sneak past ya here."

I feel the librarian's back brush against my shoulders.

Aandn tagesAdv12advion antofAffagesir mativeAct Dis

"Mark, dear. This is silly, I know, but have you got a pass, sweetie?"

I hear the wooden legs of a library chair hit the carpet next to me. The chair scoots forward.

"Mark." Mrs. Isaac's face, on the side of my screen. "Mark. There ya are. Mark, you want to come . . . here, take a sip of this water, sweetie. Joan's on her way. Even tough guys need some water."

She talks to me like a child.

Advantages 12 and Dis

I snap back from somewhere. Turn my head to look at her. "Sorry." I exhale, sniffle a little. Push my chair back. "I'm so sorry." I shake my head. "I . . . fu—oh . . . I just . . . I'm late."

"Here, I'll take ya to Joan"—the school nurse—"it'll just take a minute. Fifth period's not goin' anywhere. It'll all be there tomorrow."

"Sorry. Sorry, no, I'm fine. Really. Just spaced out there. *Wooo.* Okay, I'm back. Just gonna go to class now. I'm fine." I turn back before I leave, and remember. "Thank you. Mrs. Isaac."

Lessons from My Brother
#11

The picture is a floor-length off-the-shoulder red dress. The Swans (whose names are actually Zeke and Jeremy) gifted it to me from their "drag closet." I don't know how they found out about the account, but the dress is definitely higher quality than the semi-DIY-thrift-store-finds I usually wear. I ask them if it's okay to paint on it. Jeremy says, "Queen! It'd be an honor!" In the garage, I borrow some paint my dad uses for molding touch-ups, and, over the left breast of the dress, I paint a white heart, broken in the middle.

The caption says this:

When horrible things happen, you're supposed to emerge with some sort of wisdom. The tragic movie ends with hope. The hurricane-hit community builds back, stronger than before. The world can't handle a tragedy that doesn't come with a lesson.

So here I sit, waiting for my wisdom. I sit, holding my broken heart, waiting for my strength. Waiting for the day when I, too, can say: Yes, it was the most awful thing that ever happened to me, but it's also what taught me strength, resilience, and the power of prayer.

Nothing comes.

Instead, I just swap around theories about who's to blame.

And even if it did come—wisdom—I'd trade all the strength and resilience in the entire world for just one more hour with my brother.

Because now, it's just me. Skinny, scared, heartbroken me.

And the scariest thought of all is: What if the wisdom never comes? What if I'm the kid who just stays sad?

And then on top of the sadness, you feel guilty, self-indulgent, disappointed that you're not further along. You're wallowing in it, you think. Move on. This isn't healthy. Pathological, even. You should be through the stages by now. One-two-three-four-five. Other people have been through worse and they emerged wiser, sooner.

I know this post is a little more down than the others, and I should be getting better, not going backward. I think a big part of the problem is that the person I used to go to for all of my advice is now the source of my pain. The only one who could get me out of this is the reason I'm in it. How is that possible?

I'm sad, but I'm also so angry at him. I hate that I'm angry at him, but I am. At first I was angry with the world and then at myself, but now I'm angry at him. If he was so smart, then why did he die? He knew everything about life except how to live it. Consider this: He had about a million foolproof tricks that can prevent you from drinking too much. And then he died from drinking too much.

Then I feel even worse. What sort of monster is angry at a dead person?

My brother could be forgiven if he stopped talking to me, but that was never his style. So I still hear his voice: *You've got to do more than just stare into the void. That would destroy anyone! Go out there and make something new.*

That's what I've tried to do with this account. The only time I feel good is when I'm trying to turn this something horrible into something a little bit beautiful. I still feel hurt, I still don't grow—but I can look at this drag queen, that's technically me, and see something pretty.

Thanks for reading. Sorry to be a bummer. Maybe we won't post this one.

Real Love

Ezra's on the floor doing homework while I'm on his basement couch looking at my phone, reading an email with details about this year's talent show.

"I almost forgot to tell you," he says, not looking up from his Spanish workbook, "we have to take a few extra pictures this Saturday. I'm gone next weekend."

"Where are you going?"

"Back to California. Paternal nuptials."

"Oh. Wow. Your dad's getting married?"

"Indeed."

"To the . . . to the woman he . . . dated after your mom."

"*During* my mom, more precisely." He leans back against the couch and turns his head up to me. "But no. Nicolette suffered the same fate as my mother. This wedding is to Veronika with a *K*."

"Are you excited? Won't the wedding at least be kind of fun?"

"Oh, Mark . . ." He laughs, not really at my question, and not really to me, more like a general, reflective laugh, to himself.

"Sorry, was that dumb?"

"I have one grand ambition for my time on this barely inhabitable planet, and that is to have my fruit fall so far from my father's apple tree, people assume apomixis."

I laugh, a little. "*Apomixis?*"

It's the wrong question.

He answers like a dictionary. "The asexual formation of a seed from the maternal tissues of the ovule. No fertilization required. In botany, apomixis. In animals, *parthenogenesis*. The growth and development of an embryo without fertilization."

"How do you remember that?"

Another wrong question.

"When I stumbled into the concept on an otherwise unremarkable day in biology, I internalized it like a fairy tale," he says, almost clinically. "Some dream of Prince Charming, I dream of apomixis. If a dandelion can live without a dad, so can I."

"Yeah, you don't really talk about your dad that much."

"You don't really like uncomfortable topics."

"Oh . . . I guess . . . that's probably true."

He gestures up, as if to my words in the air, as if to say, *Exhibit A.*

He continues. "Also evidenced by the fact that I just told you I hate my father and we're now talking about botany."

Botany.

Blood Alcohol Levels.

The questions I ask to avoid the ones that matter.

Or: how I manage to love someone, and still not know them at all.

I press my tongue to the roof of my mouth. Focus on my breathing. Tips to prevent crying.

"You're not a horrible person, Mark," Ezra says, as if reading my mind. He's like Eric that way. He's like Eric . . . he . . . sees me getting sad and knows just what to say. I have problems and he helps me. I'm selfish and he fixes me. Tells me exactly what to do. Ezra and Eric . . . he, he just . . . he helps me, and I don't . . . I don't do anything but be helped.

Ezra continues, matter-of-fact. "You like to stay on the surface of things, that's all. And coming from a family that talks about bad things incessantly and repetitively, it's kind of refreshing. To continue with botany, you're like one of those birds who sucks the nectar out of a flower but *while doing so* gets a seed stuck to his foot and carries that seed to another forest, thereby giving that seed a much better life. You help me without even realizing it. Look at this beautiful new forest."

I look at Ezra. I think about Ezra. I try my best to think about Ezra as Ezra. Not Ezra my boyfriend, not Ezra my soul mate, not Ezra my fairy drag-father.

Ezra as Ezra.

"Let's back up. *Back away from the botany*," I say, like a museum guard, buying time to think of a better question. I scoot Ezra forward and situate myself behind him, and put him in my arms. "What's your dad like?"

He pauses, and for a moment I think he won't answer.

Instead, he talks like he's had something to say for a long time now.

"He's a stereotype. My father is a stereotype, plain and simple. He's a type A patriarchal figure whose entire emotional landscape stops and starts at himself. The deepest emotion he can muster is *grumpy* when he doesn't get what he wants.

"Even before they divorced, I knew I hated him. I knew. My very first memory is of him seizing a bouncy ball from me when I was a child because he was reading. I was just sitting there holding it in my hands, I wasn't even bouncing the bouncy ball, but he was convinced that I *would* bounce it if I held on to it any longer. A pre-emptive punishment for the possi*bility* of disrupting his reading.

"I believe I was three. And for the record I never got the bouncy ball back."

He leans into me, nuzzles his head under my chin; his hair tickles my cheek.

"How'd you feel," I ask, "after the divorce?"

"I felt however they didn't *expect* I would! After a divorce there are various rubrics professionals use to assess your development. Are you angry? Are you demanding to spend more time out of the house? Are you less involved in school? What new unhealthy habits have you developed? Tell me about your relationships—are you overly cautious? Do you give up on relationships as soon as problems arise?"

"Oh God." I shake my fists up at the ceiling. "Like everyone's the same. Like everyone will deal with it all the same way!"

"So I, with a palpable lack of creativity, simply examined what they told me I *would* do—and did the opposite. I trained myself to be indifferent about the divorce, levelheaded in all things, studious at school, not to mention a paragon of emotional commitment." He leans forward and then falls back into me. "So yes, you just *try* to get rid of me, I dare you. Because I have a higher calling—I'm fucking with their data set."

"Is there anything worse than having a therapist be right about you?" I ask, gently rubbing his stomach under his T-shirt, hoping this isn't another wrong question.

"The worrrrrrrst," he groans. "As if your entire personality is no more original than a pathology. A 'type' in a textbook."

He tells me more. I listen. I see him, not just as a confident boyfriend who'd drop anything to help me—but as a person. A person who's felt pain and a person who might need help, too.

"I could go with you . . . if you wanted? I mean, these types of things probably need an RSVP and stuff."

He rests his eyes in mine, asks, "What about homework?"

"It's a long flight, I bet."

"And parental permission?"

"Ezra, you drove me to my brother's funeral. My parents would probably come *with* us if you asked them."

His small smile unfolds, and I know for certain I don't want to spend the rest of my life being a selfish bird sucking nectar out of a flower that grew without a father.

Lessons from My Brother
#17

The picture is me in a dress I made by tucking a basketball jersey (borrowed from Damien) into the bottom of a damaged wedding dress Goodwill was about to throw away. Crystal comes over to help me do my makeup. She takes the picture while Damien art-directs, way too anxiously, like this is a cover shoot for *Vogue*. It's the only picture I post myself.

The flight is long enough to write the caption, and the caption says this:

If you'll allow me a brief betrayal of format, I'd like to tell you about my boyfriend.

Without him there would be no pictures, no drag, no fun, no light, and very close to nothing at all. Ezra, you are not the wind beneath my wings. You are my wings. And even that isn't accurate, because you are so much more than "my" anything. But this past year, you've been my everything.

Maybe this isn't so different from every other post, because it does tie back to a lesson from my brother: If you have someone in your life wonderful enough to love you, the least you can do is learn how to love them back.

I used to wish I was more independent—didn't need help so much, from my brother, or anyone. But maybe independence is the wrong goal? Maybe the right goal is just to make sure the people you depend on can also depend on you.

Ezra: I love you. And from here until forever, I will love you the way you deserve to be loved. And as a start, here's a poem I wrote a long time ago. It's not very good, which I guess is why I didn't give it to you. But it's true.

There's a place in your arms where I forget to be sad.
A spot on your body that reminds me of life.
For a moment, a minute, or twenty,
our world makes the world disappear.

Nowadays the world is dipped in sadness.
A wrinkly raisin of a planet, dipped in sadness.
But in here,
there is only this minute, these candles, and you.
Mrs. Parsons told us poems don't have to rhyme,
But I like it better when they do.

There's only one spot where the waves don't crash,
It's in your arms, where I forget to be sad.

Could I remember the words I knew before,
I'd say thank you, I love you, and so much more.
#LessonsFromMyBrother

I use every dime I ever made from lawn mowing and buy a ticket to California.

I post the picture when we land.

Vows

"I am getting to be an old man," Ezra's father says to Veronika with a *K* as they stand barefoot under an altar made of sticks and twine. The scene would be almost simple if it weren't for the white-tipped waves crashing a dozen feet behind them. The wind makes the vows hard to hear, so Ezra's father moves the microphone closer to his lips.

"I am getting to be an old man. Even still, this feels like the first day of my life."

Ezra whispers to me, "If this is the first day of his life, then my theory of apomixis might just hold up."

We'd arrived the night before, a little late to the rehearsal dinner. He spoke to his father cordially, almost like old coworkers who'd fallen out of touch. Then his father shook my hand.

"I'm not sure Veronika got the plus-one in time, Ezra. Tonight's buffet style, so you will be fine, but your friend should check with the wedding planner for tomorrow."

Our white, cushioned folding chairs nestle into the sand as we listen to Veronika, in a white dress with cream shoulders and a low-cut V-neck, exchange her vows. "I promise to love you deeper every day." Ezra holds my hand, pressing into my palm with a need I'd never felt before.

Long strands of white fabric flow in the wind as she walks back up the sandy aisle, pumping a bouquet of white roses with the hand that isn't holding her new husband's.

It smells like summer and seaweed. The guests wear dresses in bold colors and sandals with sequined straps. They circle around tables with crisp white linens and take shrimp skewers from melting ice sculptures, talking loudly about weather and house renovations.

"Mark the Queen would look great in that purple number." Ezra points to a woman with proudly gray hair as a man in a black tuxedo offers us a tray of tuna tartare.

The sun sets over the ocean and everyone takes a picture. Ezra's most animated aunt—I guess everyone has one—demands we do the same.

He pauses in my eyes as we fix our windblown hair. "Thank you for coming."

The dinner is long, and the toasts describe a man he's never met, Ezra says. And a woman he never will.

"It'd almost be easier if he was a jerk to everyone."

We sleep in a hotel and I feel nothing at all like a person in high school.

We make love and for the first time I understand the phrase.

Before the sun rises the next morning, we go to the airport.

He rests his head on my shoulder and sleeps the entire flight home.

Family Meeting

"**W**hatcha doin' in here, big guy?" my dad asks from outside my bedroom door on one completely unremarkable Saturday afternoon. "You want to come down and sit with me and your mother in the family room for a minute?"

Nothing good has ever come from any child being asked to "come down and sit with me and your mother." I carry a pen from upstairs and nervously, repeatedly, click it open, click it closed.

"Take a seat," Dad says, pointing to the open chair opposite his recliner. The chair's way too comfy to have a serious conversation in. I sit and it swallows me.

Mom's on the couch and puts her iPad down. She looks over to my dad, gives him a head nod, and then looks back at me, with a plastic smile.

My eyes dart, eyebrows arch skeptically. *What's going on?*

"So," my dad says, too chipper. "Tell us about this social media project."

"Oh," I say, surprised and for some reason instantly ashamed. "You know about it?"

"Seems the whole city knows about it. And then some."

"Oh, I didn't . . . yeah, I don't really—keep track of all the . . . I just kind of do the pictures, and stuff. Ezra does the internet parts."

"Why didn't you tell me and your mom about it?"

"I don't know. It was kind of a personal thing."

"Personal? Mark, it's public on the internet."

I can't figure out his tone.

"Yeah, I guess . . . I don't know. I didn't really think about it."

"These are the kinds of things we need to think about, bud. This stuff on the internet, it's forever. Colleges—I just read that colleges now *Google* every applicant. For their social media."

Mom intervenes. "Your father means, we like that you have a creative outlet. We do. It's wonderful, Mark. We love that it's about your brother."

"Okay?"

"A lot of people seem to like it," my dad adds. "Do you enjoy dressing up like that?"

"I guess I do? Or else we wouldn't be having this supremely awkward conversation."

"We're not 'awkward,' Mark."

"Go on, Duke." Duke's trying to get someone to pet him, and my mom snaps for him to go lie down by the door.

Dad continues, "We just want to make sure you're thinking through everything. That's our job, as parents."

"What should I be thinking through?"

"Come on, Mark. We just . . . don't want you to limit your future."

"Duke. Go on."

"Not everyone will be on board with something like this."

He's speaking diplomatically, but I'm starting to figure out his tone. I look him in the eyes. "Are you on board with something like this?"

"Of course. I'm your father, and I'd love you no matter what." He takes a breath. "I can't say it's how I ever dreamed of seeing my son." He's speaking delicately. Clarifies. "It's about colleges, Mark. Jobs, down the road."

Mom steps in quickly. "Your father just means, we wish you would have told us, instead of us finding out from the neighbors."

"That's not what Dad said at all."

"Mark, now, we're just talking," Dad adds, "don't make it a big deal."

"Am I getting yelled at for not telling you? Or for making it a big deal?"

"*Tone*, Mark," he warns. "And you're not getting yelled at. We're trying to understand where this is coming from."

"You're trying to get your son to stop wearing dresses."

"You're—that's not it at all, honey. This isn't how—let's start this over again. I think it's just a little thing with how the words came out. You and your father, just—Mark . . ."

I don't stomp. I have no energy left for stomping. I just leave.

I'm on my bed, staring at the ceiling. Empty and annoyed.

I'd rather have him just say it—just say what he actually feels—rather than tiptoe around it with some BS about jobs.

A knock on my door. Gentle, the kind where you knock with just one knuckle.

"Come in."

My dad slowly creaks the door open. Takes a single step.

He speaks softly, reflectively. "I'm sorry, Mark."

It's more surprising than if he'd come into my bedroom speaking Japanese.

I look over from my bed and try to hide my confusion.

He always talks so slow. "That was not how we wanted it to go, and not what I wanted to say. And I'm sorry. It's a tough time, still. No one knows how long these things will take and, well, I think it's taken us a little longer than we expected. We're all just learnin' as we go."

I've never heard him say that, either. *It's a tough time.* Obviously, but to say it, to each other . . . it's not really our style. I feel guilty immediately. Embarrassed, even. For being the cause of his apology. For bringing even one more ounce of pain into this house.

"So, if you'll humor your old man. Talk me through it."

"Through what?"

"What do you like about wearing dresses?"

"Dad, you're the one making it an issue. I didn't say anything at all. You're making it an issue." I always get so defensive, so quickly with him.

He looks at me with earnest, almost innocent eyes. The eyes of a kid inside the body of a man. He's being kind, and I'm still being a dick. He sits on the edge of my bed. I curl up my legs. "I want to know you," he says.

"You created me. You know me."

"Son, I want to know you. So just help me with that, all right? Help your dad understand." He takes a long pause, but I don't fill the silence because it looks like there's something more he wants to say. "Eric was . . . easier for me to know."

It couldn't be, but I feel like this might be the first time I've heard my dad say Eric's name since the day he had to make all those phone calls.

He continues. "Help me know you."

"I . . ." don't know what to say. "What do you want to know?"

"Well, the dresses. Let's start with the dresses. Why dresses? We read what you wrote, under the pictures, downstairs just now. We hadn't seen that before. You know your mom and I aren't the best on these social media things. And they're beautiful. The words. It's really special, son. What you're telling people about your brother. Sharing him with the world. But why not put pictures of *you*? The guy Eric knew. Why put on a dress?"

"They are pictures of me," I say, too aggressively.

"Son, yes. Of course. But you know what I mean." Another pause. "You're not making this very easy."

"I don't know what you want me to say. They are pictures of me. Me in a dress. But still me." I feel my face getting hot.

He talks like he's dismantling a bomb, and I'm the bomb. "Do you like dresses more than what you normally wear? More than the types of clothes you wear at home? Or to school?"

"Not more than, no. Just . . . It feels—pretty. It's all horrible and this feels pretty."

"Me and your mom haven't missed somethin', have we? Do you want to be a girl?"

"Oh my God . . ."

"It's okay, Mark, we're just trying to understand. We can't . . . well, we can't do anything if we don't understand."

"Not . . . well . . . I just want to be a boy who wears dresses sometimes. Who gets to be pretty sometimes."

"Do you not like being a boy?"

"I don't even know. No . . ." I try to calm down, find my footing. Something about his words—the black and white of his words—pisses me off. But it also feels bizarre that I haven't thought about any of this yet. It feels like the obvious questions I should have already asked myself. "No, I don't not like being a boy. I just . . . I don't know. I like wearing dresses. I think it's fun to be, sort of a character, but a character that's just other parts of me that maybe I don't show when I'm in, like, a pair of khakis."

"Don't get worked up, Mark. I'm just trying to understand. I've never wanted to wear a dress, so I'm just trying to understand. Don't be emotional."

"Don't tell me how to be, Dad!" My dad and I always go to anger. "Just let me be. Okay? Let me get worked up. Let me wear a dress. I don't like being a boy. Okay? I don't like being a boy the way boys are supposed to be, a boy who doesn't get worked up and doesn't cry and eats steak and crushes it at soccer practice. I like being a boy the way *I* want to be a boy, which is a boy who writes cheesy picture poems and wears pretty dresses that his boyfriend helps him pick out. I like being that kind of a boy—or whatever fucking genderless fairy nymph that is."

"Don't swear, Mark."

"Oh my God."

"There are still rules. Things are different, but there are still rules, and one of them is don't swear at your father."

"You came in here asking, and now I'm trying to explain, and rather than actually listening to me, all you care about is a fucking swear word."

"Enough." He says it stern.

"It's always been like this and it'll always be like this and it'll only get worse now that our *moderator* is gone because none of us knew what to do to help him."

My words land like a punch.

"Is that what you think?"

"Obviously! Think of *all the times*. Thanksgiving. Christmas. And *every single time* you lied about why you were going to Evanston. None of it helped! And now we don't even . . . we just watch TV and go for walks and eat ice cream and we don't even—"

"Because it's too hard to talk about it!"

"It's harder not to!"

"So what do you want to know? What do you want to talk about? You want to know that your mother hasn't slept through the night since your brother died? Would that help you?"

"I don't want to know that." I can't help crying.

"You want to know that I haven't stopped replaying *every single conversation*?"

"I don't . . ." I didn't expect . . .

"That as soon as their pity runs out, I'm gonna lose my job because all I can focus on is what I should have done?"

"No, Dad. I don't want to know that. I don't."

"That I know that a father's first job is to keep his sons alive. Even animals know that. Even animals know to keep their children alive. And they'll tell you tough love, and then they'll tell you go easy, and there's no way to know which one is gonna keep him alive and which one is gonna kill him. There's no way to know until it's done."

"Stop. Dad, please."

"And then they tell you there's nothing you coulda done, but you know they don't believe that and they blame you as much as you blame you. We didn't *lie* to you Mark, we tried to protect you because we thought it was gonna all end up fine, and a father is supposed to protect his children! And you're my *son*, Mark. You're my *son*. You're what I've got left and I'm damn sure not gonna not know you. You can walk around with a goddamn airplane on your head, but I'm damn sure not gonna *not* know you!"

I have never hugged my father.

I've hugged him goodbye, hugged him good night. But I've never *really* hugged my father.

I hug him.

I inhale, to speak. All that comes out is an unsteady sigh, almost like a shiver. He grips my forearm with his hand. His hand feels so big, and he tells me that he's sorry and it's gonna be okay.

"I'm still sad." I finally speak. "Almost all the time."

My mom stands outside the door. Gentle steps on soft carpet. She doesn't wipe my tears or hers.

She puts her hand on my shoulder, and her eyes are wide. Perhaps for the first time, I notice that they're green. Her voice is low.

"Me too, honey." Her soft apology.

A long pause. My dad sits straighter. "The quiet times are the hardest." He pauses. "The nights."

Mom nods slowly. She still holds my shoulder, knuckles pale with the pressure. Her grip feels strong, but her fingers feel fragile, like the bones of a bird.

Could it be that I never knew her eyes were green?

"What if we never get better?" I speak with my head down, like a bedtime prayer. A garage door closes in the distance. A car beeps locked. Quieter, still, a question as confession. "Like, really better?"

I fall into her hug like a cloth doll. My mom hugs me. Her hands interlock at my shoulder and I smell her shampoo.

"We've got each other." She hugs me, and says again, quieter, but steadier, "We've got each other."

Quieter. "We've got each other."

Family Dinner

A week or so later, the dinner conversation pauses.

"Awkward silence!" Eric always used to shout during moments like this. He'd shout it enthusiastically, like he'd just found someone in hide-and-seek.

A fork taps on a plate. My mom picks up a piece of chicken.

A knife scrapes ceramic. My dad cuts into his sweet potato.

"Ya never did tell us why you like wearing dresses."

"Oh, you're kidding me," I moan.

"You wanna know what I think?" my dad asks.

"Don't pretend like I have a choice." I smile to offset the sarcasm.

He pauses.

"I've been noodlin' on this, so I got a theory. I think . . ." He takes a breath. ". . . that you're brave. I think you're tougher than anybody. I think most people just kind of look at the world, and play the part. And I think it takes a lot of courage to—question . . . or challenge . . . things like that. That's courage, Mark, and there's nothing that would make a father more proud. Maybe I don't understand it all the time—no big secret that I wasn't a brain like you and your brother—but maybe I don't need to. I do think it's bigger than me, and I think it's beautiful, Mark. Whatever it is."

A small smile, like parting clouds. It's exactly the opposite of what I thought he was going to say, and it strikes me that it's possible that I don't know my father at all. That I've been his housemate for over seventeen years, but somehow I don't know him at all. My mouth is dry. My mom's eyes are still green. I swallow. "Well, as soon as I figure out what it is, you'll be the first to know."

"Take your time," he says, "Figuring things out . . ." He takes another bite of chicken, and points with his fork. "Some of the best questions don't have answers." He puts his fork down, and looks philosophically at his plate, then me. "Life isn't a math test."

I wait for more, but that's it. He never was poetic like Eric, but he's trying. And I can, too.

A Eulogy

I'm so calm it makes me nervous.

My makeup brushes do not mock me. They do not tell me to get ready to look ridiculous.

My dress does not scare me. It does not tell me to remember the last time I wore women's clothes in a talent show.

My pulse, oblivious to the broader calm, races like a hamster on amphetamines.

Progress, not perfection, I guess.

I'm singing a song that I wrote. I don't know how to write songs, so I took a Praise Band song and wrote kind of a poem about Eric that could match the music. Carmen from Find Your Faith is playing the piano.

I reach in for the night's outfit: a *pink* princess dress with puffy sleeves. I had two options, and when I presented plan B, Ezra just shook his head. "I didn't give up half my Saturdays so you could wear an understated aubergine!"

⬦ ⬦ ⬦

"Mark, I have to tell you something before you go out there, just so it's not a surprise," Ezra says urgently, backstage. "It's—well, I'm not trying to make you nervous, but—there are a lot of people out there."

"Okay," I answer, confused. The talent show is always a full auditorium, and you can't get fuller than full.

"A *lot* a lot of people. You're the only person left who doesn't realize the extent of it, but . . . you're popular. Very popular. You have 'fans,' Mark. And I *told you* they were asking for appearances, and, well, they brought signs. And some are already chanting 'Mark the Queen.'"

With a full face of makeup, I tilt my head and look him in the eye.

"Well. I guess the name had enough pizzazz after all."

I step onto the dark stage.

The applause comes before I reach the light.

A single spotlight shines.

Light is a wave. It transports energy without the transport of matter.

Sound is a wave, too.

Grief comes in waves, at least that's what they say.

And so, I suppose, does hope.

The spotlight whispers invisible energy that sounds like light and warms like my brother's smile.

I wish I would have written you a happier song, I say, just to Eric, through silent waves of my own. But it's happy enough, and it's true.

Carmen plays.

I sing.

> *I wrote a song for you*
> *But I apologize*
> *I don't know anything*
> *About writing a song*
>
> *I know you'd say to me*
> *If you could say to me*
> *"Please do not sing for me*
> *It's time to start movin' along."*
>
> *So I apologize*
> *About this song for you*
> *Because it's sad, and true.*
> *But hey, at least it's not long.*

And I keep singing to Eric, about how, growing up, he was always strong enough for both of us.

And when he left, he went away and took the both of us.

And the pain never goes away.

I sing about a time, growing up, when life was nothing but love.

All I knew was all he taught me.

The pain never goes away.

They tell you it gets better with time.

But do they know that with time, he gets further away?

And the pain.

The pain never goes away.

I look up at the light, adjust my dress, lean forward, so far my heels lift off the ground. Carmen stops playing and I sing a cappella to a silent auditorium.

This should be the part where the song gets happy. The part I share my strength with them. The chorus! Belt it out like it's a musical. Because a song cannot end without a lesson. A life cannot end without a lesson. Everything happens for a reason. Jesus God, reveal the reason.

I wanted happiness. Smiles and choruses. But, I apologize, some songs just stay sad.

So I hurt, and live with him. I cry, and live for him. I listen, and listen for him.

He says be strong enough for both of us. Love strong enough for both of us. Hope hard enough for both of us. Smile wide enough for both of us. Live big enough for both of us.

> *From here until forever,*
> *Like any other two.*
> *We'll do everything together,*
> *Your Little Brother and You.*

Hall of Fame

The light stays bright, and now I know for sure: Eric did not go up to be an angel; he was never the spectating kind. I wave to the wings for Ezra to come onstage. Carmen pulls out a neon-green wig I'd hidden in the piano bench. I pull Ezra into the spotlight, and Miss Pound-town takes a bow. Crystal's in the front row, wearing her mustache. Damien's next to her in the most unusual clip-on earrings I've ever seen.

Outside the auditorium, in the Athletics Hall of Fame hallway, I wobble against Ezra as an unfathomable number of people share kind words and tell me stories of their pain, stories where Eric's words came at just the right time. Bashfully in the back stand my parents.

"If you talk to that old man back there"—I point at my dad—"I bet he'd show you where Eric's picture is in this hallway."

"It's up here twice, actually!" Dad shouts back, and marches up to show the way.

My mom hugs me so urgently that the flowers she'd been carrying drop to the floor. The hug parts the clouds inside my chest and starts spreading sunshine, everywhere, warming my heart and wrapping its rays around every single rib, going up to my shoulders and down through my arms, down to my elbows and fingers and warming the pit of my stomach, spreading sunbeams down, down, down through every inch of my thighs and my knees and my shins through my calves until it massages my feet with warm rays of everything's-going-to-be-okay.

It's not okay, but we'll be okay.

"Are you Mrs. Davis?" asks a girl who looks to be about Eric's age. My mom gently nods her head. "Thank you," the girl says from inside a tight hug. "You're an incredible mother."

Graduation Day

Very early morning

Just Me and My Brother

It's my first time here.

Mom and Dad go every Sunday, right after church. But I've never gone with.

I look down at the little diagram Dad drew me, the world's most morbid scavenger hunt. I'm supposed to turn left at the big oak tree, walk toward a gravestone that looks like a miniature Washington Monument, and Eric's is three after that.

I'm nervous, for some reason. I walk slowly, buy time, stop at other people's graves, subtract the year they were born from the year they died. Some were younger than Eric. It's just too many sad families. The world has too many sad families.

I read the grave marker two down from the Washington Monument one. The one, according to my dad's drawing, that will be right before Eric's. It's for a couple: William and Tanya Johnson. Carved into their granite gravestone, a dove holds a ribbon in its beak, weaves it into the shape of a heart, overlapping a cross. I trace the ribbon with my eyes. William died three years ago, in December. Tanya's date of death is blank. Empty, just waiting. I wonder what she's doing right now, Tanya. If she's waiting, too.

I try not to look, but I can see his stone. I remember it from the funeral.

Maybe I can just stay with William and Tanya. Well, just William.

I have long since passed the denial stage—but have I?

I try not to look.

I try to just keep staring at the frozen patch of dirt in front of William and Ta—

His name. In stone.

Eric Davis.

In a cemetery.

It feels like a movie. Like I'm watching myself in some kind of sad movie.

On that family trip to D.C., when we went to the building where they keep the Constitution, my dad couldn't wrap his head around the fact that this, right in front of us, was the *real* Constitution. "*That* is the Constitution." He got so close the guard told him to back up. "The *real* Constitution. The same one!"

Eric Davis. The real Eric Davis.

It says his birthday on the grave.

I clench my jaw. I *told* myself I wouldn't cry, to show him that I'm okay, that I'm strong, that he doesn't need to feel bad because I'm strong and I'm okay. But here, a cemetery, a grave . . . he feels, somehow, more dead than he was before. Of course I knew he was dead. But graveyard dead? As dead as, like, Ulysses S. Grant? Impossible.

I look to the sky and try to rewind the tears back into my eyes.

"One moment please," I say to the stone, as my chin shakes. "Please hold."

The sun is starting to come up. Other people might be here soon. I got here early to be alone. I take a deep breath and stare at an empty patch of grass on the other side of Eric's grave. That side doesn't have a stone in it. Just empty, waiting. The grass is thin and trampled. Talking to a gravestone, like in a movie.

I shift weight, awkwardly.

The tombstone feels like it's expecting something.

"It's pretty morbid here, huh?" I laugh, small, then sniffle. Exhale, again, and inhale, deeply, bite my upper lip hard enough so it hurts. It's so hot out, already. There's something I came here to say, but now that I'm here, I just—

"Back sweat is the worst." I peel my T-shirt off my back, shift my eyes from the tombstone. "It's gonna be *so* hot in those gowns." I press my thumb into my palm, stare at a tree in the distance.

"Okay! That's all I wanted to say! See ya, Eric!" I turn around and pretend to leave.

I giggle, to myself (well, who else?), but then it builds, like a wave, until I'm cracking up, laughing maniacally like an actual crazy person. I put my hands against my face as the laugh transitions to sobs that require my entire body.

I cry, hard, hit myself in the chest. Come on.

"Fuckkk!" I exhale into the trampled dirt. I look back at the grave. "Heck of a year, huh?" I laugh, smaller, and inhale, mess with the random pocket on the side of my shorts.

"Dr. Amato told me I 'use humor' as a way to deflect from my emotions." I close the pocket.

"I told him anyone who says 'use humor' probably doesn't know how to." I kick the dirt.

"I thought that was pretty good." I tap the tip of my dirty tennis shoe on a blade of grass.

"But yeah, if you ever get outta here, I'm gonna kick your ass for being the reason I have to go to this fucking grief counselor." I wipe my eyes. "Dr. Amato, if you're listening"—I look up to the clouds for some reason—"I know he's not coming back.

"So I obviously don't really know what to say." I wipe my eyes for hopefully the last time. "I also don't really know what I have to, like, catch you up on." I laugh. "I mean, are you like *God* now, and see everything? Or are you, like, doin' your own thing in heaven and just kind of pop down when we talk to you?" I look at the dead grass. "Or are you just *here*." I rub my heel into the dirt. "You better pop down when we talk to you. Mom talks to you all the time. So you better pop down.

"I do hope you're not *here*, because this place is not fun."

I shuffle my feet.

"I graduate later today. That's one thing." I give him side-eye like he's right in front of me. "In case you're not aware, you won the GPA competition." There are so many graves. "You can thank Dr. Sanders for that. Asshole. Oh, and I got into college, and me and Damien are going t—" I stop, just in time. I can feel them coming. "*That* we will discuss later. You were so excited to go to coll—

"Okay! That's not why I'm here!" I hit myself in the thigh,

hard. "I could've cried in my own bedroom. *Fuck*." I sniffle and promise myself it will be the last sniffle. Talk, again, faster. "Okay, the *other*, just, life update thing is—you know how you were so corny when you were down here?" I laugh. "Well, I started this account where I share all the corny stuff you said. Kidding. Well, not about the account. I did do that. And I share all the things you said. You always knew what to say. *In contrast . . .*" I motion to myself and stare at the ground. The roots of the big oak tree reach all the way over here.

"Oh, and I wear pretty dresses in the pictures." I smile, proud. "Well, some are pretty. Some are pretty ugly—but they look cute in the pictures. I think you'd like it. I'm definitely being my 'full sequin-y self.' It's actually kind of crazy. Like, thousands of people follow it; Ezra would know how many. Oh, and that's the other thing. Remember Ezra? We're still together. And that's really awesome. He's . . . awesome. So much more the guy for me than John was. I can hear your *told-you-so* from all the way down here. Or up here. Wherever you are. I think you'd really like him. He's smarter than both of us put together, though, so maybe you'd hate that. Oh, and Crystal is moving to Colorado because she got thi—

"Okay, now I'm just babbling." I cut myself off. "Probably nervous to actually get to the point of why I'm here. In addition to, you know, just like, finally seeing you, or whatever, there are two things I wanted to say." I roll my eyes at myself. "God, now it feels like a speech. 'Be sure to signpost in the introduction so your audience knows what to expect.' *Anyway . . .*"

On the horizon, light starts to shine, oranges and reds pushing out the dark blue night.

That's maybe the wildest part about it all. The world keeps on spinning.

I talk to my brother.

"The first is sort of stupid, but I guess, so, my biggest fear . . . is that you're gonna fade away. That someday I'm gonna wake up and not remember what your laugh sounded like or not remember what side of your mouth you smiled with. And I think the hardest thing for me to think about is in, like, a year, or whenever, when I start living a year of life that you didn't technically get to. Like, when I turn twenty. I think that'll be really hard. Because I still get your help all the time. But when I turn twenty, you might think, well, 'Oh, he's older than me, so he doesn't need me.' But I *do* need you. All the time. So even if I have a kid, or, you know, do something totally outside of anything you ever did—still just . . . I don't know what I'd do without your help. I can't . . . I can't lose you again.

"Okay, that sniffle about a million sniffles ago was supposed to be the last sniffle. *Jesus*. I'm supposed to be showing you how strong I am. But actually, well, strong people can cry. That's probably the better lesson, and it's related to the, I guess . . . the second thing I want to say. Which is even dumber than the first, if you can believe it. But, like I said, I don't even know if I really have a sense of where I think you are. I don't know if I believe in heaven, or angels, or any of that. But if there is this proper *Heaven*, and that's where you are, then this totally makes no sense, but I just think about it a lot, so I'll say it anyway.

"My biggest fear of all is that you're sad.

"That you're up in heaven, and there are all these heaven

things going on, but you can't enjoy them, because you're sad. Sad about how you died, or sad about how sad you made us. So just in case there is sadness in heaven, which I know doesn't make sense, I just need you to know it's okay. To be sad. Even if there's all this pressure to be perfect, and all the other heaven people are looking at you like you're an idiot because you're sad in heaven—it's okay. To feel sad. To feel so sad that it doesn't even feel like a feeling, it feels like your entire existence. To have the sadness take up so much space that there's not room for anything else. It's okay, Eric, to feel that kind of sad.

"You don't have to be the happiest angel. You can be the one who needs help.

"I told you it was dumb. You're *you*! But, if you do need help, and all the goody-goodies up in heaven aren't cutting it, well. I'm here.

"And before I go, and get the fuck out of this cemetery—*no offense*—there's this voice memo you left me. I mean, who makes voice memos? But I listen to it every single day. In the month or whatever after you . . . I would just listen to it over and over and over and over. And Dr. Amato would probably say that's pathological, but it helped. So, I just kind of wanted to say the same thing to you. And then, you know, you can think back on it. Okay, I feel stupid, but I'll just say it."

I take a deep breath, lift my eyes, and talk to Eric.

"Ladies and gentlemen, this is to record, for all of human history, how much I fucking love my brother. And with that, good night!"

"Okay, well, yeah. That's what you said to me, and what I wanted to say to you.

"It's weird to say goodbye, so, I think I'm just gonna go.

"But—I love you, like I just said.

"And even if I live to a million years old, meet a million more people, and do a trillion more things, my favorite thing I ever was, was your little brother."

I stay just a little while longer. The cemetery isn't empty anymore. Six plots down from Eric's, in the same row, two people, maybe a mom and dad, stand silently by a grave. Farther away, on the other side of the big oak tree, a woman holds the hand of a very young girl, and the girl holds a flower. They walk like they know where they're going.

You can fully see the sun now, shining through the gaps in the black iron fence. A car joins the parking lot. It has a whole family in it. Them, me, the mom and dad six graves down, the woman and her daughter on the other side of the big oak tree—we are the people who visit cemeteries. Separately, but probably at the same time, we wonder if we'll ever stop crying. We know things that other people don't know: like how you can be long past denial, but still not believe it. And we know we have to move on. We know they would *want* us to move on. And we do move on. But through the light waves of the rising sun, this is something we can only tell each other: We don't. Not really.

So we know the limits of language. We know there should be a whole world of words in between grief and life. Or just one word, maybe, for love that's forever even after it's gone. Or a word for what it's like to move forward, but not on.

I pass the family on the way to my car. Two kids, a mom, and a dad.

"Morning," the mom says quietly. Her voice catches, but by now, she knows how to clench her jaw in such a way to stop the tears. Words are hard, so these are things we know.

No one in the world knows what it's like, except almost everyone.

"Good morning."

Acknowledgments

From the bottom of my heart, thank you so much to anyone reading. Thank you for giving Mark, Eric, Ezra, and this story a little bit of your day. I could never fully express how grateful I am for your time, but "thank you" seems a good place to start.

A special message of love to anyone whose life has been affected by substance abuse, alcoholism, addiction, or loss. This book came from a very personal place, and I'm sending you more love than you could ever imagine.

So many people have helped make this dream a reality. I have to start with **Brent Taylor.** Thank you for being not only an incredibly skilled agent, but also a thoughtful editor and a caring collaborator. I'm grateful every day for your guidance.

And to the team at **Roaring Brook** and **Macmillan:** I could not imagine a happier home for the Davis Family. My brilliant editor **Mekisha Telfer**, the love and insight you brought to this manuscript made the story so much better, and the humor and diligence you brought to the process made everything so smooth and rewarding. I'm honored to work with you. To **Mia Moran, Jackie Dever, Katy**

Miller, and **Emily Stone**, thank you for your thoughtful and precise edits. **Aurora Parlagreco**, thank you for your creative vision and for treating this book with such tenderness and care. And **Jasjyot Singh Hans**, I'm so honored Mark came to life in your beautiful work. I couldn't have dreamed of a more fitting cover.

So many people have provided kindness, encouragement, and guidance on the winding path to publication. To **K.L. Going** for the manuscript critique that turned an idea into a book, and the encouragement that helped me stick with it. To **Rob Costello** for the most instructive and inspiring feedback, and for getting to know these characters as well as I did. I'm forever grateful. To **Hanna Gibeau** for that life-changing email, early support, and immensely instructive editing. To **Ross Weiner** and **Heather Karpas** for all you did to kickstart my writing career. **Tina Dubois**, for generous reads and eye-opening manuscript suggestions. **Sarah Passick** and **Celeste Fine** for transformative conversations. To the entire staff at **Highlights Foundation**, especially my teachers **K.L. Going** and **Clara Gillow Clark**, for the workshop that unlocked it all, and to **Liz Kossnar** for your kindness and encouragement. Thank you to **Kelly Delaney** for incredibly helpful notes, and to **Ashley Reisinger** for an especially insightful reader's report. To **MasterClass** for assembling the instructor lineup of my dreams, and to the **New York Public Library** for the hundreds of books (and countless hours) that helped me learn how to write.

And to **my parents**. What to say about the world's most wonderful parents? You have always made me feel so perfectly supported, encouraged, and loved—and I love you very, very much. To my sisters, **Samantha** and **Missy**, who hype me up and make me feel like the luckiest brother around. And to all the **Clays** and **Hugdahls** and **Fiedlers** and **Kraetzers** out there—thank you. To **Javier** for being the embodiment of love and support, to **Nick** for being the first reader, to **Zev** for truly everything, to **Barrett** for always and constantly making me smile, to **Ilyse** for being the best book buddy, to **Daniel** and **Larnelle** for college and beyond, **Tanner** for the world's best friend dates, **Alex** for the world's best dance parties, **Maggie** for the authorly inspiration, **Patrick** and **Andrew** for forever friendship, **Matt** and **Brendan** for that first foray into creative writing, and a world of friends who make me feel like the luckiest man on the planet.

And finally, to everyone who has ever left a kind comment or sent a little love to Carrie Dragshaw. I never would have dared to dream of writing a book without your encouraging words and your life-changing kindness.

Reading has meant so much to me throughout my life, and the idea of adding a book to the library of the world is simply beyond comprehension. Thank you again to everyone who helped make it happen and, especially, to you, the reader. I am forever grateful.

Sending love,

Dan

Drew Gurian

DAN CLAY is a writer and drag queen thrilled to be making his debut as a novelist with *Becoming a Queen*. Until now, he focused on spreading love and positivity online through his drag persona, Carrie Dragshaw. His writing as Carrie has been featured in hundreds of magazines, newspapers, and television shows and his TED Talk on being your "whole self" details his firsthand experience with the healing power of drag. When he's not writing, Dan works for a climate change nonprofit and a New York-based branding agency. He lives in New York.

Instagram @dan_clay | writerdanclay.com